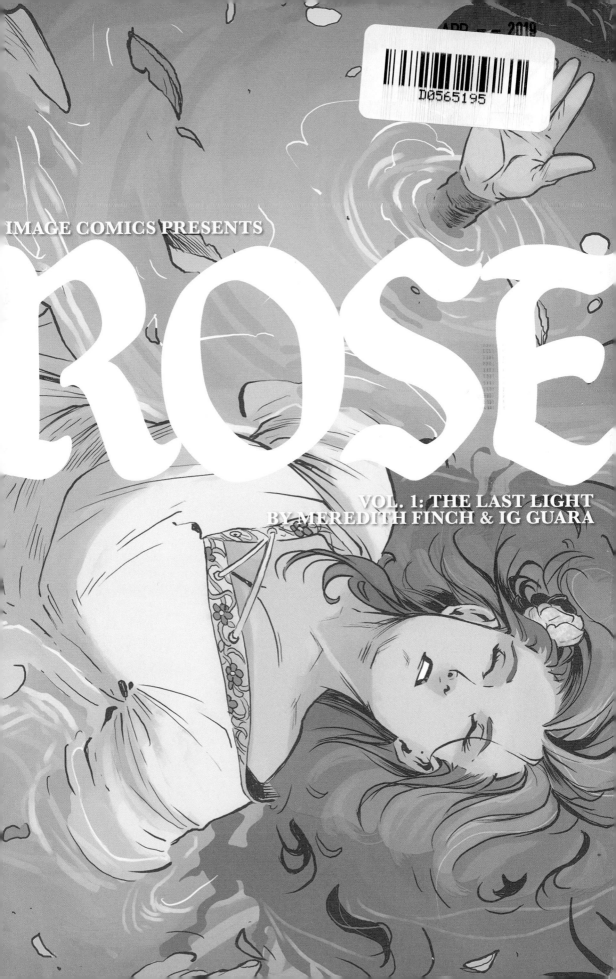

IMAGE COMICS PRESENTS

ROSE

VOL. 1: THE LAST LIGHT
BY MEREDITH FINCH & IG GUARA

IMAGE COMICS, INC.

/ Robert Kirkman: Chief Operating Officer / Erik Larsen: Chief Financial Officer / Todd McFarlane: President / Marc Silvestri: Chief Executive Officer / Jim Valentino: Vice President /

Eric Stephenson: Publisher / Corey Murphy: Director of Sales / Jeff Boison: Director of Publishing Planning & Book Trade Sales / Chris Ross: Director of Digital Sales / Jeff Stang: Director of Specialty Sales / Kat Salazar: Director of PR & Marketing / Branwyn Bigglestone: Controller / Kali Dugan: Senior Accounting Manager / Sue Korpela: Accounting & HR Manager / Drew Gill: Art Director / Heather Doornink: Production Director / Leigh Thomas: Print Manager / Tricia Ramos: Traffic Manager / Briah Skelly: Publicist / Aly Hoffman: Events & Conventions Coordinator / Sasha Head: Sales & Marketing Production Designer / David Brothers: Branding Manager / Melissa Gifford: Content Manager / Drew Fitzgerald: Publicity Assistant / Vincent Kukua: Production Artist / Erika Schnatz: Production Artist / Ryan Brewer: Production Artist / Shanna Matuszak: Production Artist / Carey Hall: Production Artist / Esther Kim: Direct Market Sales Representative / Emilio Bautista: Digital Sales Representative / Leanna Caunter: Accounting Analyst / Chloe Ramos-Peterson: Library Market Sales Representative / Marla Eizik: Administrative Assistant /

IMAGECOMICS.COM

ROSE, VOL. 1.: THE LAST LIGHT. First printing. November 2017. Published by Image Comics, Inc. Office of publication: 2701 NW Vaughn St., Suite 780, Portland, OR 97210. Copyright © 2017 Meredith Finch. All rights reserved. Contains material originally published in single magazine form as ROSE #1-6. "ROSE," its logos, and the likenesses of all characters herein are trademarks of Meredith Finch, unless otherwise noted. "Image" and the Image Comics logos are registered trademarks of Image Comics, Inc. No part of this publication may be reproduced or transmitted, in any form or by any means (except for short excerpts for journalistic or review purposes), without the express written permission of Meredith Finch, or Image Comics, Inc. All names, characters, events, and locales in this publication are entirely fictional. Any resemblance to actual persons (living or dead), events, or places, without satiric intent, is coincidental. Printed in the USA. For information regarding the CPSIA on this printed material call: 203-595-3636 and provide reference #RICH-766093. For international rights, contact: foreignlicensing@imagecomics.com. ISBN: 978-1-5343-0341-6.

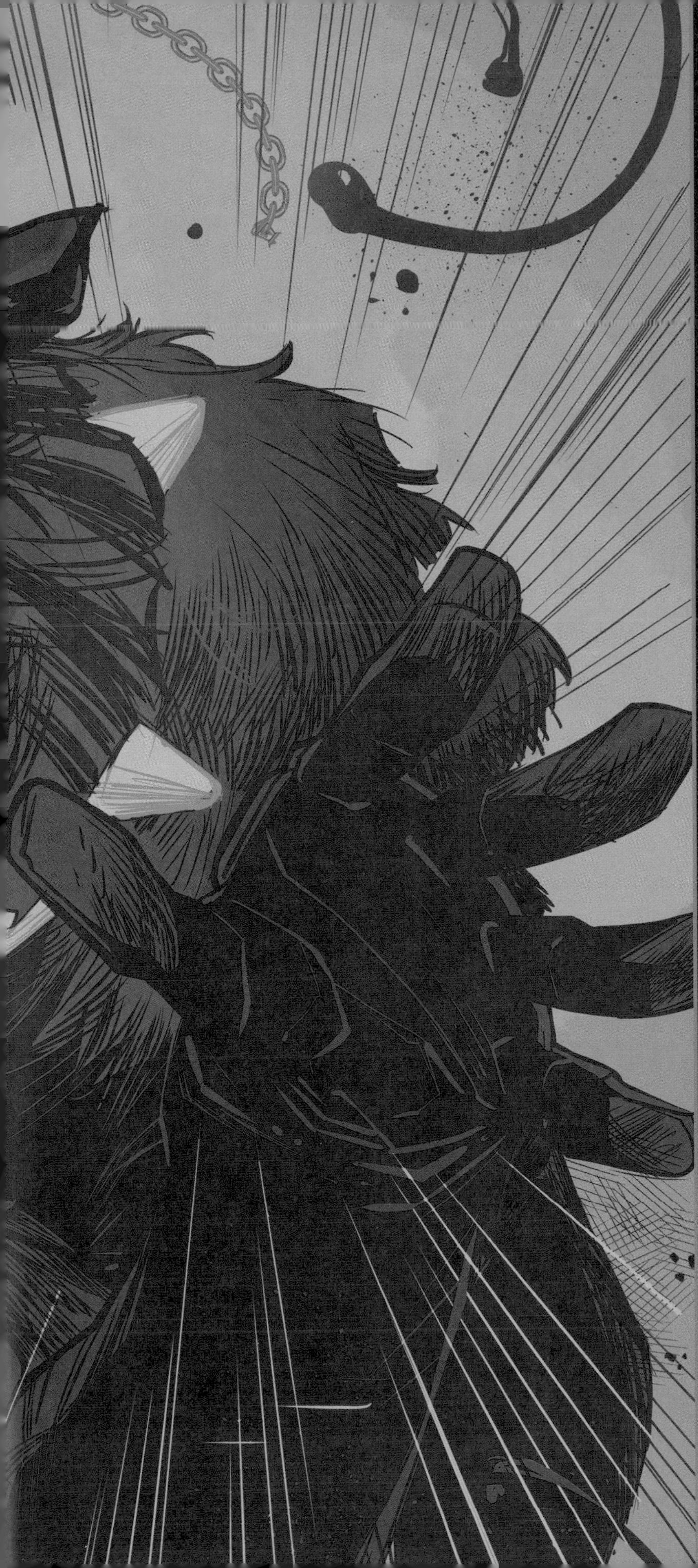

written by
MEREDITH
FINCH

pencils & inks by
IG GUARA

colors by
TRIONA FARRELL

letters by
CARDINAL RAE

collection cover by
IG GUARA &
TRIONA FARRELL

collection design by
VINCENT KUKUA

ROSE created by
MEREDITH
FINCH

Dear Reader,

As you join me in embarking on this journey with ROSE and THORNE, I would like to take a minute to thank the many people who have made this project possible.

First and foremost, I want to thank my incredible husband David. Without his support and encouragement, I would never have been brave enough to put my writing out into the world. His unfailing belief in me made the book you are about to read possible. He is my soul mate and my best friend, and I would be lost without him.

To my beautiful boys, Hayden, Everett and Isaac; thank you for being my biggest cheerleaders. Being your mother will always be my greatest accomplishment, and I can only hope that I am able to communicate through Rose a small part of the depth of my love and devotion to you.

To my teammates, Ig Guara and Triona Farrell. The beauty of what the two of you have created takes my breath away, and the emotional arc that takes place on each and every page is a masterpiece of storytelling. This is what comics were meant to be.

Any writing needs good editing, and I have been incredibly blessed to have the expertise and talents of Andy Schmidt from Comics Experience on this project. Andy has an uncanny ability to cut to the heart of what is missing and push me beyond my comfort zone in the process of ensuring I am writing the best possible story.

To my friend Erica Schultz: I can not tell you how much your support, encouragement and incredible patience has meant to me. God bless DC and their writers class for bringing you into my life.

To my local comic book shop, Rogues Gallery, and its owner, Shawn Cousineau: thank you for your support and your willingness to give me an open and honest response to my first draft of ROSE. You helped shape the story that unfolds on these pages.

Thank you to Eric Stephenson, and all of the staff at IMAGE COMICS, for believing in ROSE, and for the incredible amount of support you have thrown behind me. This experience has far exceeded anything I could have hoped for.

Finally, I want to thank you, the reader, for joining me on this journey with ROSE and THORNE. It is my hope that you will find something in this book that will speak to your heart as we each strive toward discovering our own personal truth.

God Bless You,

Meredith Finch

ONE

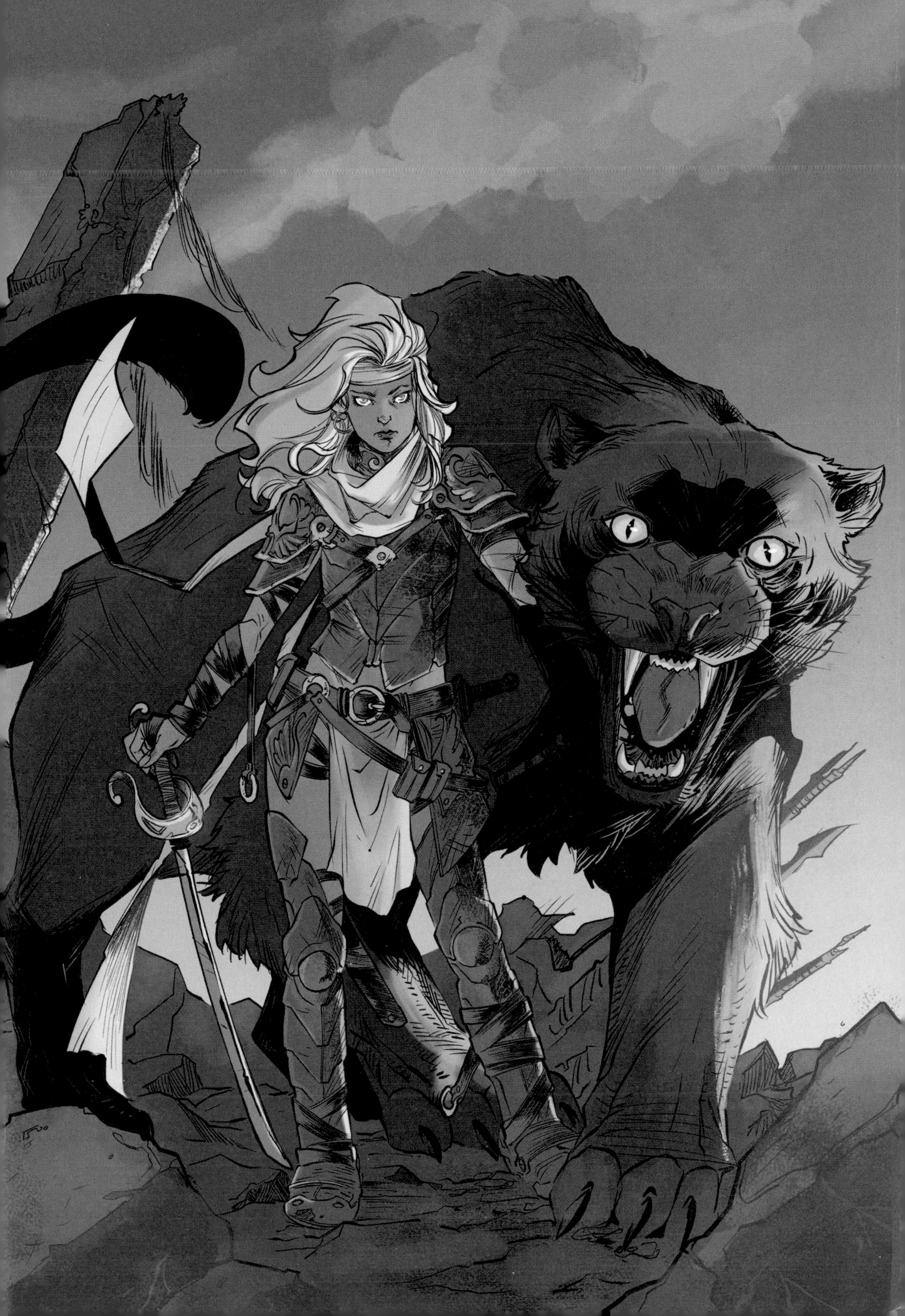

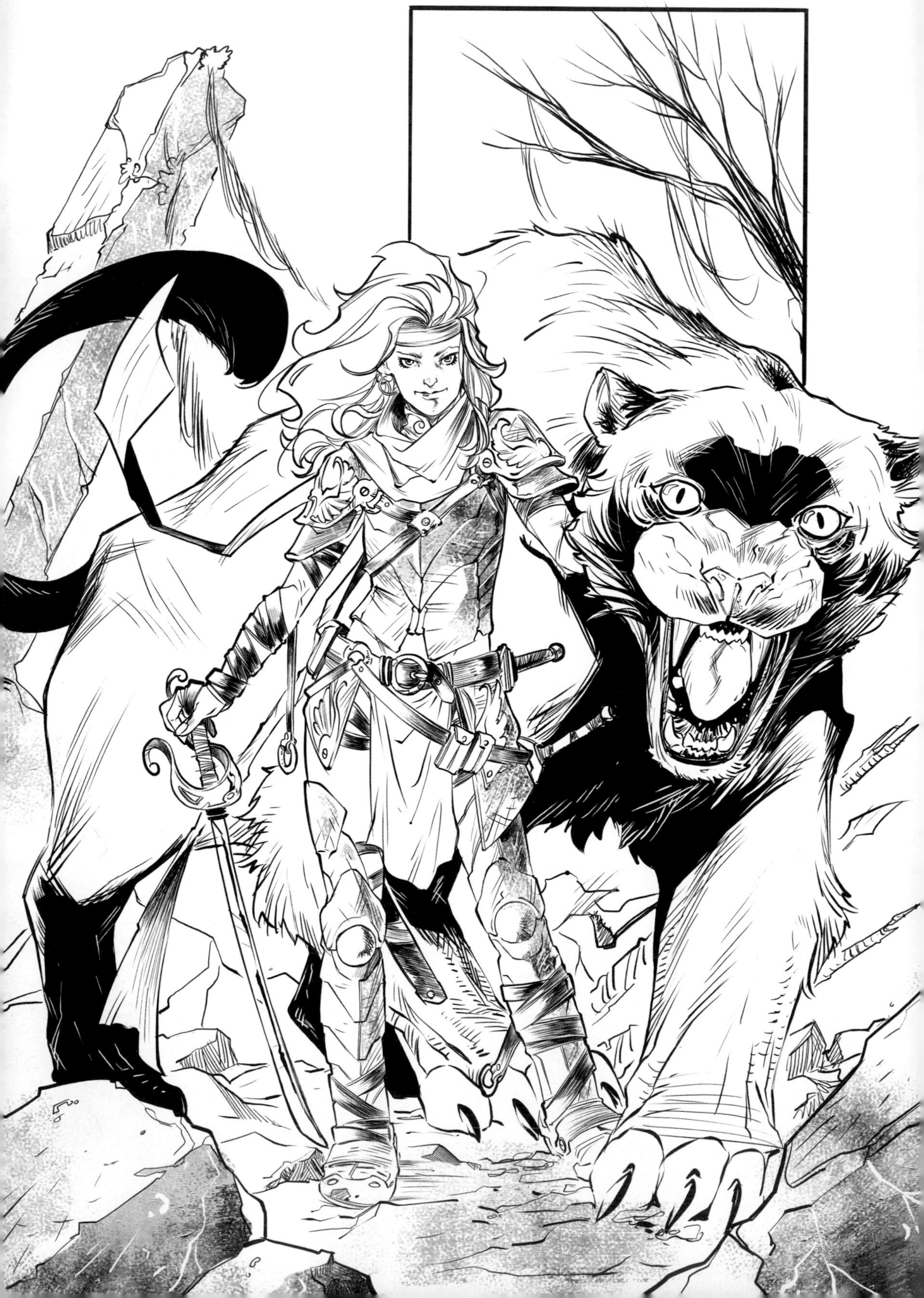

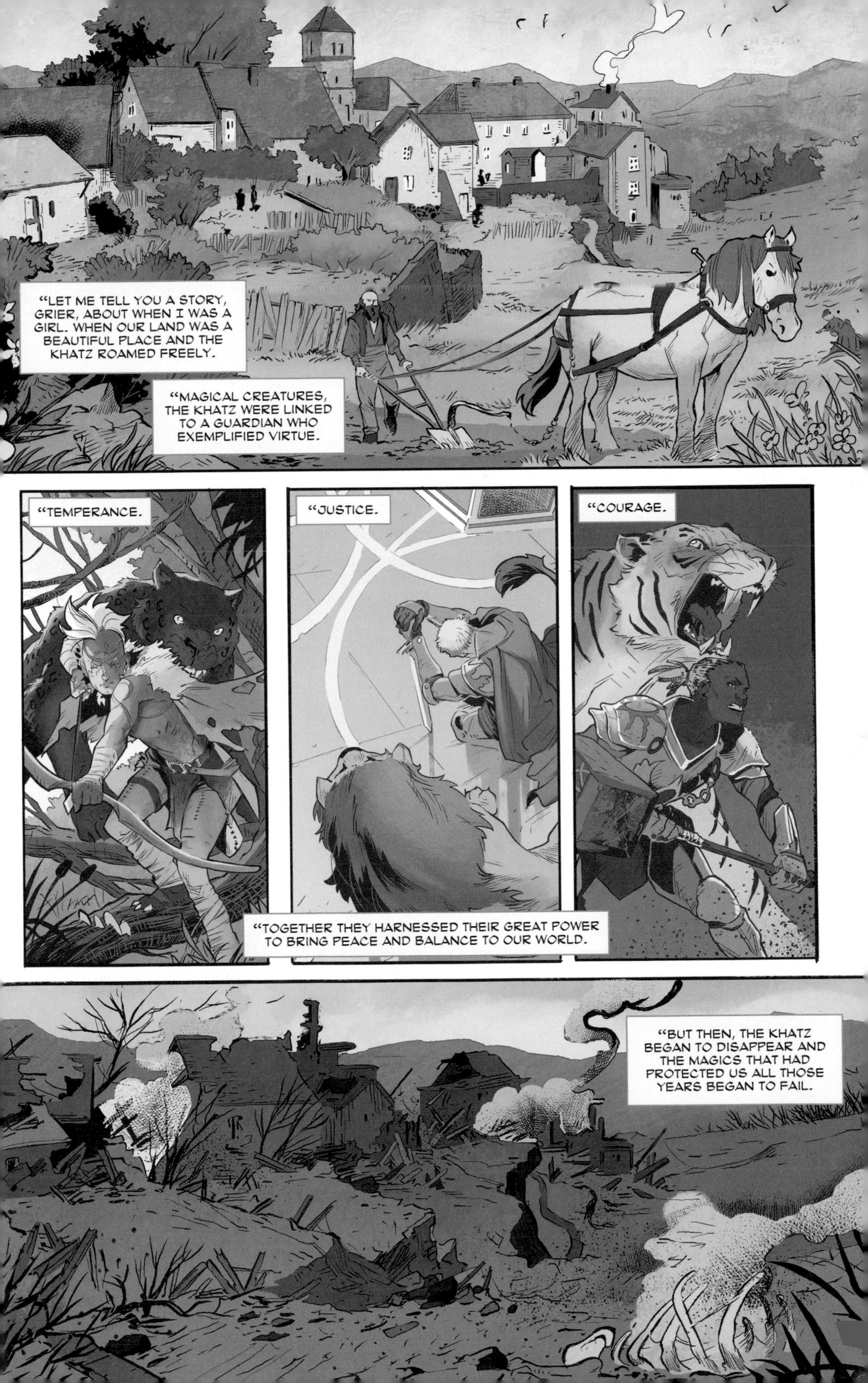

"LET ME TELL YOU A STORY, GRIER, ABOUT WHEN I WAS A GIRL. WHEN OUR LAND WAS A BEAUTIFUL PLACE AND THE KHATZ ROAMED FREELY.
"MAGICAL CREATURES, THE KHATZ WERE LINKED TO A GUARDIAN WHO EXEMPLIFIED VIRTUE.
"TEMPERANCE.
"JUSTICE.
"COURAGE.
"TOGETHER THEY HARNESSED THEIR GREAT POWER TO BRING PEACE AND BALANCE TO OUR WORLD.
"BUT THEN, THE KHATZ BEGAN TO DISAPPEAR AND THE MAGICS THAT HAD PROTECTED US ALL THOSE YEARS BEGAN TO FAIL.

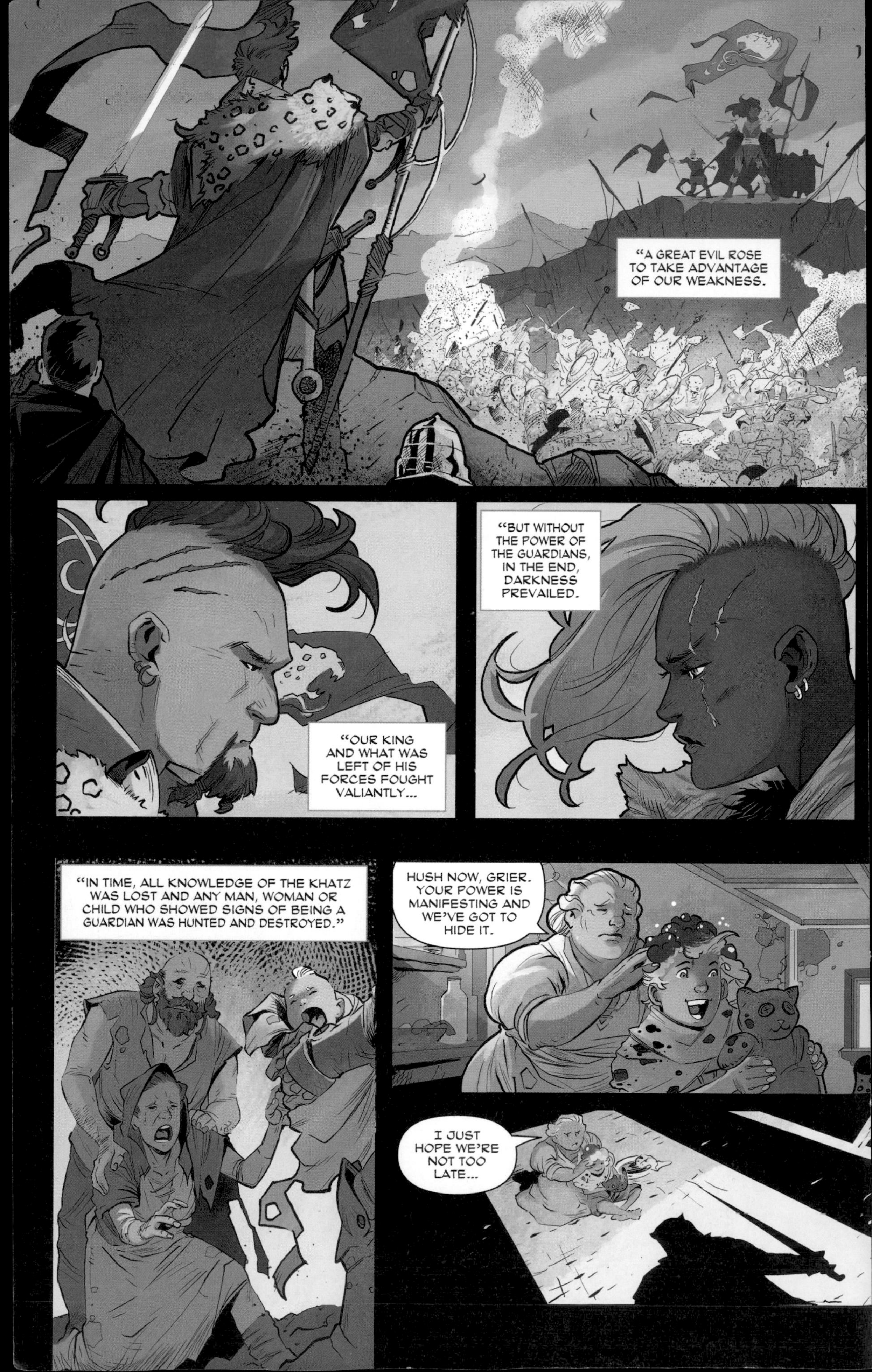
"A GREAT EVIL ROSE TO TAKE ADVANTAGE OF OUR WEAKNESS.
"OUR KING AND WHAT WAS LEFT OF HIS FORCES FOUGHT VALIANTLY...
"BUT WITHOUT THE POWER OF THE GUARDIANS, IN THE END, DARKNESS PREVAILED.
"IN TIME, ALL KNOWLEDGE OF THE KHATZ WAS LOST AND ANY MAN, WOMAN OR CHILD WHO SHOWED SIGNS OF BEING A GUARDIAN WAS HUNTED AND DESTROYED."
HUSH NOW, GRIER. YOUR POWER IS MANIFESTING AND WE'VE GOT TO HIDE IT.
I JUST HOPE WE'RE NOT TOO LATE...

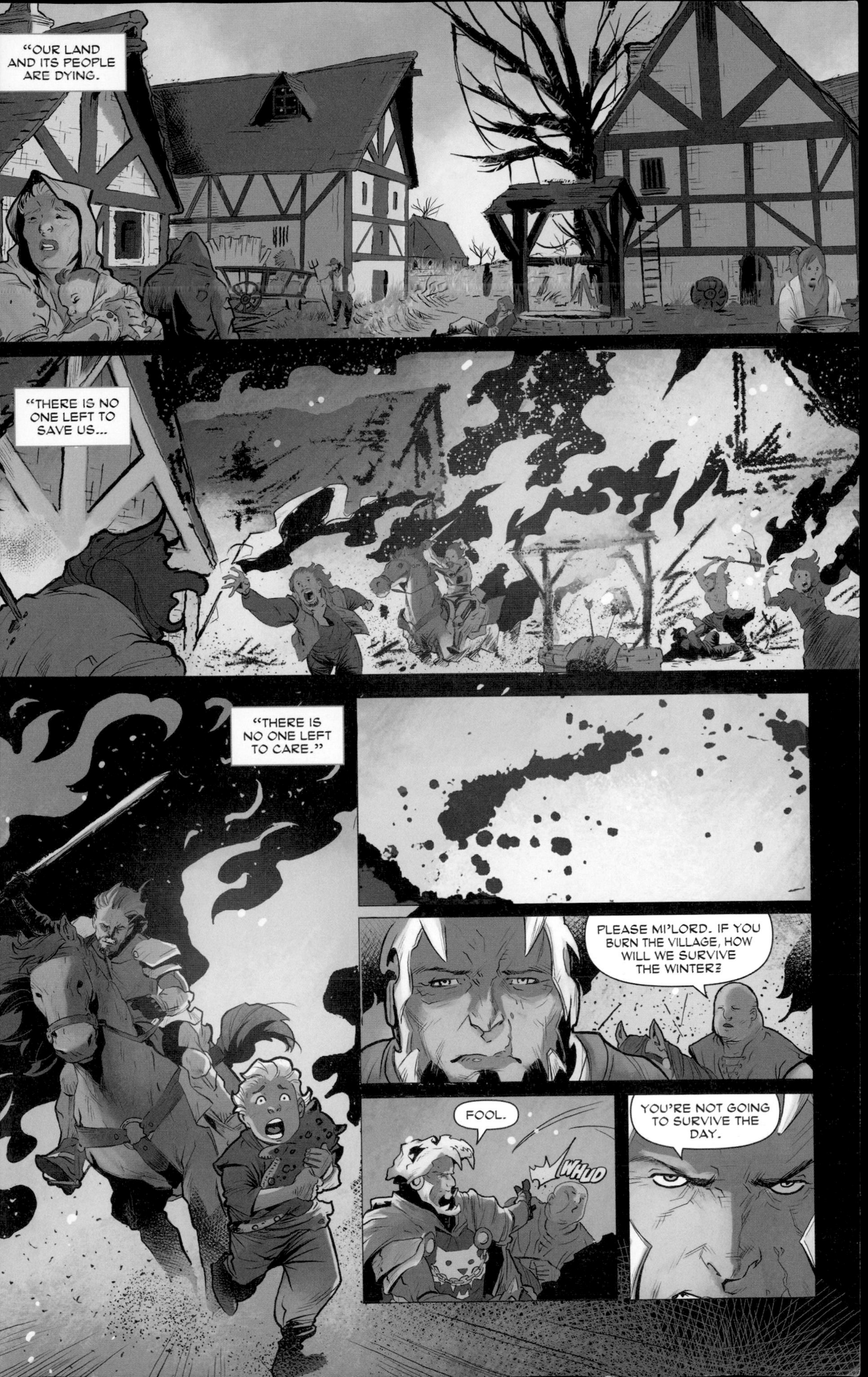
"OUR LAND AND ITS PEOPLE ARE DYING.
"THERE IS NO ONE LEFT TO SAVE US...
"THERE IS NO ONE LEFT TO CARE."
PLEASE MI'LORD. IF YOU BURN THE VILLAGE, HOW WILL WE SURVIVE THE WINTER?
FOOL.
WHUD
YOU'RE NOT GOING TO SURVIVE THE DAY.

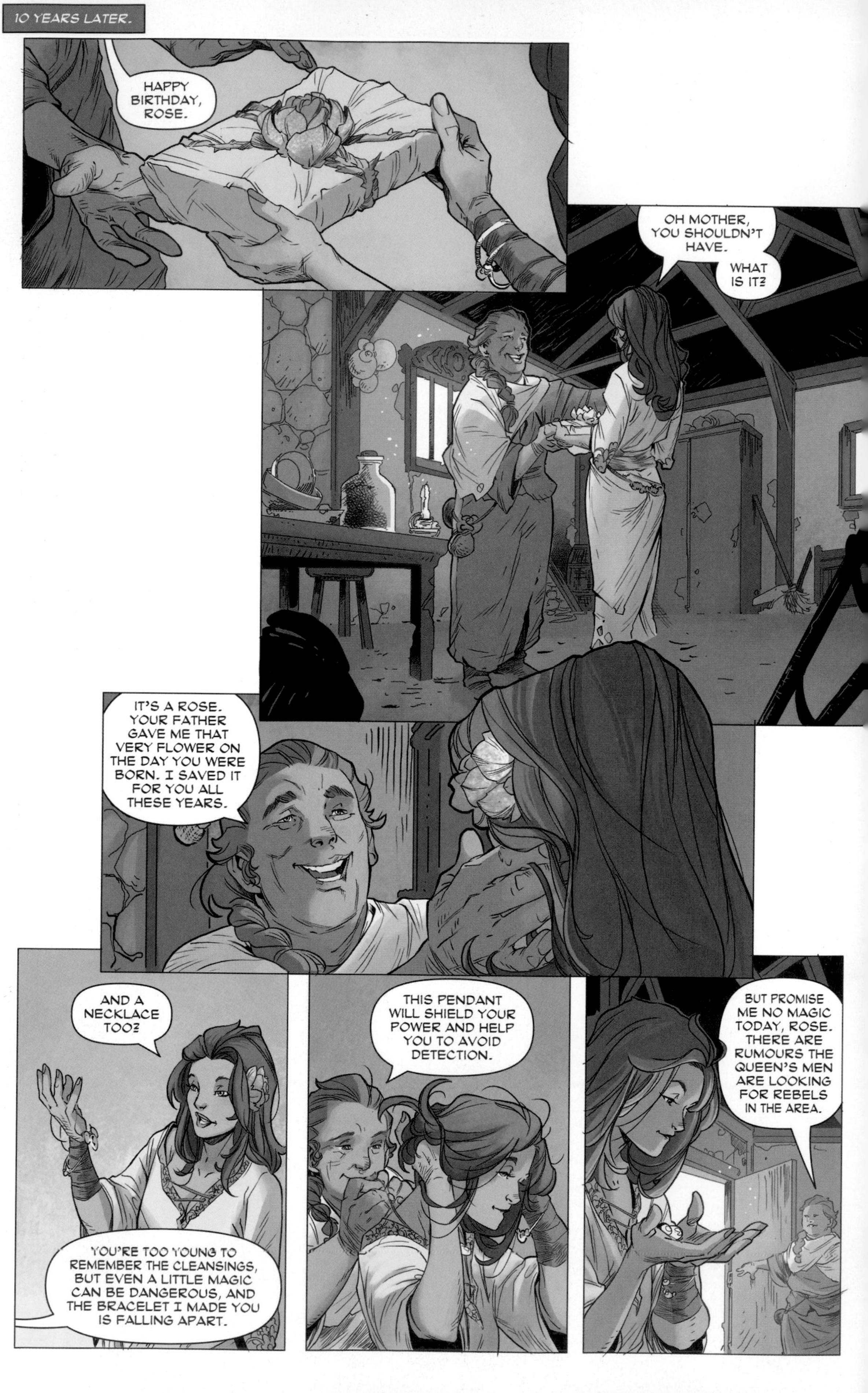
10 YEARS LATER.
HAPPY BIRTHDAY, ROSE.
OH MOTHER, YOU SHOULDN'T HAVE.
WHAT IS IT?
IT'S A ROSE. YOUR FATHER GAVE ME THAT VERY FLOWER ON THE DAY YOU WERE BORN. I SAVED IT FOR YOU ALL THESE YEARS.
AND A NECKLACE TOO?
YOU'RE TOO YOUNG TO REMEMBER THE CLEANSINGS, BUT EVEN A LITTLE MAGIC CAN BE DANGEROUS, AND THE BRACELET I MADE YOU IS FALLING APART.
THIS PENDANT WILL SHIELD YOUR POWER AND HELP YOU TO AVOID DETECTION.
BUT PROMISE ME NO MAGIC TODAY, ROSE. THERE ARE RUMOURS THE QUEEN'S MEN ARE LOOKING FOR REBELS IN THE AREA.

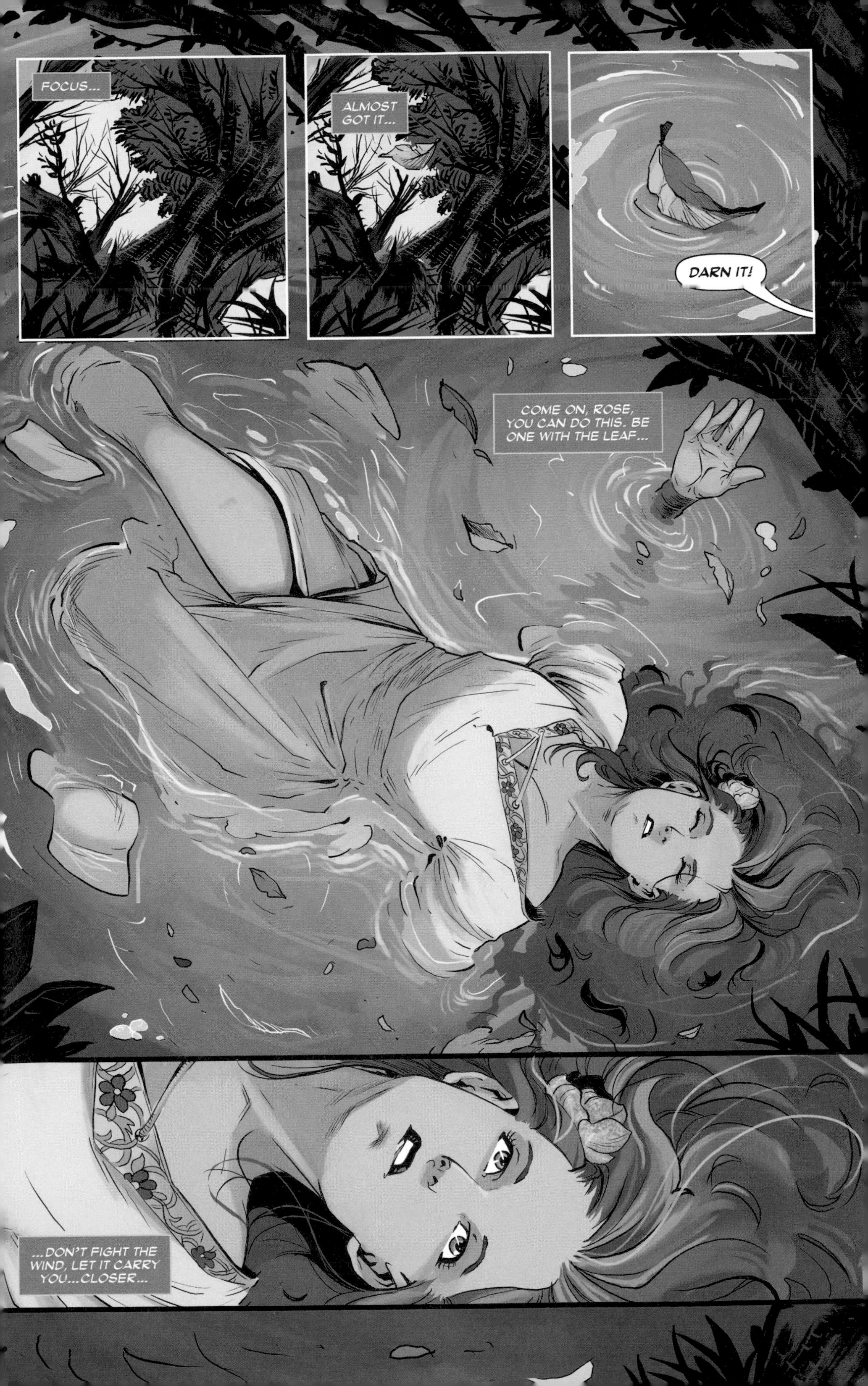
FOCUS...
ALMOST GOT IT...
DARN IT!
COME ON, ROSE, YOU CAN DO THIS. BE ONE WITH THE LEAF...
...DON'T FIGHT THE WIND, LET IT CARRY YOU...CLOSER...

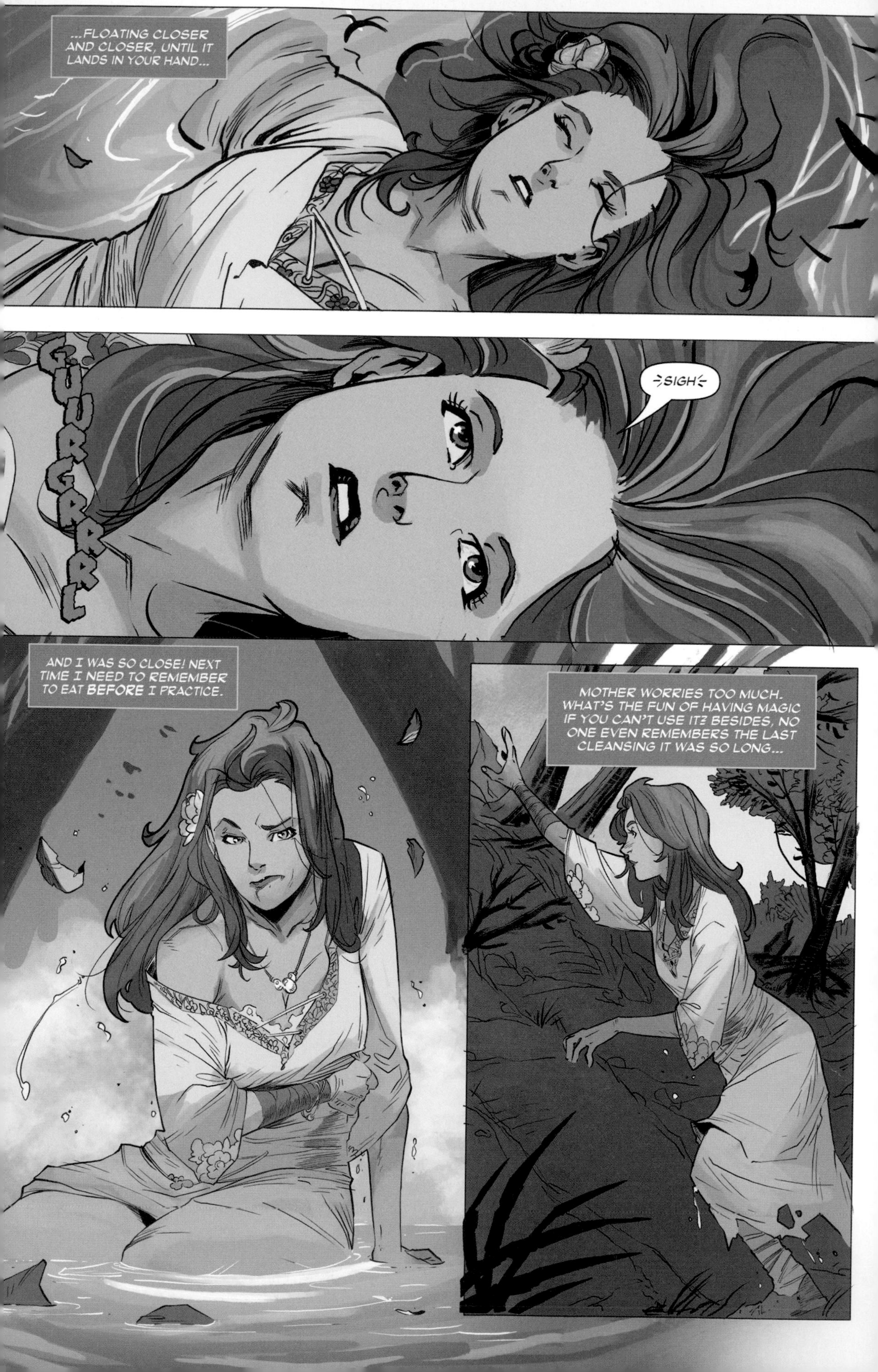
...FLOATING CLOSER AND CLOSER, UNTIL IT LANDS IN YOUR HAND...
GUURGRRRL
SIGH
AND I WAS SO CLOSE! NEXT TIME I NEED TO REMEMBER TO EAT BEFORE I PRACTICE.
MOTHER WORRIES TOO MUCH. WHAT'S THE FUN OF HAVING MAGIC IF YOU CAN'T USE IT? BESIDES, NO ONE EVEN REMEMBERS THE LAST CLEANSING IT WAS SO LONG...

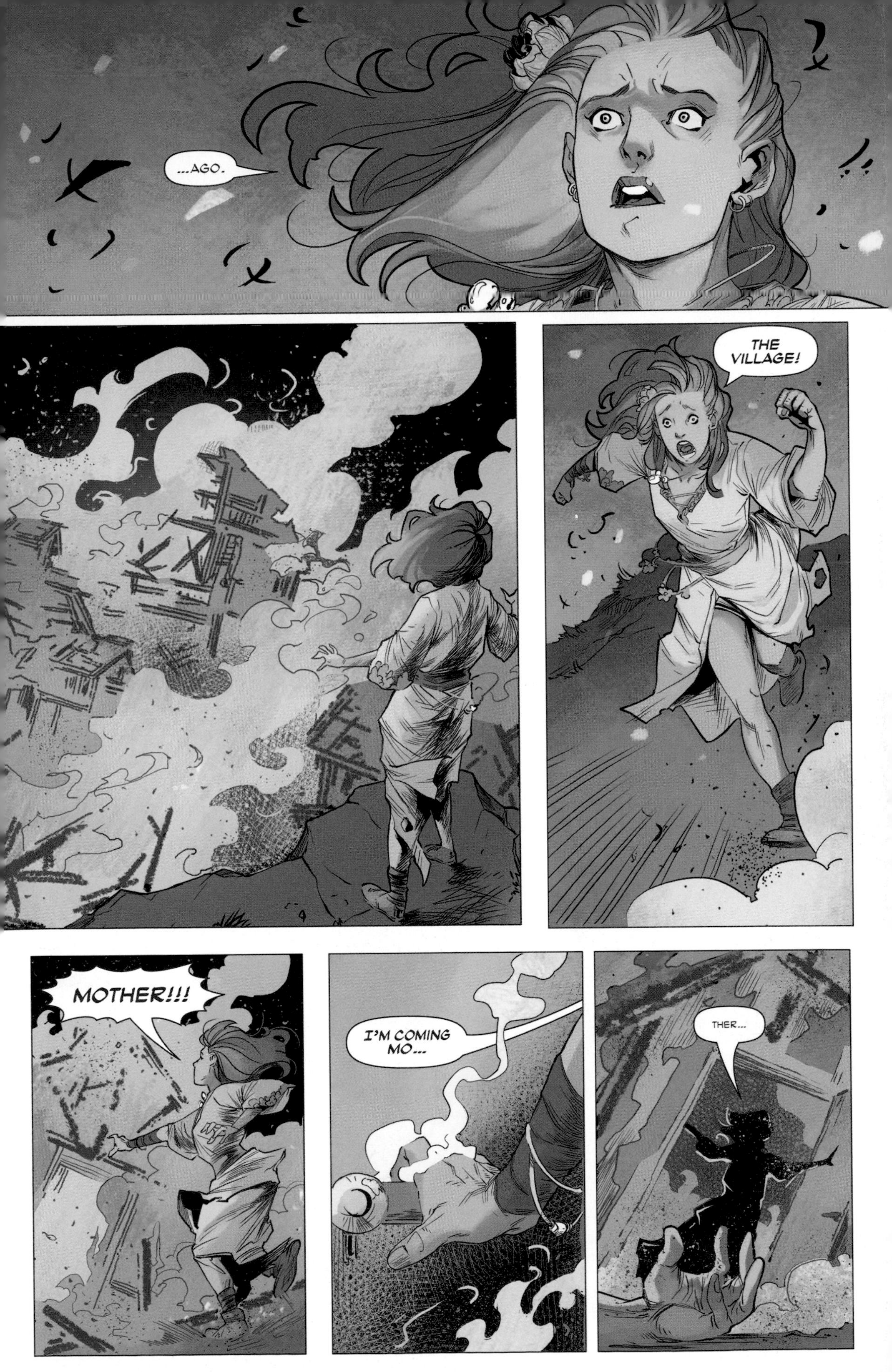
...AGO.
THE VILLAGE!
MOTHER!!!
I'M COMING MO...
THER...

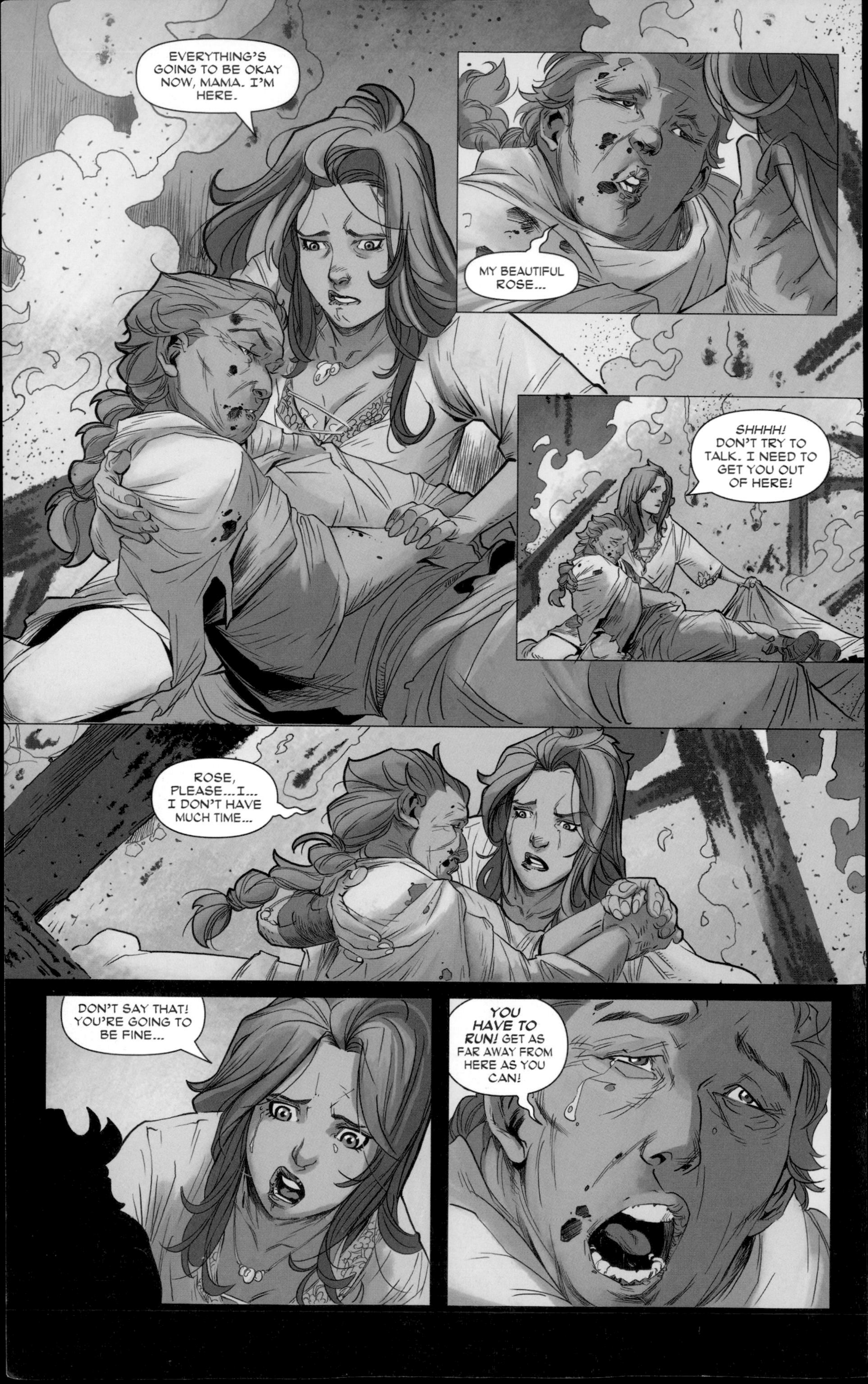
EVERYTHING'S GOING TO BE OKAY NOW, MAMA. I'M HERE.
MY BEAUTIFUL ROSE...
SHHHH! DON'T TRY TO TALK. I NEED TO GET YOU OUT OF HERE!
ROSE, PLEASE...I... I DON'T HAVE MUCH TIME...
DON'T SAY THAT! YOU'RE GOING TO BE FINE...
YOU HAVE TO RUN! GET AS FAR AWAY FROM HERE AS YOU CAN!

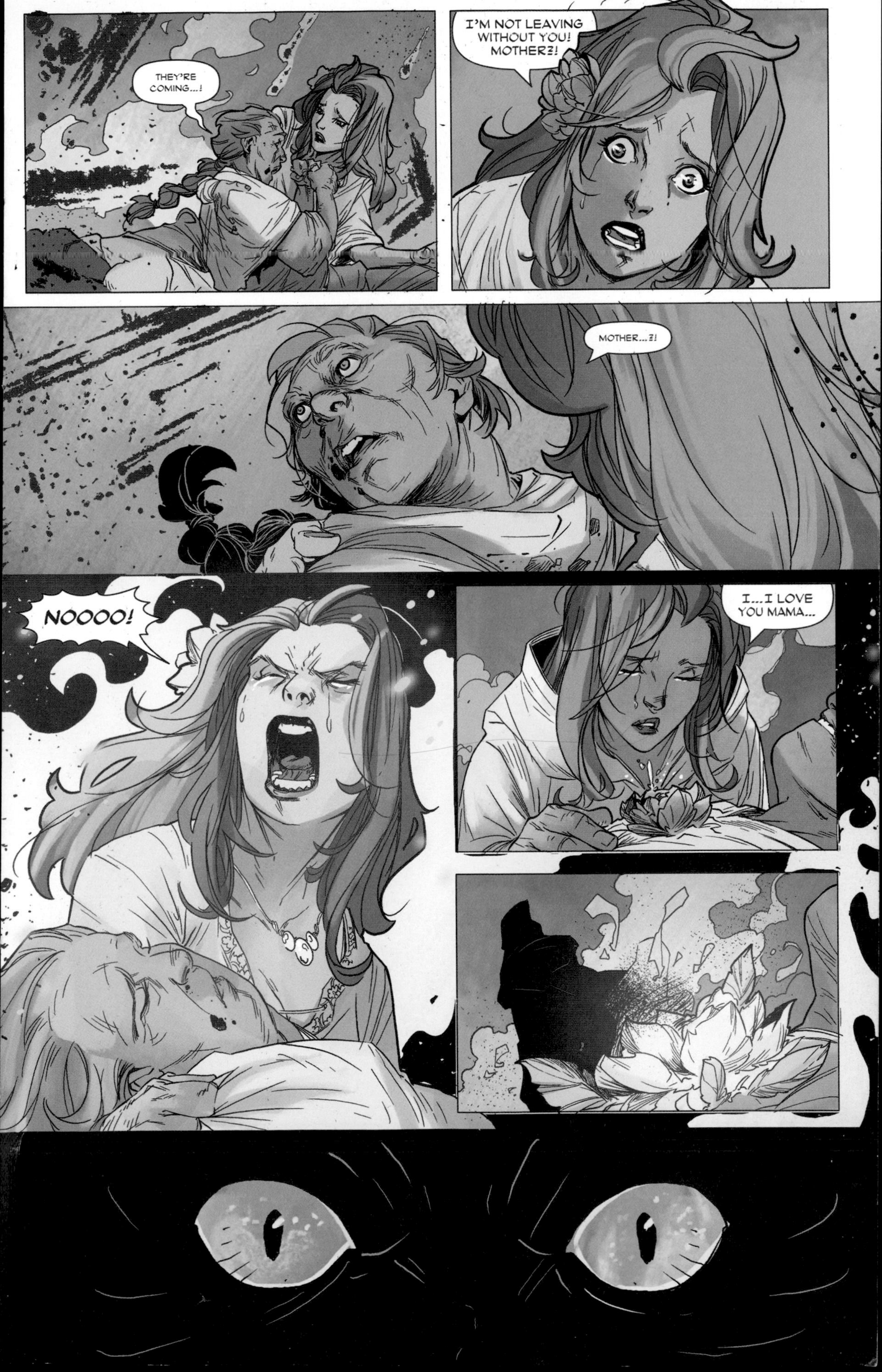
THEY'RE COMING...!
I'M NOT LEAVING WITHOUT YOU! MOTHER?!
MOTHER...?!
NOOOO!
I...I LOVE YOU MAMA...

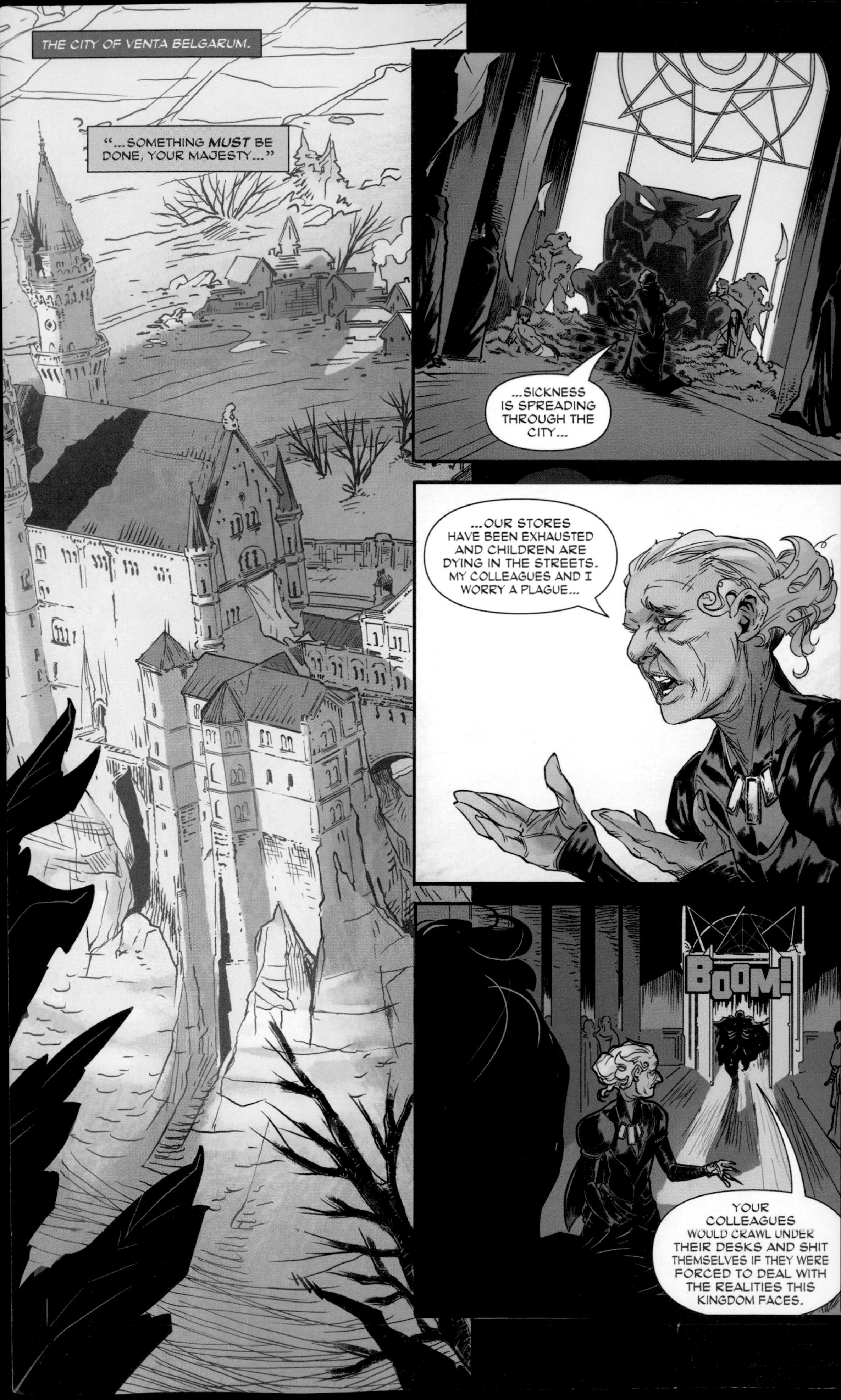
THE CITY OF VENTA BELGARUM.
"...SOMETHING MUST BE DONE, YOUR MAJESTY..."
...SICKNESS IS SPREADING THROUGH THE CITY...
...OUR STORES HAVE BEEN EXHAUSTED AND CHILDREN ARE DYING IN THE STREETS. MY COLLEAGUES AND I WORRY A PLAGUE...
BOOM!
YOUR COLLEAGUES WOULD CRAWL UNDER THEIR DESKS AND SHIT THEMSELVES IF THEY WERE FORCED TO DEAL WITH THE REALITIES THIS KINGDOM FACES.

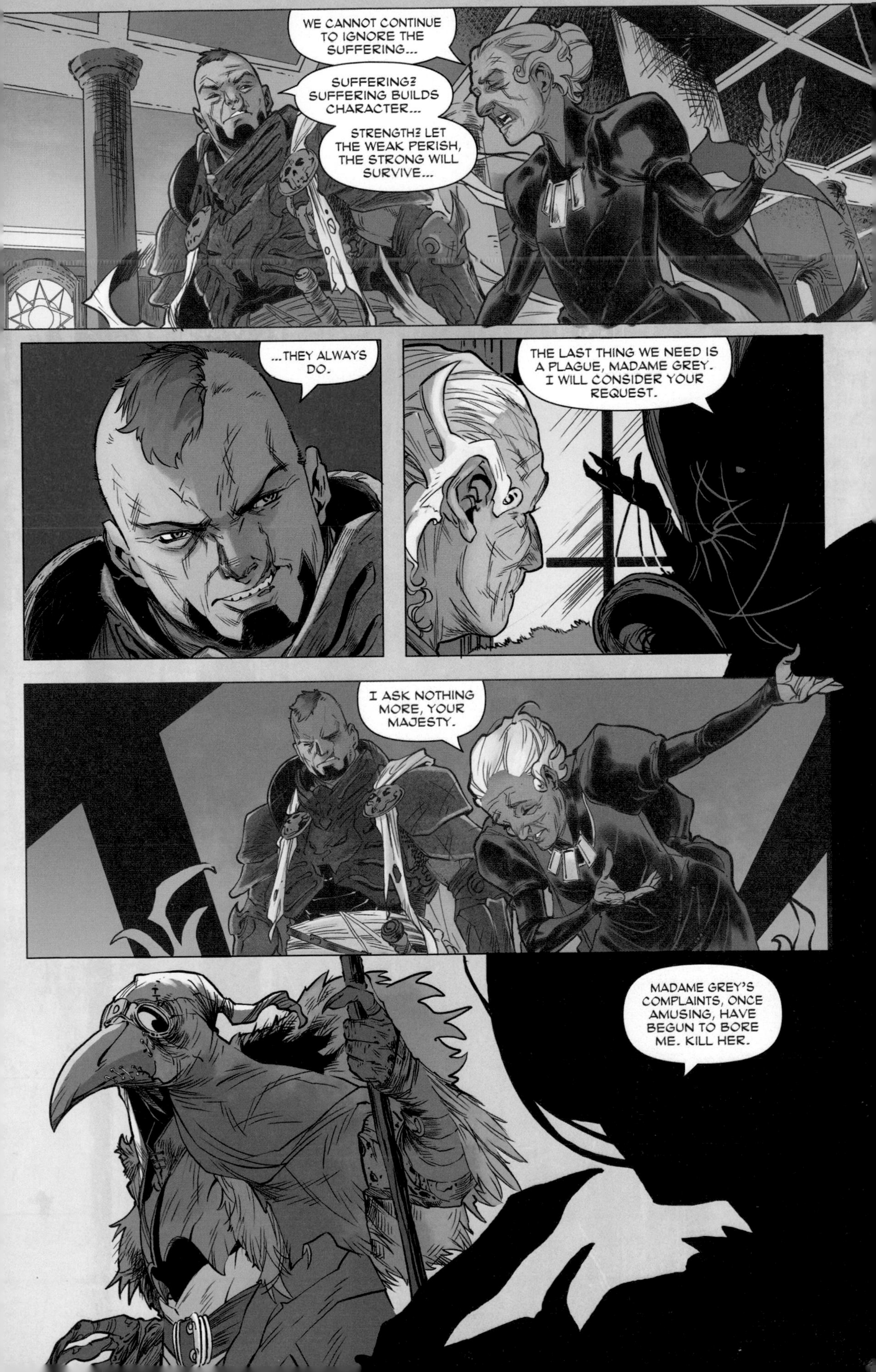
WE CANNOT CONTINUE TO IGNORE THE SUFFERING...
SUFFERING? SUFFERING BUILDS CHARACTER...
STRENGTH? LET THE WEAK PERISH, THE STRONG WILL SURVIVE...
...THEY ALWAYS DO.
THE LAST THING WE NEED IS A PLAGUE, MADAME GREY. I WILL CONSIDER YOUR REQUEST.
I ASK NOTHING MORE, YOUR MAJESTY.
MADAME GREY'S COMPLAINTS, ONCE AMUSING, HAVE BEGUN TO BORE ME. KILL HER.

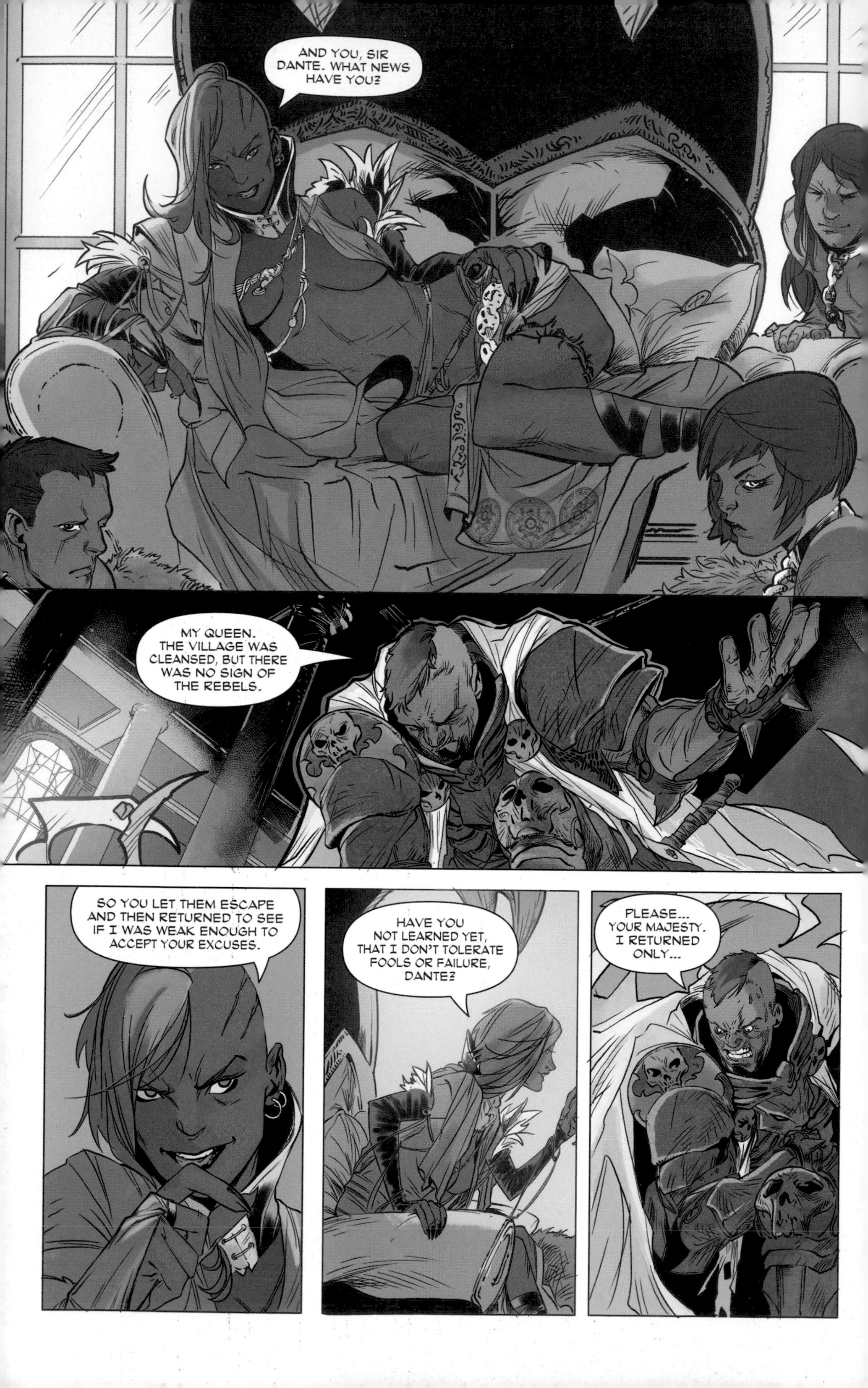
AND YOU, SIR DANTE. WHAT NEWS HAVE YOU?
MY QUEEN. THE VILLAGE WAS CLEANSED, BUT THERE WAS NO SIGN OF THE REBELS.
SO YOU LET THEM ESCAPE AND THEN RETURNED TO SEE IF I WAS WEAK ENOUGH TO ACCEPT YOUR EXCUSES.
HAVE YOU NOT LEARNED YET, THAT I DON'T TOLERATE FOOLS OR FAILURE, DANTE?
PLEASE... YOUR MAJESTY. I RETURNED ONLY...

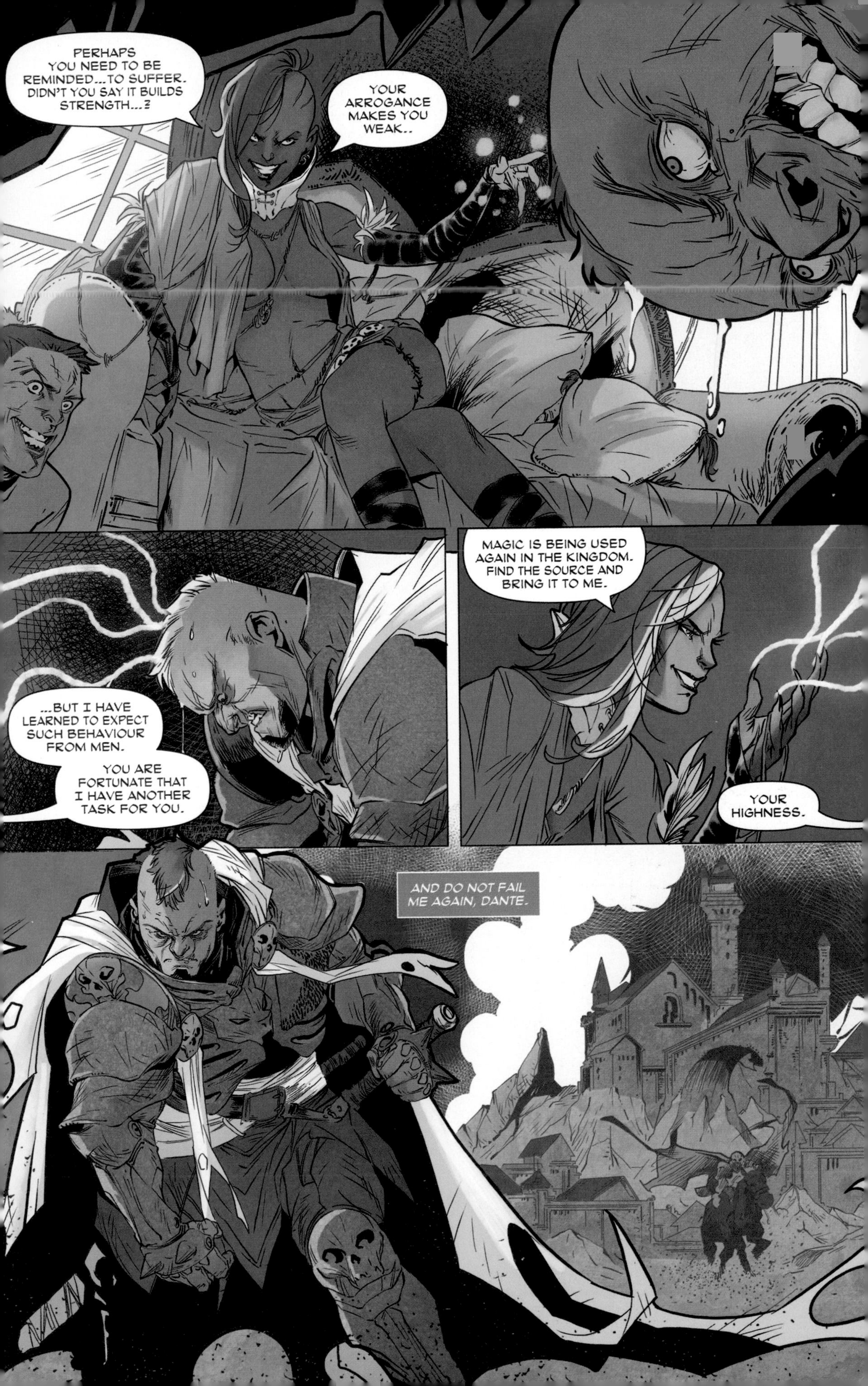

PERHAPS YOU NEED TO BE REMINDED...TO SUFFER. DIDN'T YOU SAY IT BUILDS STRENGTH...?
YOUR ARROGANCE MAKES YOU WEAK..
...BUT I HAVE LEARNED TO EXPECT SUCH BEHAVIOUR FROM MEN.
YOU ARE FORTUNATE THAT I HAVE ANOTHER TASK FOR YOU.
MAGIC IS BEING USED AGAIN IN THE KINGDOM. FIND THE SOURCE AND BRING IT TO ME.
YOUR HIGHNESS.
AND DO NOT FAIL ME AGAIN, DANTE.

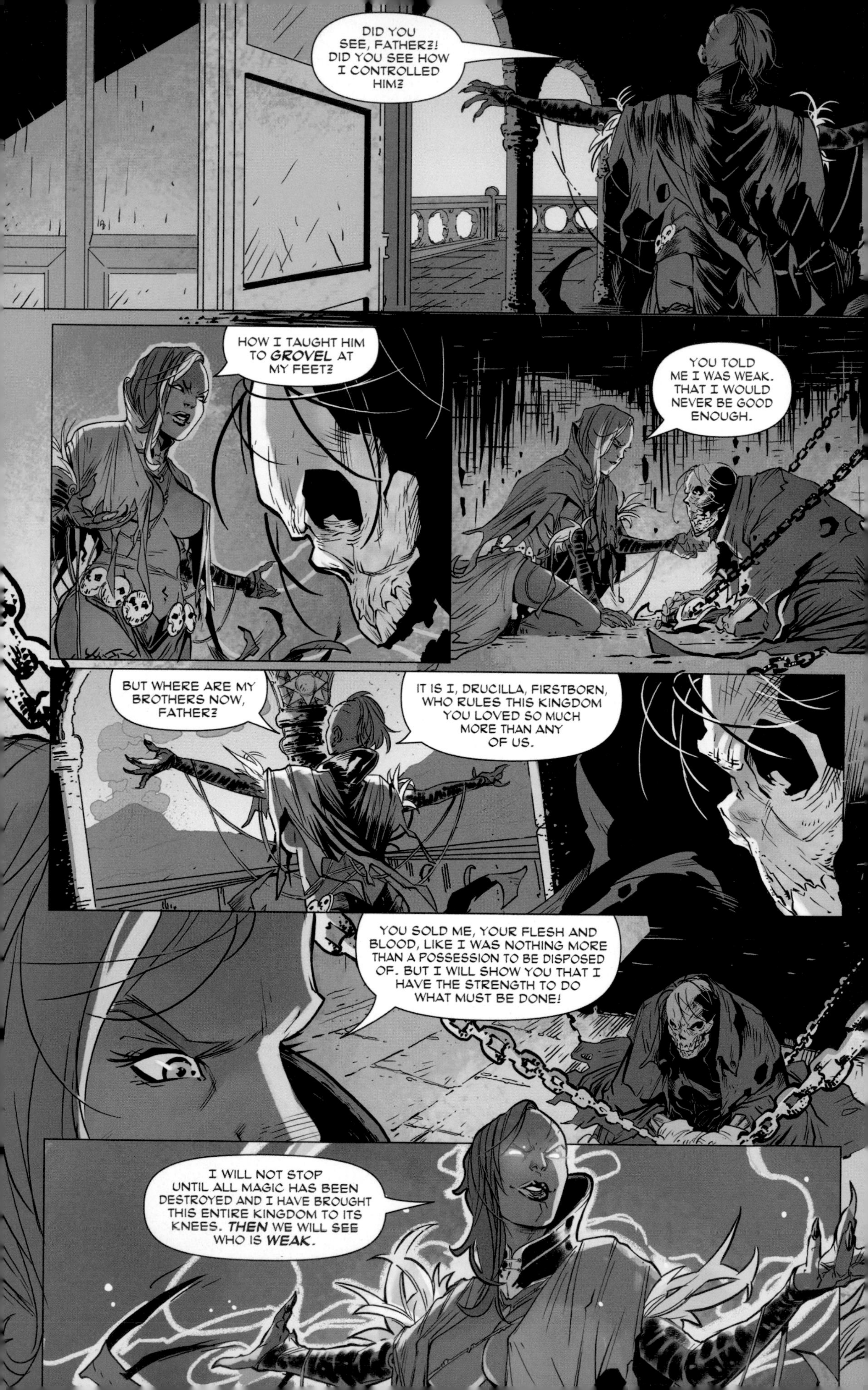
DID YOU SEE, FATHER?! DID YOU SEE HOW I CONTROLLED HIM?
HOW I TAUGHT HIM TO GROVEL AT MY FEET?
YOU TOLD ME I WAS WEAK. THAT I WOULD NEVER BE GOOD ENOUGH.
BUT WHERE ARE MY BROTHERS NOW, FATHER?
IT IS I, DRUCILLA, FIRSTBORN, WHO RULES THIS KINGDOM YOU LOVED SO MUCH MORE THAN ANY OF US.
YOU SOLD ME, YOUR FLESH AND BLOOD, LIKE I WAS NOTHING MORE THAN A POSSESSION TO BE DISPOSED OF. BUT I WILL SHOW YOU THAT I HAVE THE STRENGTH TO DO WHAT MUST BE DONE!
I WILL NOT STOP UNTIL ALL MAGIC HAS BEEN DESTROYED AND I HAVE BROUGHT THIS ENTIRE KINGDOM TO ITS KNEES. THEN WE WILL SEE WHO IS WEAK.

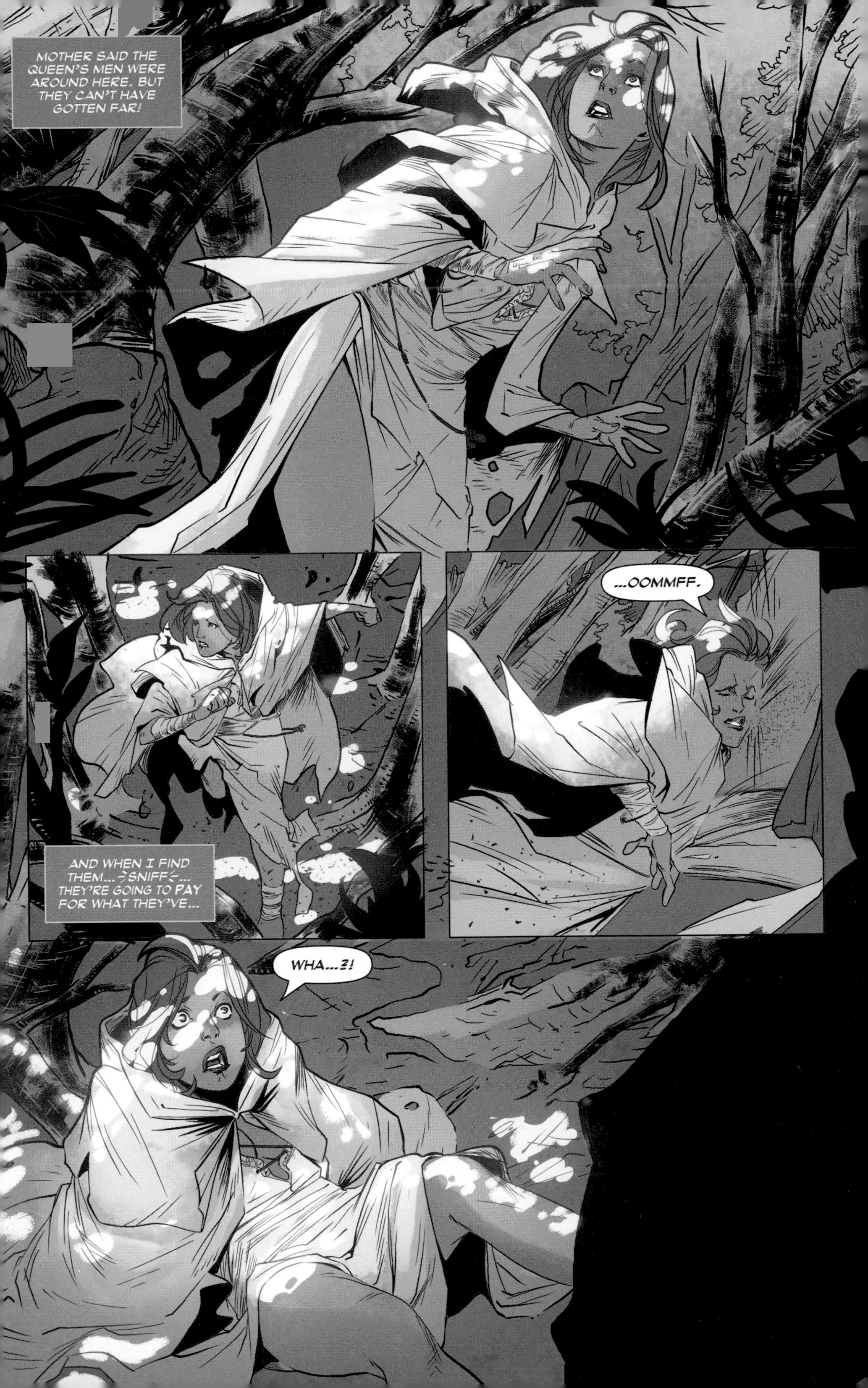
MOTHER SAID THE QUEEN'S MEN WERE AROUND HERE. BUT THEY CAN'T HAVE GOTTEN FAR!
AND WHEN I FIND THEM... >SNIFF<... THEY'RE GOING TO PAY FOR WHAT THEY'VE...
...OOMMFF.
WHA...?!

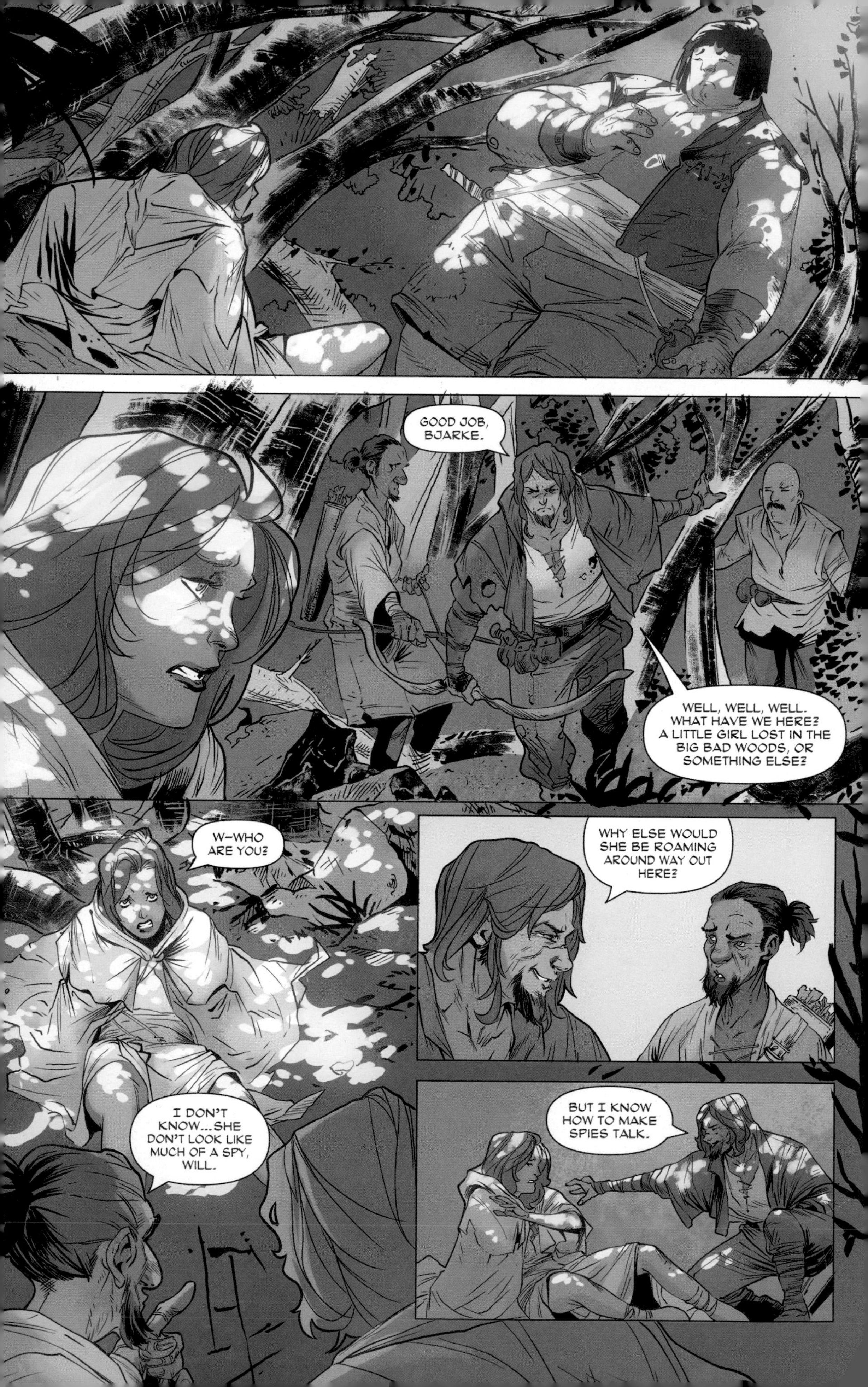
GOOD JOB, BJARKE.
WELL, WELL, WELL. WHAT HAVE WE HERE? A LITTLE GIRL LOST IN THE BIG BAD WOODS, OR SOMETHING ELSE?
W-WHO ARE YOU?
WHY ELSE WOULD SHE BE ROAMING AROUND WAY OUT HERE?
I DON'T KNOW...SHE DON'T LOOK LIKE MUCH OF A SPY, WILL.
BUT I KNOW HOW TO MAKE SPIES TALK.

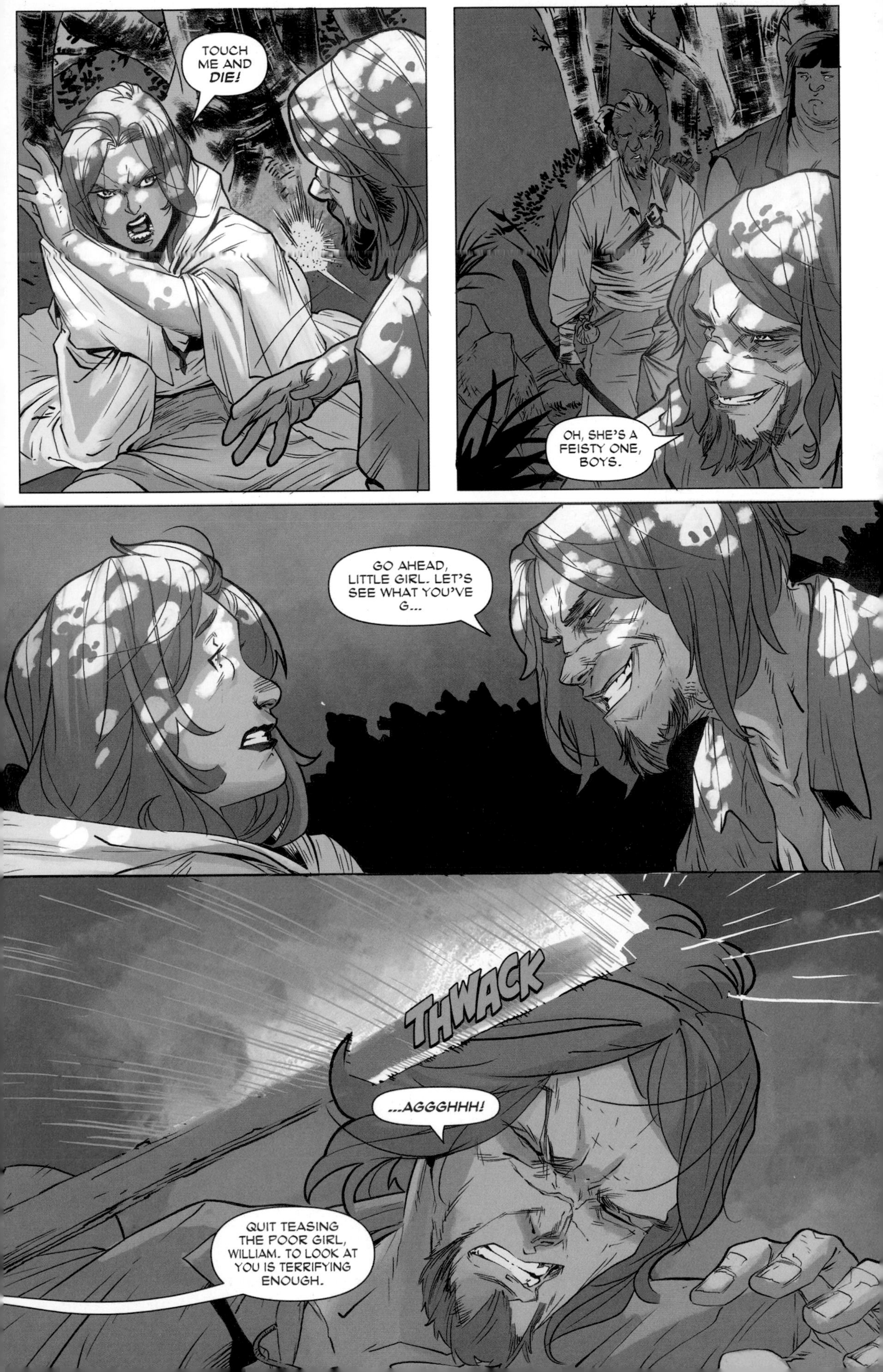
TOUCH ME AND *DIE!*
OH, SHE'S A FEISTY ONE, BOYS.
GO AHEAD, LITTLE GIRL. LET'S SEE WHAT YOU'VE G...
THWACK
...AGGGHHH!
QUIT TEASING THE POOR GIRL, WILLIAM. TO LOOK AT YOU IS TERRIFYING ENOUGH.

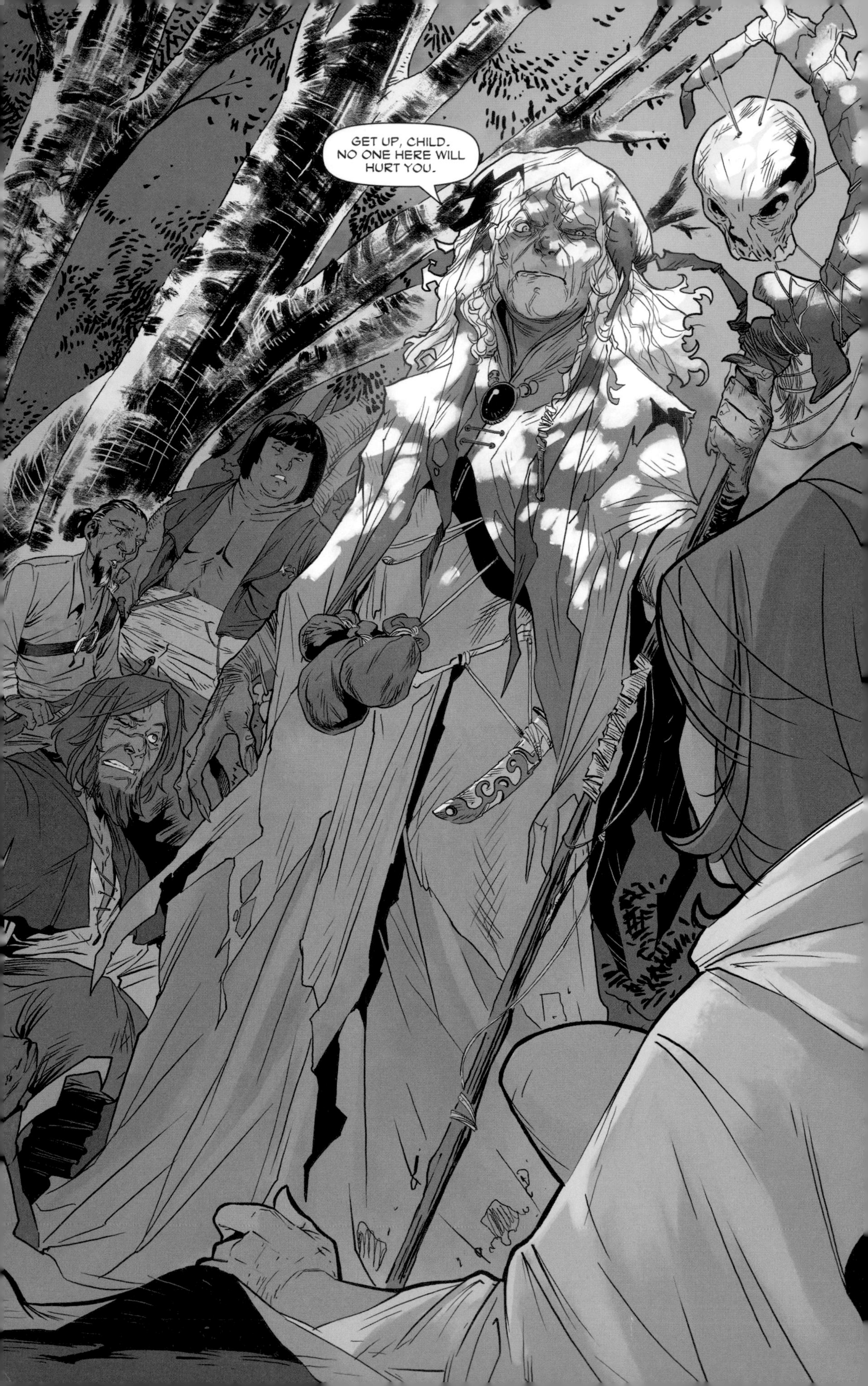
GET UP, CHILD. NO ONE HERE WILL HURT YOU.

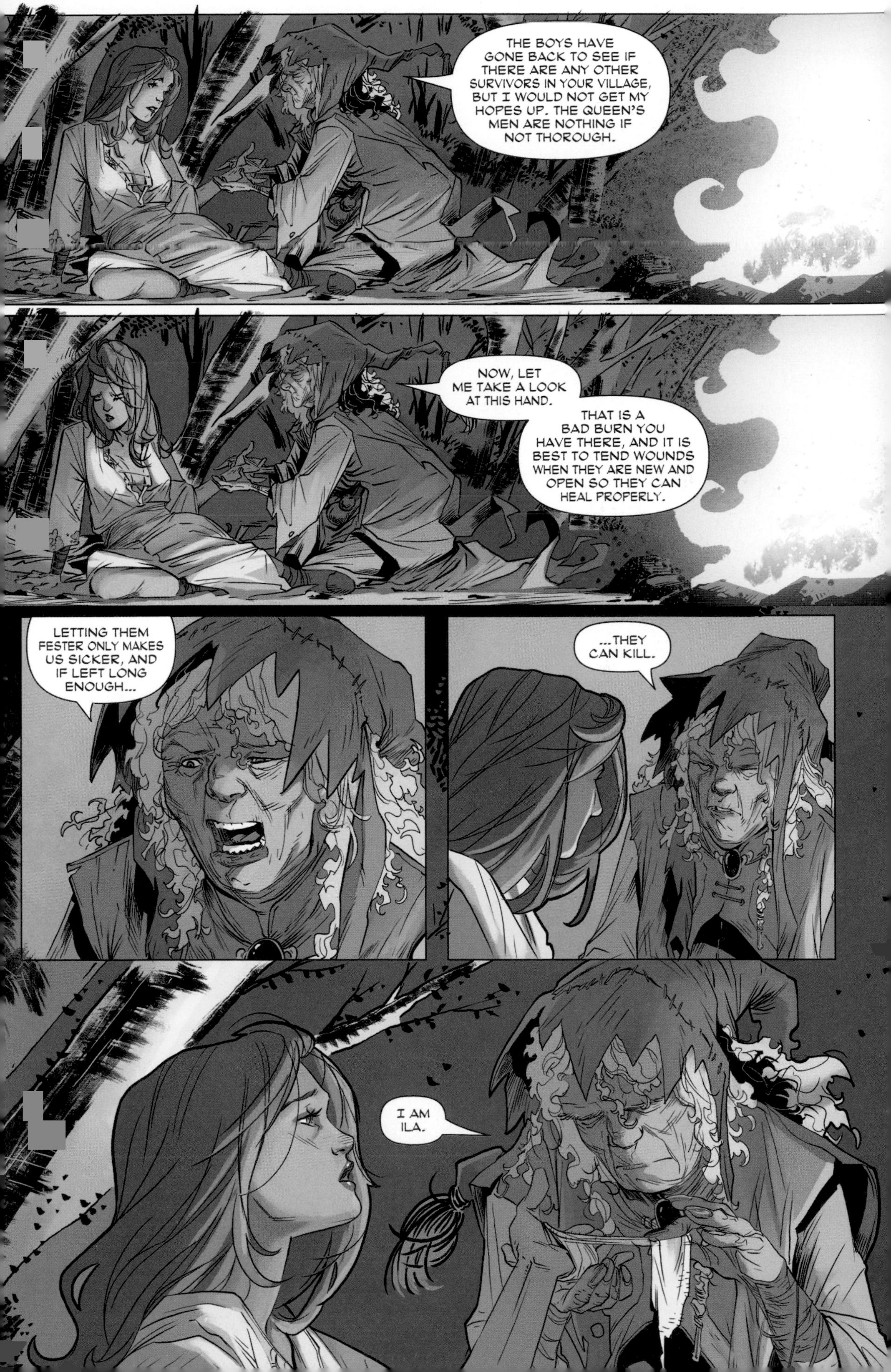
THE BOYS HAVE GONE BACK TO SEE IF THERE ARE ANY OTHER SURVIVORS IN YOUR VILLAGE, BUT I WOULD NOT GET MY HOPES UP. THE QUEEN'S MEN ARE NOTHING IF NOT THOROUGH.
NOW, LET ME TAKE A LOOK AT THIS HAND.
THAT IS A BAD BURN YOU HAVE THERE, AND IT IS BEST TO TEND WOUNDS WHEN THEY ARE NEW AND OPEN SO THEY CAN HEAL PROPERLY.
LETTING THEM FESTER ONLY MAKES US SICKER, AND IF LEFT LONG ENOUGH...
...THEY CAN KILL.
I AM ILA.

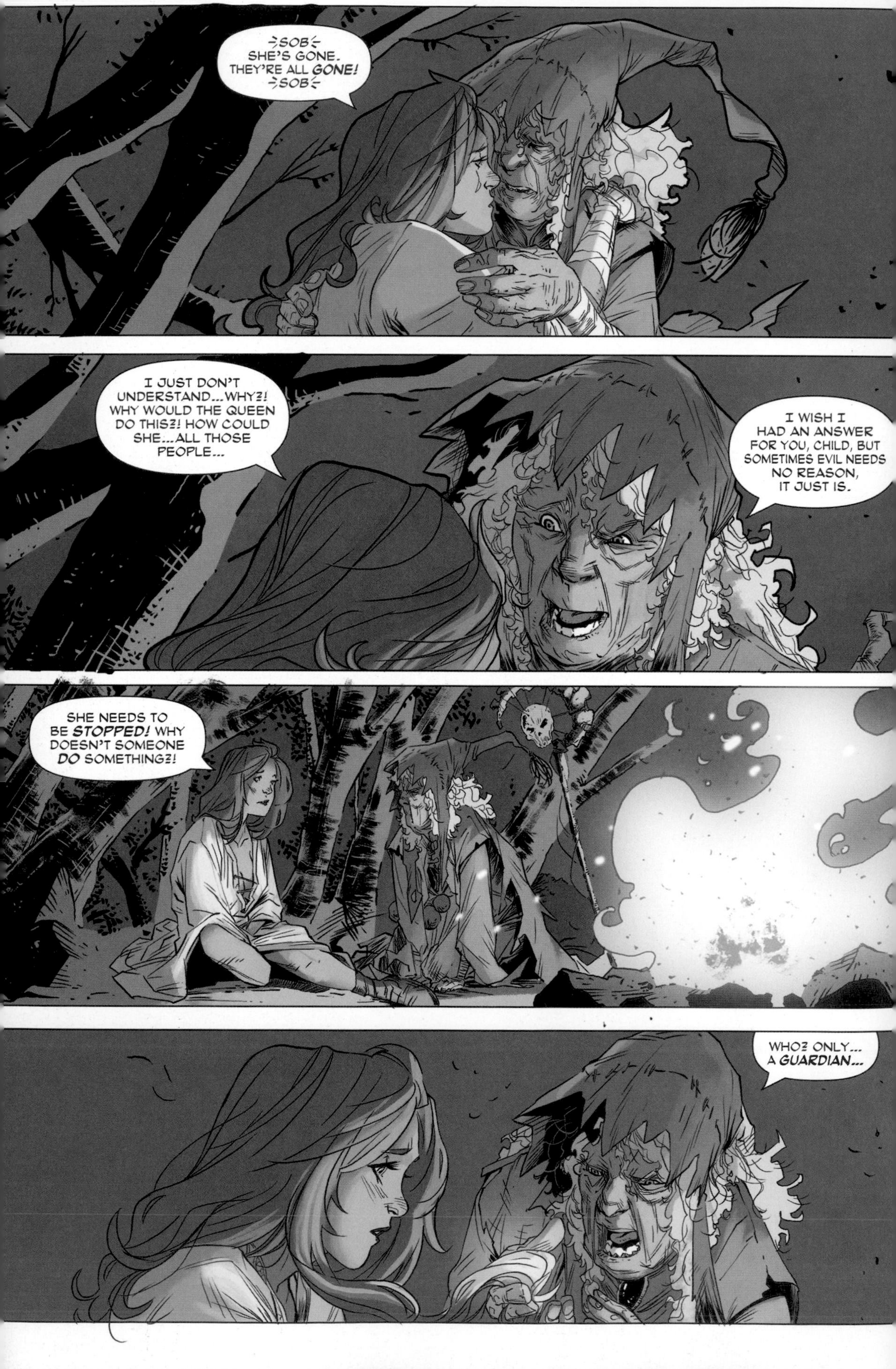
-SOB- SHE'S GONE. THEY'RE ALL GONE! -SOB-
I JUST DON'T UNDERSTAND...WHY?! WHY WOULD THE QUEEN DO THIS?! HOW COULD SHE...ALL THOSE PEOPLE...
I WISH I HAD AN ANSWER FOR YOU, CHILD, BUT SOMETIMES EVIL NEEDS NO REASON, IT JUST IS.
SHE NEEDS TO BE STOPPED! WHY DOESN'T SOMEONE DO SOMETHING?!
WHO? ONLY... A GUARDIAN...

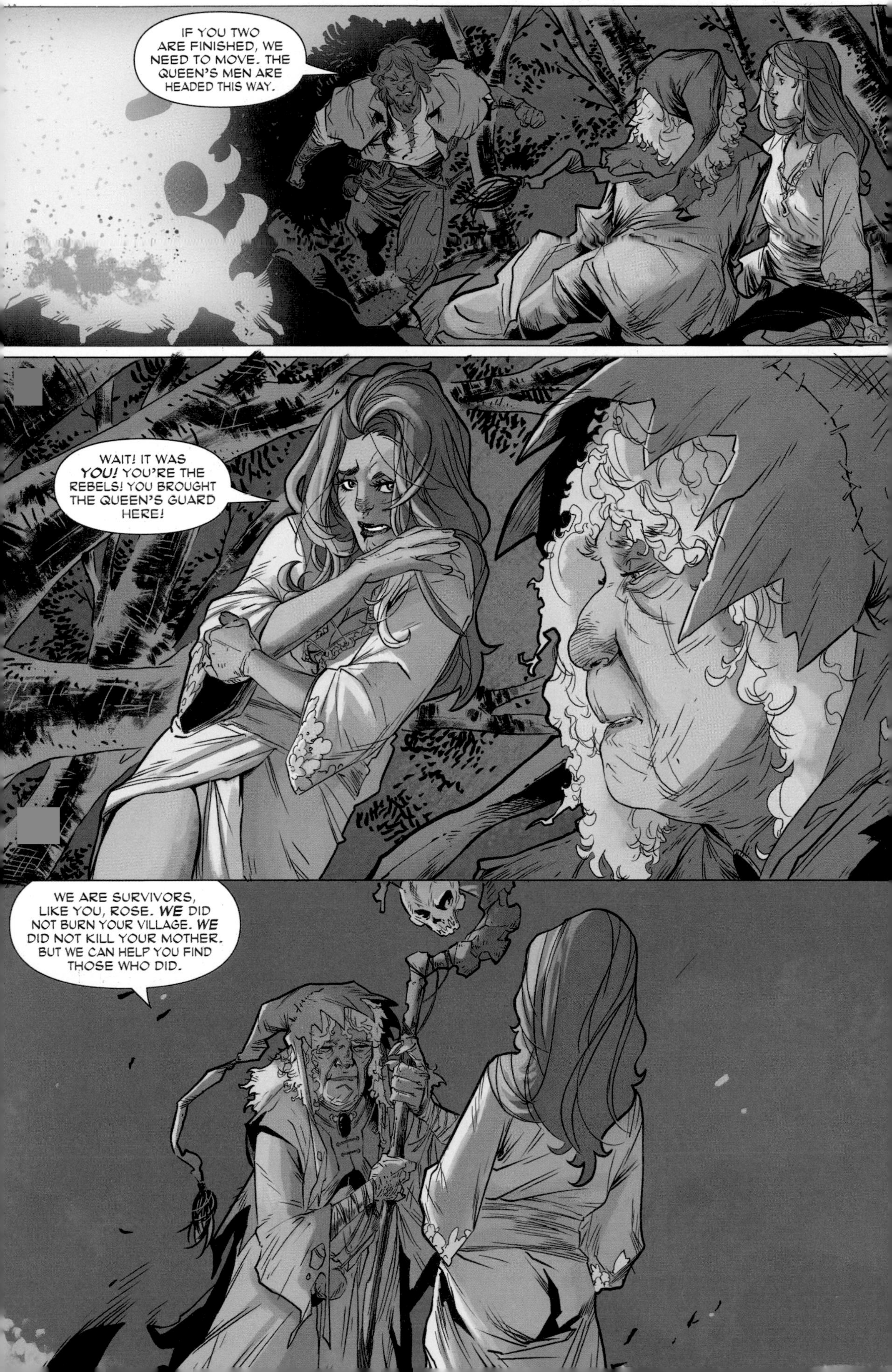
IF YOU TWO ARE FINISHED, WE NEED TO MOVE. THE QUEEN'S MEN ARE HEADED THIS WAY.
WAIT! IT WAS *YOU!* YOU'RE THE REBELS! YOU BROUGHT THE QUEEN'S GUARD HERE!
WE ARE SURVIVORS, LIKE YOU, ROSE. *WE* DID NOT BURN YOUR VILLAGE. *WE* DID NOT KILL YOUR MOTHER. BUT WE CAN HELP YOU FIND THOSE WHO DID.

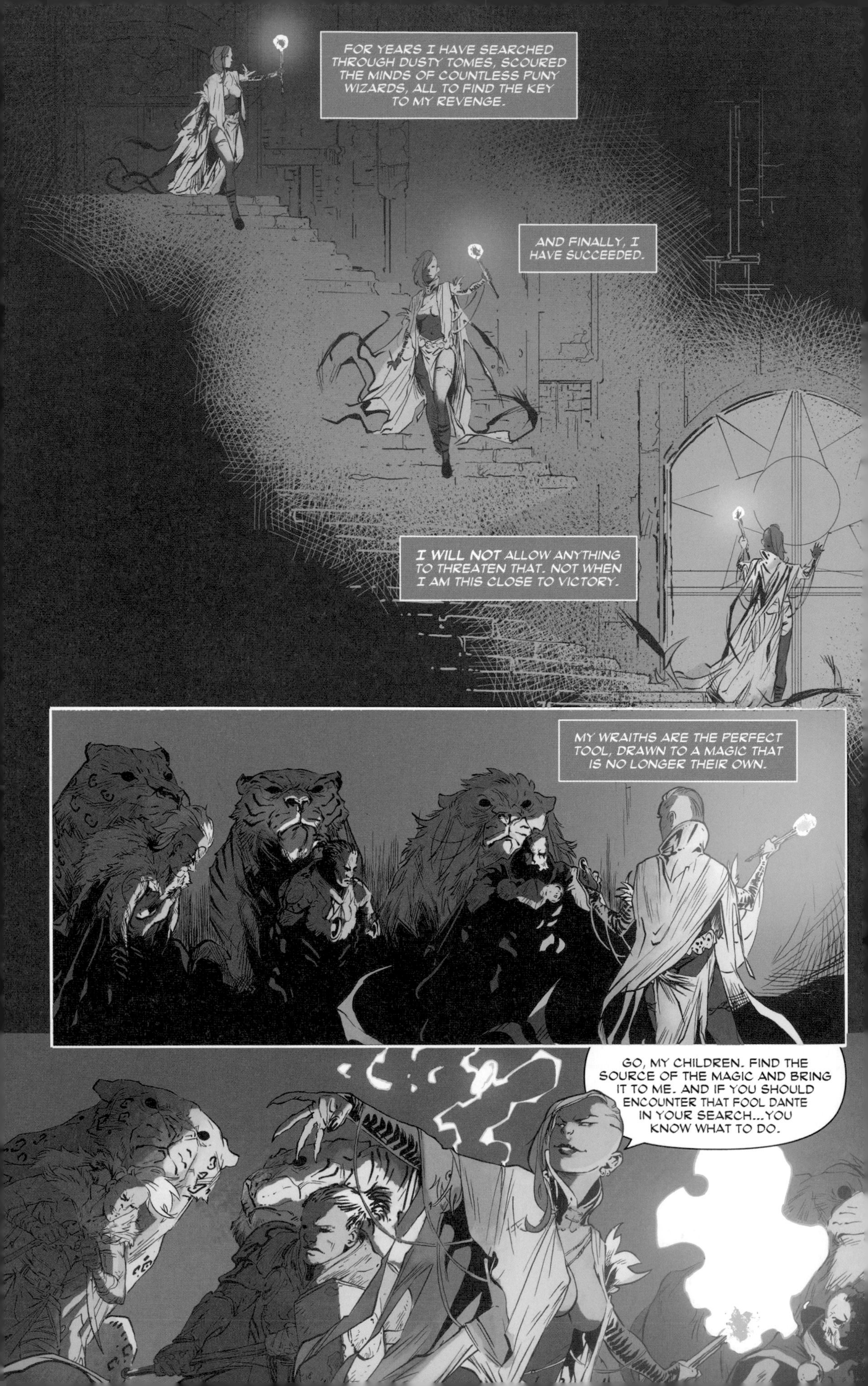
FOR YEARS I HAVE SEARCHED THROUGH DUSTY TOMES, SCOURED THE MINDS OF COUNTLESS PUNY WIZARDS, ALL TO FIND THE KEY TO MY REVENGE.
AND FINALLY, I HAVE SUCCEEDED.
I WILL NOT ALLOW ANYTHING TO THREATEN THAT. NOT WHEN I AM THIS CLOSE TO VICTORY.
MY WRAITHS ARE THE PERFECT TOOL, DRAWN TO A MAGIC THAT IS NO LONGER THEIR OWN.
GO, MY CHILDREN. FIND THE SOURCE OF THE MAGIC AND BRING IT TO ME. AND IF YOU SHOULD ENCOUNTER THAT FOOL DANTE IN YOUR SEARCH...YOU KNOW WHAT TO DO.

TWO

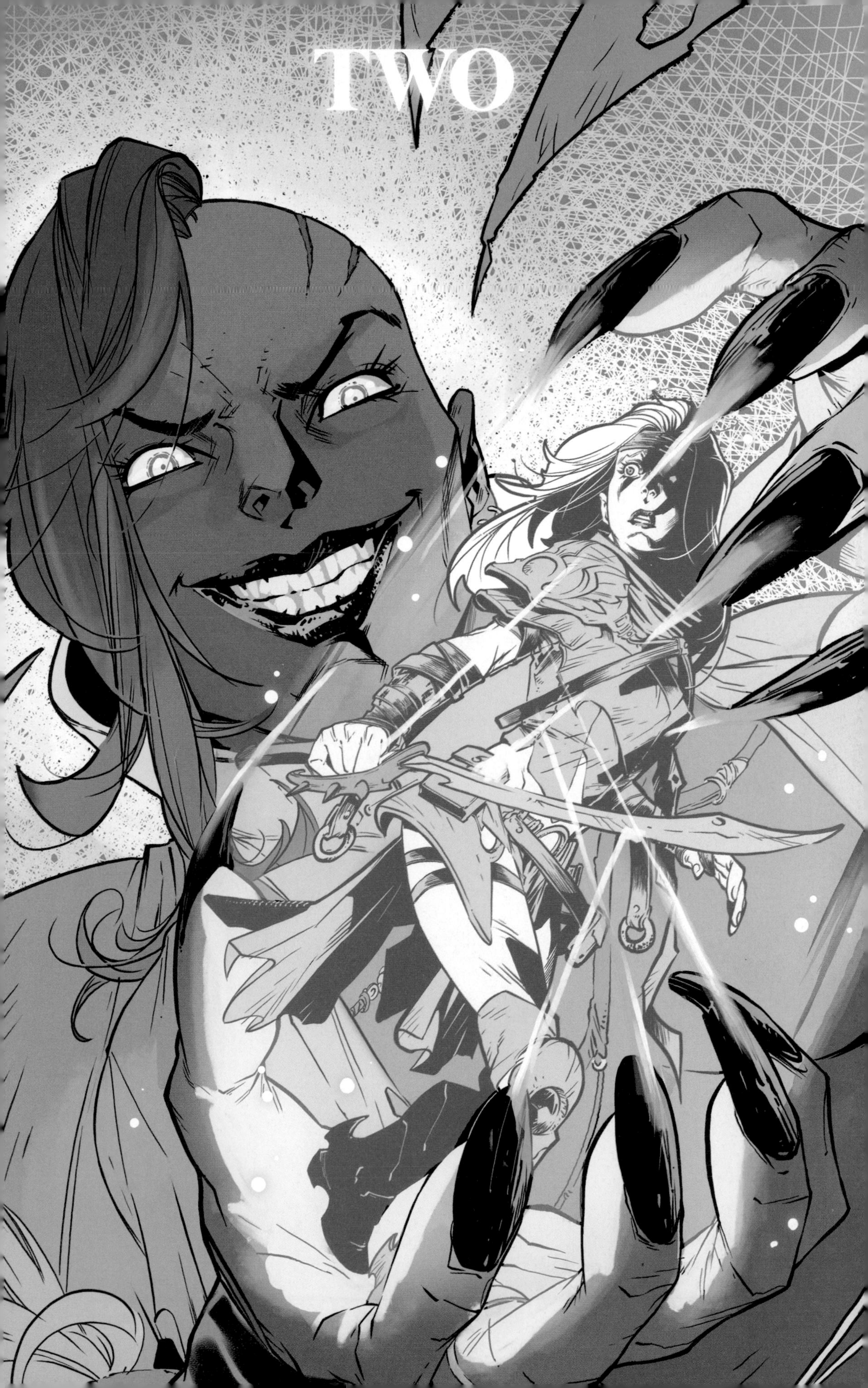

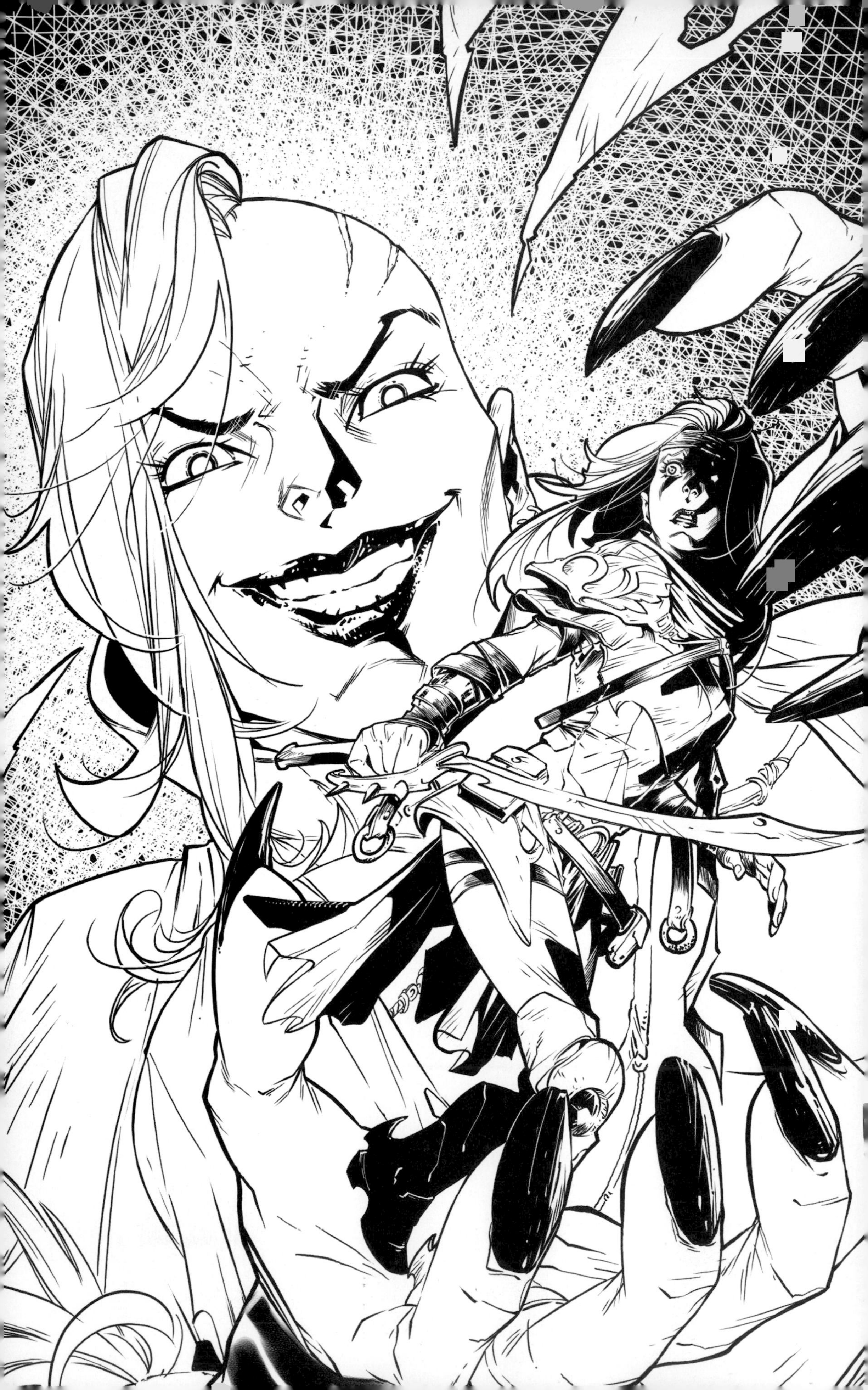

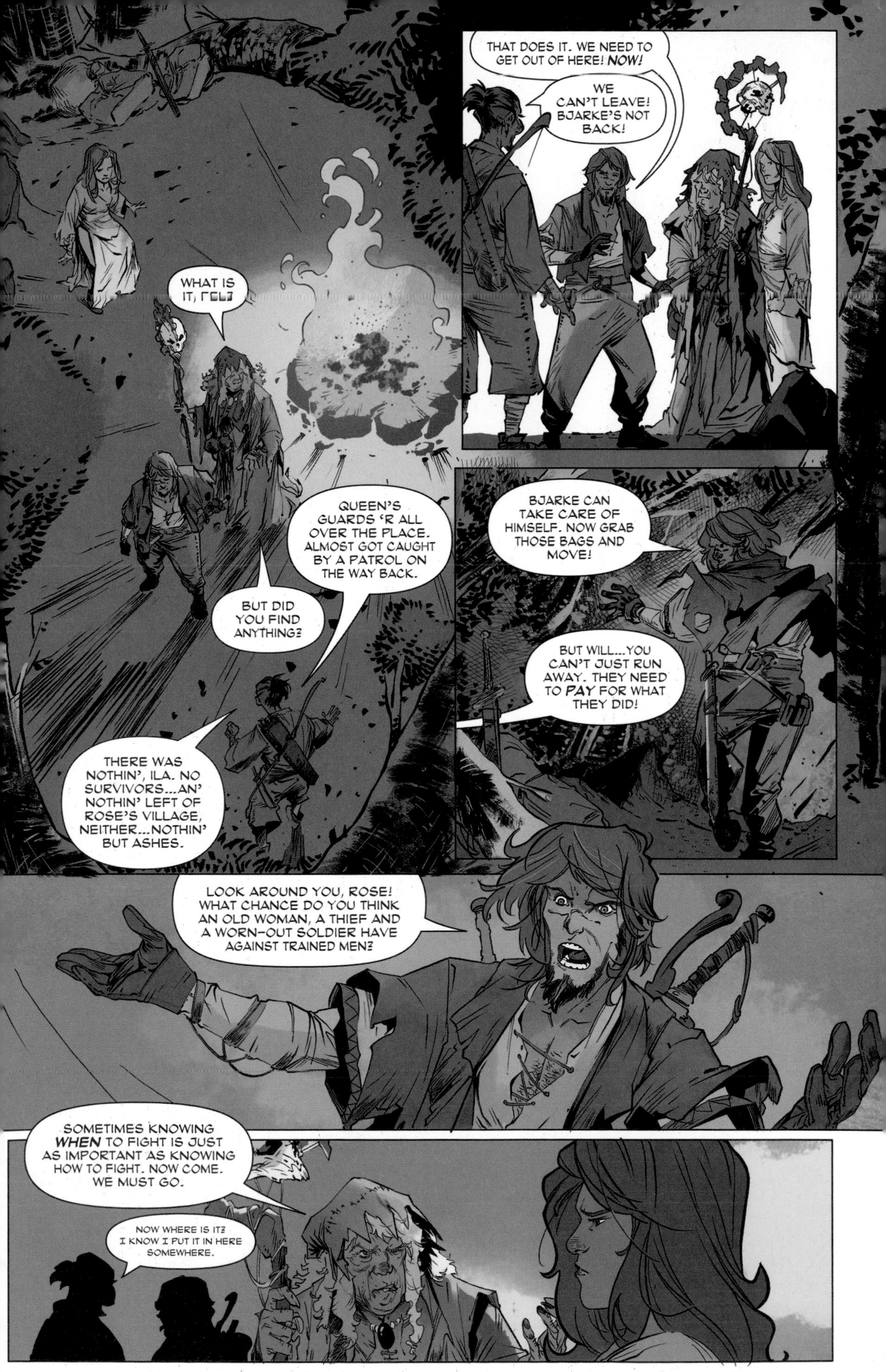
WHAT IS IT, FEL?
QUEEN'S GUARDS 'R ALL OVER THE PLACE. ALMOST GOT CAUGHT BY A PATROL ON THE WAY BACK.
BUT DID YOU FIND ANYTHING?
THERE WAS NOTHIN', ILA. NO SURVIVORS...AN' NOTHIN' LEFT OF ROSE'S VILLAGE, NEITHER...NOTHIN' BUT ASHES.
THAT DOES IT. WE NEED TO GET OUT OF HERE! *NOW!*
WE CAN'T LEAVE! BJARKE'S NOT BACK!
BJARKE CAN TAKE CARE OF HIMSELF. NOW GRAB THOSE BAGS AND MOVE!
BUT WILL...YOU CAN'T JUST RUN AWAY. THEY NEED TO *PAY* FOR WHAT THEY DID!
LOOK AROUND YOU, ROSE! WHAT CHANCE DO YOU THINK AN OLD WOMAN, A THIEF AND A WORN-OUT SOLDIER HAVE AGAINST TRAINED MEN?
SOMETIMES KNOWING ***WHEN*** TO FIGHT IS JUST AS IMPORTANT AS KNOWING HOW TO FIGHT. NOW COME. WE MUST GO.
NOW WHERE IS IT? I KNOW I PUT IT IN HERE SOMEWHERE.

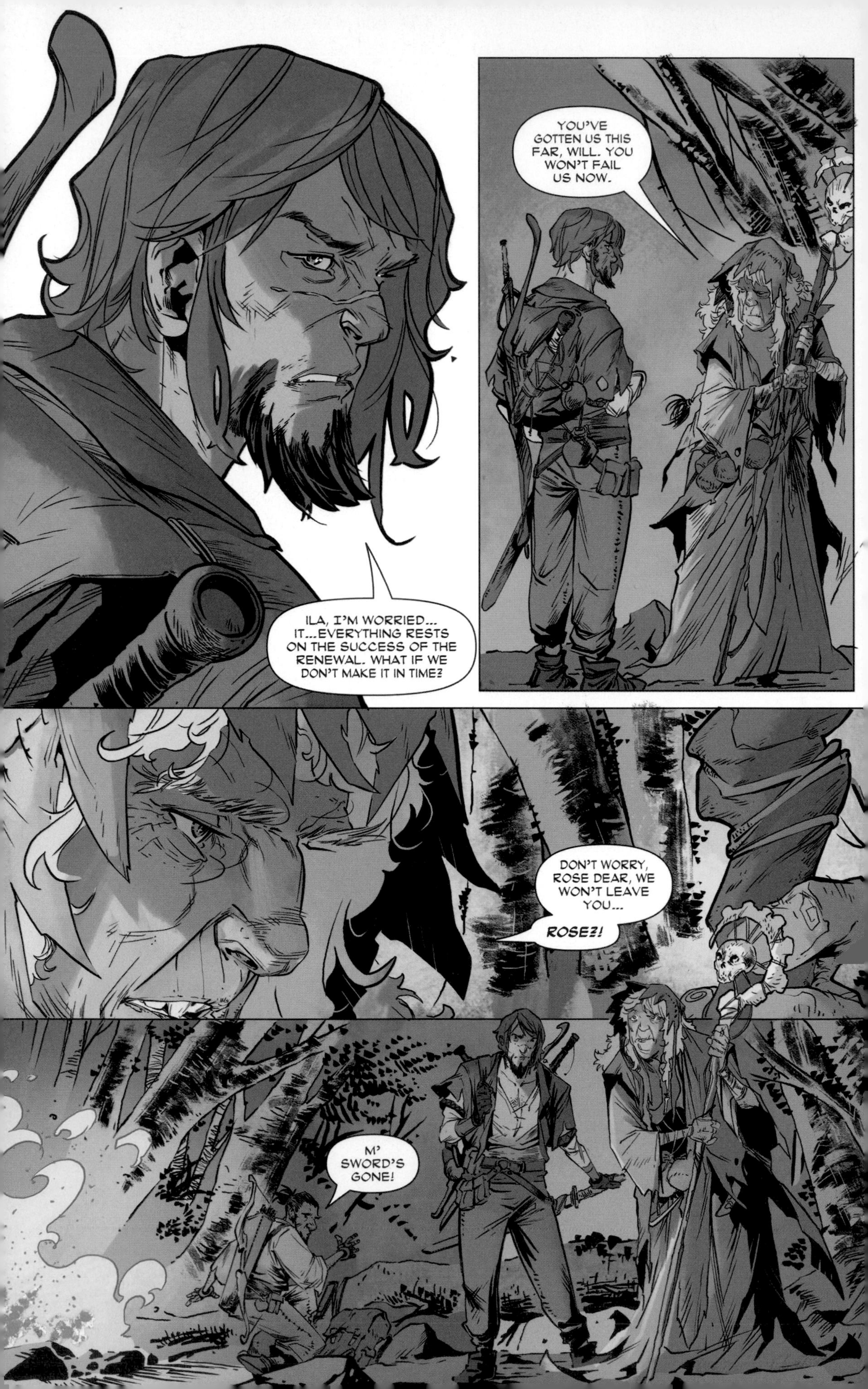
ILA, I'M WORRIED... IT...EVERYTHING RESTS ON THE SUCCESS OF THE RENEWAL. WHAT IF WE DON'T MAKE IT IN TIME?
YOU'VE GOTTEN US THIS FAR, WILL. YOU WON'T FAIL US NOW.
DON'T WORRY, ROSE DEAR, WE WON'T LEAVE YOU...
ROSE?!
M' SWORD'S GONE!

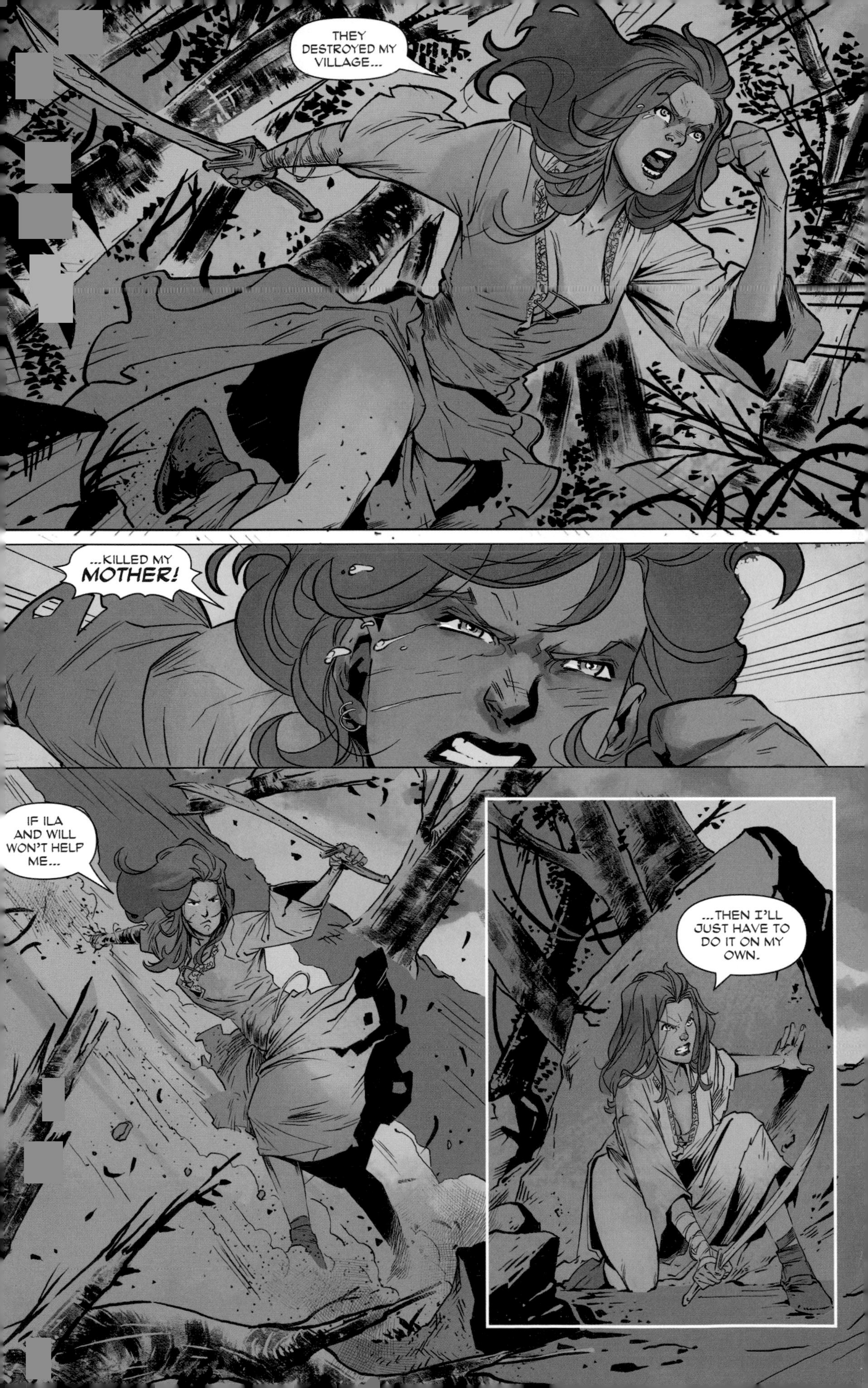
THEY DESTROYED MY VILLAGE...
...KILLED MY MOTHER!
IF ILA AND WILL WON'T HELP ME...
...THEN I'LL JUST HAVE TO DO IT ON MY OWN.

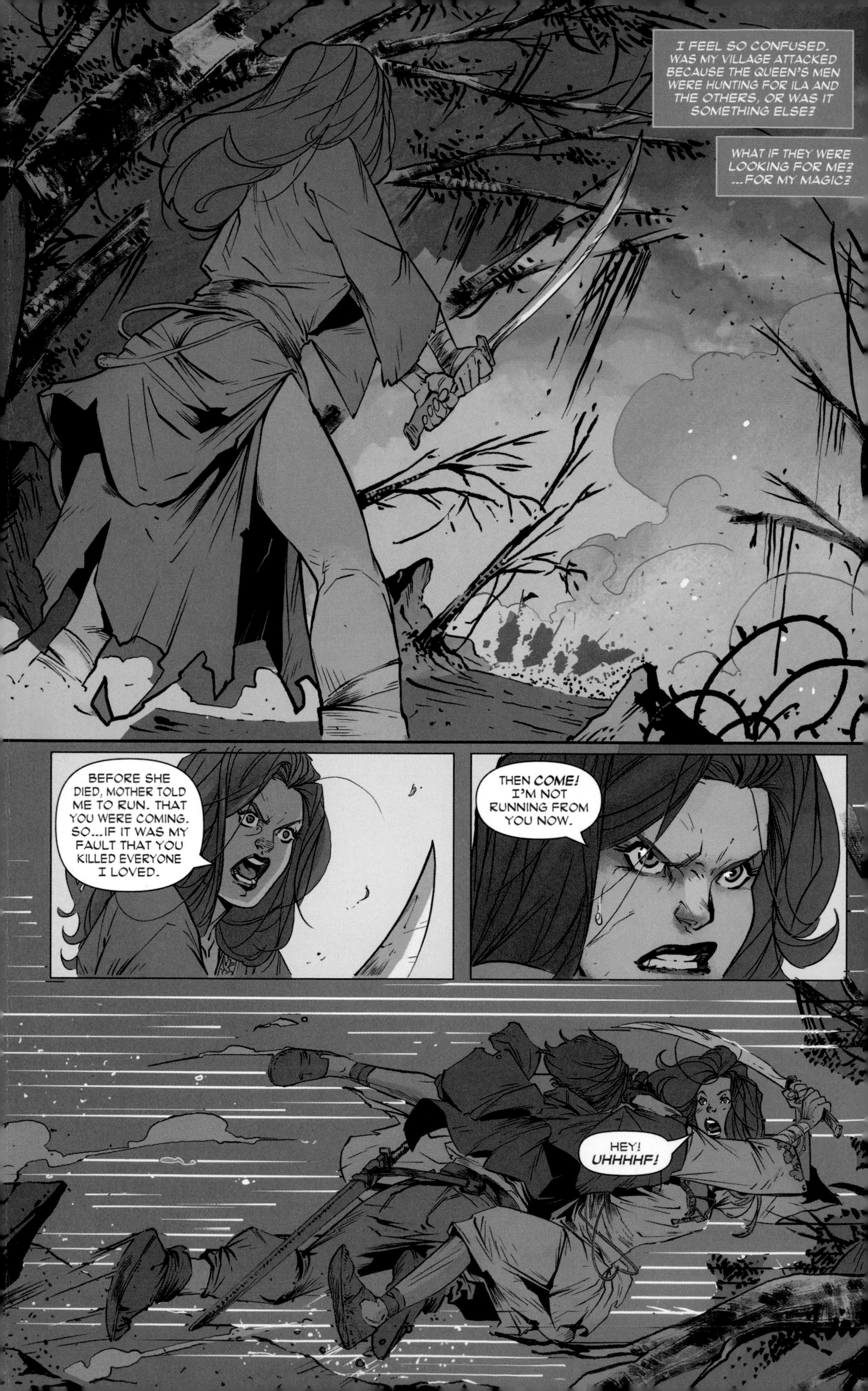
I FEEL SO CONFUSED. WAS MY VILLAGE ATTACKED BECAUSE THE QUEEN'S MEN WERE HUNTING FOR ILA AND THE OTHERS, OR WAS IT SOMETHING ELSE?
WHAT IF THEY WERE LOOKING FOR ME? ...FOR MY MAGIC?
BEFORE SHE DIED, MOTHER TOLD ME TO RUN. THAT YOU WERE COMING. SO...IF IT WAS MY FAULT THAT YOU KILLED EVERYONE I LOVED.
THEN *COME!* I'M NOT RUNNING FROM YOU NOW.
HEY! *UHHHHF!*

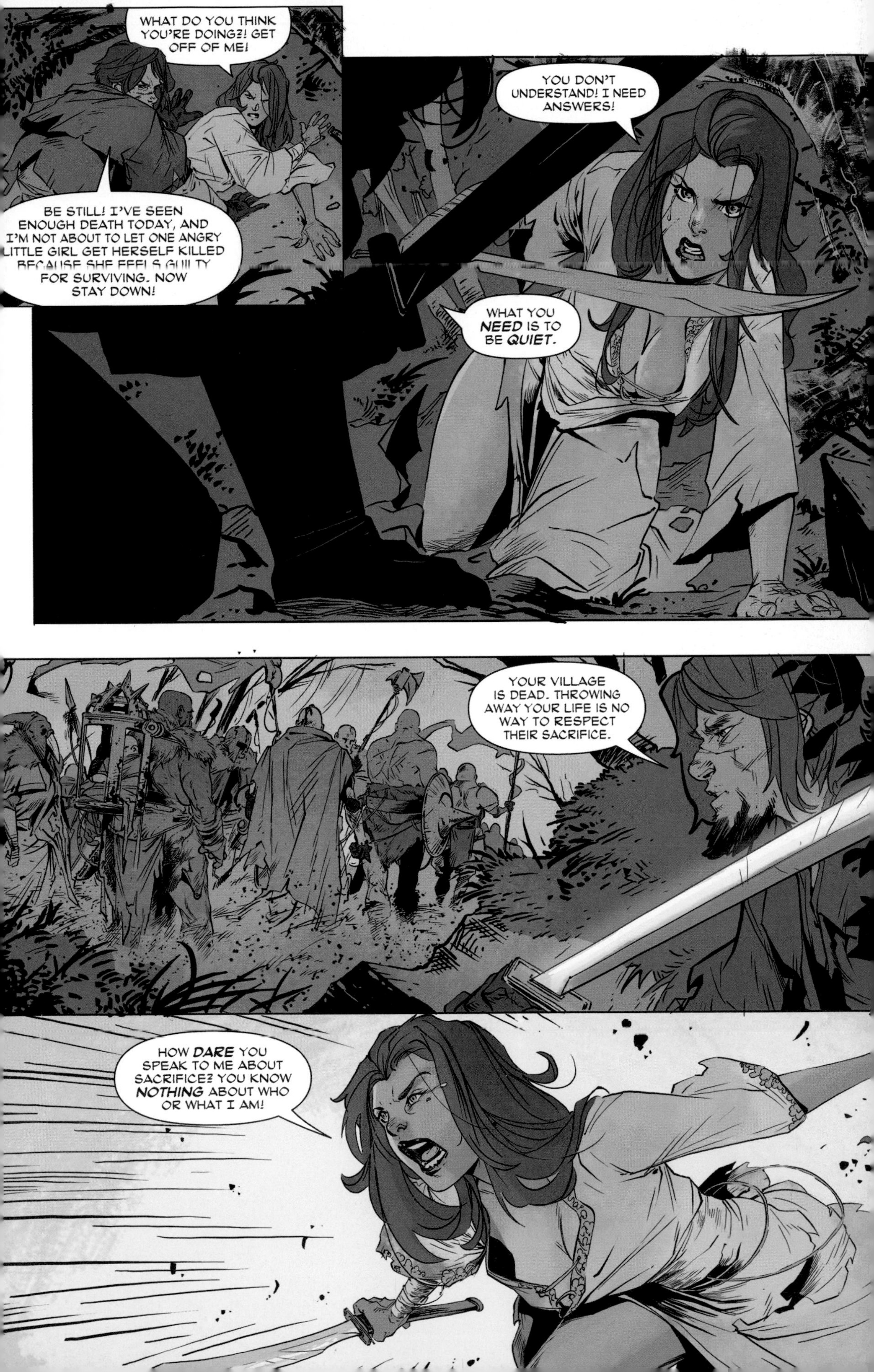
WHAT DO YOU THINK YOU'RE DOING?! GET OFF OF ME!
BE STILL! I'VE SEEN ENOUGH DEATH TODAY, AND I'M NOT ABOUT TO LET ONE ANGRY LITTLE GIRL GET HERSELF KILLED BECAUSE SHE FEELS GUILTY FOR SURVIVING. NOW STAY DOWN!
YOU DON'T UNDERSTAND! I NEED ANSWERS!
WHAT YOU NEED IS TO BE QUIET.
YOUR VILLAGE IS DEAD. THROWING AWAY YOUR LIFE IS NO WAY TO RESPECT THEIR SACRIFICE.
HOW DARE YOU SPEAK TO ME ABOUT SACRIFICE? YOU KNOW NOTHING ABOUT WHO OR WHAT I AM!

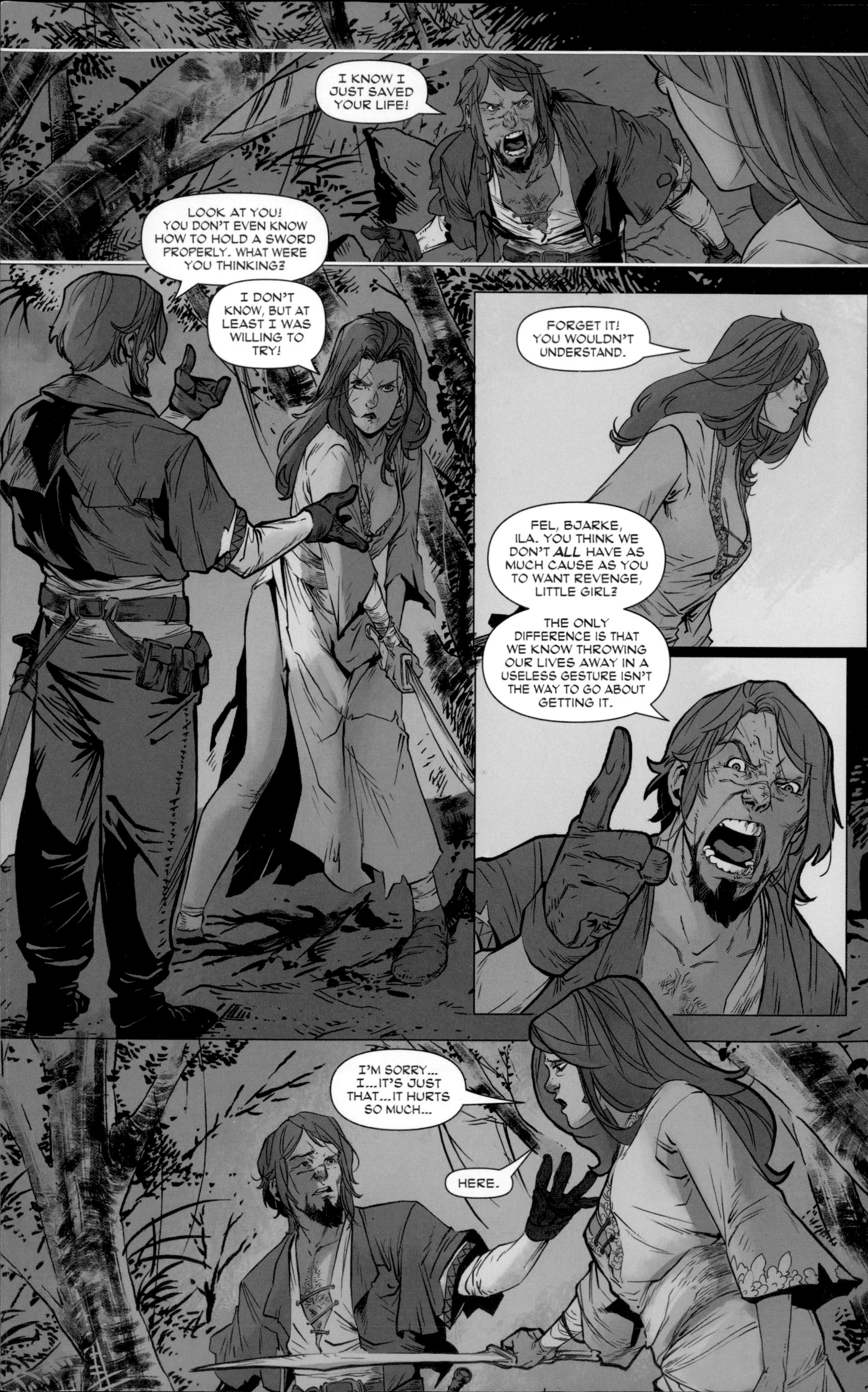
I KNOW I JUST SAVED YOUR LIFE!
LOOK AT YOU! YOU DON'T EVEN KNOW HOW TO HOLD A SWORD PROPERLY. WHAT WERE YOU THINKING?
I DON'T KNOW, BUT AT LEAST I WAS WILLING TO TRY!
FORGET IT! YOU WOULDN'T UNDERSTAND.
FEL, BJARKE, ILA. YOU THINK WE DON'T ALL HAVE AS MUCH CAUSE AS YOU TO WANT REVENGE, LITTLE GIRL?
THE ONLY DIFFERENCE IS THAT WE KNOW THROWING OUR LIVES AWAY IN A USELESS GESTURE ISN'T THE WAY TO GO ABOUT GETTING IT.
I'M SORRY... I...IT'S JUST THAT...IT HURTS SO MUCH...
HERE.

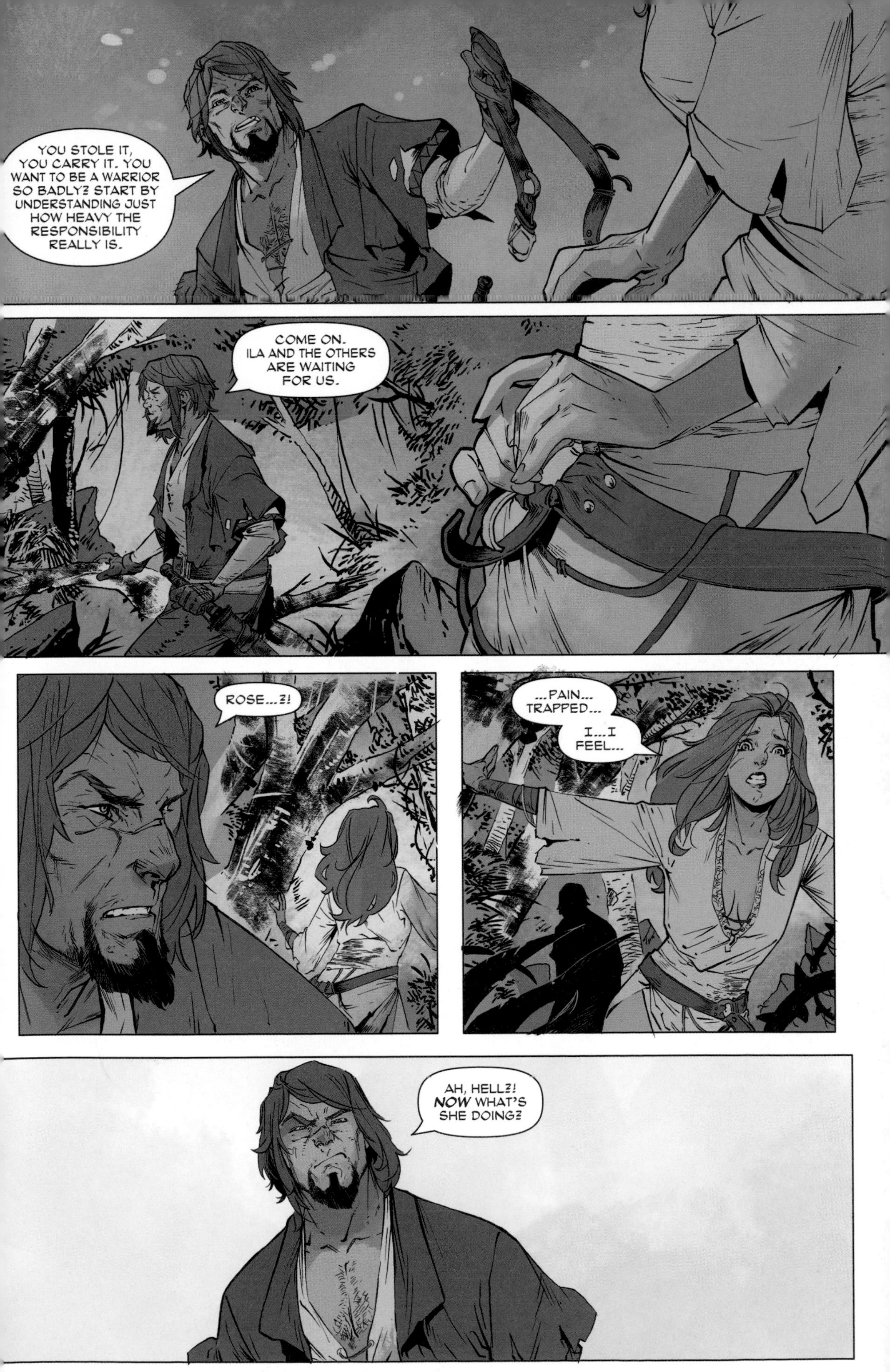
YOU STOLE IT, YOU CARRY IT. YOU WANT TO BE A WARRIOR SO BADLY?! START BY UNDERSTANDING JUST HOW HEAVY THE RESPONSIBILITY REALLY IS.
COME ON. ILA AND THE OTHERS ARE WAITING FOR US.
ROSE...?!
...PAIN... TRAPPED...
I...I FEEL...
AH, HELL?! NOW WHAT'S SHE DOING?

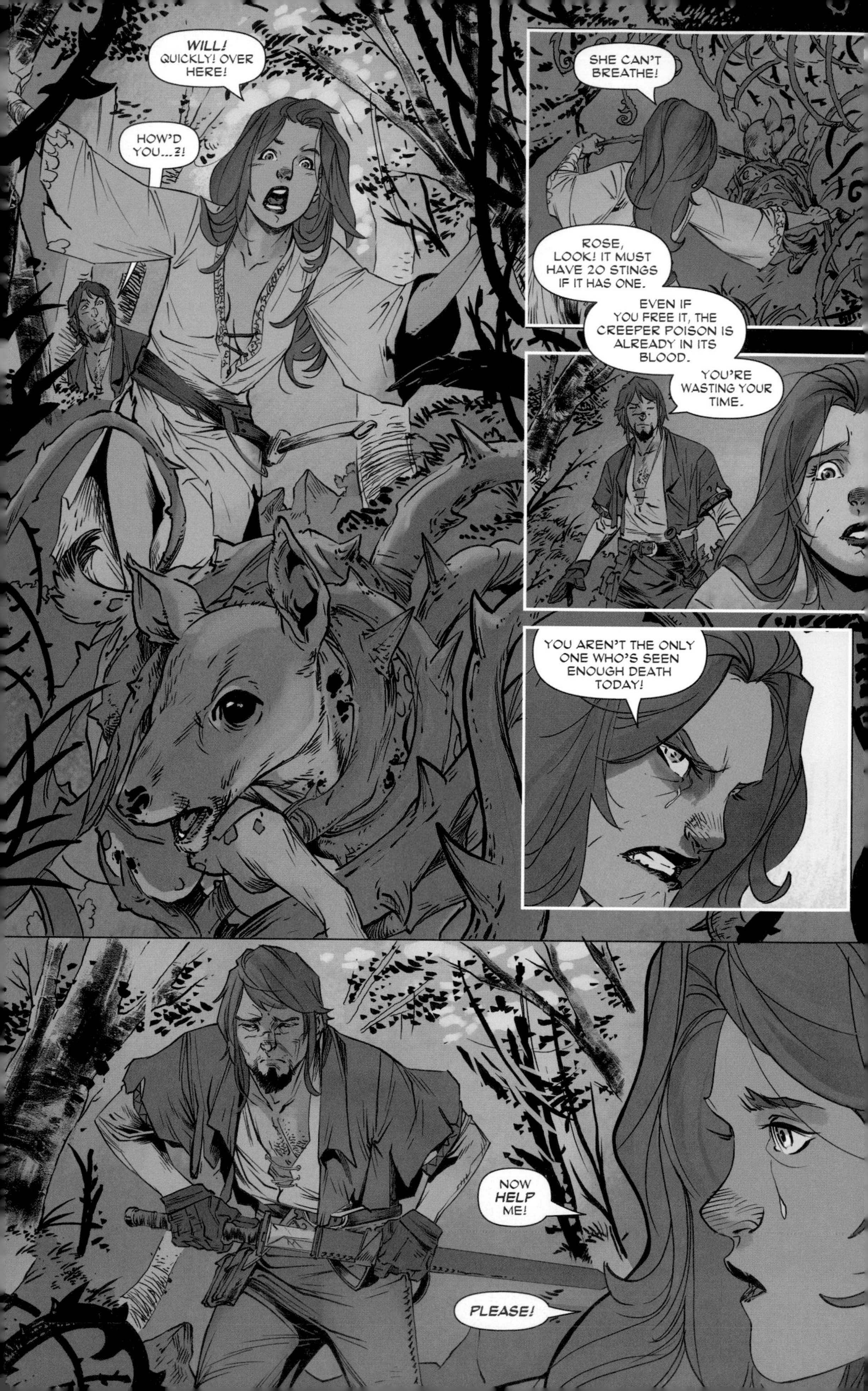
WILL! QUICKLY! OVER HERE!
HOW'D YOU...?!
SHE CAN'T BREATHE!
ROSE, LOOK! IT MUST HAVE 20 STINGS IF IT HAS ONE.
EVEN IF YOU FREE IT, THE CREEPER POISON IS ALREADY IN ITS BLOOD.
YOU'RE WASTING YOUR TIME.
YOU AREN'T THE ONLY ONE WHO'S SEEN ENOUGH DEATH TODAY!
NOW HELP ME!
PLEASE!

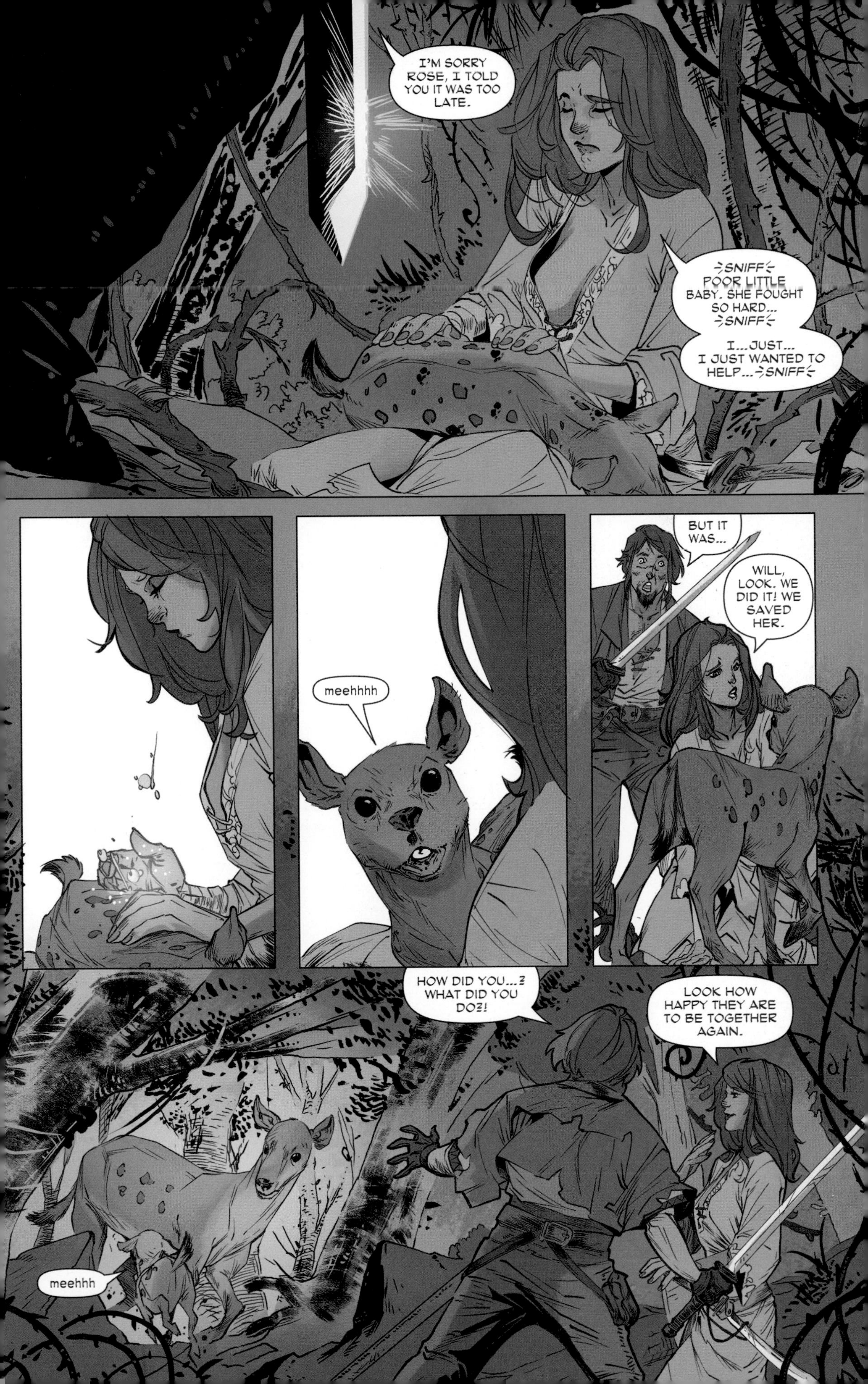
I'M SORRY ROSE, I TOLD YOU IT WAS TOO LATE.
⚡SNIFF⚡ POOR LITTLE BABY. SHE FOUGHT SO HARD... ⚡SNIFF⚡
I...JUST... I JUST WANTED TO HELP...⚡SNIFF⚡
meehhhh
BUT IT WAS...
WILL, LOOK. WE DID IT! WE SAVED HER.
HOW DID YOU...? WHAT DID YOU DO?!
LOOK HOW HAPPY THEY ARE TO BE TOGETHER AGAIN.
meehhh

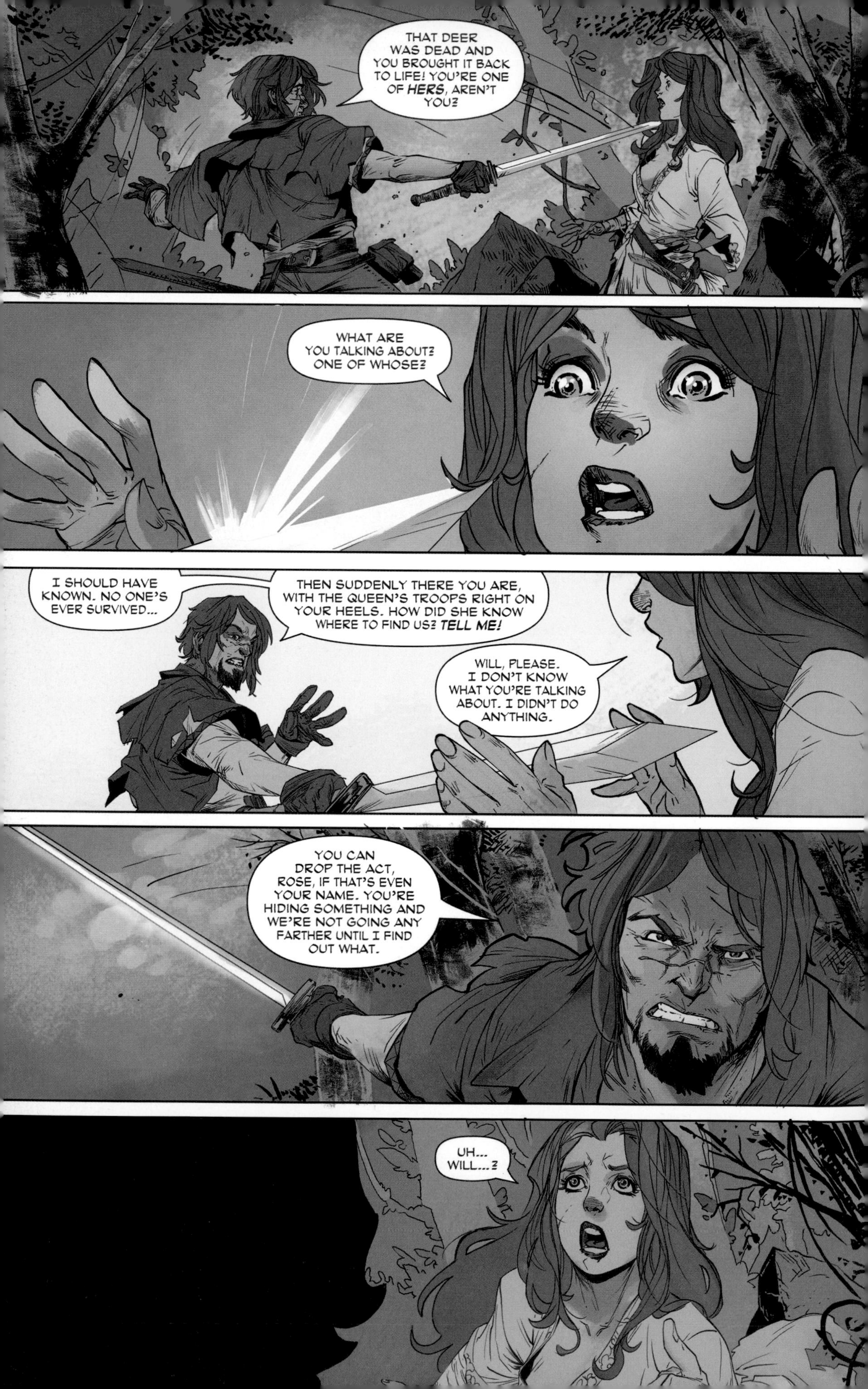
THAT DEER WAS DEAD AND YOU BROUGHT IT BACK TO LIFE! YOU'RE ONE OF ***HERS***, AREN'T YOU?
WHAT ARE YOU TALKING ABOUT? ONE OF WHOSE?
I SHOULD HAVE KNOWN. NO ONE'S EVER SURVIVED...
THEN SUDDENLY THERE YOU ARE, WITH THE QUEEN'S TROOPS RIGHT ON YOUR HEELS. HOW DID SHE KNOW WHERE TO FIND US? ***TELL ME!***
WILL, PLEASE. I DON'T KNOW WHAT YOU'RE TALKING ABOUT. I DIDN'T DO ANYTHING.
YOU CAN DROP THE ACT, ROSE, IF THAT'S EVEN YOUR NAME. YOU'RE HIDING SOMETHING AND WE'RE NOT GOING ANY FARTHER UNTIL I FIND OUT WHAT.
UH... WILL...?

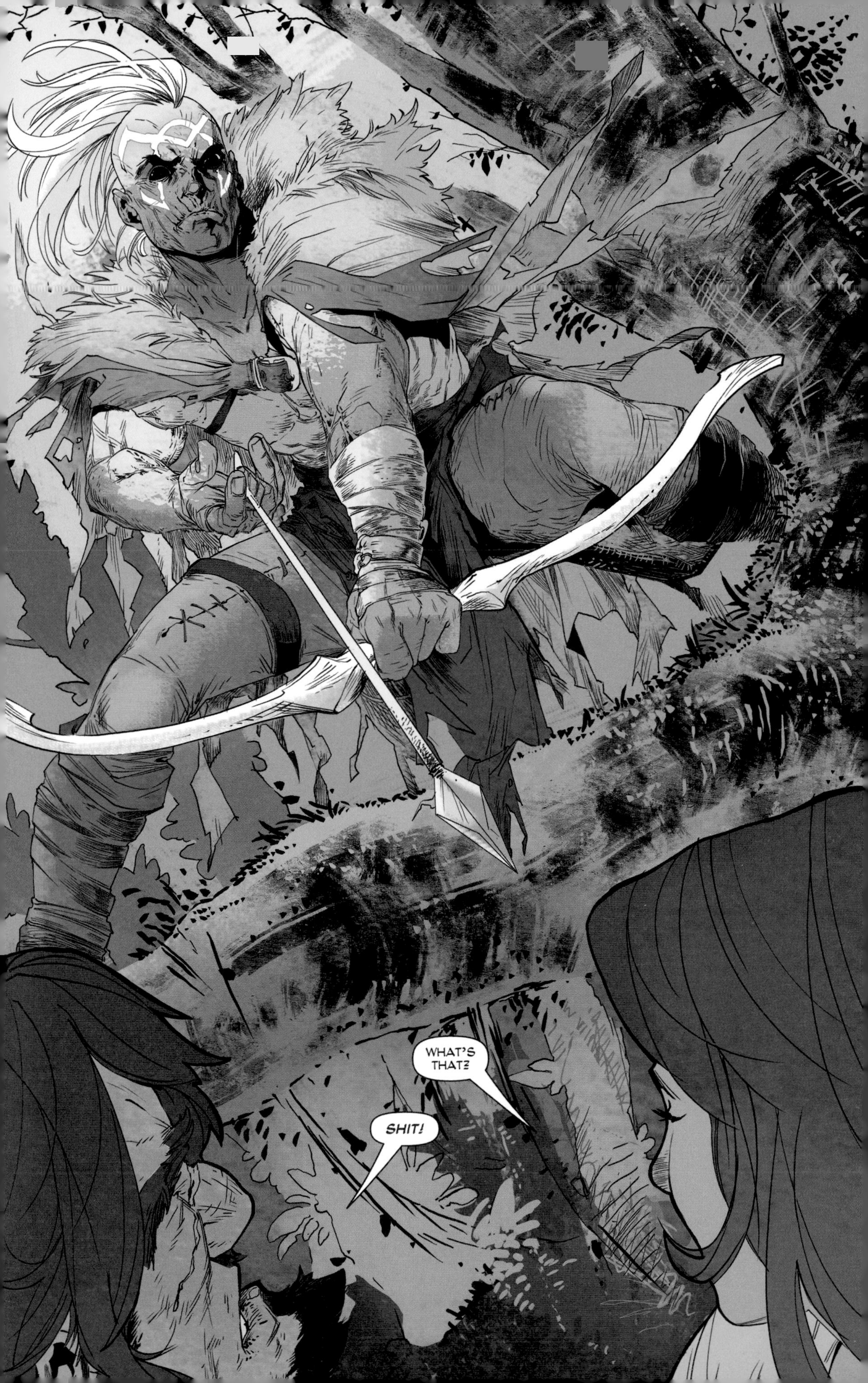
WHAT'S THAT?
SHIT!

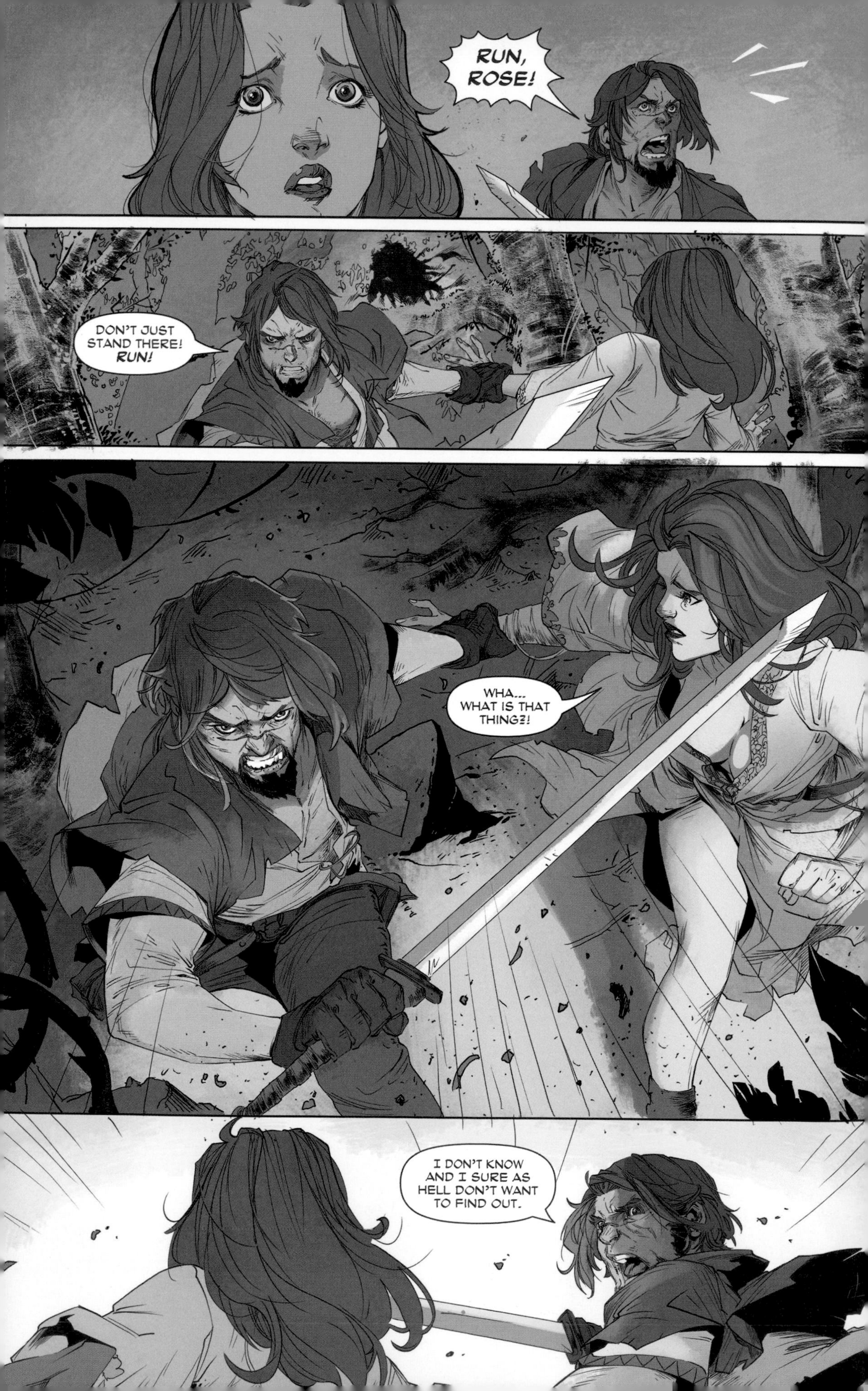
RUN, ROSE!
DON'T JUST STAND THERE! RUN!
WHA... WHAT IS THAT THING?!
I DON'T KNOW AND I SURE AS HELL DON'T WANT TO FIND OUT.

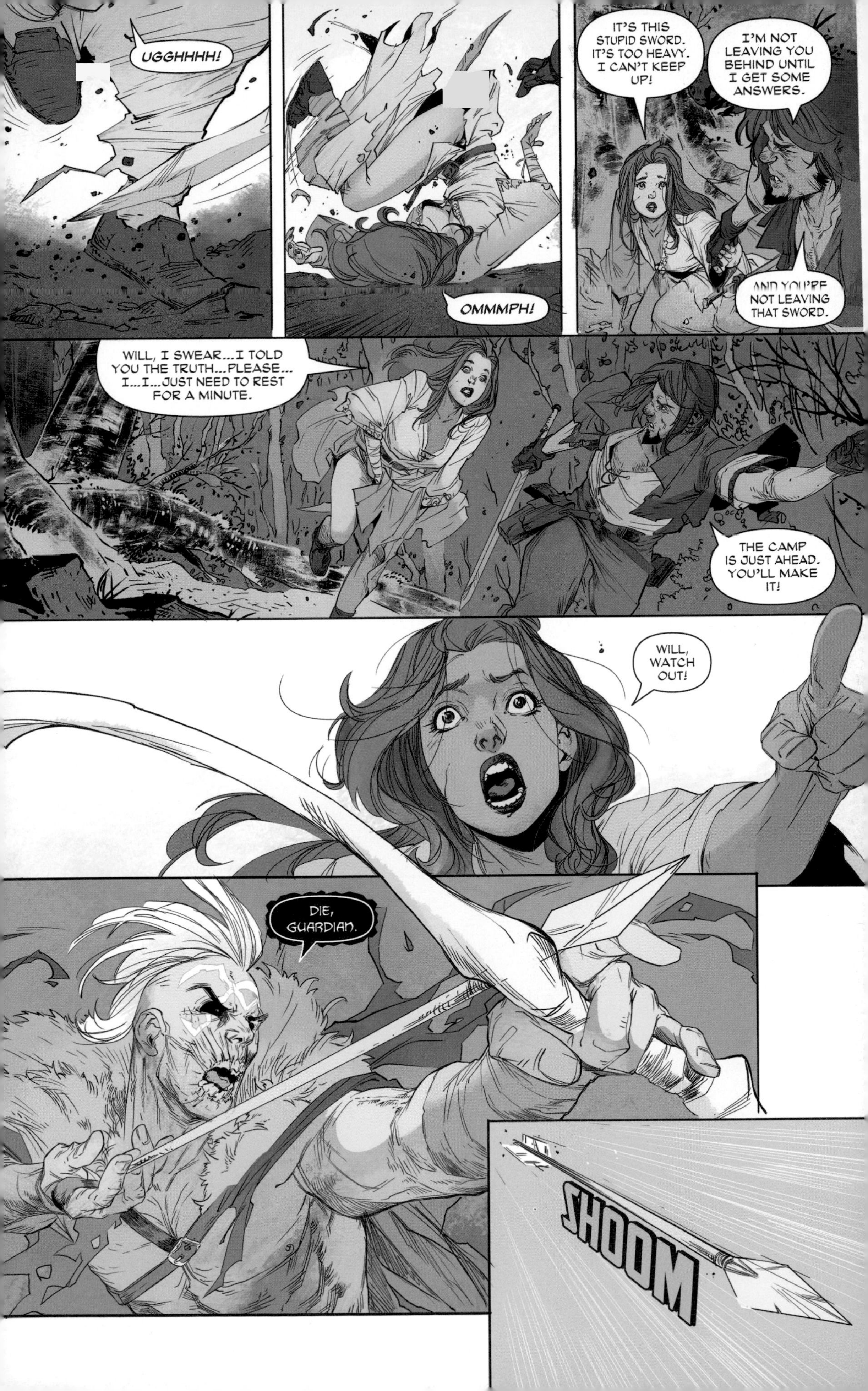

UGGHHHH!
OMMMPH!
IT'S THIS STUPID SWORD. IT'S TOO HEAVY. I CAN'T KEEP UP!
I'M NOT LEAVING YOU BEHIND UNTIL I GET SOME ANSWERS.
AND YOU'RE NOT LEAVING THAT SWORD.
WILL, I SWEAR...I TOLD YOU THE TRUTH...PLEASE... I...I...JUST NEED TO REST FOR A MINUTE.
THE CAMP IS JUST AHEAD. YOU'LL MAKE IT!
WILL, WATCH OUT!
DIE, GUARDIAN.
SHOOM

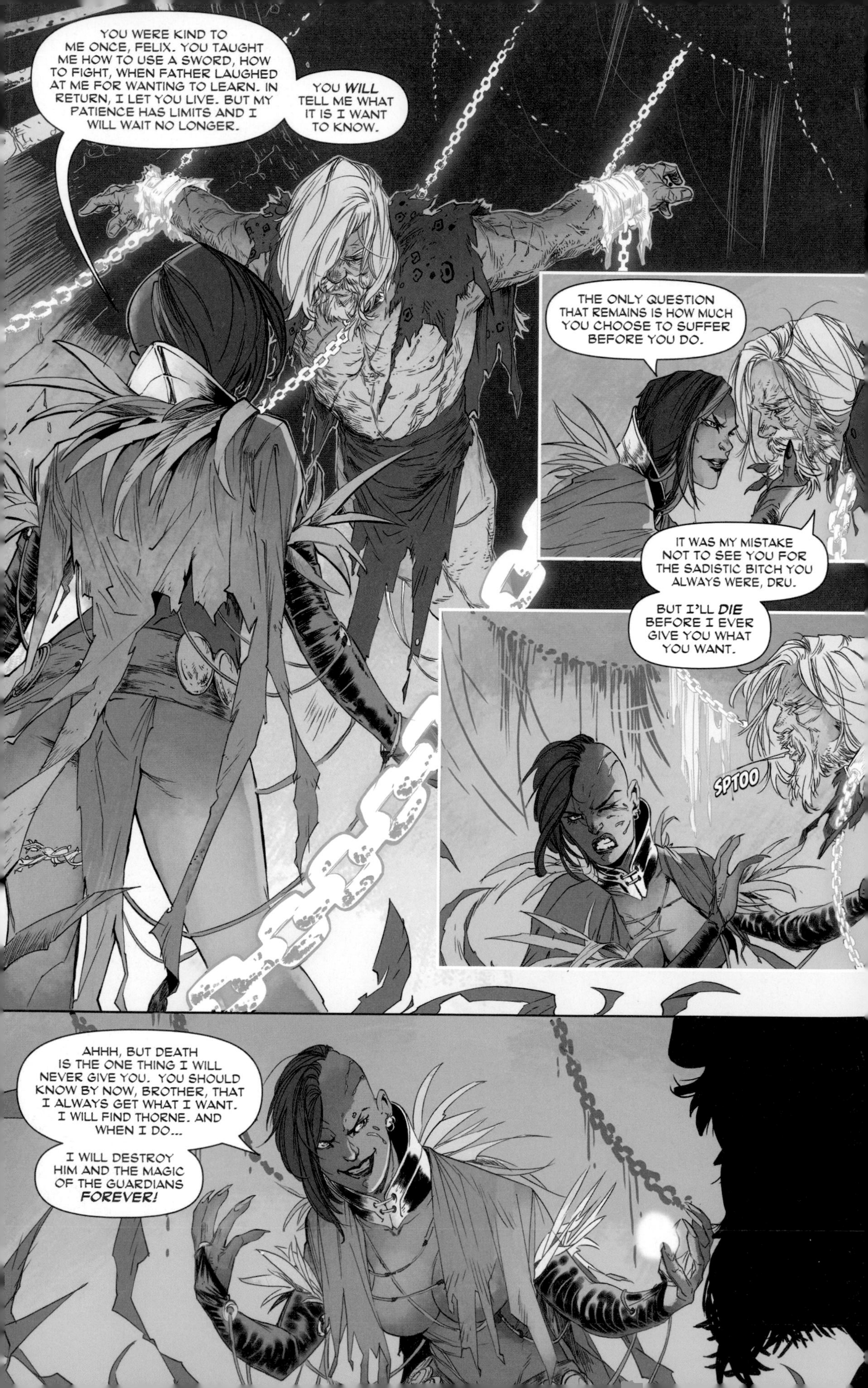
YOU WERE KIND TO ME ONCE, FELIX. YOU TAUGHT ME HOW TO USE A SWORD, HOW TO FIGHT, WHEN FATHER LAUGHED AT ME FOR WANTING TO LEARN. IN RETURN, I LET YOU LIVE. BUT MY PATIENCE HAS LIMITS AND I WILL WAIT NO LONGER.
YOU *WILL* TELL ME WHAT IT IS I WANT TO KNOW.
THE ONLY QUESTION THAT REMAINS IS HOW MUCH YOU CHOOSE TO SUFFER BEFORE YOU DO.
IT WAS MY MISTAKE NOT TO SEE YOU FOR THE SADISTIC BITCH YOU ALWAYS WERE, DRU.
BUT I'LL *DIE* BEFORE I EVER GIVE YOU WHAT YOU WANT.
SPTOO
AHHH, BUT DEATH IS THE ONE THING I WILL NEVER GIVE YOU. YOU SHOULD KNOW BY NOW, BROTHER, THAT I ALWAYS GET WHAT I WANT. I WILL FIND THORNE. AND WHEN I DO...
I WILL DESTROY HIM AND THE MAGIC OF THE GUARDIANS *FOREVER!*

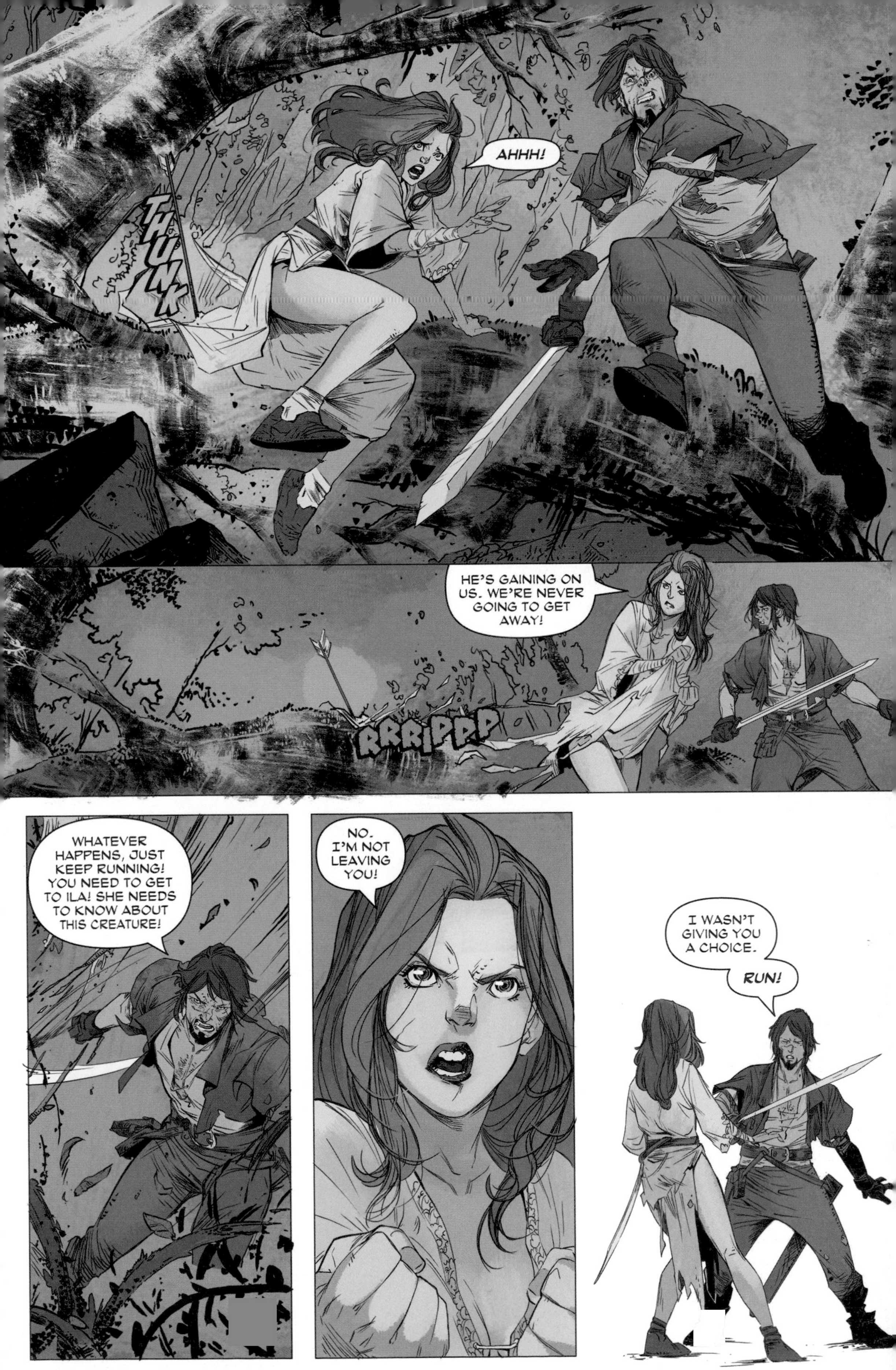
AHHH!
THUNK
HE'S GAINING ON US. WE'RE NEVER GOING TO GET AWAY!
RRRIPPP
WHATEVER HAPPENS, JUST KEEP RUNNING! YOU NEED TO GET TO ILA! SHE NEEDS TO KNOW ABOUT THIS CREATURE!
NO. I'M NOT LEAVING YOU!
I WASN'T GIVING YOU A CHOICE.
RUN!

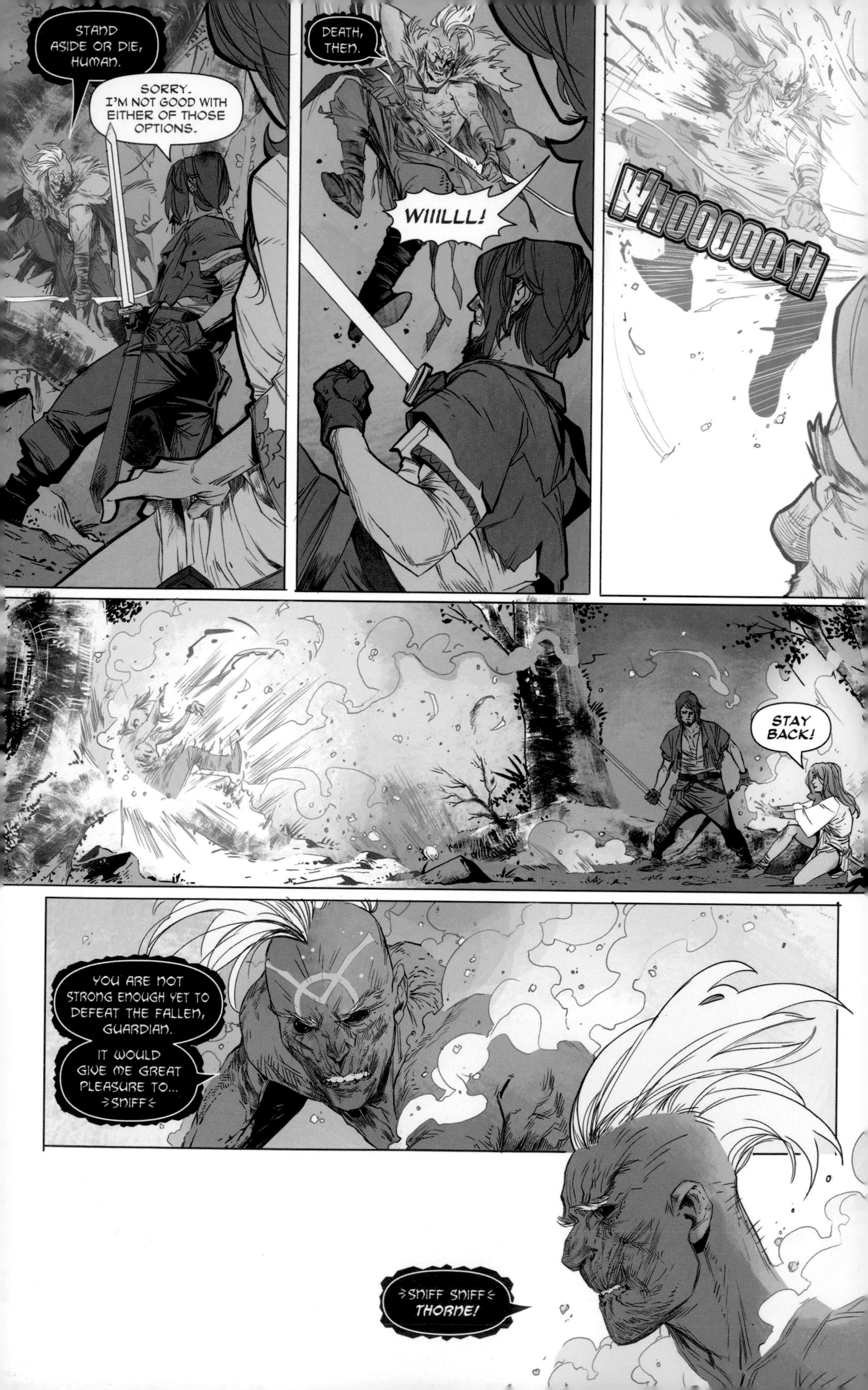
STAND ASIDE OR DIE, HUMAN.
SORRY. I'M NOT GOOD WITH EITHER OF THOSE OPTIONS.
DEATH, THEN.
WIIILLL!
WHOOOOOOSH
STAY BACK!
YOU ARE NOT STRONG ENOUGH YET TO DEFEAT THE FALLEN, GUARDIAN.
IT WOULD GIVE ME GREAT PLEASURE TO... >SNIFF<
>SNIFF SNIFF< THORNE!

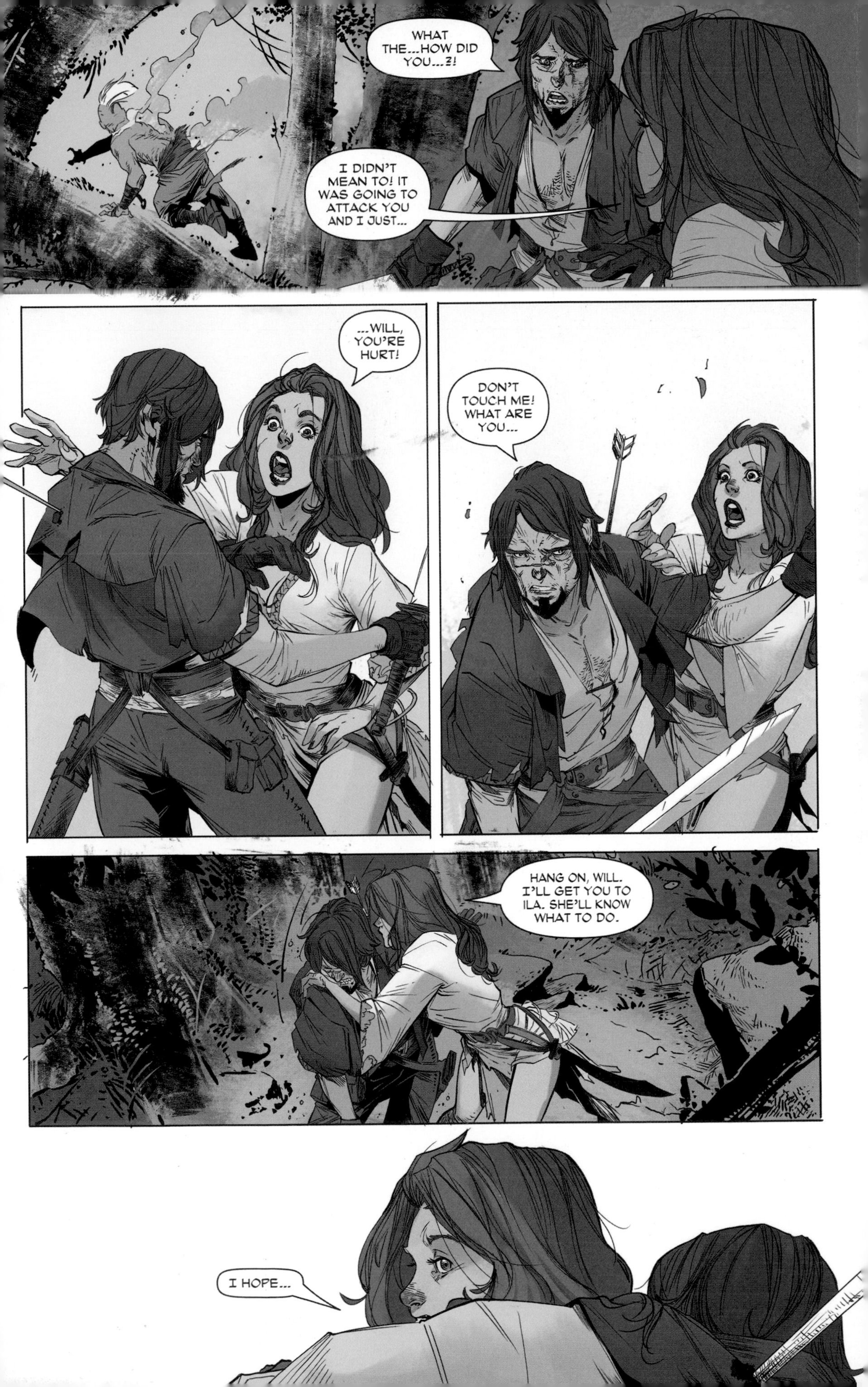
WHAT THE...HOW DID YOU...?!
I DIDN'T MEAN TO! IT WAS GOING TO ATTACK YOU AND I JUST...
...WILL, YOU'RE HURT!
DON'T TOUCH ME! WHAT ARE YOU...
HANG ON, WILL. I'LL GET YOU TO ILA. SHE'LL KNOW WHAT TO DO.
I HOPE...

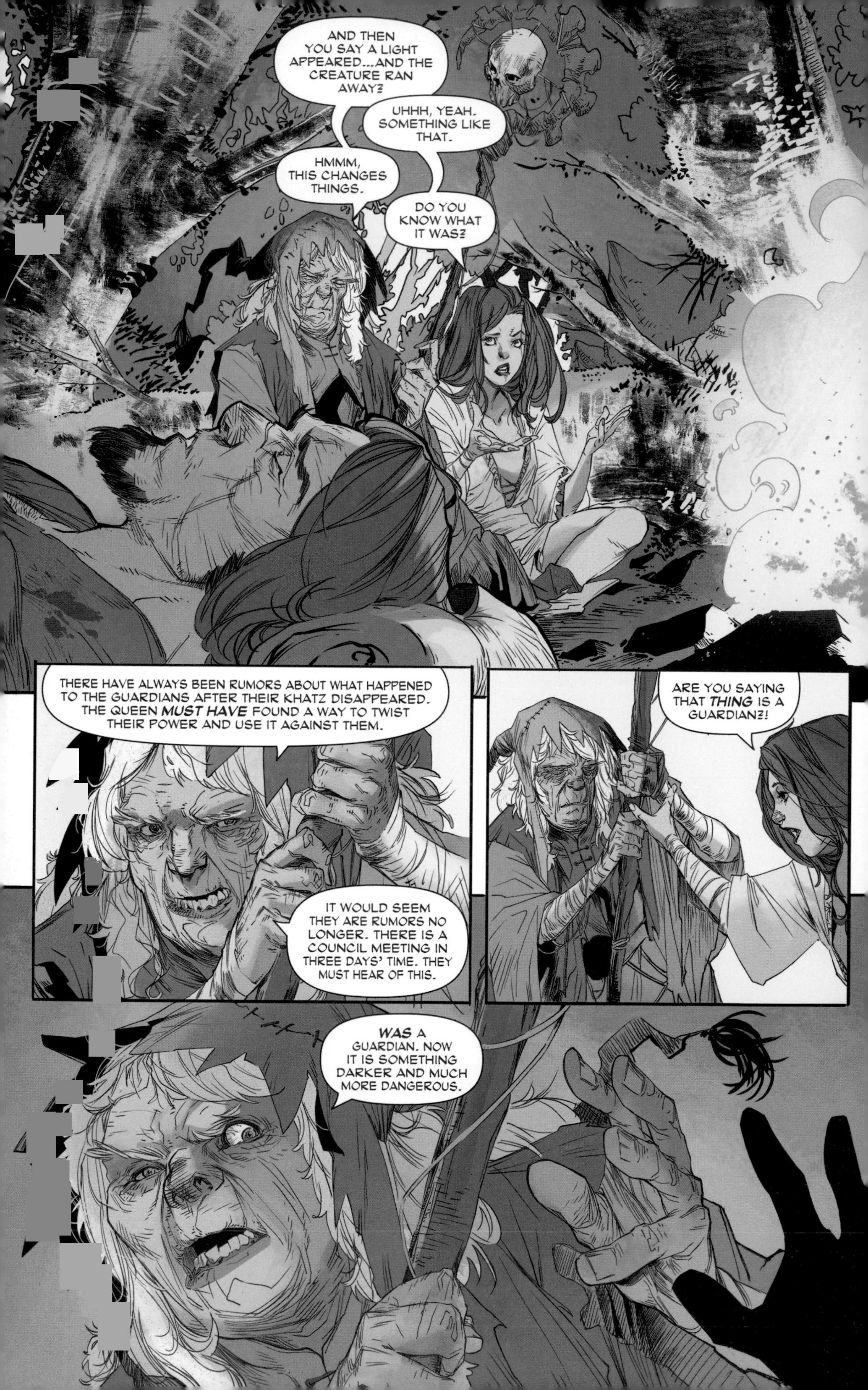
AND THEN YOU SAY A LIGHT APPEARED...AND THE CREATURE RAN AWAY?
UHHH, YEAH. SOMETHING LIKE THAT.
HMMM, THIS CHANGES THINGS.
DO YOU KNOW WHAT IT WAS?
THERE HAVE ALWAYS BEEN RUMORS ABOUT WHAT HAPPENED TO THE GUARDIANS AFTER THEIR KHATZ DISAPPEARED. THE QUEEN MUST HAVE FOUND A WAY TO TWIST THEIR POWER AND USE IT AGAINST THEM.
IT WOULD SEEM THEY ARE RUMORS NO LONGER. THERE IS A COUNCIL MEETING IN THREE DAYS' TIME. THEY MUST HEAR OF THIS.
ARE YOU SAYING THAT THING IS A GUARDIAN?!
WAS A GUARDIAN. NOW IT IS SOMETHING DARKER AND MUCH MORE DANGEROUS.

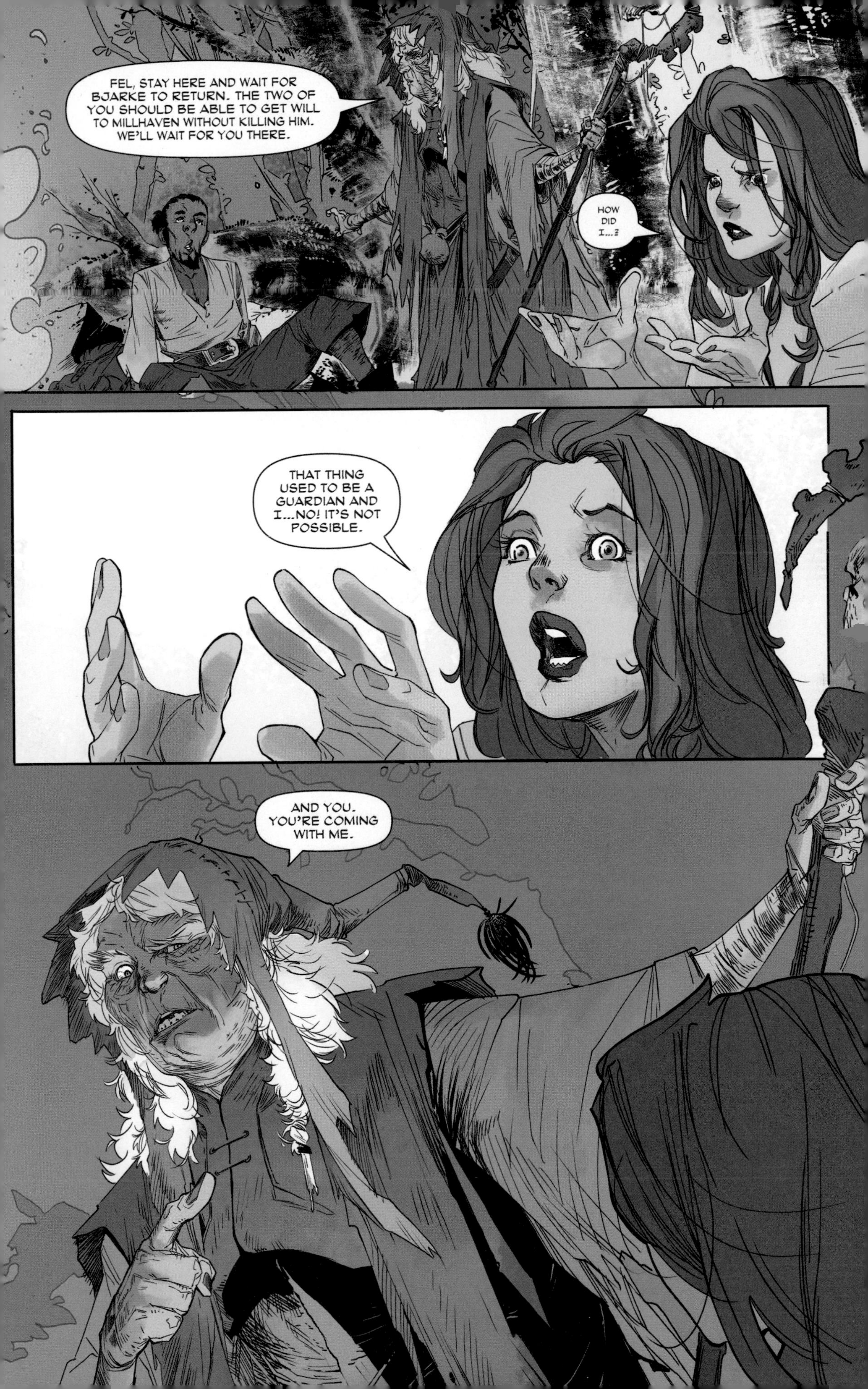
FEL, STAY HERE AND WAIT FOR BJARKE TO RETURN. THE TWO OF YOU SHOULD BE ABLE TO GET WILL TO MILLHAVEN WITHOUT KILLING HIM. WE'LL WAIT FOR YOU THERE.
HOW DID I...?
THAT THING USED TO BE A GUARDIAN AND I...NO! IT'S NOT POSSIBLE.
AND YOU. YOU'RE COMING WITH ME.

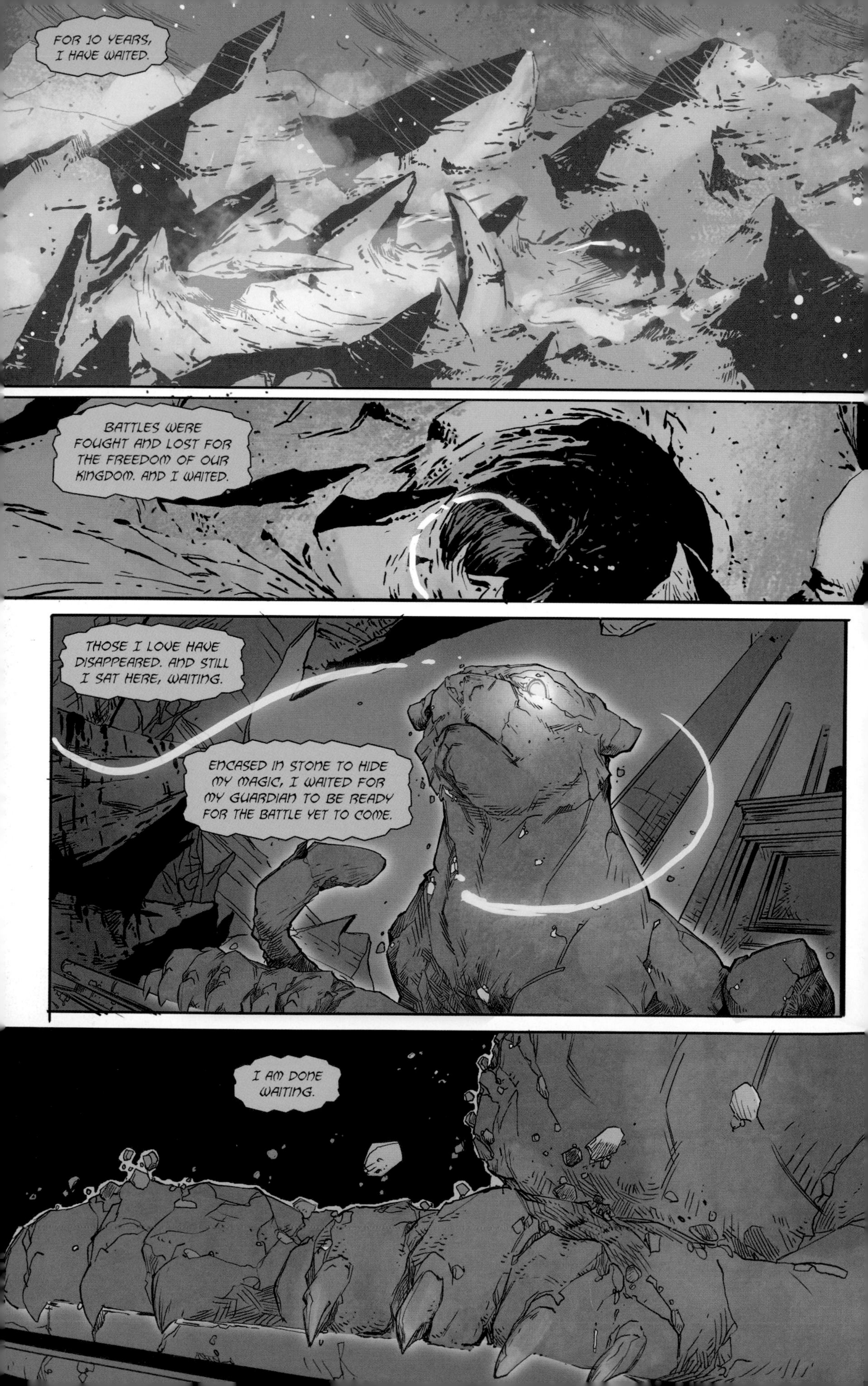
FOR 10 YEARS, I HAVE WAITED.
BATTLES WERE FOUGHT AND LOST FOR THE FREEDOM OF OUR KINGDOM. AND I WAITED.
THOSE I LOVE HAVE DISAPPEARED. AND STILL I SAT HERE, WAITING.
ENCASED IN STONE TO HIDE MY MAGIC, I WAITED FOR MY GUARDIAN TO BE READY FOR THE BATTLE YET TO COME.
I AM DONE WAITING.

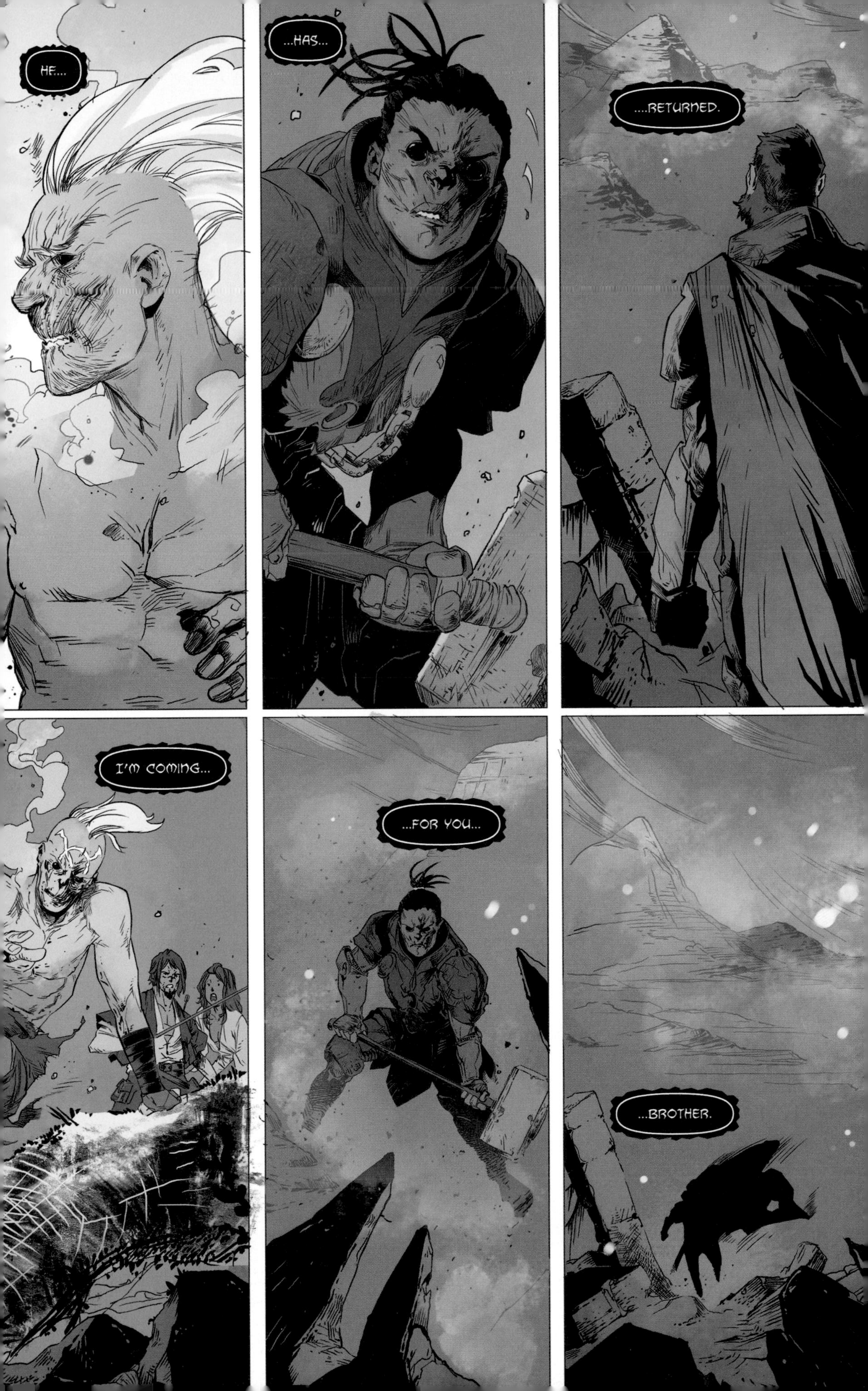
HE...
...HAS...
....RETURNED.
I'M COMING...
...FOR YOU...
...BROTHER.

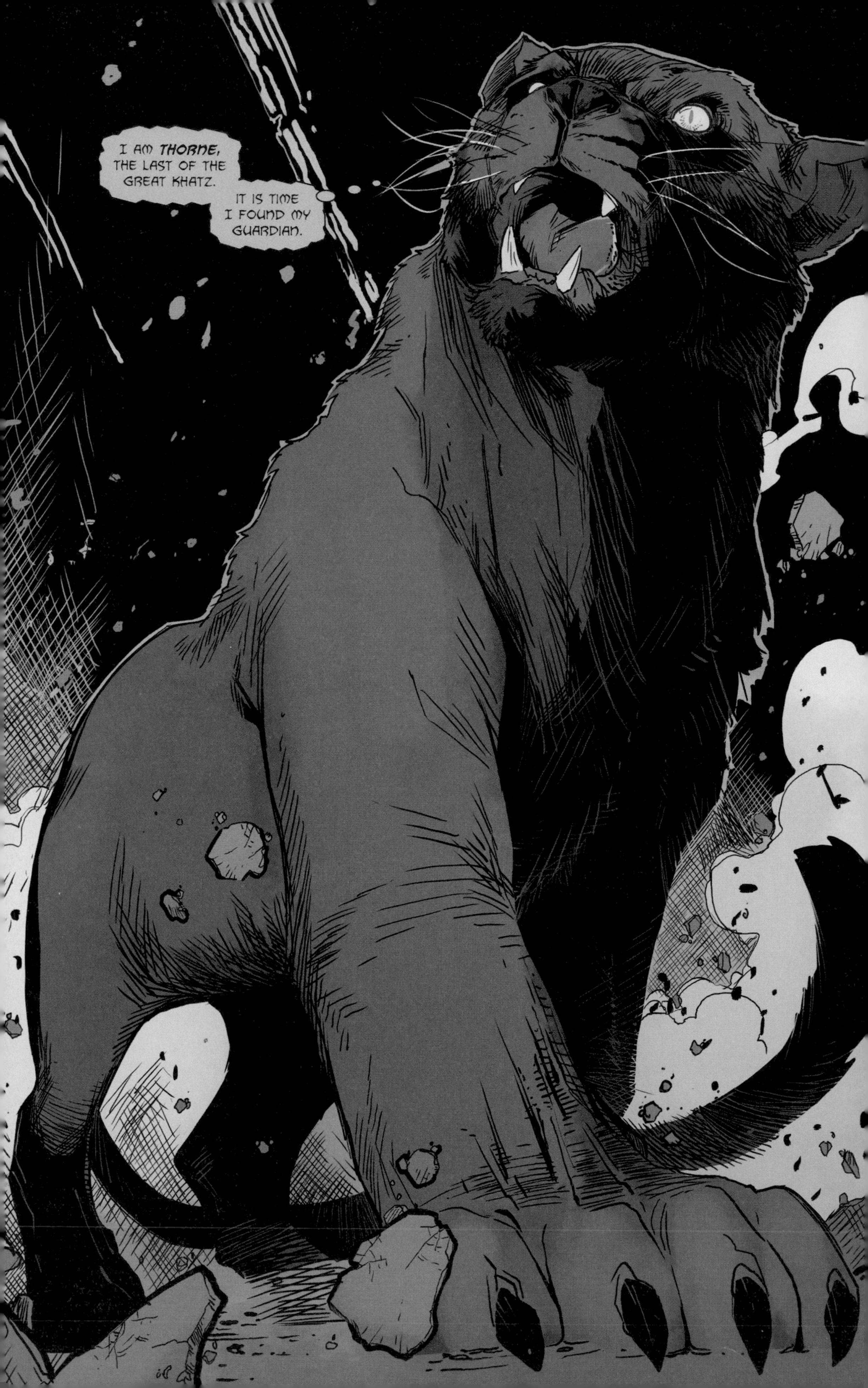
I AM THORNE, THE LAST OF THE GREAT KHATZ.
IT IS TIME I FOUND MY GUARDIAN.

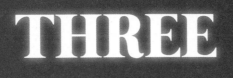

THREE

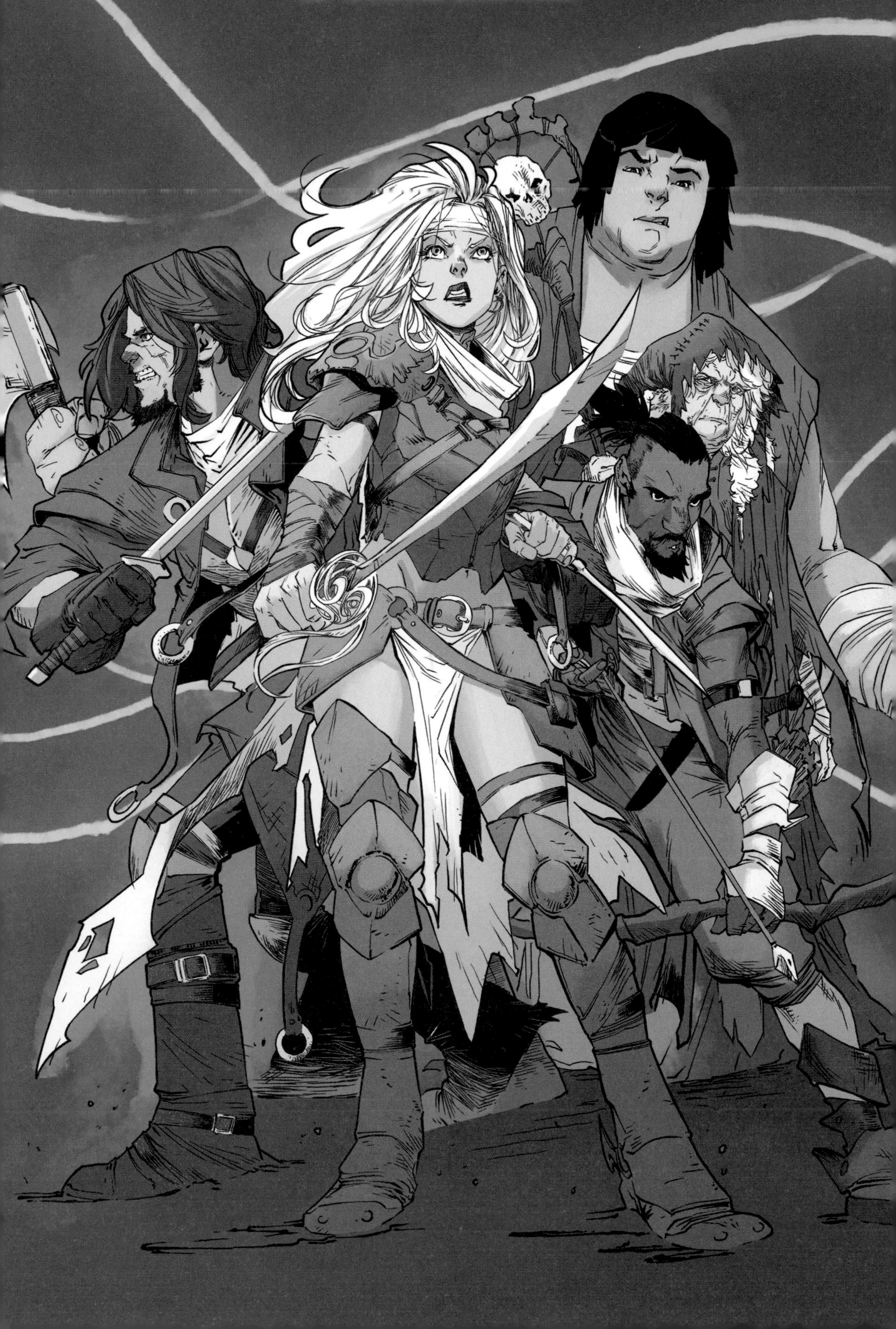

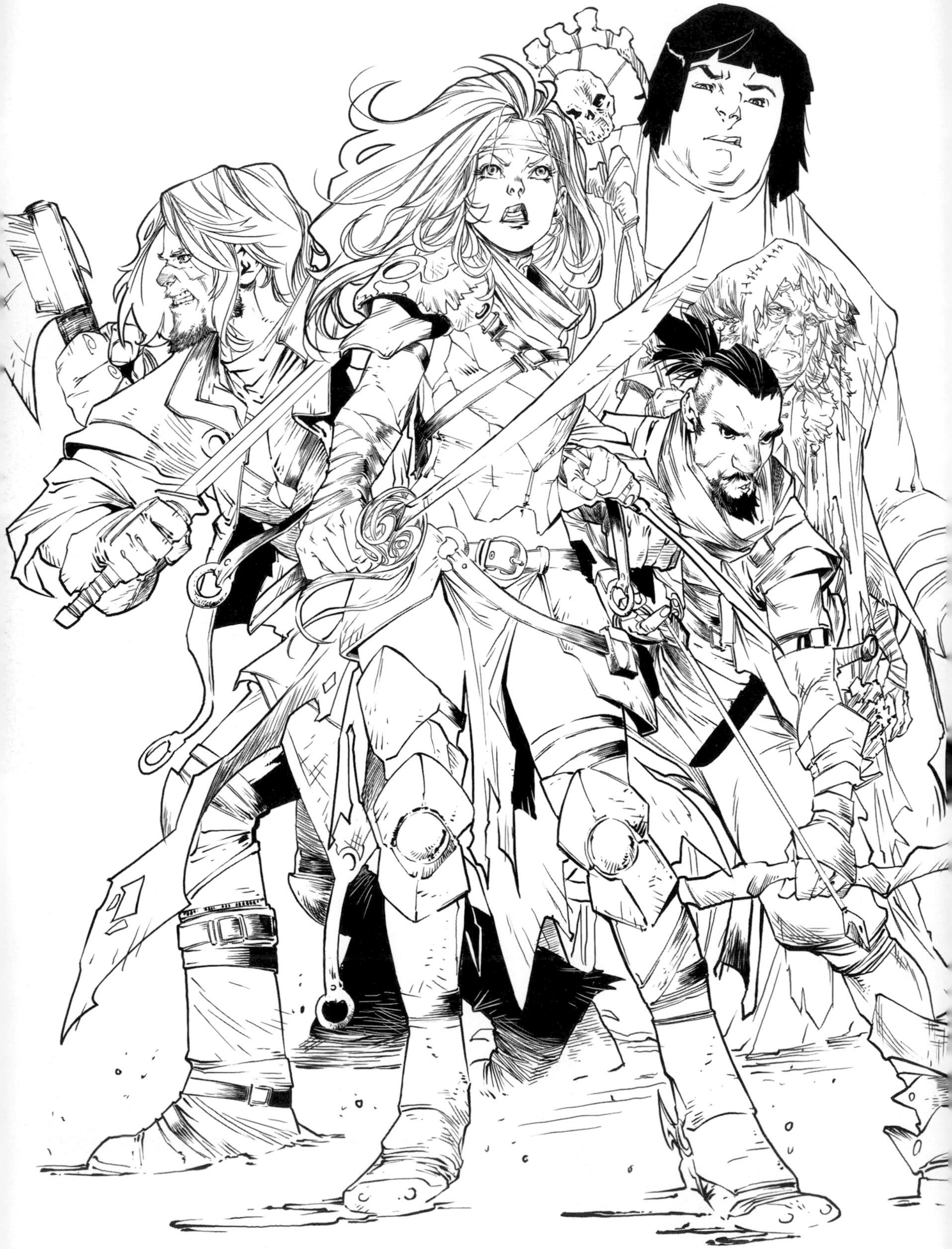

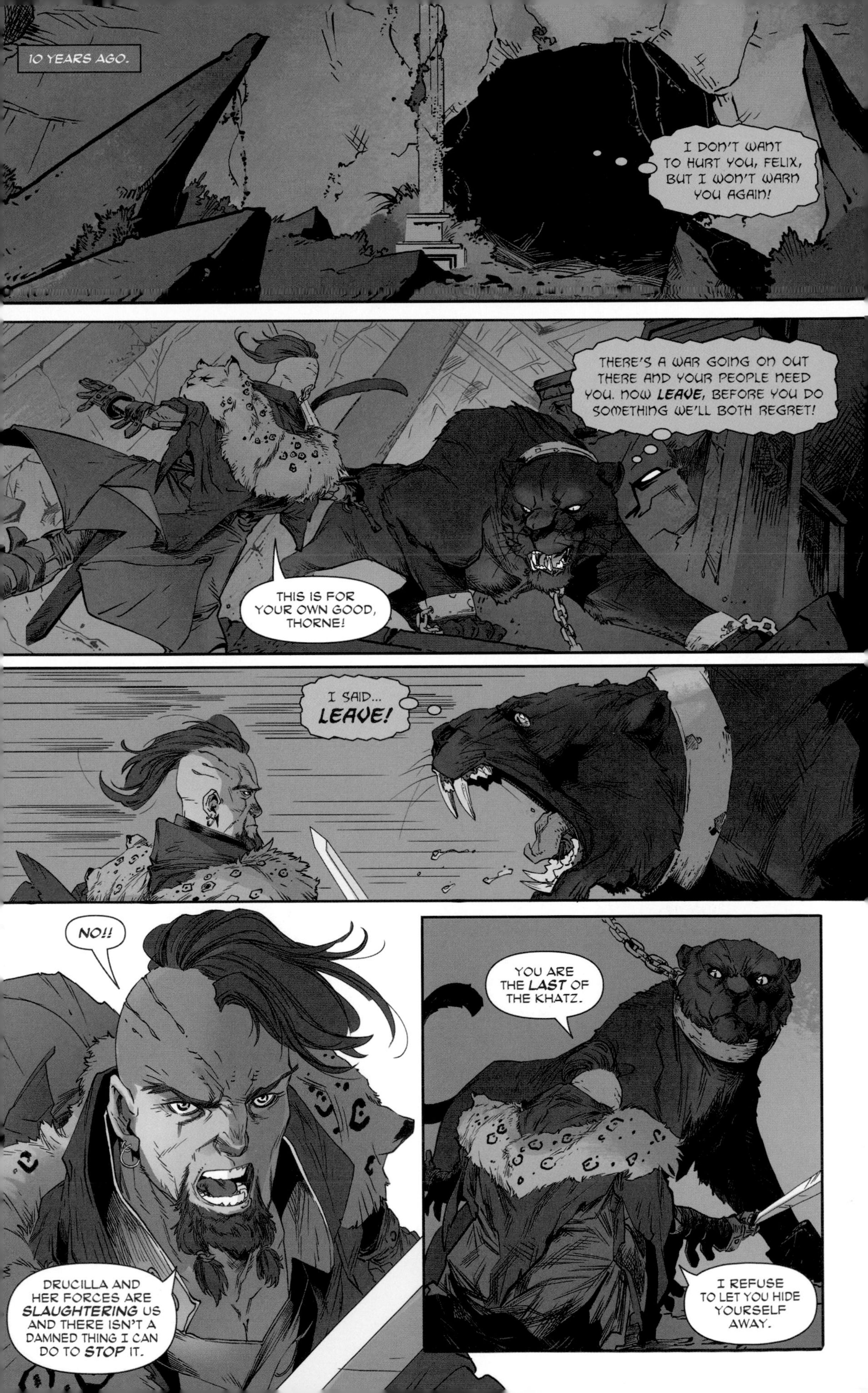
10 YEARS AGO.
I DON'T WANT TO HURT YOU, FELIX, BUT I WON'T WARN YOU AGAIN!
THERE'S A WAR GOING ON OUT THERE AND YOUR PEOPLE NEED YOU. NOW LEAVE, BEFORE YOU DO SOMETHING WE'LL BOTH REGRET!
THIS IS FOR YOUR OWN GOOD, THORNE!
I SAID... LEAVE!
NO!!
DRUCILLA AND HER FORCES ARE SLAUGHTERING US AND THERE ISN'T A DAMNED THING I CAN DO TO STOP IT.
YOU ARE THE LAST OF THE KHATZ.
I REFUSE TO LET YOU HIDE YOURSELF AWAY.

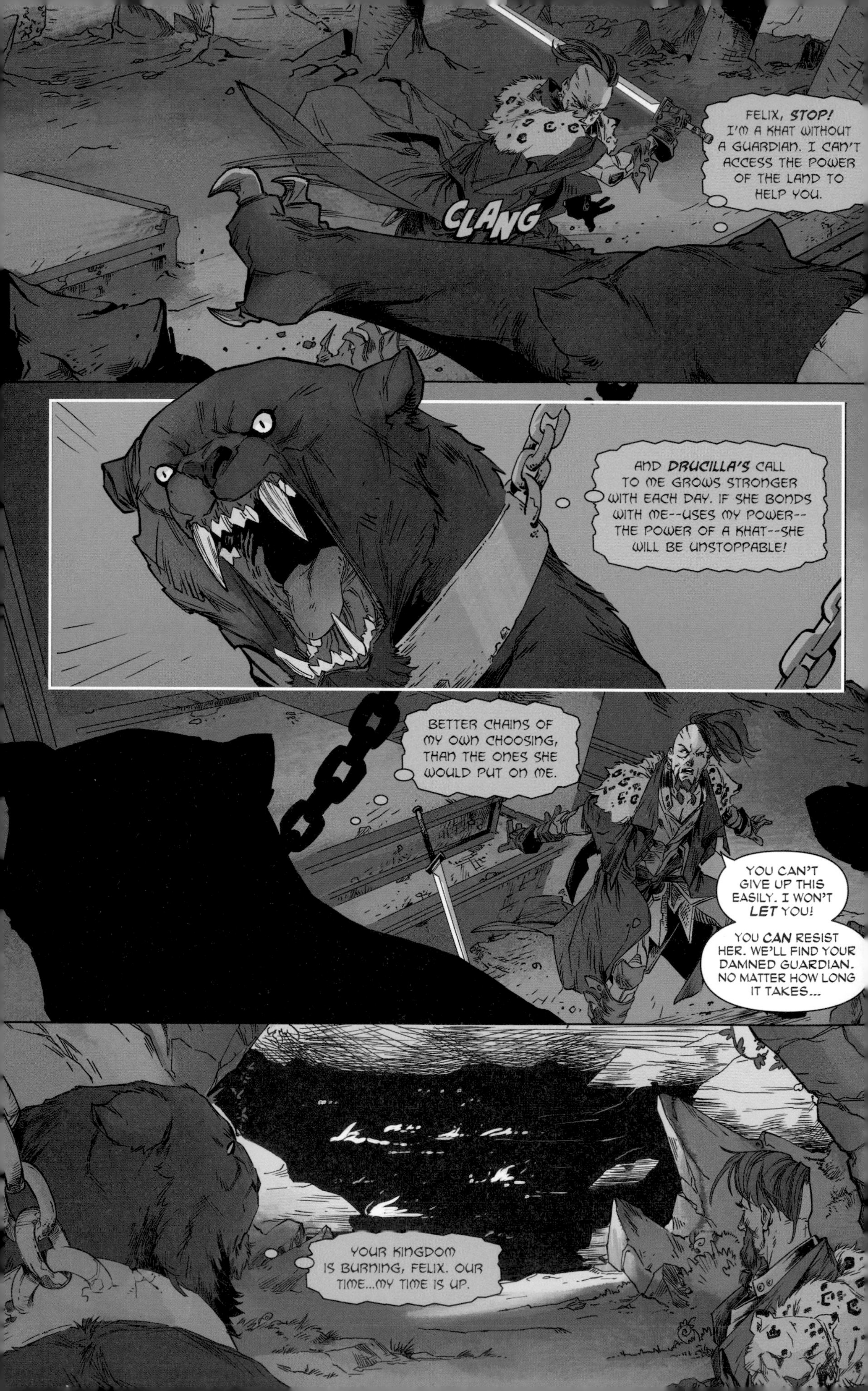
FELIX, STOP! I'M A KHAT WITHOUT A GUARDIAN. I CAN'T ACCESS THE POWER OF THE LAND TO HELP YOU.
CLANG
AND DRUCILLA'S CALL TO ME GROWS STRONGER WITH EACH DAY. IF SHE BONDS WITH ME--USES MY POWER--THE POWER OF A KHAT--SHE WILL BE UNSTOPPABLE!
BETTER CHAINS OF MY OWN CHOOSING, THAN THE ONES SHE WOULD PUT ON ME.
YOU CAN'T GIVE UP THIS EASILY. I WON'T LET YOU!
YOU CAN RESIST HER. WE'LL FIND YOUR DAMNED GUARDIAN. NO MATTER HOW LONG IT TAKES...
YOUR KINGDOM IS BURNING, FELIX. OUR TIME...MY TIME IS UP.

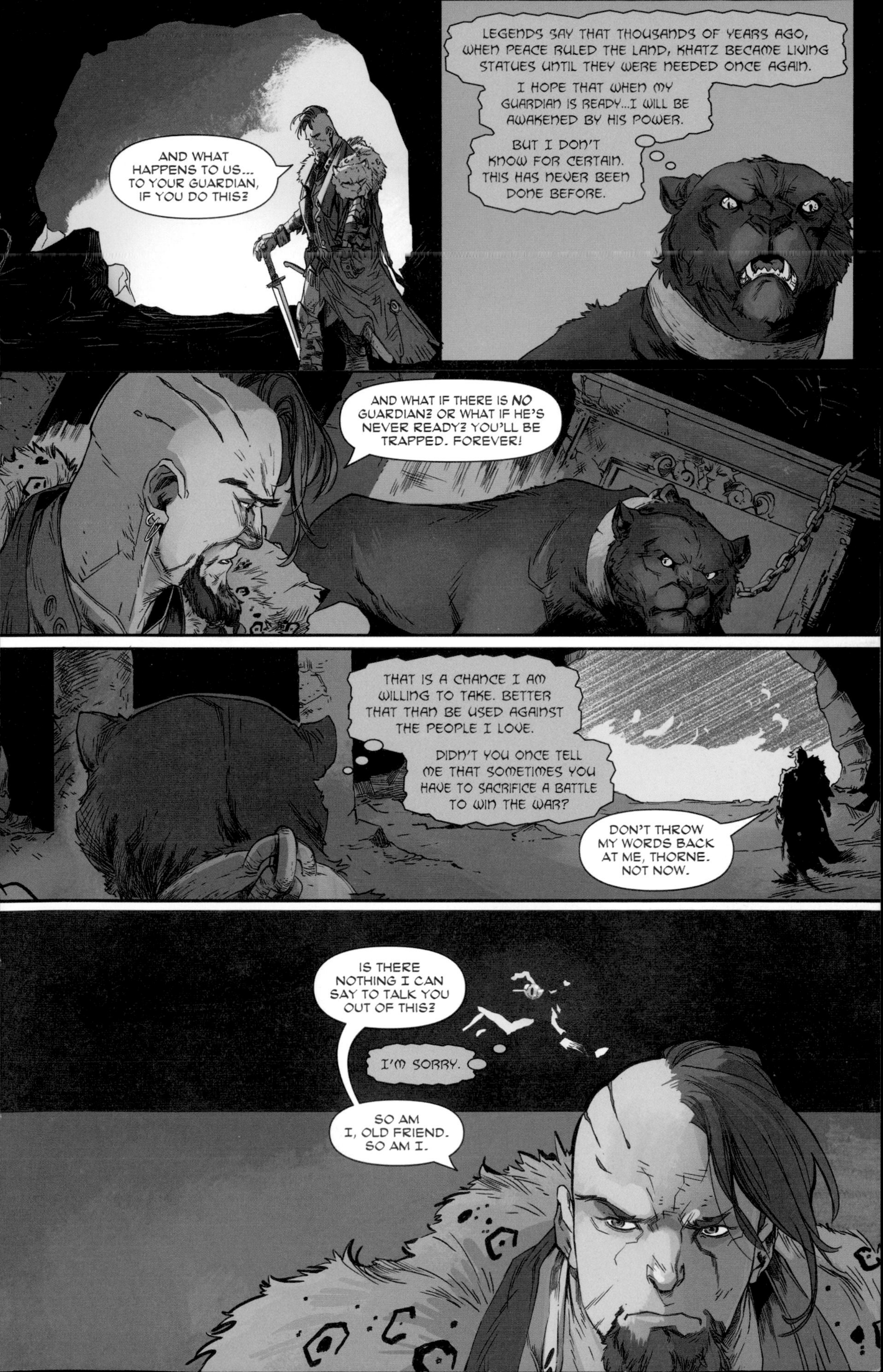
AND WHAT HAPPENS TO US... TO YOUR GUARDIAN, IF YOU DO THIS?
LEGENDS SAY THAT THOUSANDS OF YEARS AGO, WHEN PEACE RULED THE LAND, KHATZ BECAME LIVING STATUES UNTIL THEY WERE NEEDED ONCE AGAIN.
I HOPE THAT WHEN MY GUARDIAN IS READY...I WILL BE AWAKENED BY HIS POWER.
BUT I DON'T KNOW FOR CERTAIN. THIS HAS NEVER BEEN DONE BEFORE.
AND WHAT IF THERE IS NO GUARDIAN? OR WHAT IF HE'S NEVER READY? YOU'LL BE TRAPPED. FOREVER!
THAT IS A CHANCE I AM WILLING TO TAKE. BETTER THAT THAN BE USED AGAINST THE PEOPLE I LOVE.
DIDN'T YOU ONCE TELL ME THAT SOMETIMES YOU HAVE TO SACRIFICE A BATTLE TO WIN THE WAR?
DON'T THROW MY WORDS BACK AT ME, THORNE. NOT NOW.
IS THERE NOTHING I CAN SAY TO TALK YOU OUT OF THIS?
I'M SORRY.
SO AM I, OLD FRIEND. SO AM I.

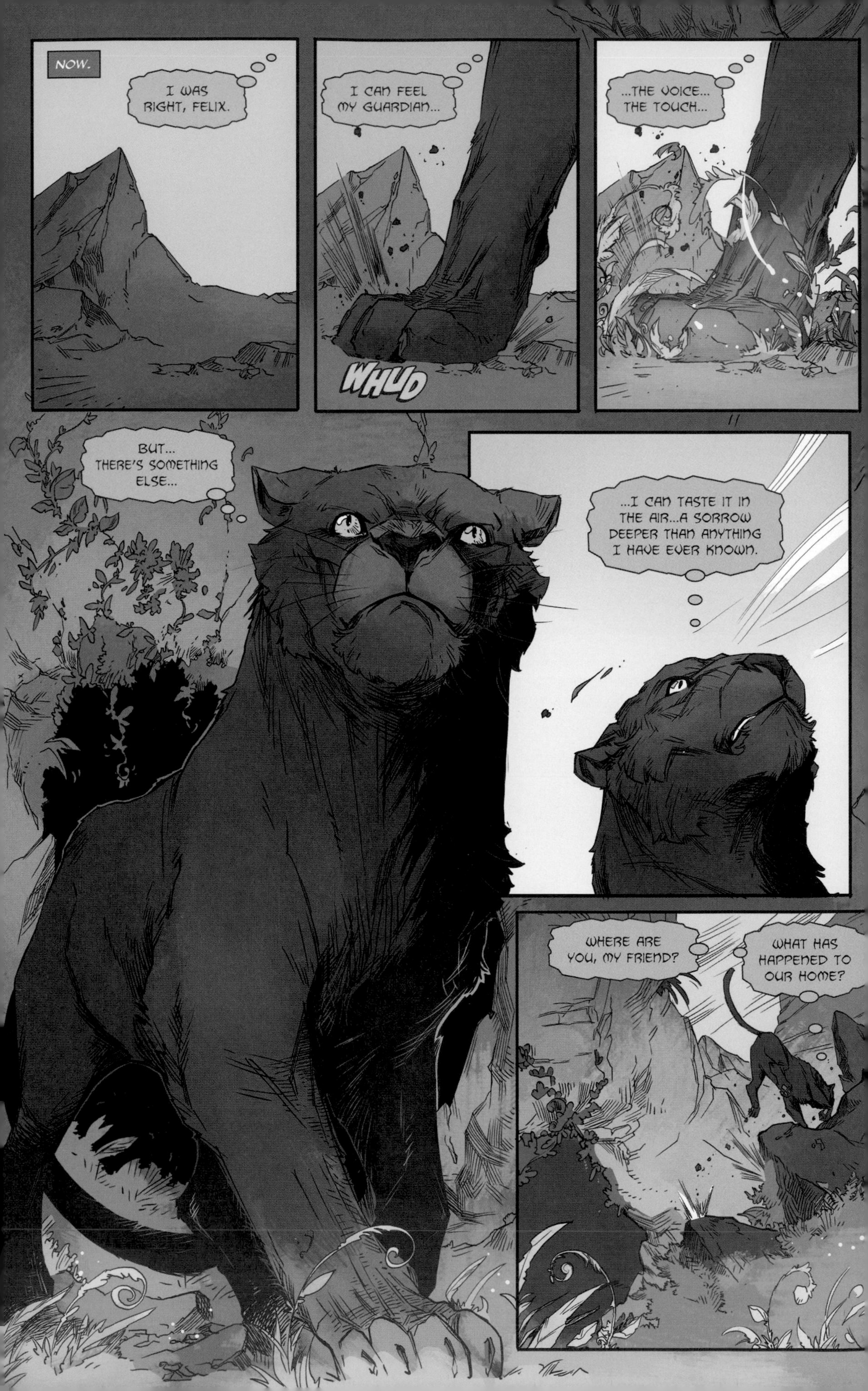
NOW.
I WAS RIGHT, FELIX.
I CAN FEEL MY GUARDIAN...
WHUD
...THE VOICE... THE TOUCH...
BUT... THERE'S SOMETHING ELSE...
...I CAN TASTE IT IN THE AIR...A SORROW DEEPER THAN ANYTHING I HAVE EVER KNOWN.
WHERE ARE YOU, MY FRIEND?
WHAT HAS HAPPENED TO OUR HOME?

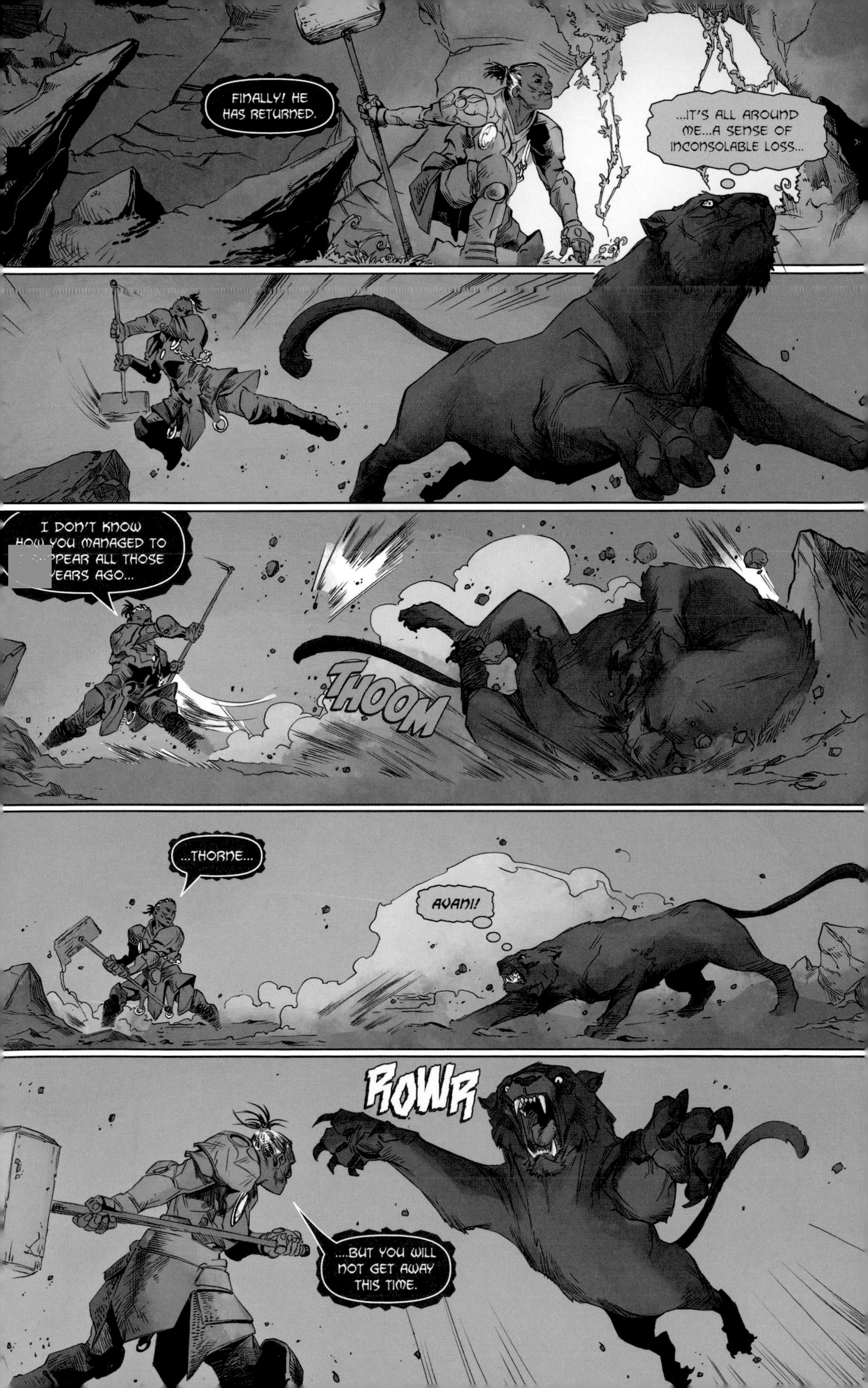
FINALLY! HE HAS RETURNED.
...IT'S ALL AROUND ME...A SENSE OF INCONSOLABLE LOSS...
I DON'T KNOW HOW YOU MANAGED TO PPEAR ALL THOSE YEARS AGO...
THOOM
...THORNE...
AVANI!
ROWR
....BUT YOU WILL NOT GET AWAY THIS TIME.

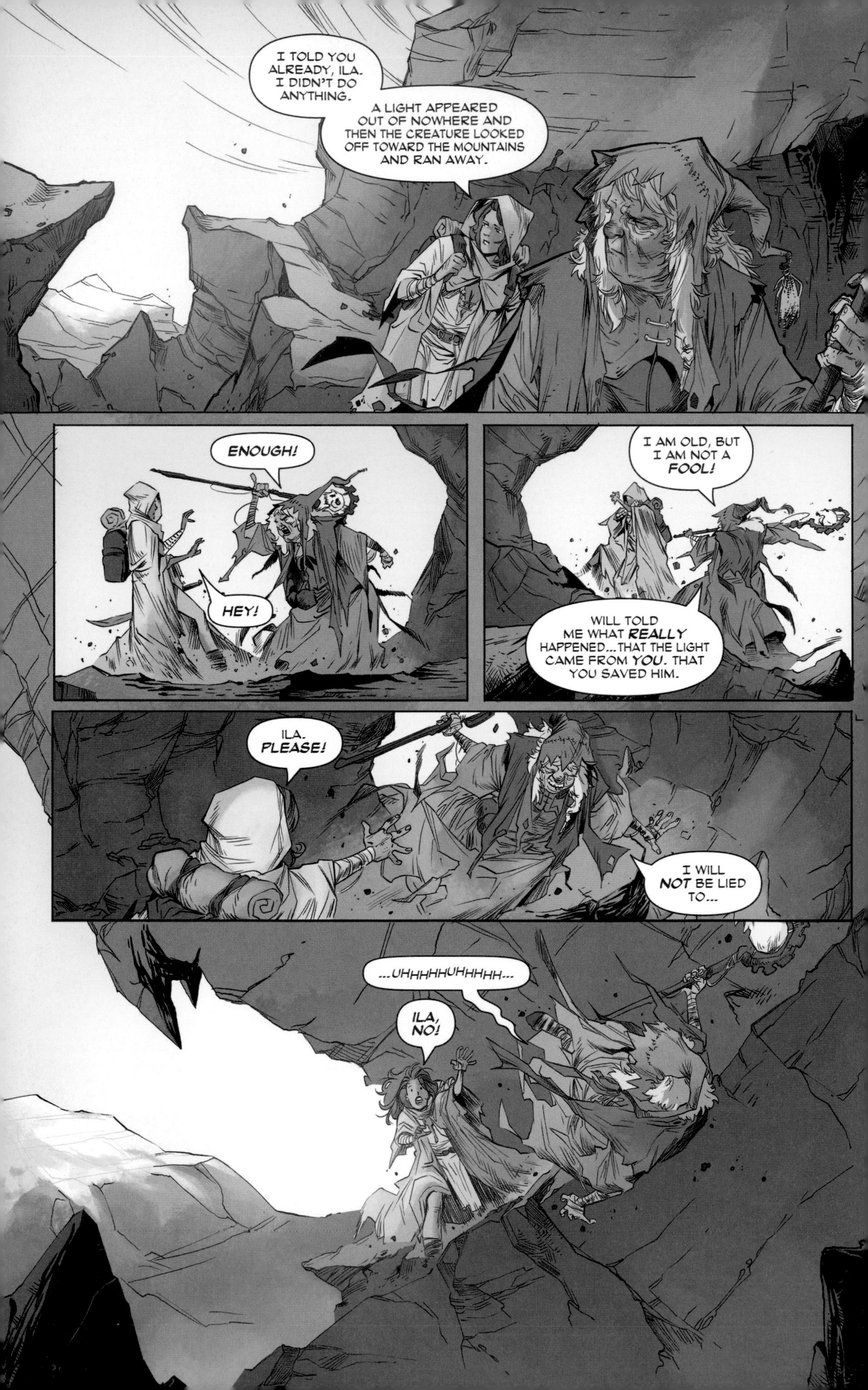
I TOLD YOU ALREADY, ILA. I DIDN'T DO ANYTHING.
A LIGHT APPEARED OUT OF NOWHERE AND THEN THE CREATURE LOOKED OFF TOWARD THE MOUNTAINS AND RAN AWAY.
ENOUGH!
HEY!
I AM OLD, BUT I AM NOT A FOOL!
WILL TOLD ME WHAT REALLY HAPPENED...THAT THE LIGHT CAME FROM YOU. THAT YOU SAVED HIM.
ILA. PLEASE!
I WILL NOT BE LIED TO...
...UHHHHHUHHHHH...
ILA, NO!

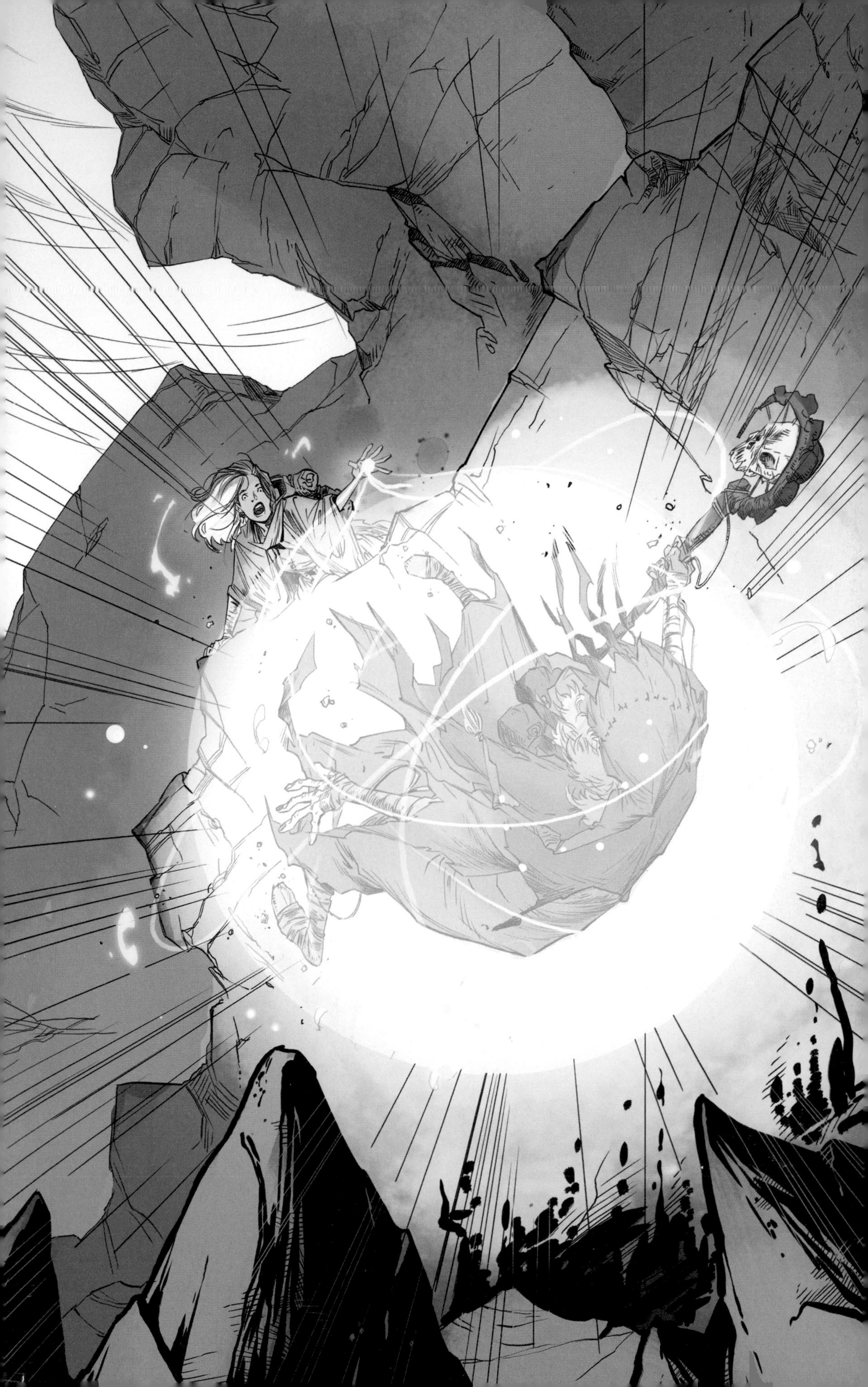

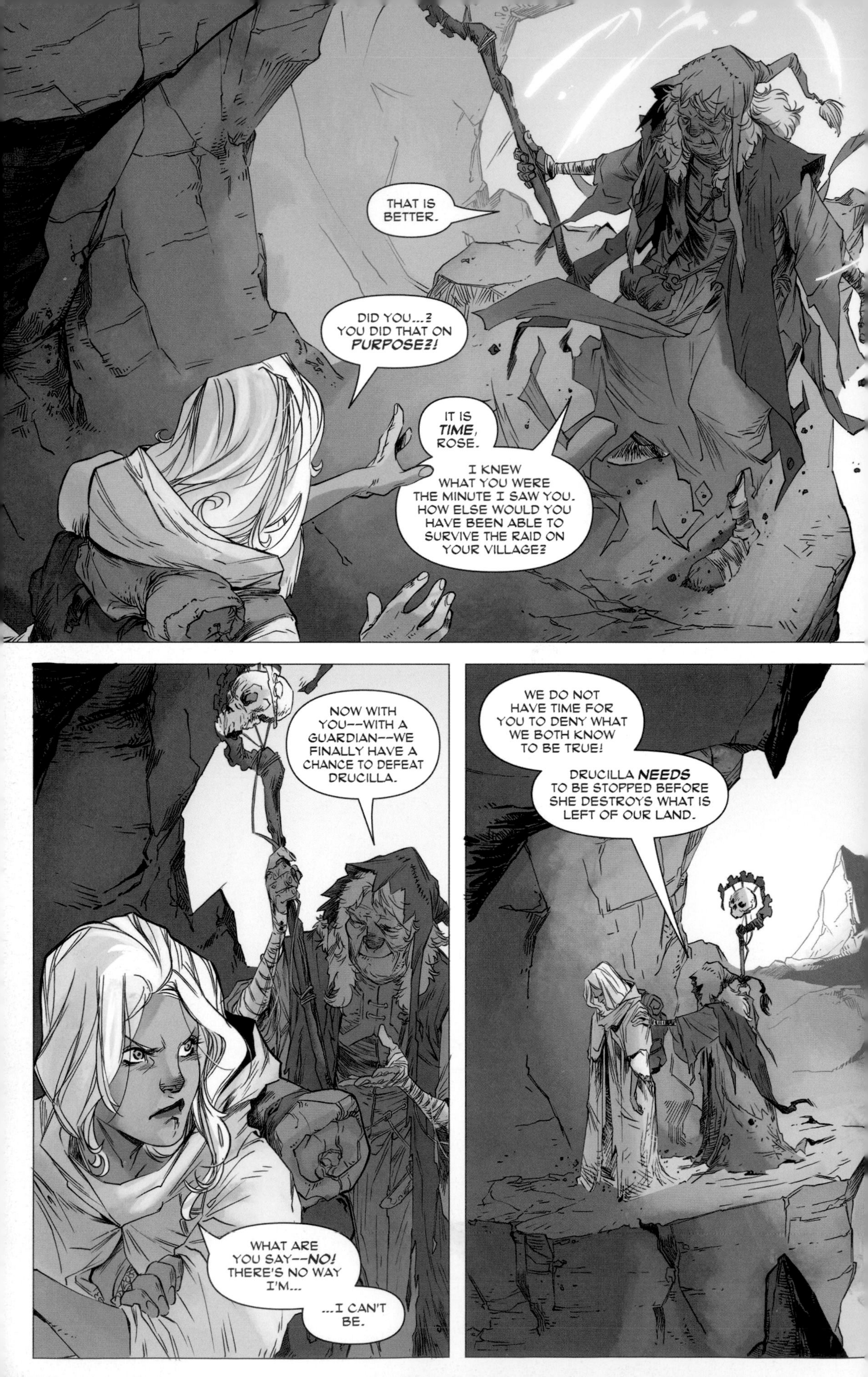
THAT IS BETTER.
DID YOU...? YOU DID THAT ON PURPOSE?!
IT IS TIME, ROSE.
I KNEW WHAT YOU WERE THE MINUTE I SAW YOU. HOW ELSE WOULD YOU HAVE BEEN ABLE TO SURVIVE THE RAID ON YOUR VILLAGE?
NOW WITH YOU--WITH A GUARDIAN--WE FINALLY HAVE A CHANCE TO DEFEAT DRUCILLA.
WHAT ARE YOU SAY--NO! THERE'S NO WAY I'M...
...I CAN'T BE.
WE DO NOT HAVE TIME FOR YOU TO DENY WHAT WE BOTH KNOW TO BE TRUE!
DRUCILLA NEEDS TO BE STOPPED BEFORE SHE DESTROYS WHAT IS LEFT OF OUR LAND.

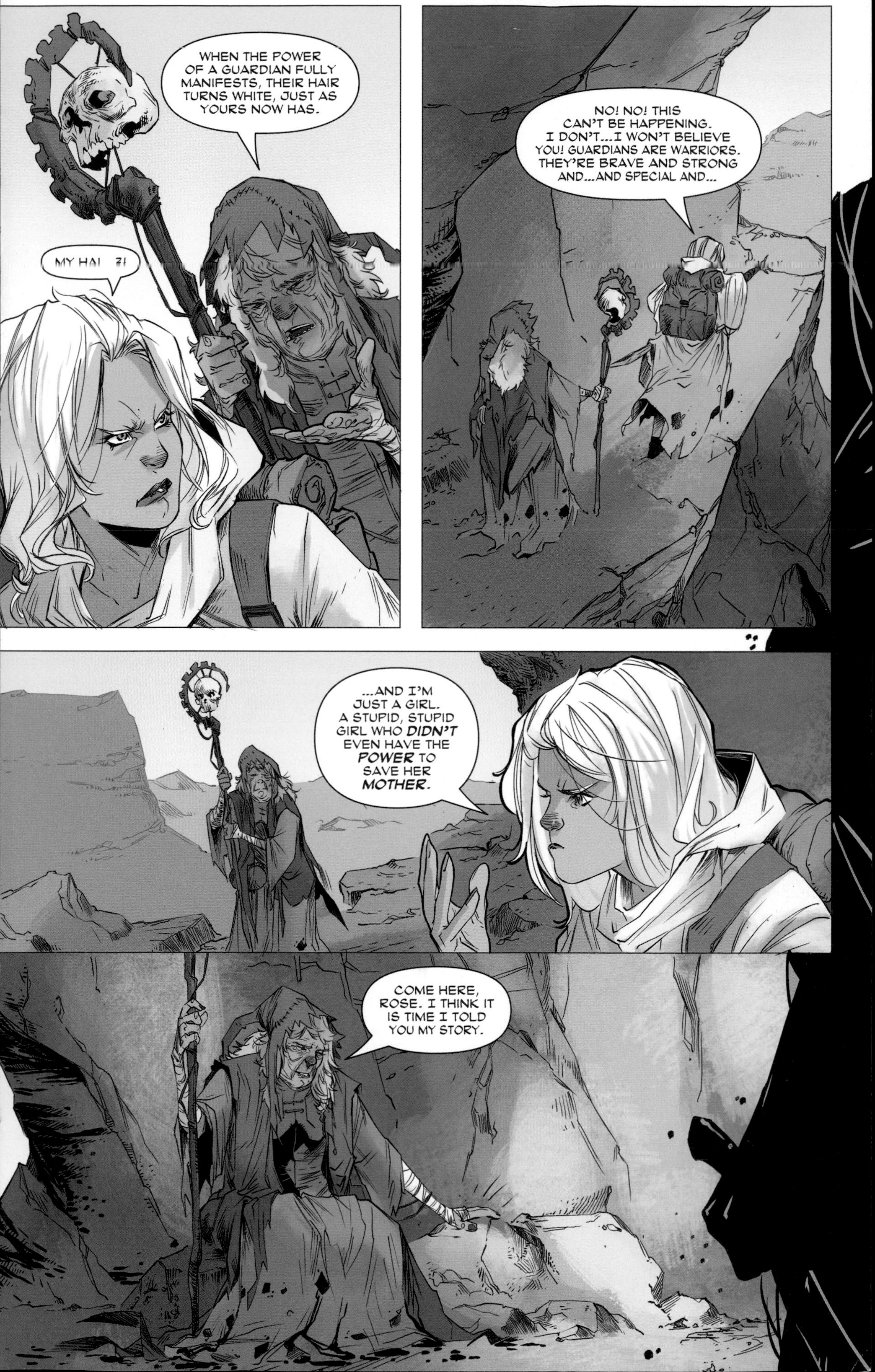
WHEN THE POWER OF A GUARDIAN FULLY MANIFESTS, THEIR HAIR TURNS WHITE, JUST AS YOURS NOW HAS.
MY HAI ?!
NO! NO! THIS CAN'T BE HAPPENING. I DON'T...I WON'T BELIEVE YOU! GUARDIANS ARE WARRIORS. THEY'RE BRAVE AND STRONG AND...AND SPECIAL AND...
...AND I'M JUST A GIRL. A STUPID, STUPID GIRL WHO *DIDN'T* EVEN HAVE THE ***POWER*** TO SAVE HER ***MOTHER***.
COME HERE, ROSE. I THINK IT IS TIME I TOLD YOU MY STORY.

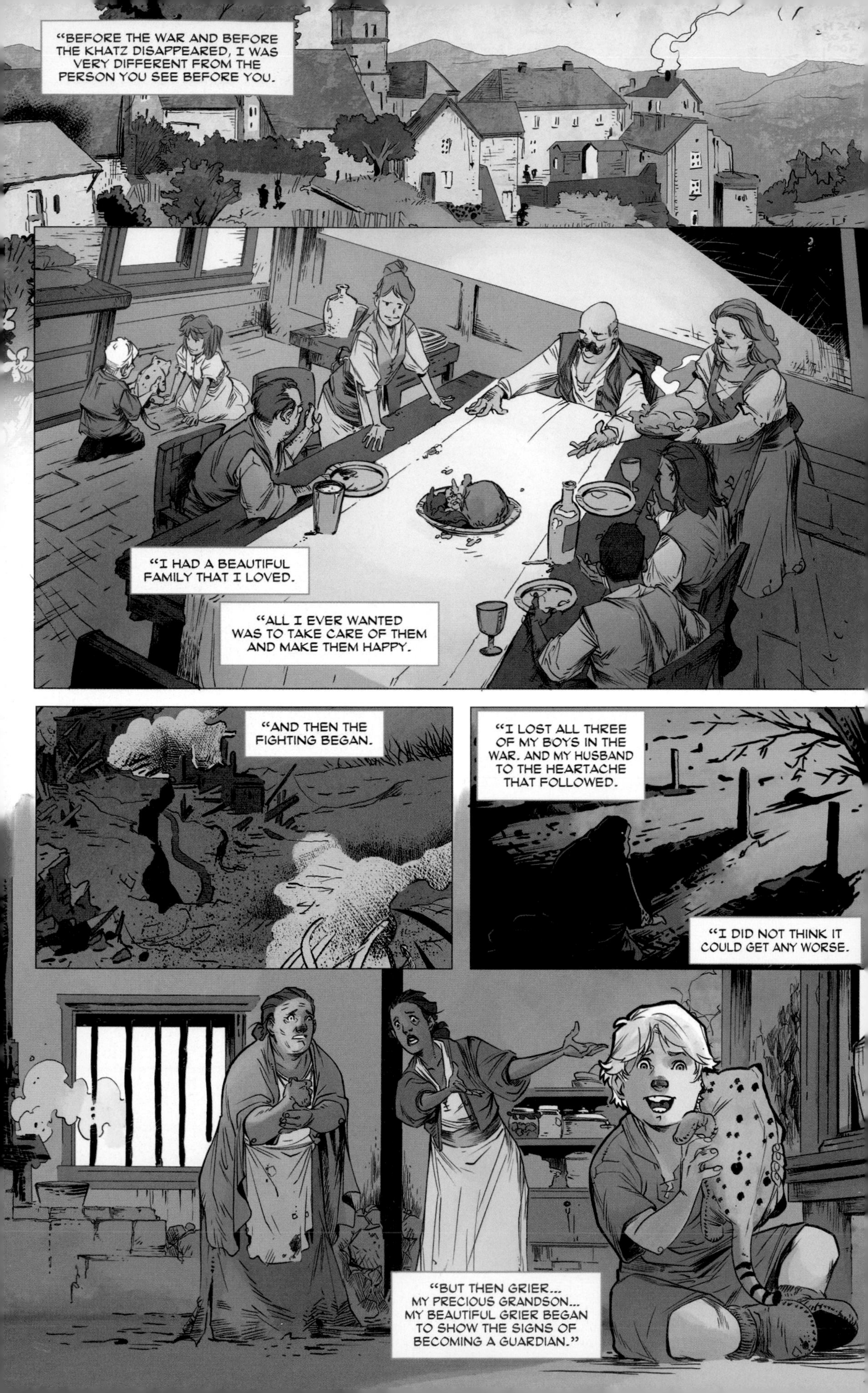
"BEFORE THE WAR AND BEFORE THE KHATZ DISAPPEARED, I WAS VERY DIFFERENT FROM THE PERSON YOU SEE BEFORE YOU.
"I HAD A BEAUTIFUL FAMILY THAT I LOVED.
"ALL I EVER WANTED WAS TO TAKE CARE OF THEM AND MAKE THEM HAPPY.
"AND THEN THE FIGHTING BEGAN.
"I LOST ALL THREE OF MY BOYS IN THE WAR. AND MY HUSBAND TO THE HEARTACHE THAT FOLLOWED.
"I DID NOT THINK IT COULD GET ANY WORSE.
"BUT THEN GRIER... MY PRECIOUS GRANDSON... MY BEAUTIFUL GRIER BEGAN TO SHOW THE SIGNS OF BECOMING A GUARDIAN."

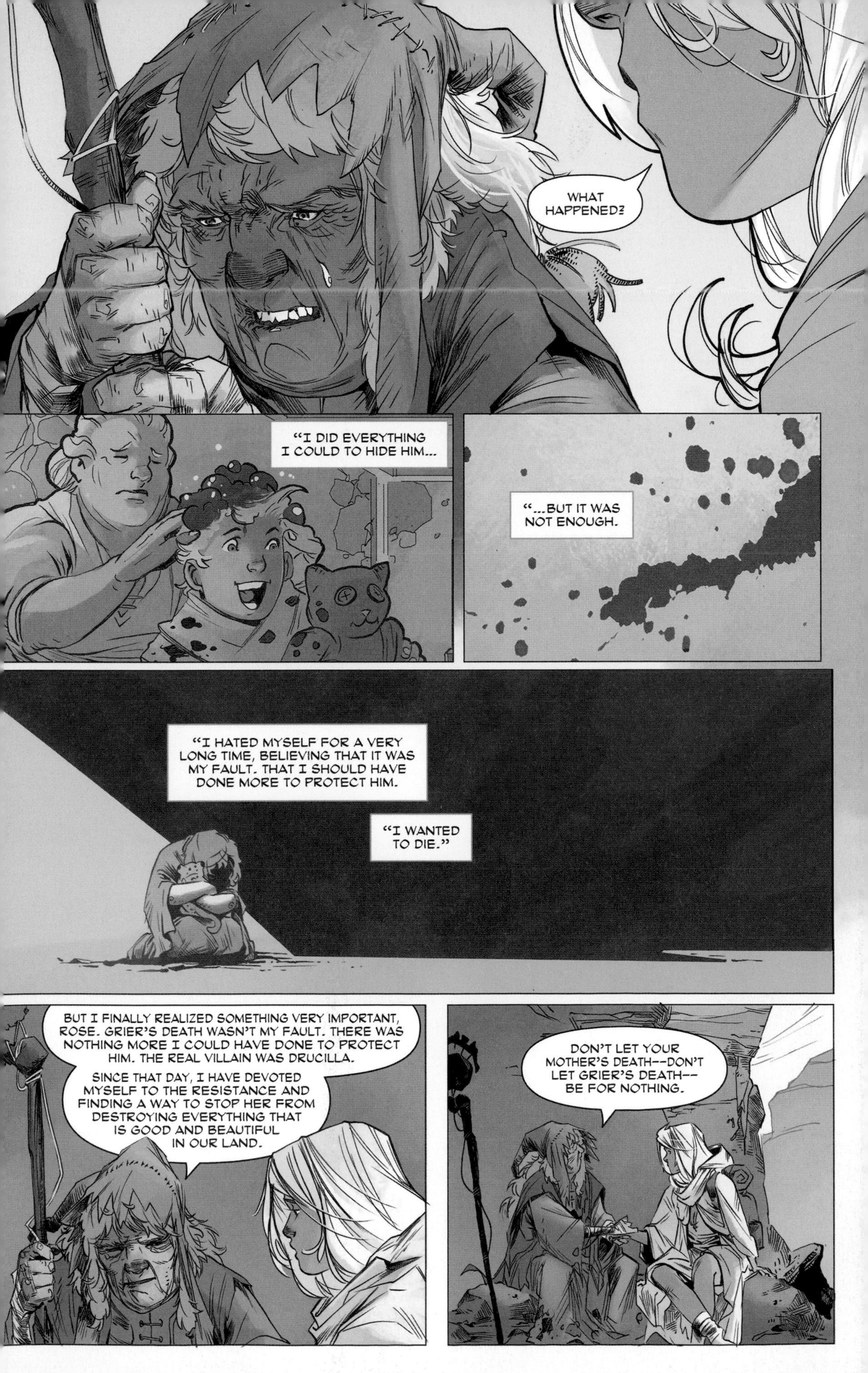
WHAT HAPPENED?
"I DID EVERYTHING I COULD TO HIDE HIM...
"...BUT IT WAS NOT ENOUGH.
"I HATED MYSELF FOR A VERY LONG TIME, BELIEVING THAT IT WAS MY FAULT. THAT I SHOULD HAVE DONE MORE TO PROTECT HIM.
"I WANTED TO DIE."
BUT I FINALLY REALIZED SOMETHING VERY IMPORTANT, ROSE. GRIER'S DEATH WASN'T MY FAULT. THERE WAS NOTHING MORE I COULD HAVE DONE TO PROTECT HIM. THE REAL VILLAIN WAS DRUCILLA.
SINCE THAT DAY, I HAVE DEVOTED MYSELF TO THE RESISTANCE AND FINDING A WAY TO STOP HER FROM DESTROYING EVERYTHING THAT IS GOOD AND BEAUTIFUL IN OUR LAND.
DON'T LET YOUR MOTHER'S DEATH--DON'T LET GRIER'S DEATH--BE FOR NOTHING.

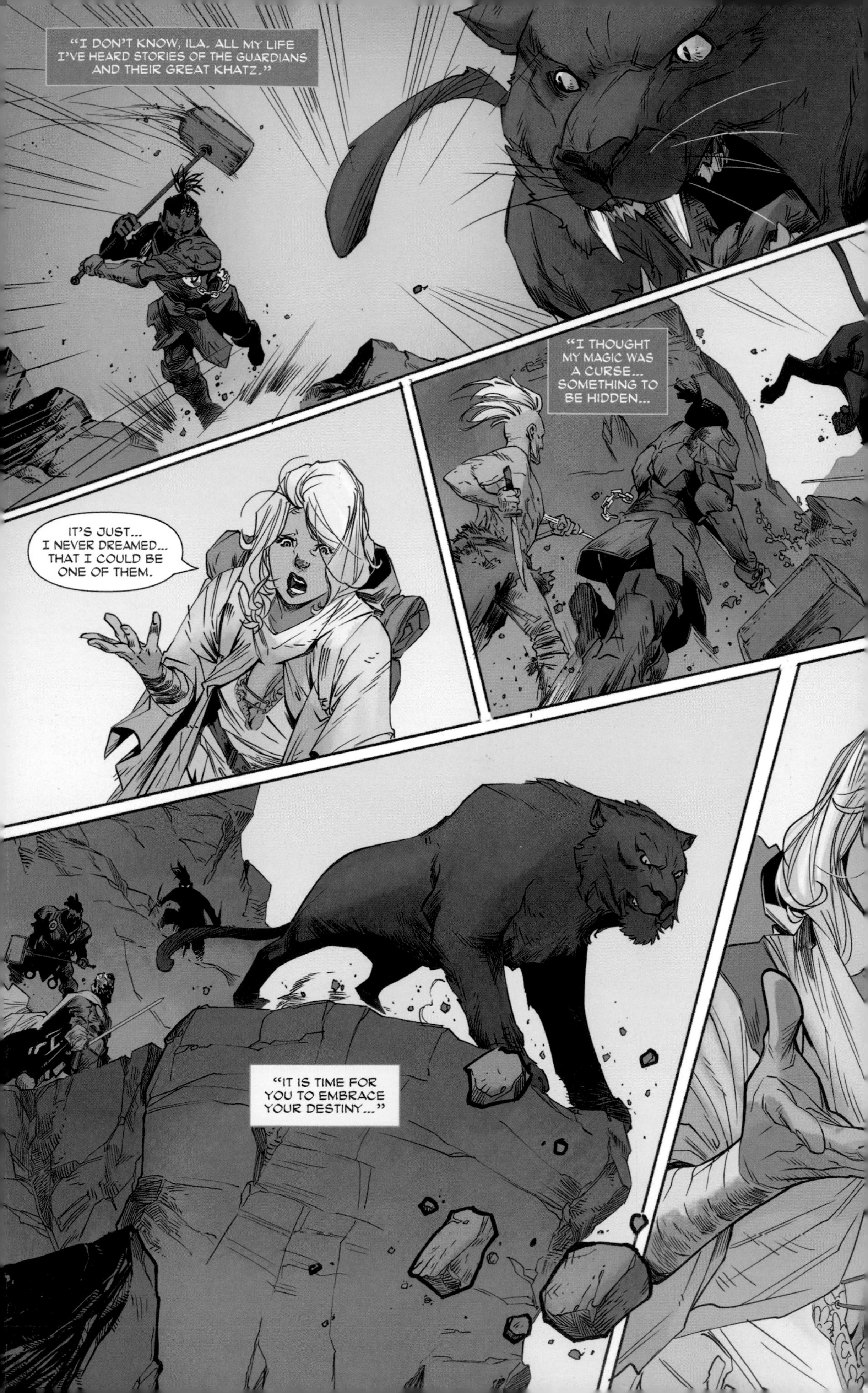
"I DON'T KNOW, ILA. ALL MY LIFE I'VE HEARD STORIES OF THE GUARDIANS AND THEIR GREAT KHATZ."
"I THOUGHT MY MAGIC WAS A CURSE... SOMETHING TO BE HIDDEN...
IT'S JUST... I NEVER DREAMED... THAT I COULD BE ONE OF THEM.
"IT IS TIME FOR YOU TO EMBRACE YOUR DESTINY..."

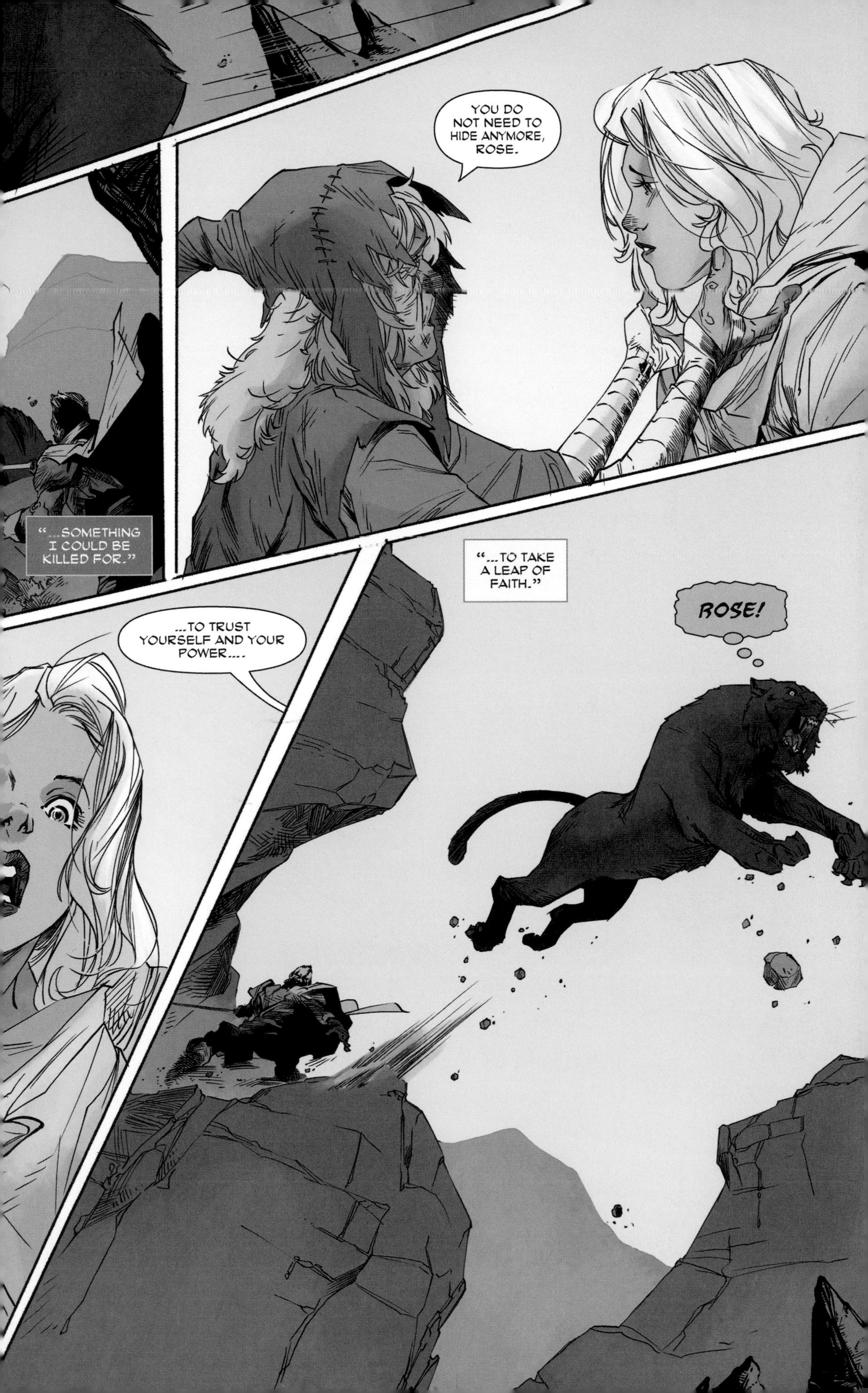
YOU DO NOT NEED TO HIDE ANYMORE, ROSE.
"...SOMETHING I COULD BE KILLED FOR."
...TO TRUST YOURSELF AND YOUR POWER....
"...TO TAKE A LEAP OF FAITH."
ROSE!

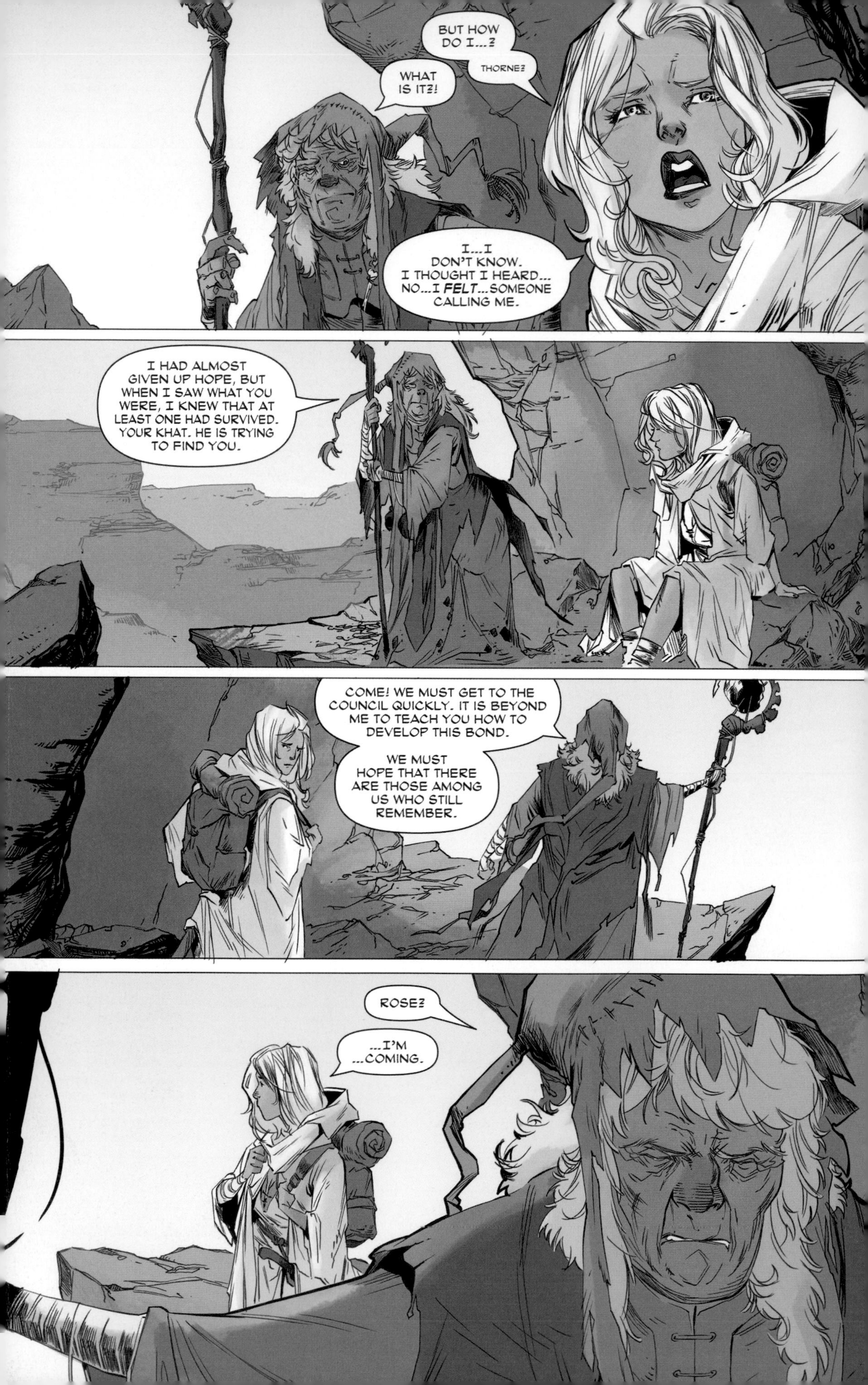
BUT HOW DO I...?
WHAT IS IT?!
THORNE?
I...I DON'T KNOW. I THOUGHT I HEARD... NO...I *FELT*...SOMEONE CALLING ME.
I HAD ALMOST GIVEN UP HOPE, BUT WHEN I SAW WHAT YOU WERE, I KNEW THAT AT LEAST ONE HAD SURVIVED. YOUR KHAT. HE IS TRYING TO FIND YOU.
COME! WE MUST GET TO THE COUNCIL QUICKLY. IT IS BEYOND ME TO TEACH YOU HOW TO DEVELOP THIS BOND.
WE MUST HOPE THAT THERE ARE THOSE AMONG US WHO STILL REMEMBER.
ROSE?
...I'M ...COMING.

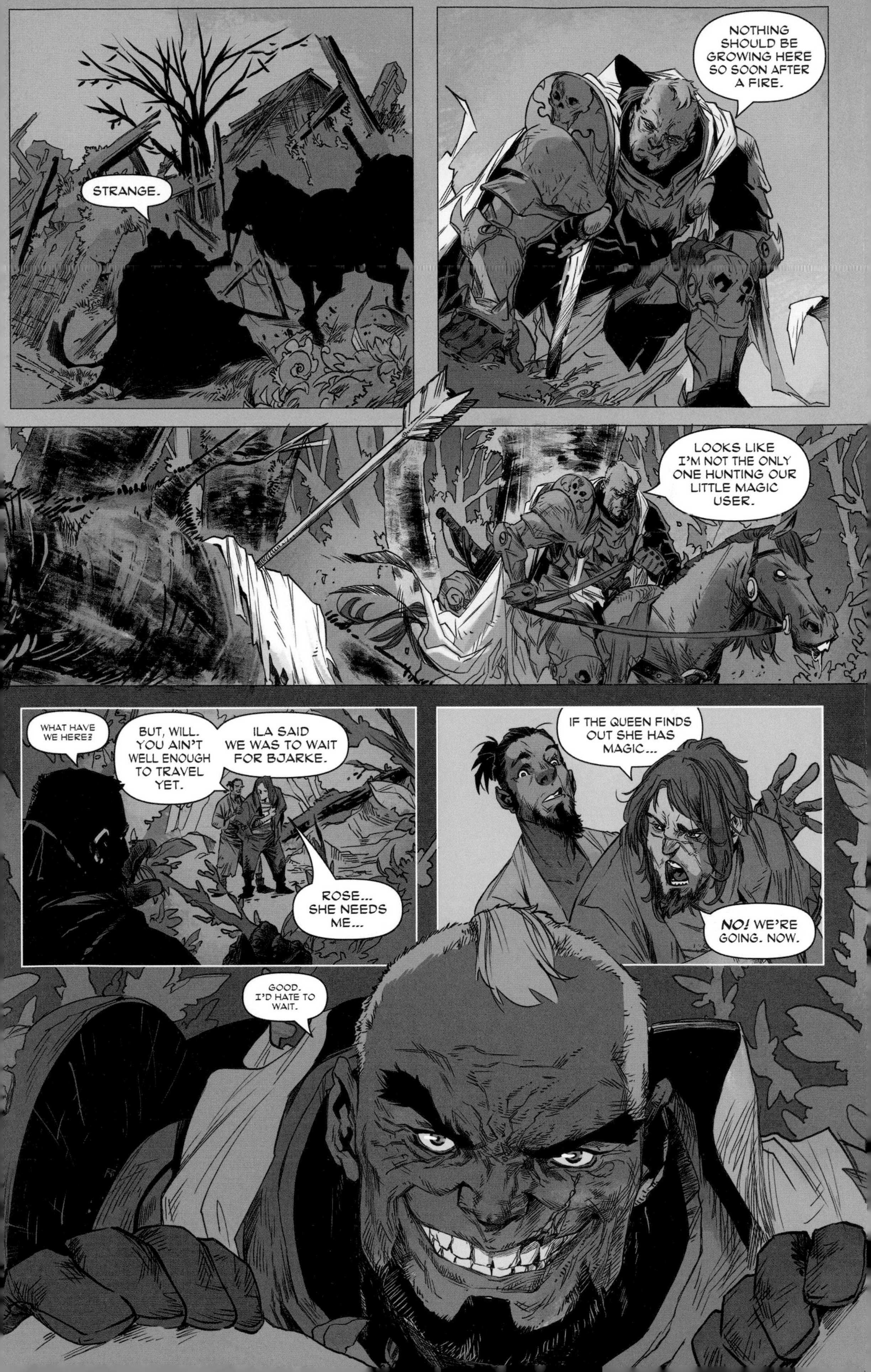
STRANGE.
NOTHING SHOULD BE GROWING HERE SO SOON AFTER A FIRE.
LOOKS LIKE I'M NOT THE ONLY ONE HUNTING OUR LITTLE MAGIC USER.
WHAT HAVE WE HERE?
BUT, WILL. YOU AIN'T WELL ENOUGH TO TRAVEL YET.
ILA SAID WE WAS TO WAIT FOR BJARKE.
ROSE... SHE NEEDS ME...
IF THE QUEEN FINDS OUT SHE HAS MAGIC...
NO! WE'RE GOING. NOW.
GOOD. I'D HATE TO WAIT.

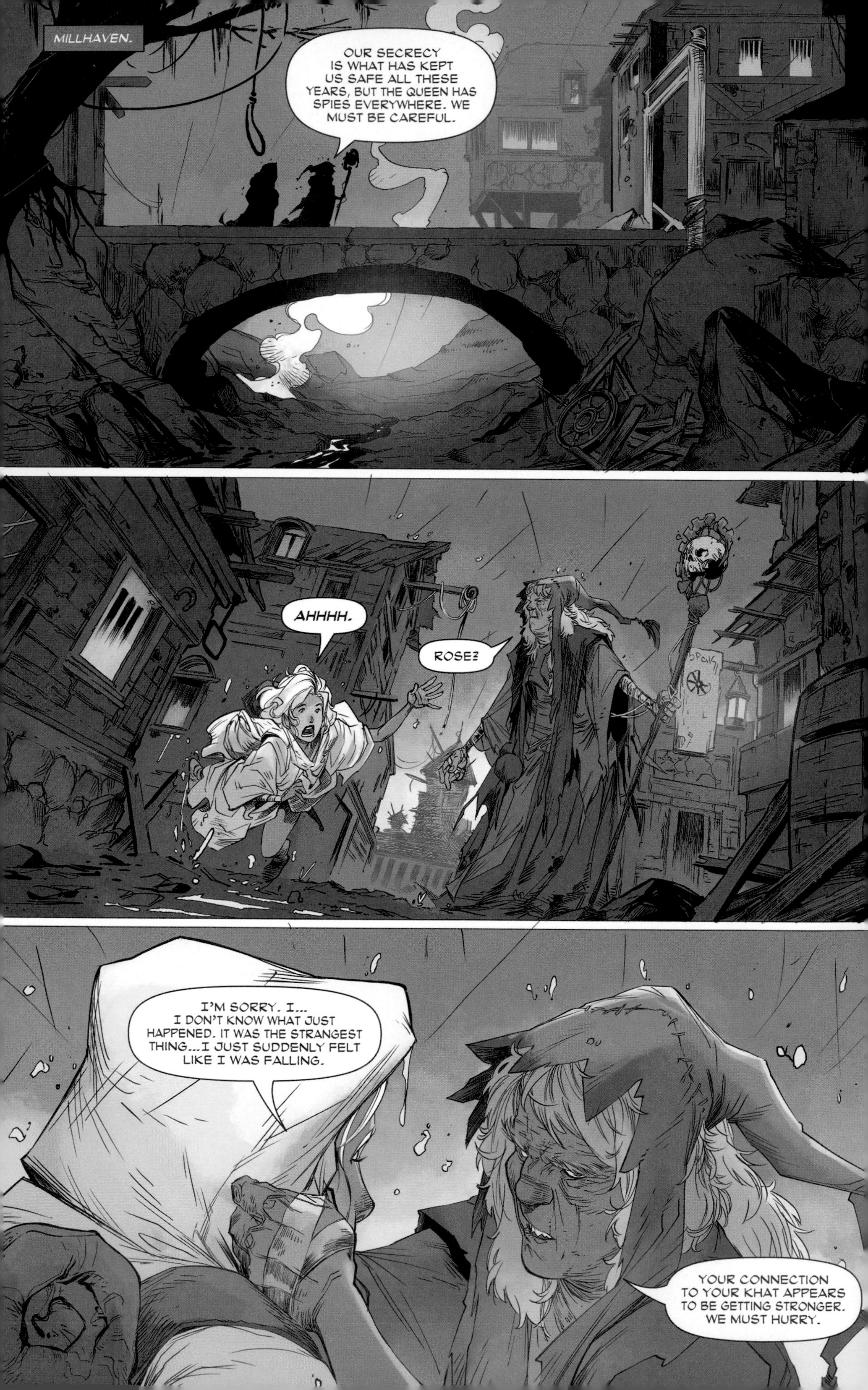
MILLHAVEN.
OUR SECRECY IS WHAT HAS KEPT US SAFE ALL THESE YEARS, BUT THE QUEEN HAS SPIES EVERYWHERE. WE MUST BE CAREFUL.
AHHHH.
ROSE?
I'M SORRY. I... I DON'T KNOW WHAT JUST HAPPENED. IT WAS THE STRANGEST THING...I JUST SUDDENLY FELT LIKE I WAS FALLING.
YOUR CONNECTION TO YOUR KHAT APPEARS TO BE GETTING STRONGER. WE MUST HURRY.

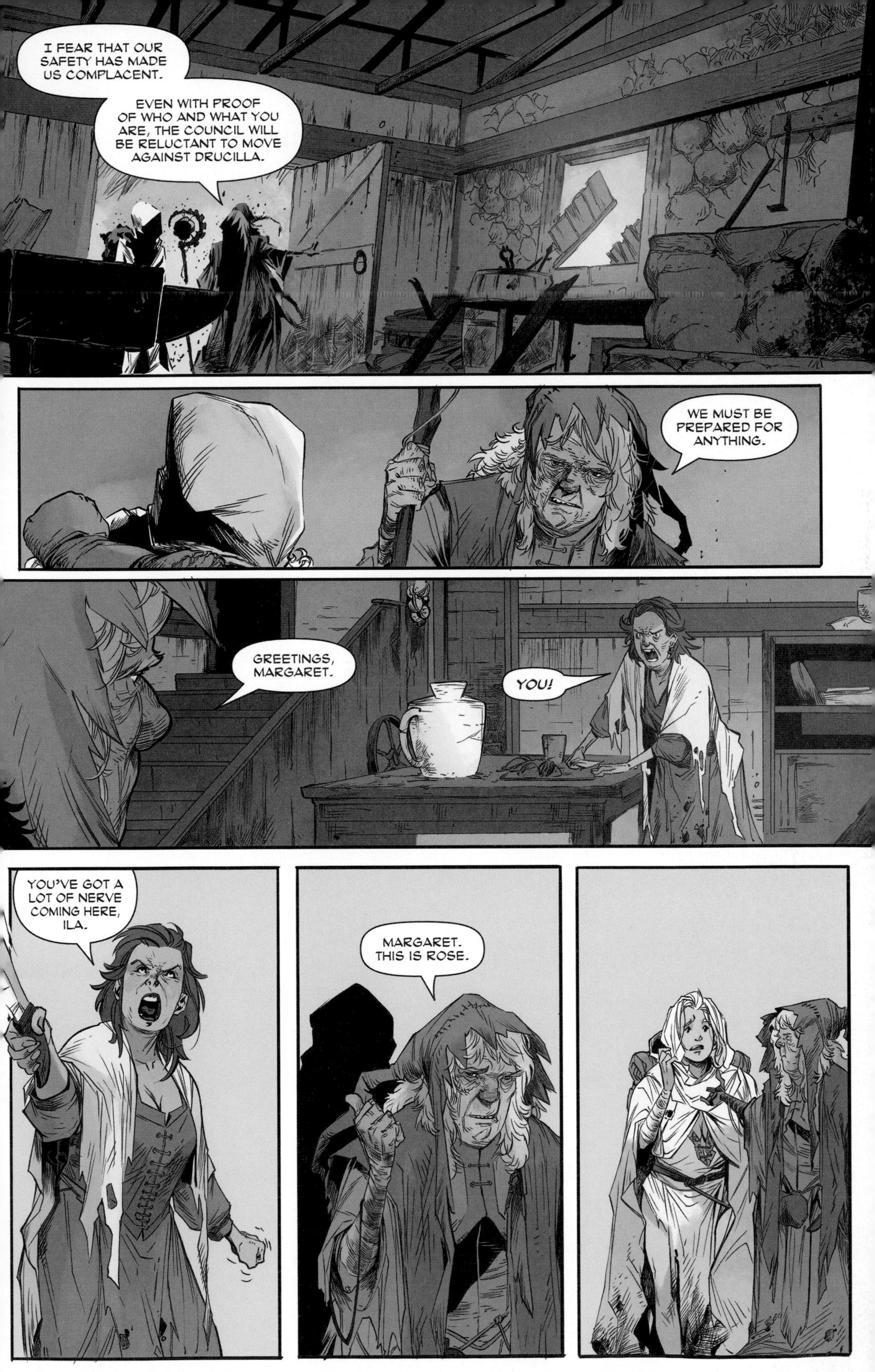
I FEAR THAT OUR SAFETY HAS MADE US COMPLACENT.
EVEN WITH PROOF OF WHO AND WHAT YOU ARE, THE COUNCIL WILL BE RELUCTANT TO MOVE AGAINST DRUCILLA.
WE MUST BE PREPARED FOR ANYTHING.
GREETINGS, MARGARET.
YOU!
YOU'VE GOT A LOT OF NERVE COMING HERE, ILA.
MARGARET. THIS IS ROSE.

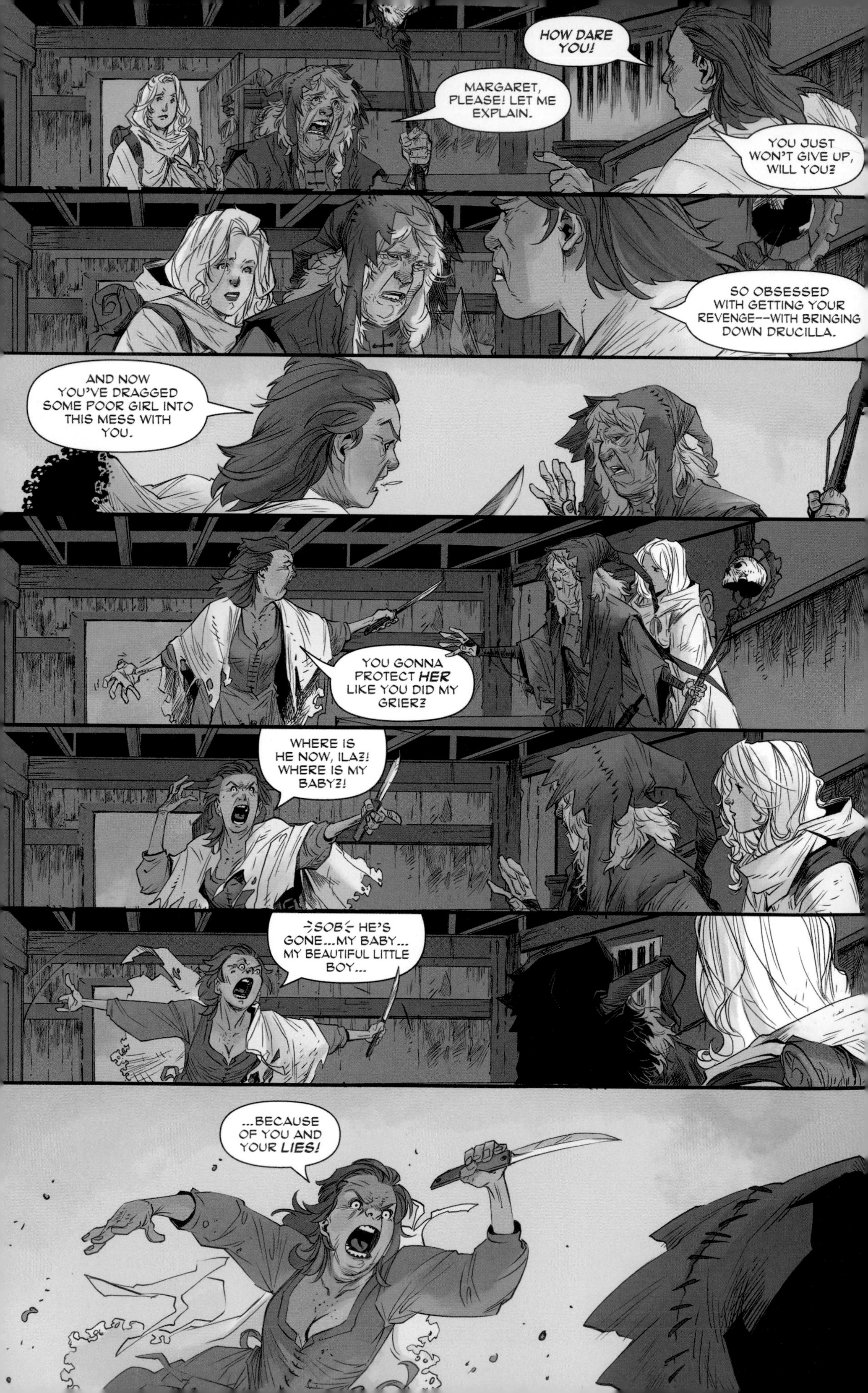
HOW DARE YOU!
MARGARET, PLEASE! LET ME EXPLAIN.
YOU JUST WON'T GIVE UP, WILL YOU?
SO OBSESSED WITH GETTING YOUR REVENGE--WITH BRINGING DOWN DRUCILLA.
AND NOW YOU'VE DRAGGED SOME POOR GIRL INTO THIS MESS WITH YOU.
YOU GONNA PROTECT HER LIKE YOU DID MY GRIER?
WHERE IS HE NOW, ILA?! WHERE IS MY BABY?!
SOB HE'S GONE... MY BABY... MY BEAUTIFUL LITTLE BOY...
...BECAUSE OF YOU AND YOUR LIES!

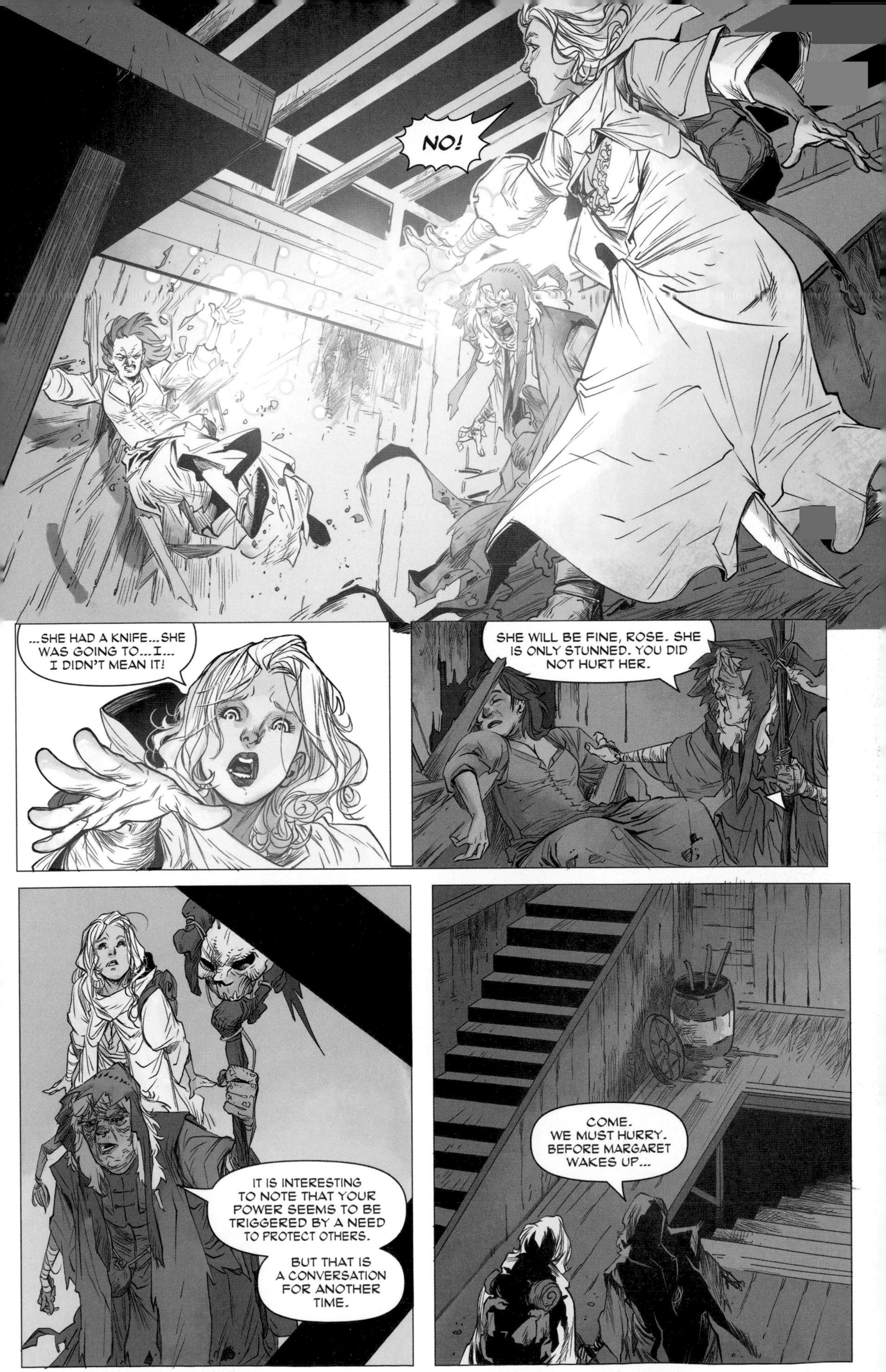
NO!
...SHE HAD A KNIFE...SHE WAS GOING TO...I... I DIDN'T MEAN IT!
SHE WILL BE FINE, ROSE. SHE IS ONLY STUNNED. YOU DID NOT HURT HER.
IT IS INTERESTING TO NOTE THAT YOUR POWER SEEMS TO BE TRIGGERED BY A NEED TO PROTECT OTHERS.
BUT THAT IS A CONVERSATION FOR ANOTHER TIME.
COME. WE MUST HURRY. BEFORE MARGARET WAKES UP...

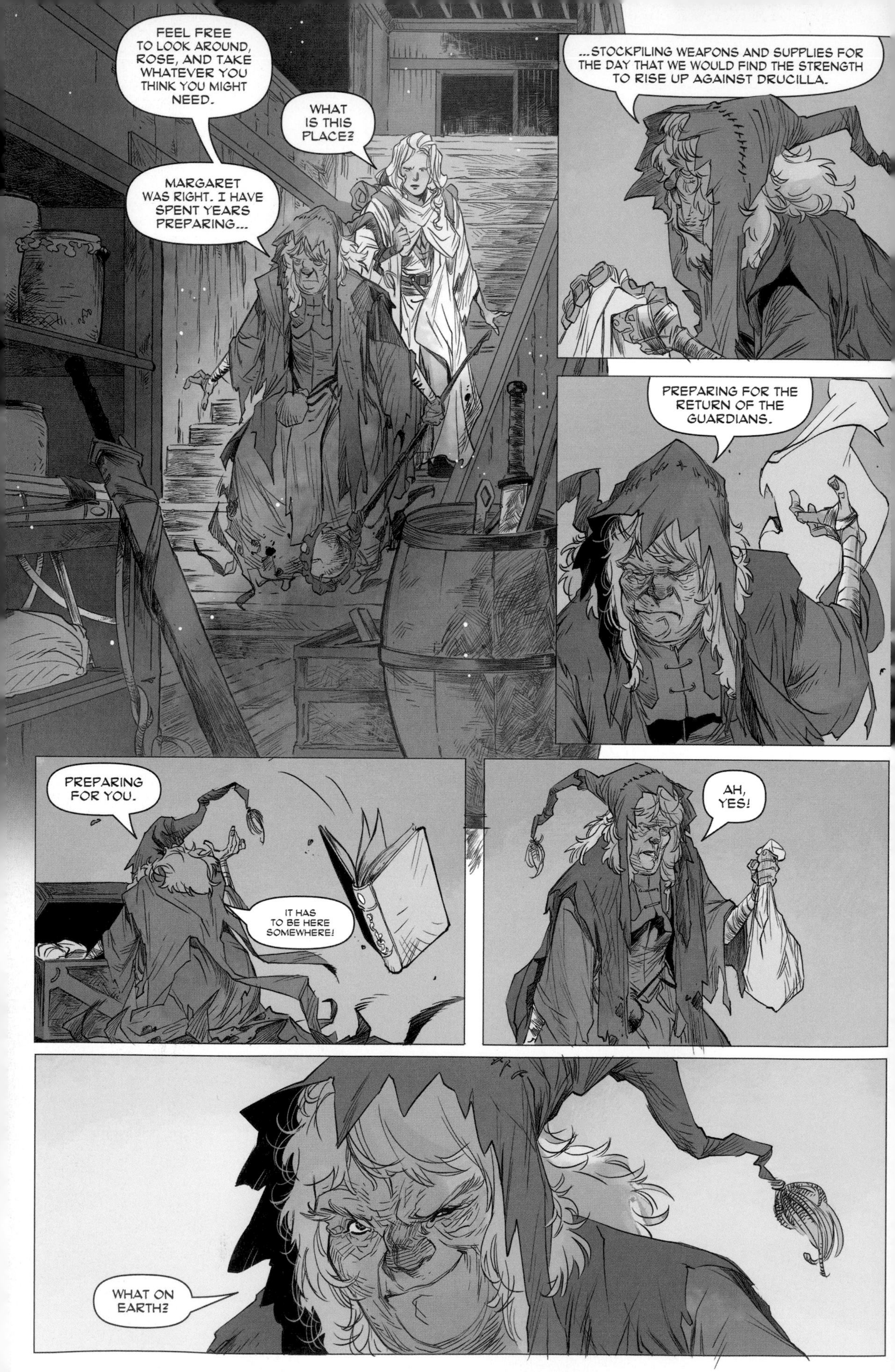
FEEL FREE TO LOOK AROUND, ROSE, AND TAKE WHATEVER YOU THINK YOU MIGHT NEED.
WHAT IS THIS PLACE?
MARGARET WAS RIGHT. I HAVE SPENT YEARS PREPARING...
...STOCKPILING WEAPONS AND SUPPLIES FOR THE DAY THAT WE WOULD FIND THE STRENGTH TO RISE UP AGAINST DRUCILLA.
PREPARING FOR THE RETURN OF THE GUARDIANS.
PREPARING FOR YOU.
IT HAS TO BE HERE SOMEWHERE!
AH, YES!
WHAT ON EARTH?

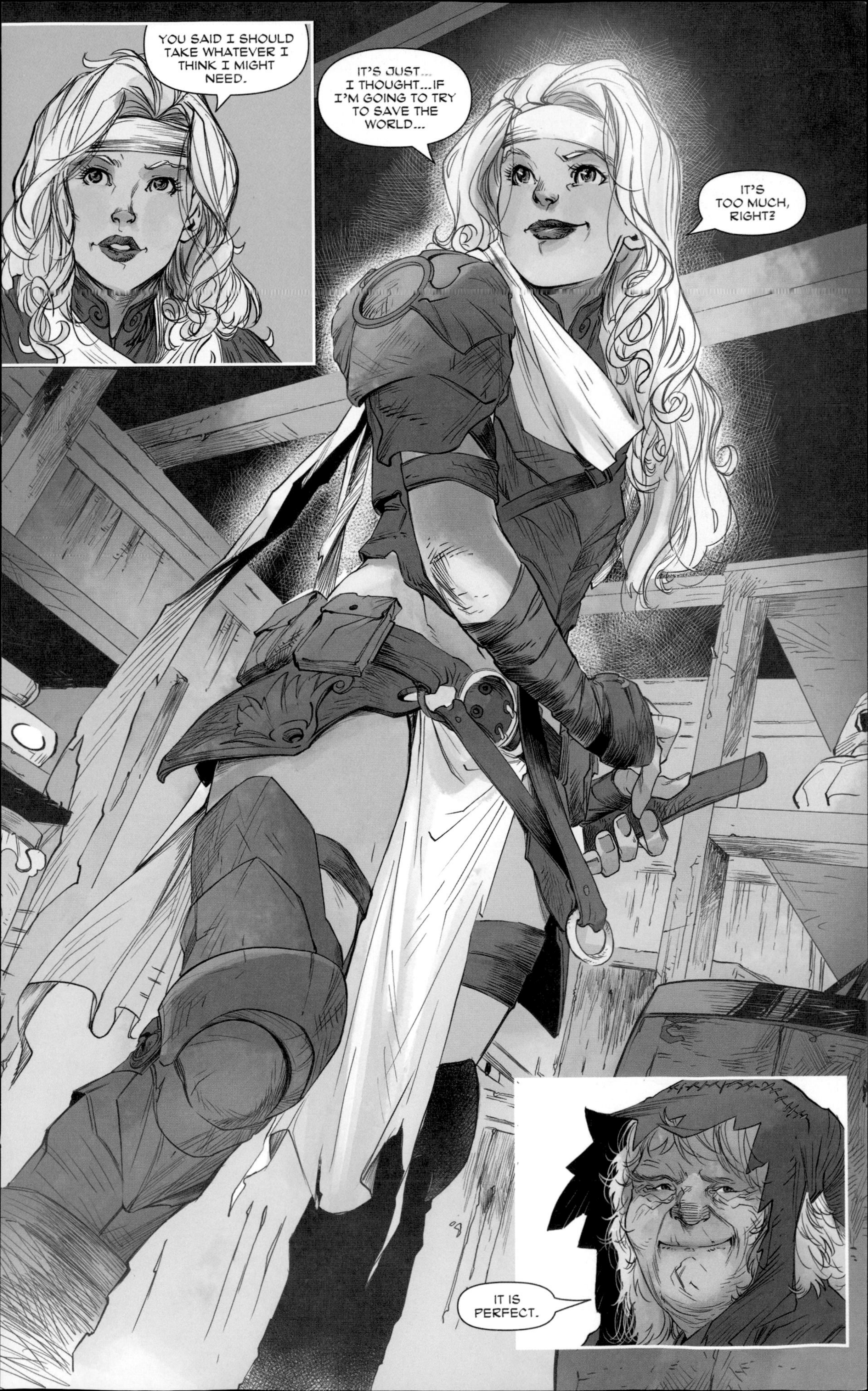
YOU SAID I SHOULD TAKE WHATEVER I THINK I MIGHT NEED.
IT'S JUST... I THOUGHT...IF I'M GOING TO TRY TO SAVE THE WORLD...
IT'S TOO MUCH, RIGHT?
IT IS PERFECT.

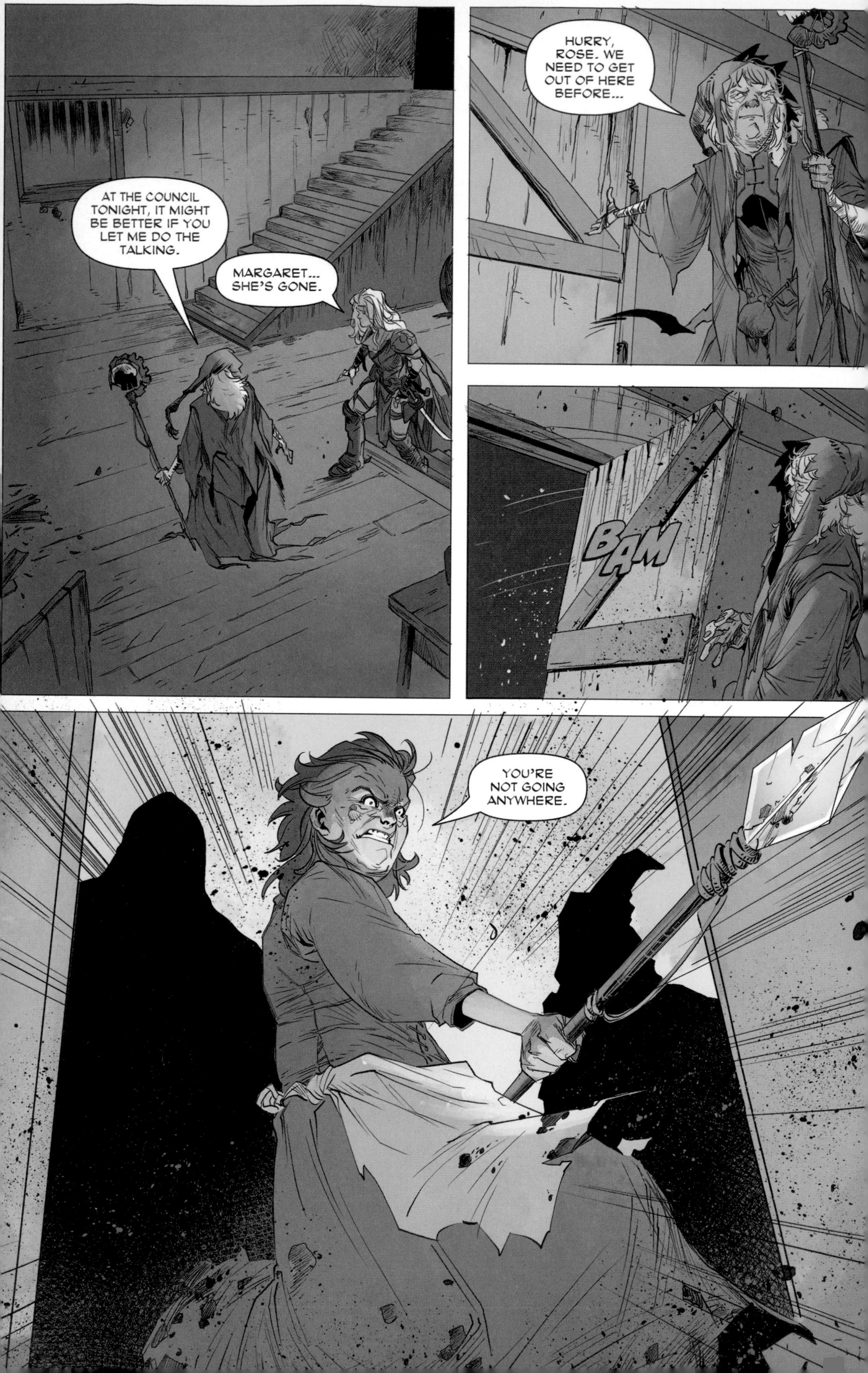
AT THE COUNCIL TONIGHT, IT MIGHT BE BETTER IF YOU LET ME DO THE TALKING.
MARGARET... SHE'S GONE.
HURRY, ROSE. WE NEED TO GET OUT OF HERE BEFORE...
BAM
YOU'RE NOT GOING ANYWHERE.

FOUR

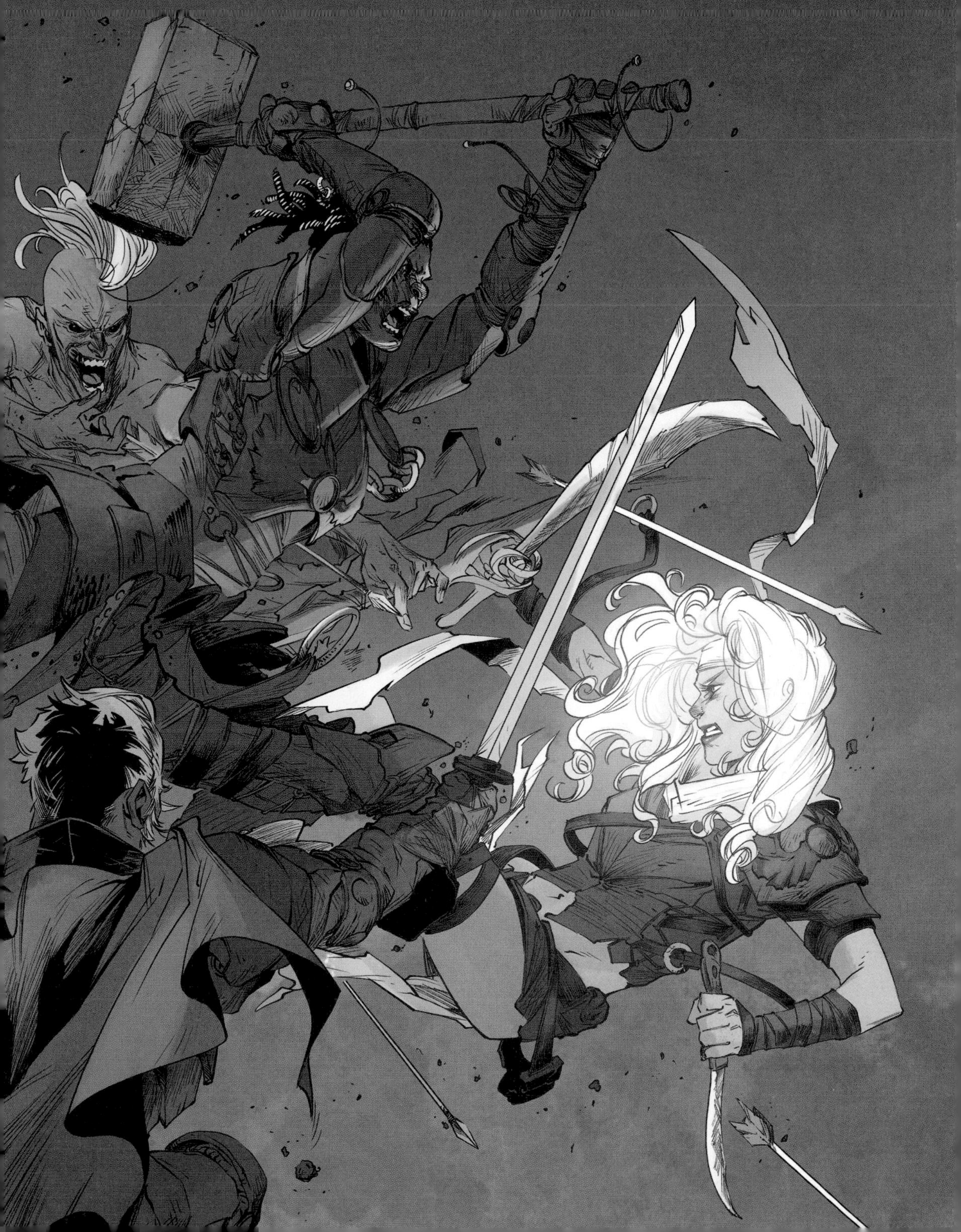

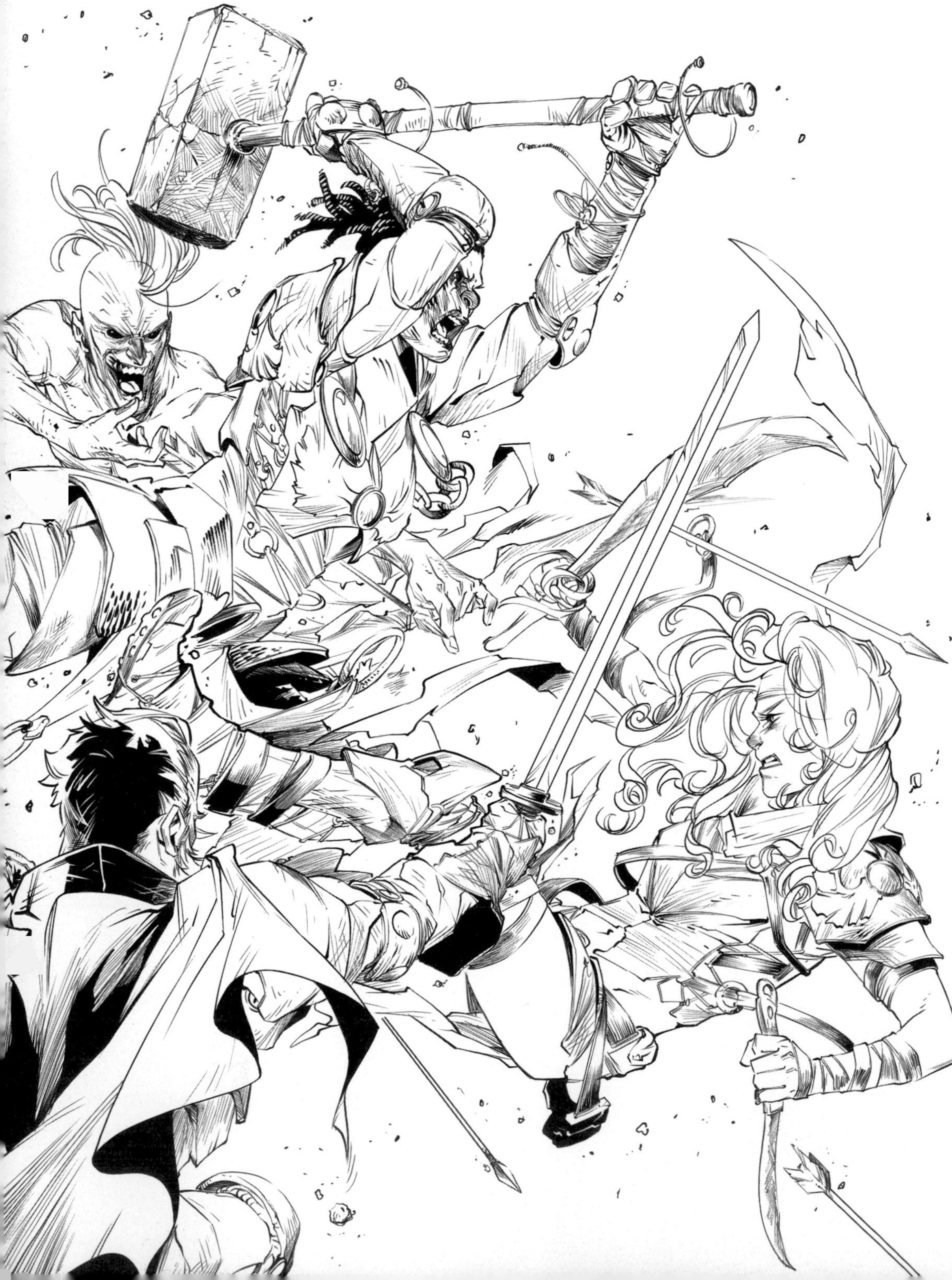

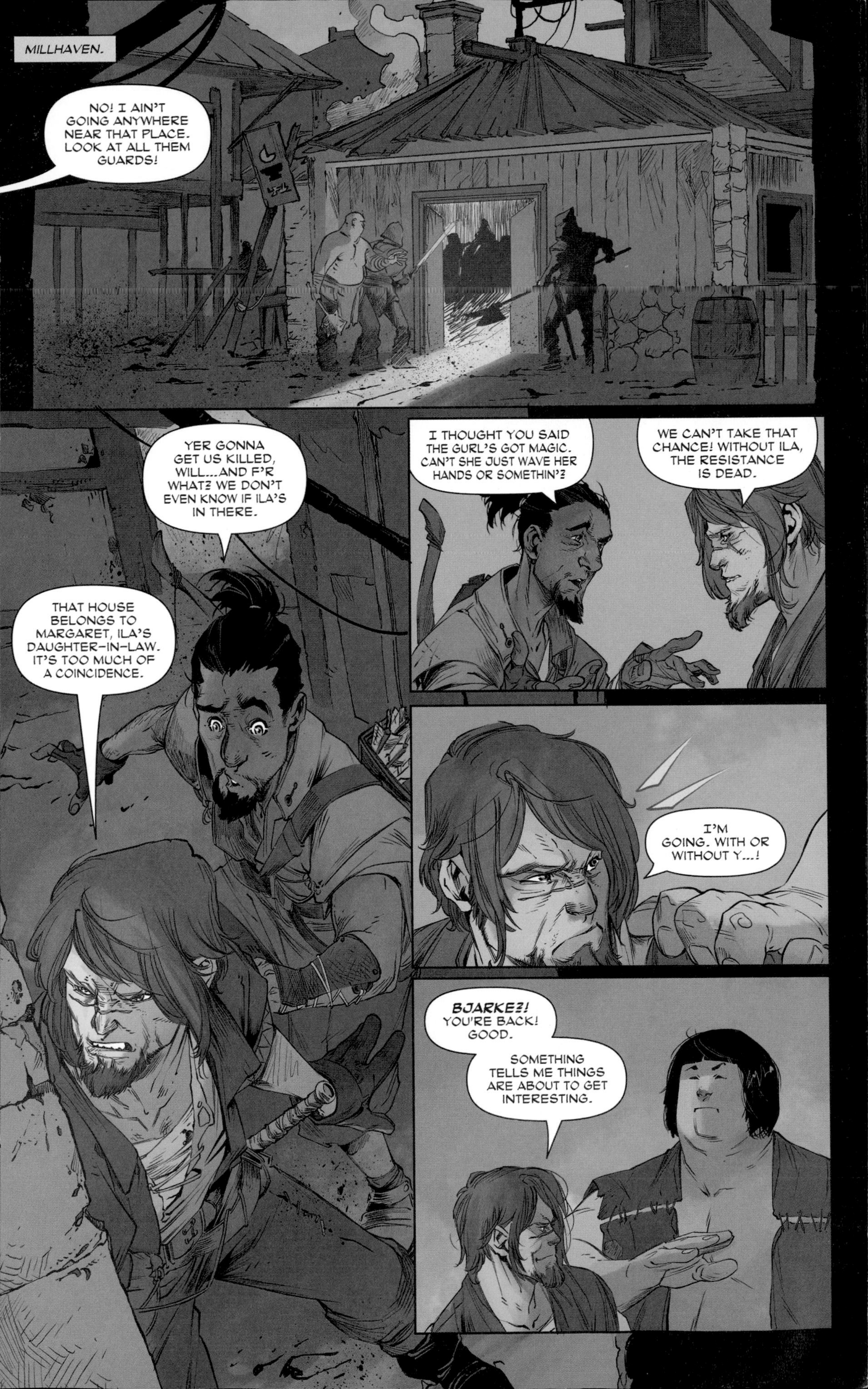
MILLHAVEN.
NO! I AIN'T GOING ANYWHERE NEAR THAT PLACE. LOOK AT ALL THEM GUARDS!
YER GONNA GET US KILLED, WILL...AND F'R WHAT? WE DON'T EVEN KNOW IF ILA'S IN THERE.
THAT HOUSE BELONGS TO MARGARET, ILA'S DAUGHTER-IN-LAW. IT'S TOO MUCH OF A COINCIDENCE.
I THOUGHT YOU SAID THE GURL'S GOT MAGIC. CAN'T SHE JUST WAVE HER HANDS OR SOMETHIN'?
WE CAN'T TAKE THAT CHANCE! WITHOUT ILA, THE RESISTANCE IS DEAD.
I'M GOING. WITH OR WITHOUT Y...!
BJARKE?! YOU'RE BACK! GOOD.
SOMETHING TELLS ME THINGS ARE ABOUT TO GET INTERESTING.

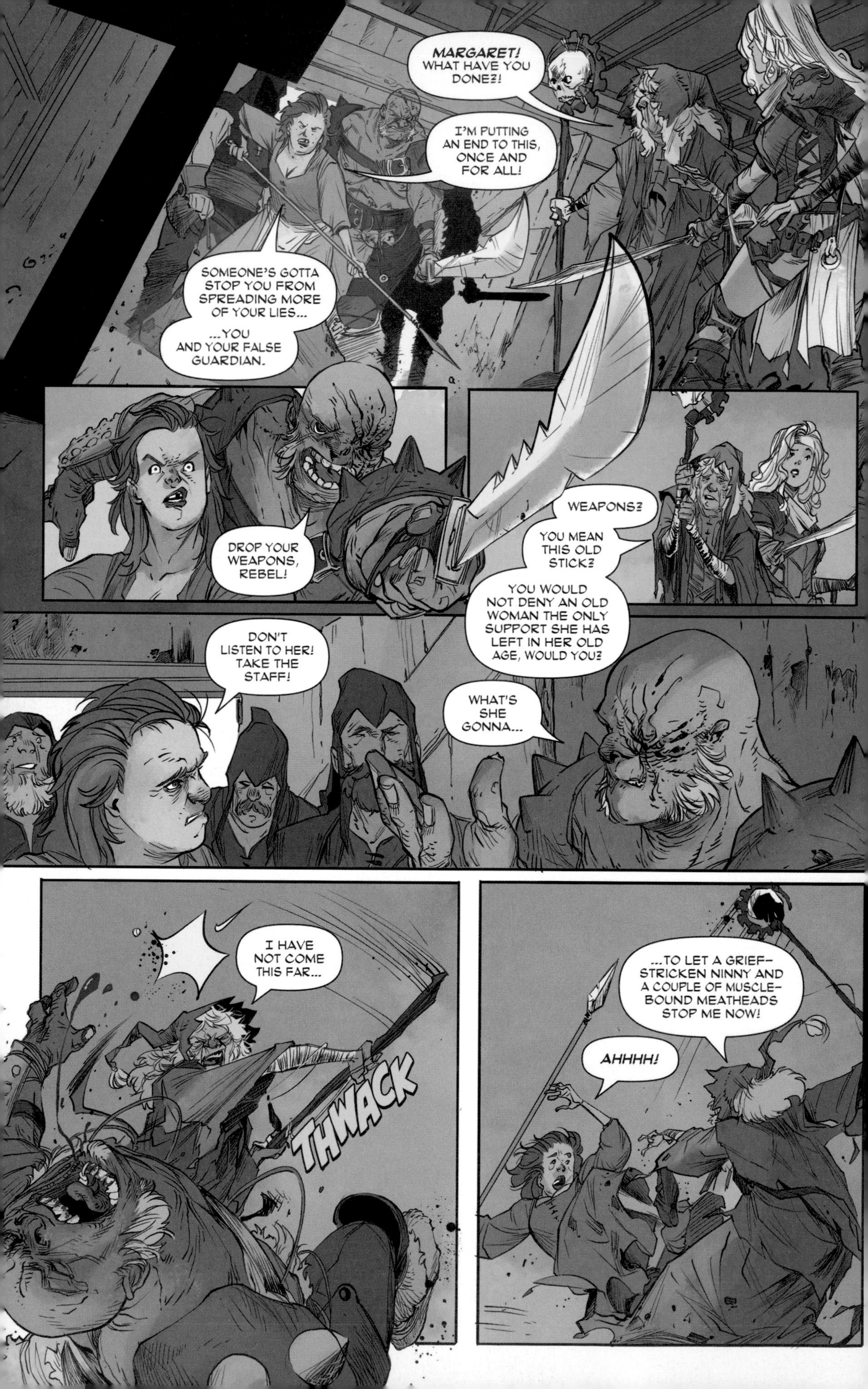
MARGARET! WHAT HAVE YOU DONE?!
I'M PUTTING AN END TO THIS, ONCE AND FOR ALL!
SOMEONE'S GOTTA STOP YOU FROM SPREADING MORE OF YOUR LIES...
...YOU AND YOUR FALSE GUARDIAN.
DROP YOUR WEAPONS, REBEL!
WEAPONS?
YOU MEAN THIS OLD STICK?
YOU WOULD NOT DENY AN OLD WOMAN THE ONLY SUPPORT SHE HAS LEFT IN HER OLD AGE, WOULD YOU?
DON'T LISTEN TO HER! TAKE THE STAFF!
WHAT'S SHE GONNA...
I HAVE NOT COME THIS FAR...
THWACK
...TO LET A GRIEF-STRICKEN NINNY AND A COUPLE OF MUSCLE-BOUND MEATHEADS STOP ME NOW!
AHHHH!

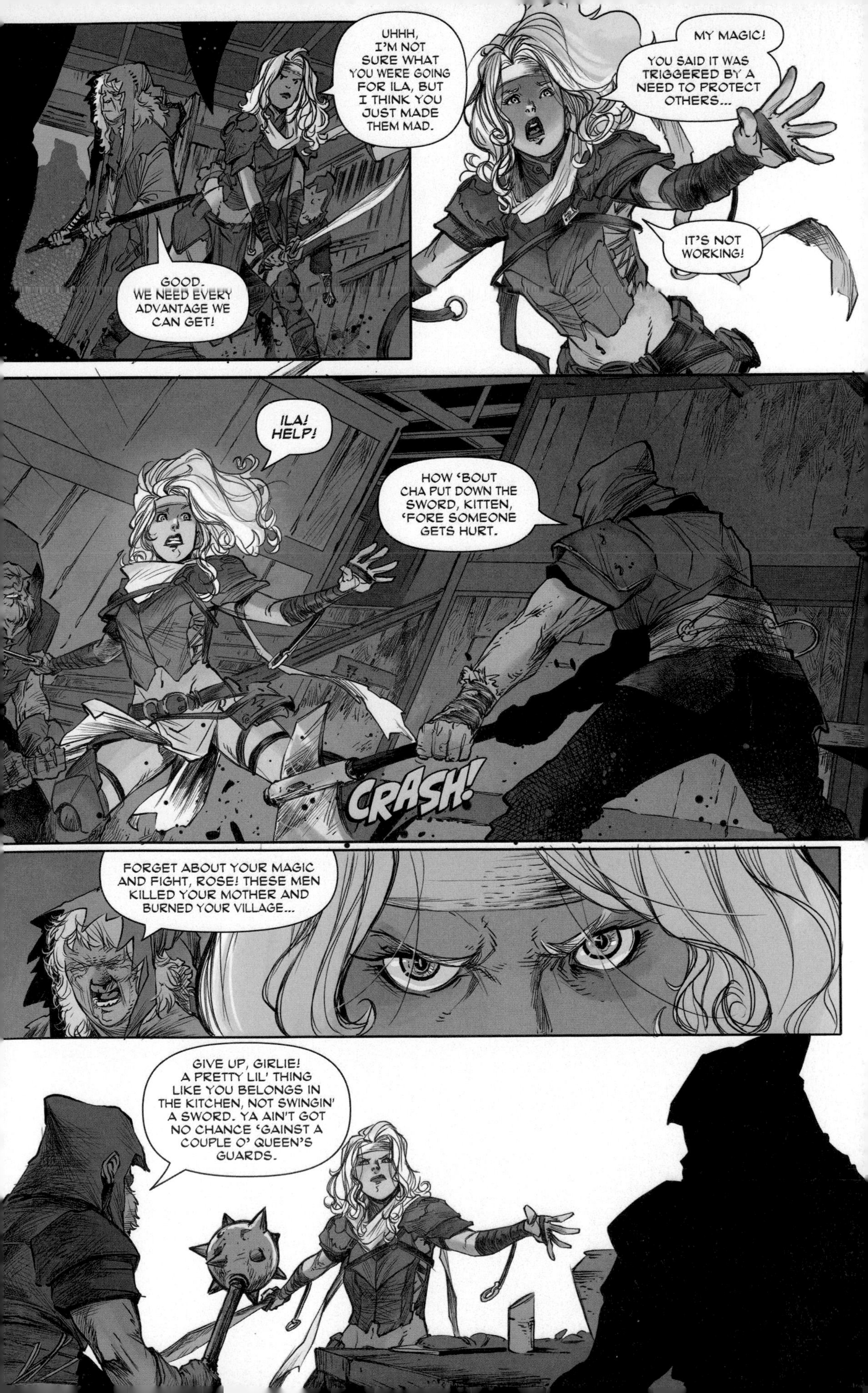
UHHH, I'M NOT SURE WHAT YOU WERE GOING FOR ILA, BUT I THINK YOU JUST MADE THEM MAD.
GOOD. WE NEED EVERY ADVANTAGE WE CAN GET!
MY MAGIC!
YOU SAID IT WAS TRIGGERED BY A NEED TO PROTECT OTHERS...
IT'S NOT WORKING!
ILA! HELP!
HOW 'BOUT CHA PUT DOWN THE SWORD, KITTEN, 'FORE SOMEONE GETS HURT.
CRASH!
FORGET ABOUT YOUR MAGIC AND FIGHT, ROSE! THESE MEN KILLED YOUR MOTHER AND BURNED YOUR VILLAGE...
GIVE UP, GIRLIE! A PRETTY LIL' THING LIKE YOU BELONGS IN THE KITCHEN, NOT SWINGIN' A SWORD. YA AIN'T GOT NO CHANCE 'GAINST A COUPLE O' QUEEN'S GUARDS.

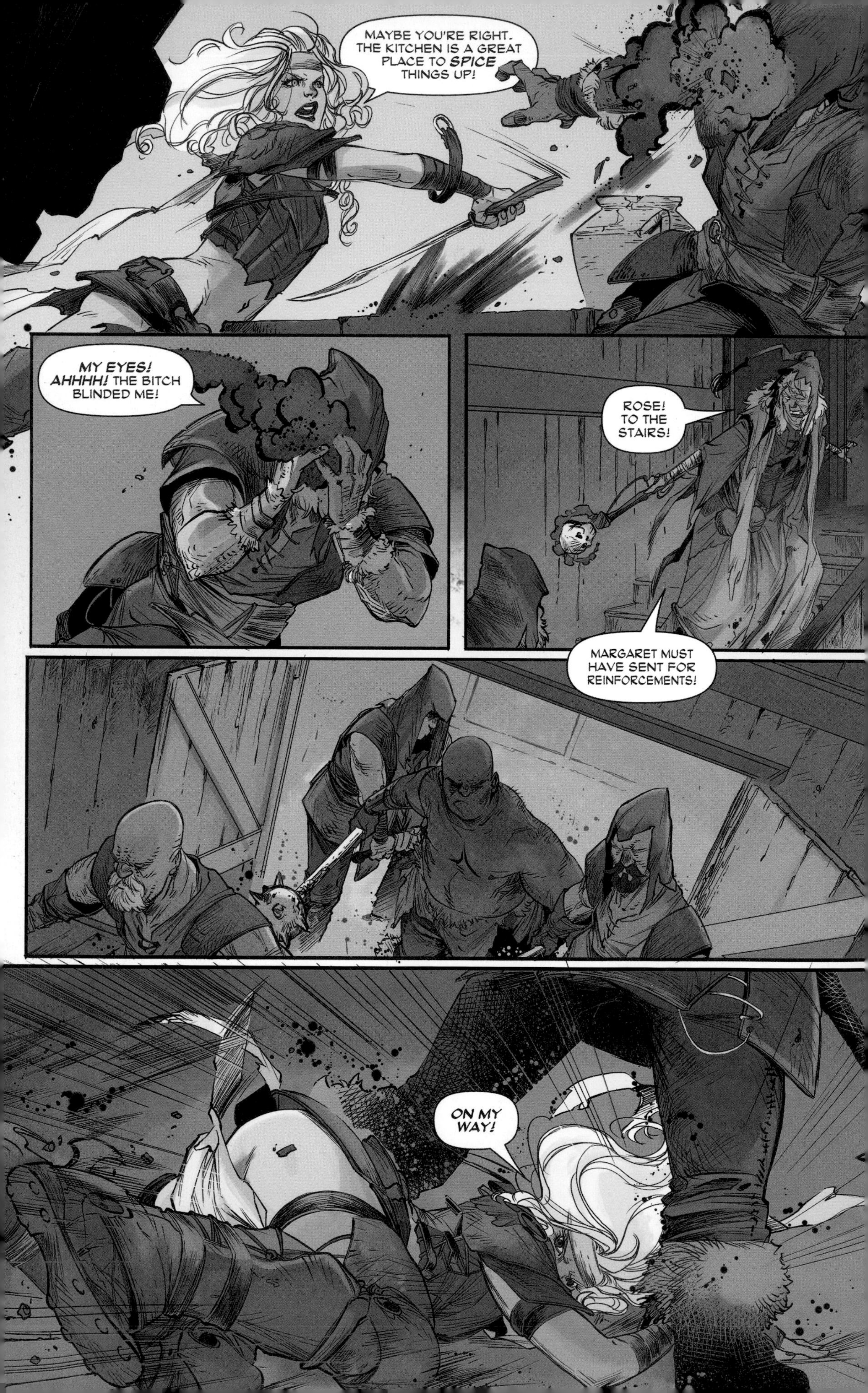
MAYBE YOU'RE RIGHT. THE KITCHEN IS A GREAT PLACE TO SPICE THINGS UP!
MY EYES! AHHHH! THE BITCH BLINDED ME!
ROSE! TO THE STAIRS!
MARGARET MUST HAVE SENT FOR REINFORCEMENTS!
ON MY WAY!

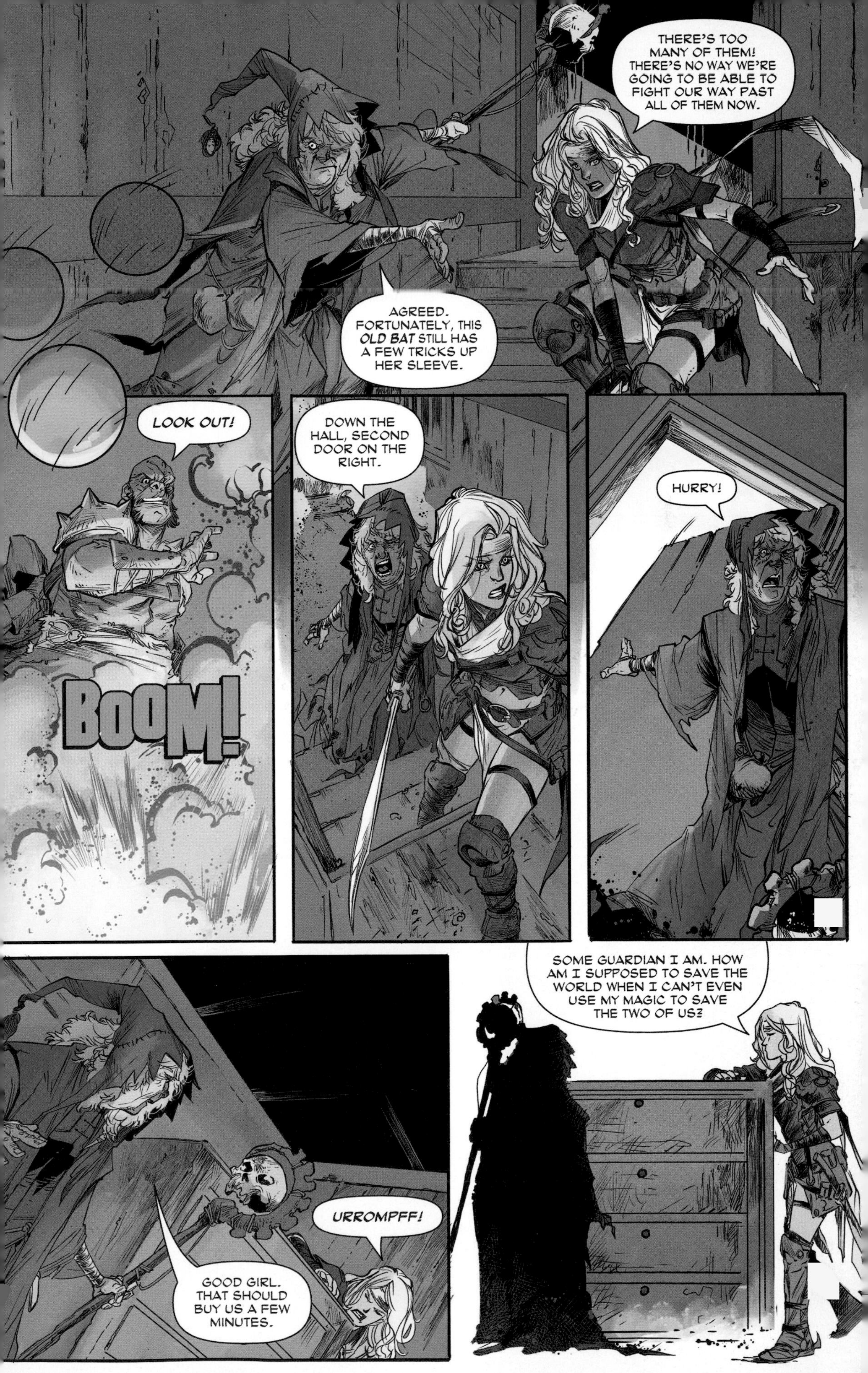

THERE'S TOO MANY OF THEM! THERE'S NO WAY WE'RE GOING TO BE ABLE TO FIGHT OUR WAY PAST ALL OF THEM NOW.
AGREED. FORTUNATELY, THIS *OLD BAT* STILL HAS A FEW TRICKS UP HER SLEEVE.
LOOK OUT!
BOOM!
DOWN THE HALL, SECOND DOOR ON THE RIGHT.
HURRY!
URROMPFF!
GOOD GIRL. THAT SHOULD BUY US A FEW MINUTES.
SOME GUARDIAN I AM. HOW AM I SUPPOSED TO SAVE THE WORLD WHEN I CAN'T EVEN USE MY MAGIC TO SAVE THE TWO OF US?

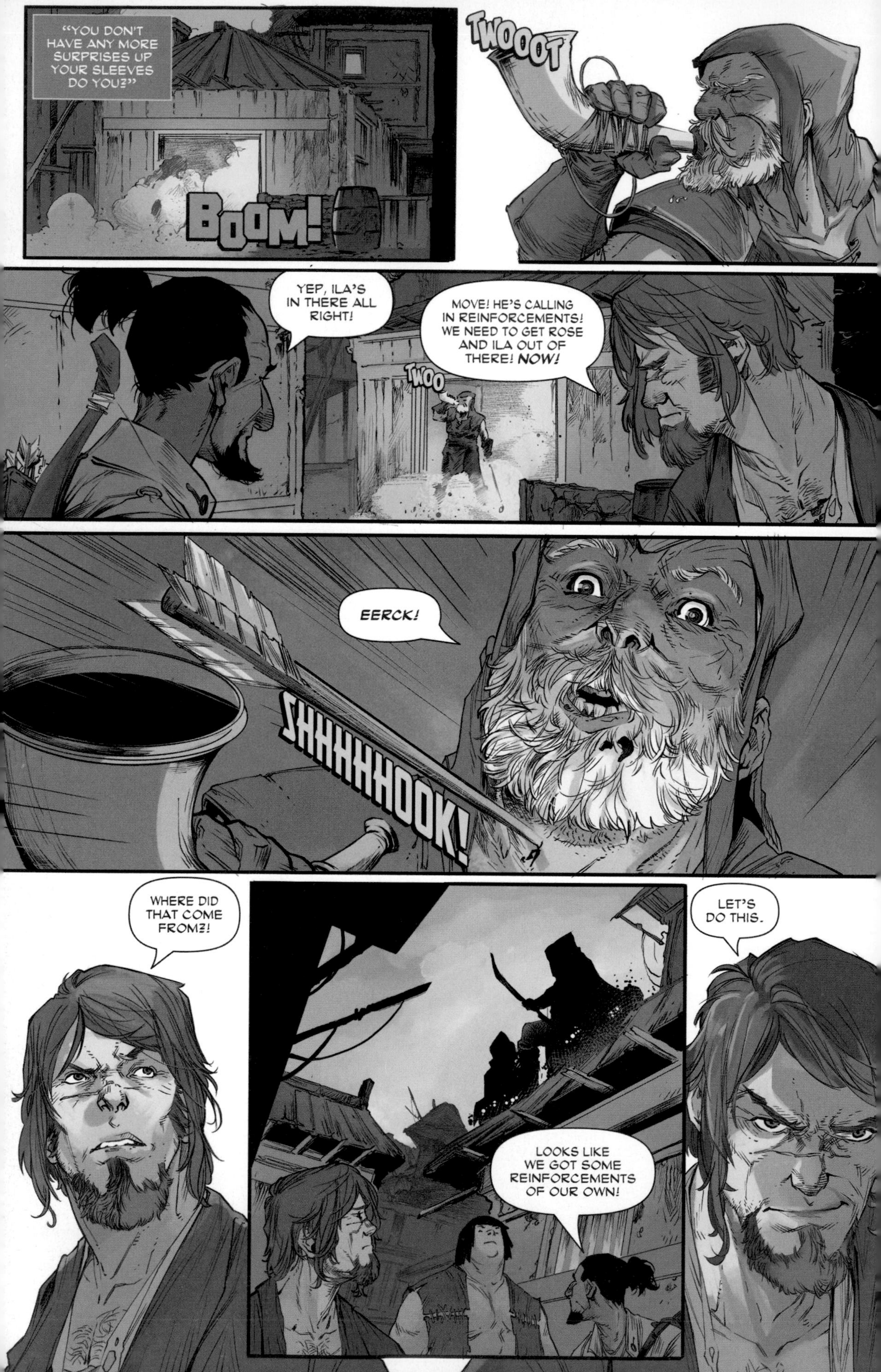
"YOU DON'T HAVE ANY MORE SURPRISES UP YOUR SLEEVES DO YOU?"
BOOM!
TWOOOT
YEP, ILA'S IN THERE ALL RIGHT!
MOVE! HE'S CALLING IN REINFORCEMENTS! WE NEED TO GET ROSE AND ILA OUT OF THERE! NOW!
TWOO
EERCK!
SHHHHHOOK!
WHERE DID THAT COME FROM?!
LOOKS LIKE WE GOT SOME REINFORCEMENTS OF OUR OWN!
LET'S DO THIS.

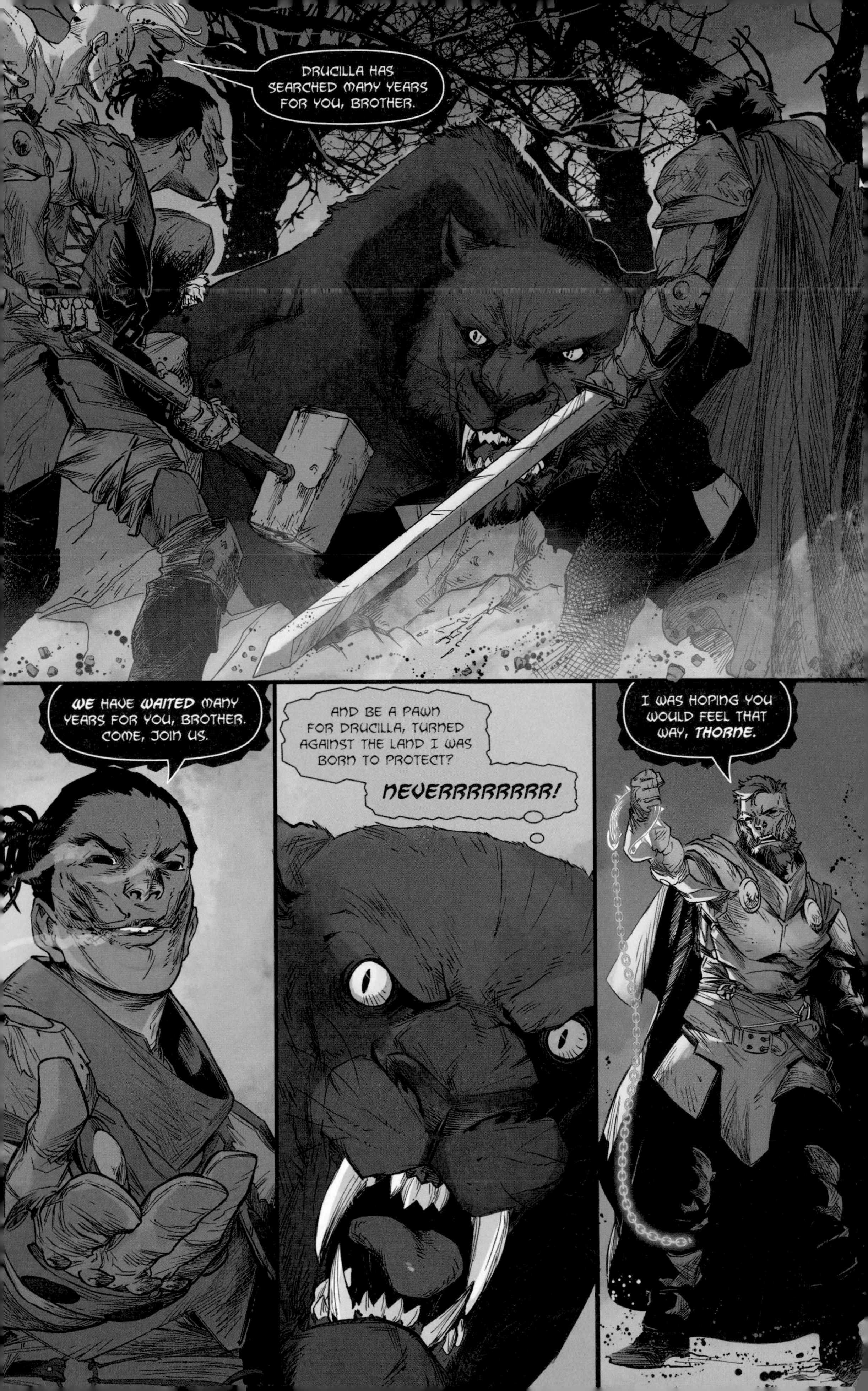

DRUCILLA HAS SEARCHED MANY YEARS FOR YOU, BROTHER.
WE HAVE WAITED MANY YEARS FOR YOU, BROTHER. COME, JOIN US.
AND BE A PAWN FOR DRUCILLA, TURNED AGAINST THE LAND I WAS BORN TO PROTECT?
NEVERRRRRRRR!
I WAS HOPING YOU WOULD FEEL THAT WAY, THORNE.

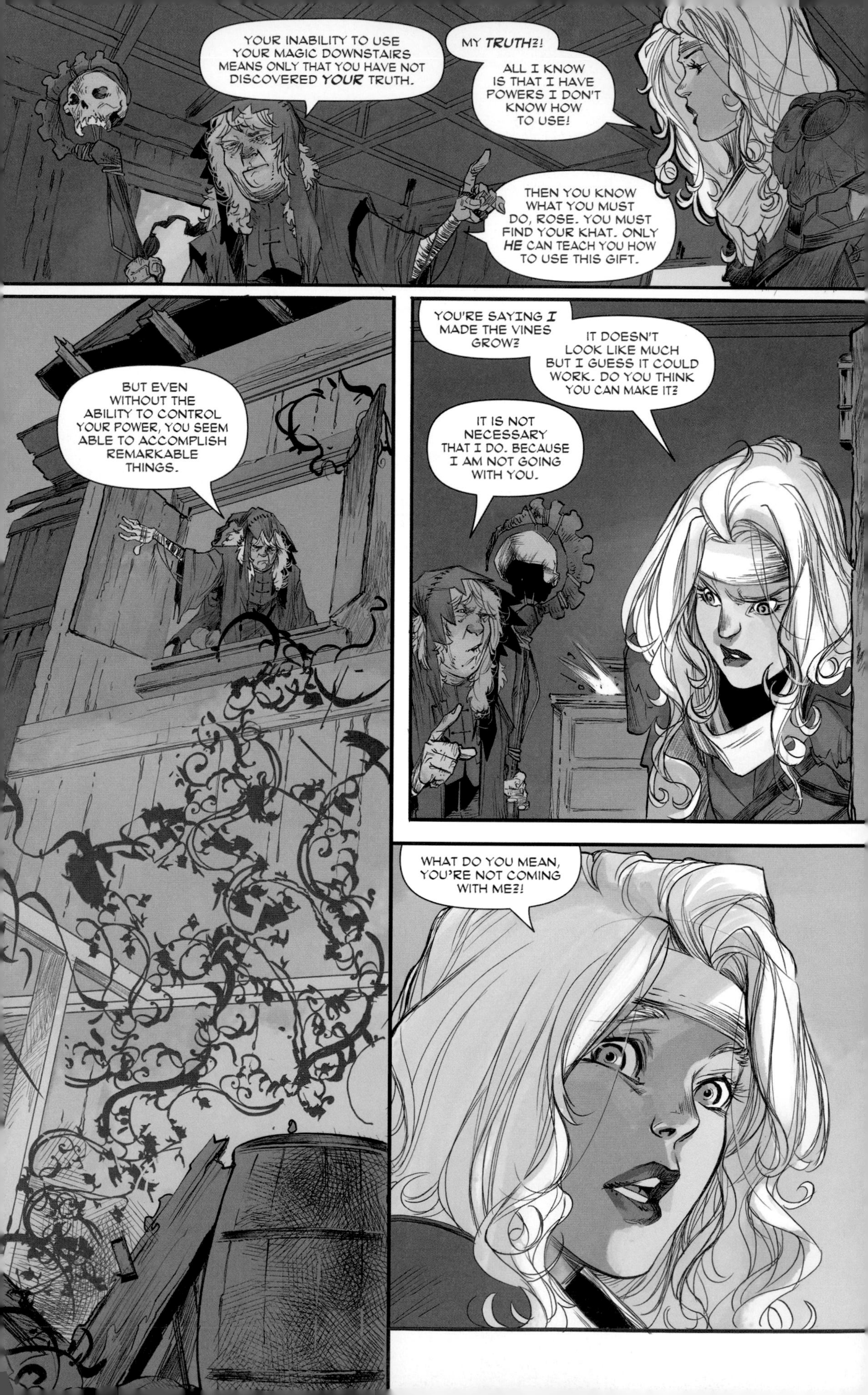
YOUR INABILITY TO USE YOUR MAGIC DOWNSTAIRS MEANS ONLY THAT YOU HAVE NOT DISCOVERED YOUR TRUTH.
MY TRUTH?!
ALL I KNOW IS THAT I HAVE POWERS I DON'T KNOW HOW TO USE!
THEN YOU KNOW WHAT YOU MUST DO, ROSE. YOU MUST FIND YOUR KHAT. ONLY HE CAN TEACH YOU HOW TO USE THIS GIFT.
BUT EVEN WITHOUT THE ABILITY TO CONTROL YOUR POWER, YOU SEEM ABLE TO ACCOMPLISH REMARKABLE THINGS.
YOU'RE SAYING I MADE THE VINES GROW?
IT DOESN'T LOOK LIKE MUCH BUT I GUESS IT COULD WORK. DO YOU THINK YOU CAN MAKE IT?
IT IS NOT NECESSARY THAT I DO. BECAUSE I AM NOT GOING WITH YOU.
WHAT DO YOU MEAN, YOU'RE NOT COMING WITH ME?!

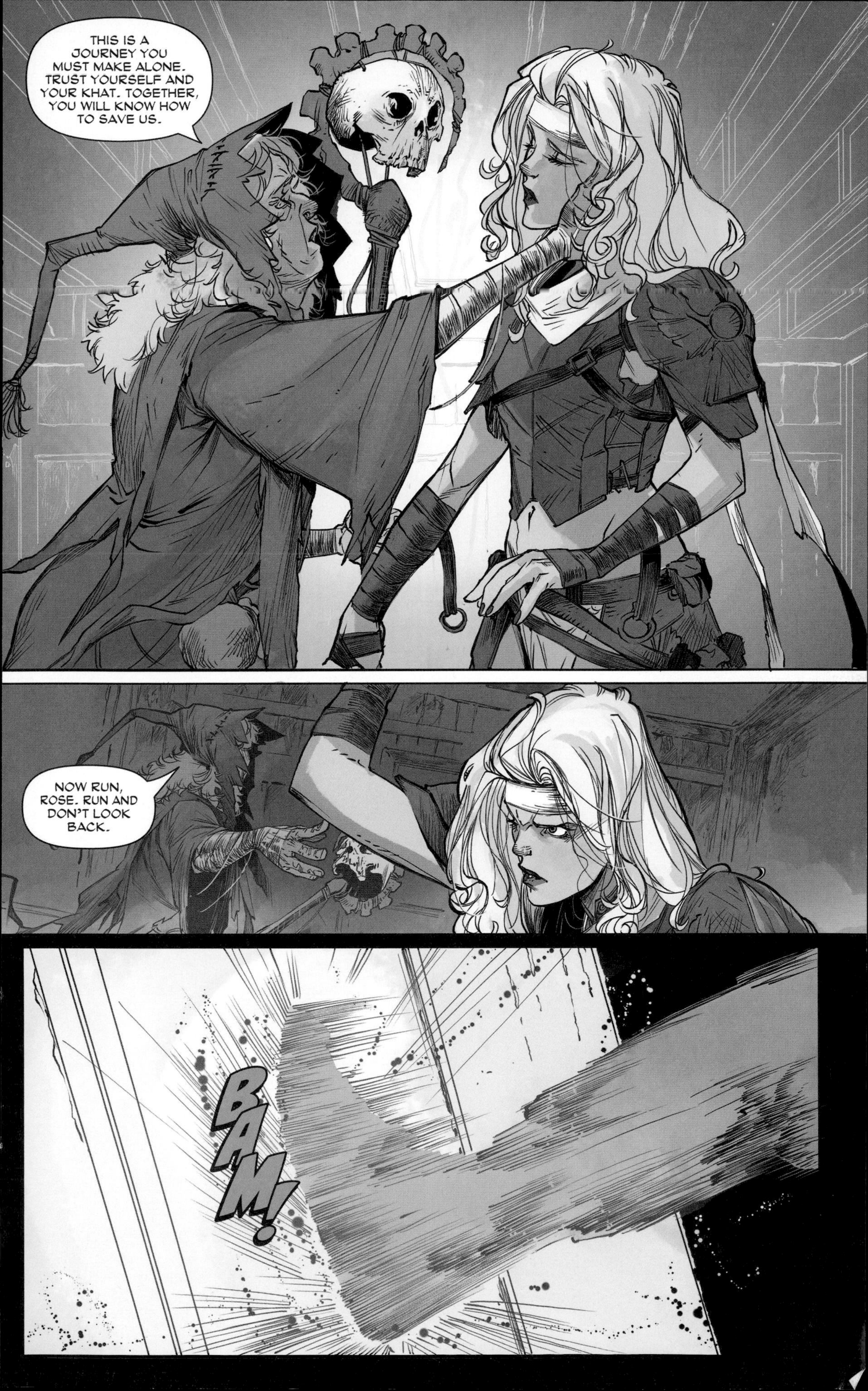
THIS IS A JOURNEY YOU MUST MAKE ALONE. TRUST YOURSELF AND YOUR KHAT. TOGETHER, YOU WILL KNOW HOW TO SAVE US.
NOW RUN, ROSE. RUN AND DON'T LOOK BACK.
BAM!

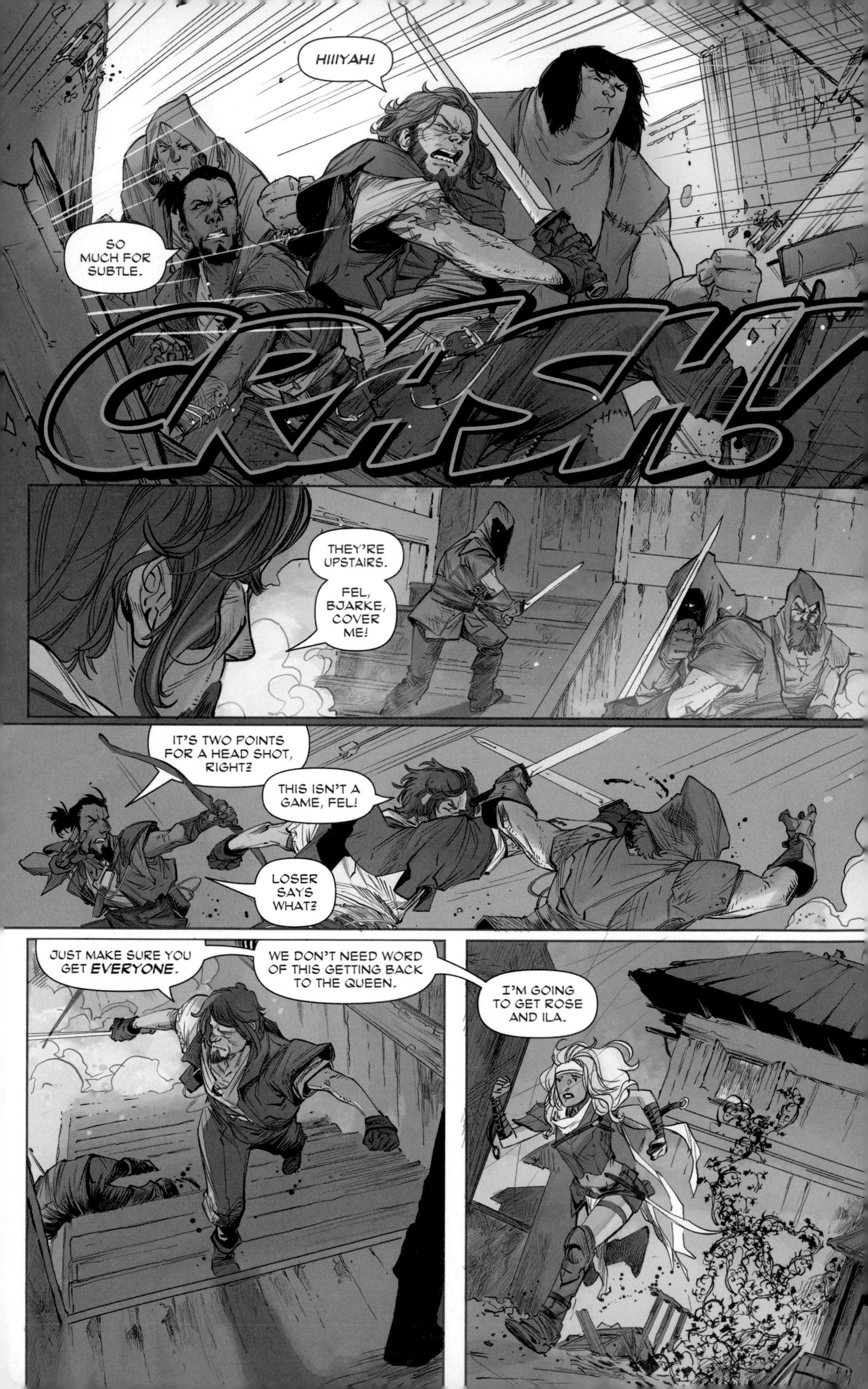
HIIIYAH!
SO MUCH FOR SUBTLE.
CRASH!
THEY'RE UPSTAIRS.
FEL, BJARKE, COVER ME!
IT'S TWO POINTS FOR A HEAD SHOT, RIGHT?
THIS ISN'T A GAME, FEL!
LOSER SAYS WHAT?
JUST MAKE SURE YOU GET EVERYONE.
WE DON'T NEED WORD OF THIS GETTING BACK TO THE QUEEN.
I'M GOING TO GET ROSE AND ILA.

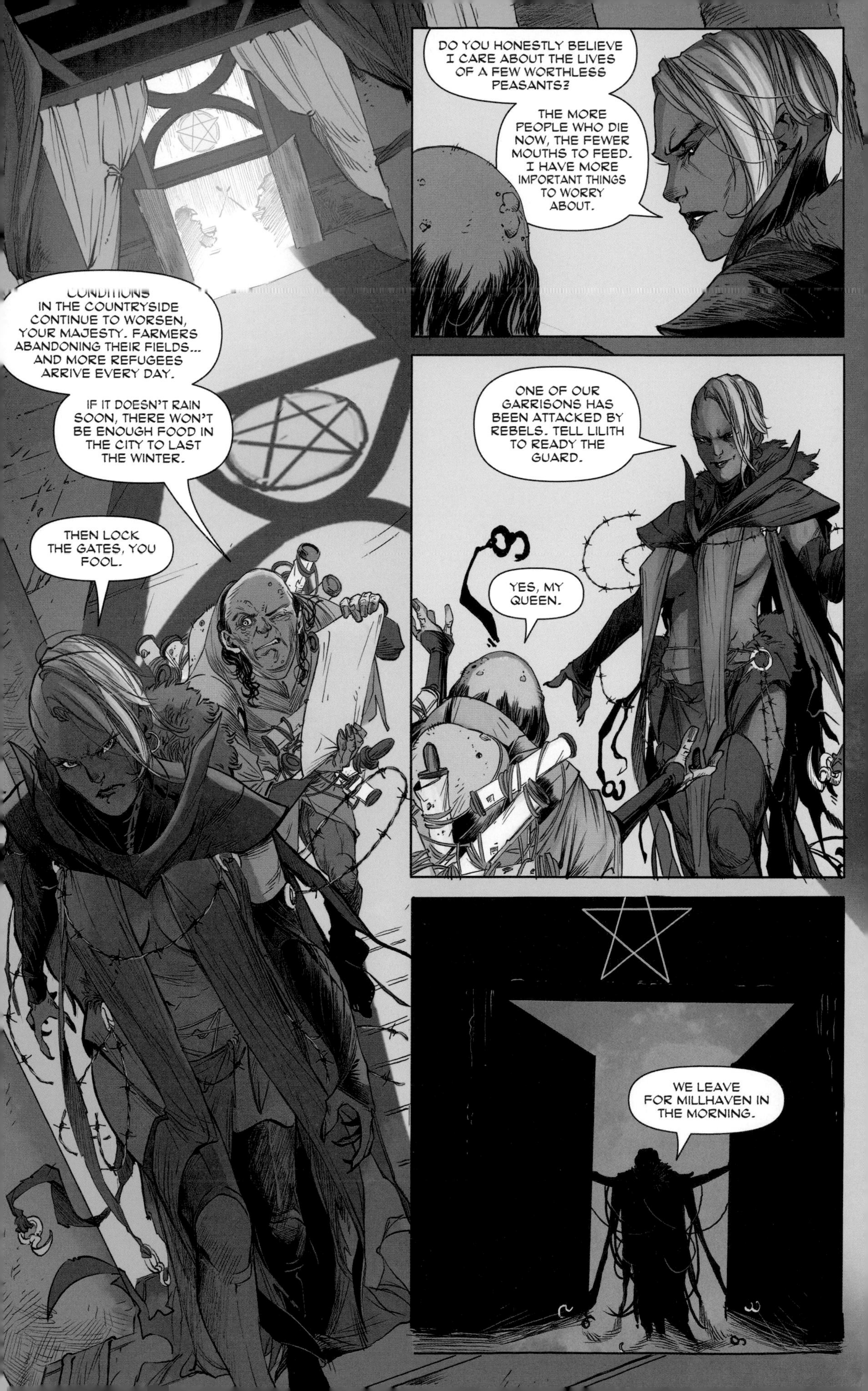
CONDITIONS IN THE COUNTRYSIDE CONTINUE TO WORSEN, YOUR MAJESTY. FARMERS ABANDONING THEIR FIELDS... AND MORE REFUGEES ARRIVE EVERY DAY.
IF IT DOESN'T RAIN SOON, THERE WON'T BE ENOUGH FOOD IN THE CITY TO LAST THE WINTER.
THEN LOCK THE GATES, YOU FOOL.
DO YOU HONESTLY BELIEVE I CARE ABOUT THE LIVES OF A FEW WORTHLESS PEASANTS?
THE MORE PEOPLE WHO DIE NOW, THE FEWER MOUTHS TO FEED. I HAVE MORE IMPORTANT THINGS TO WORRY ABOUT.
ONE OF OUR GARRISONS HAS BEEN ATTACKED BY REBELS. TELL LILITH TO READY THE GUARD.
YES, MY QUEEN.
WE LEAVE FOR MILLHAVEN IN THE MORNING.

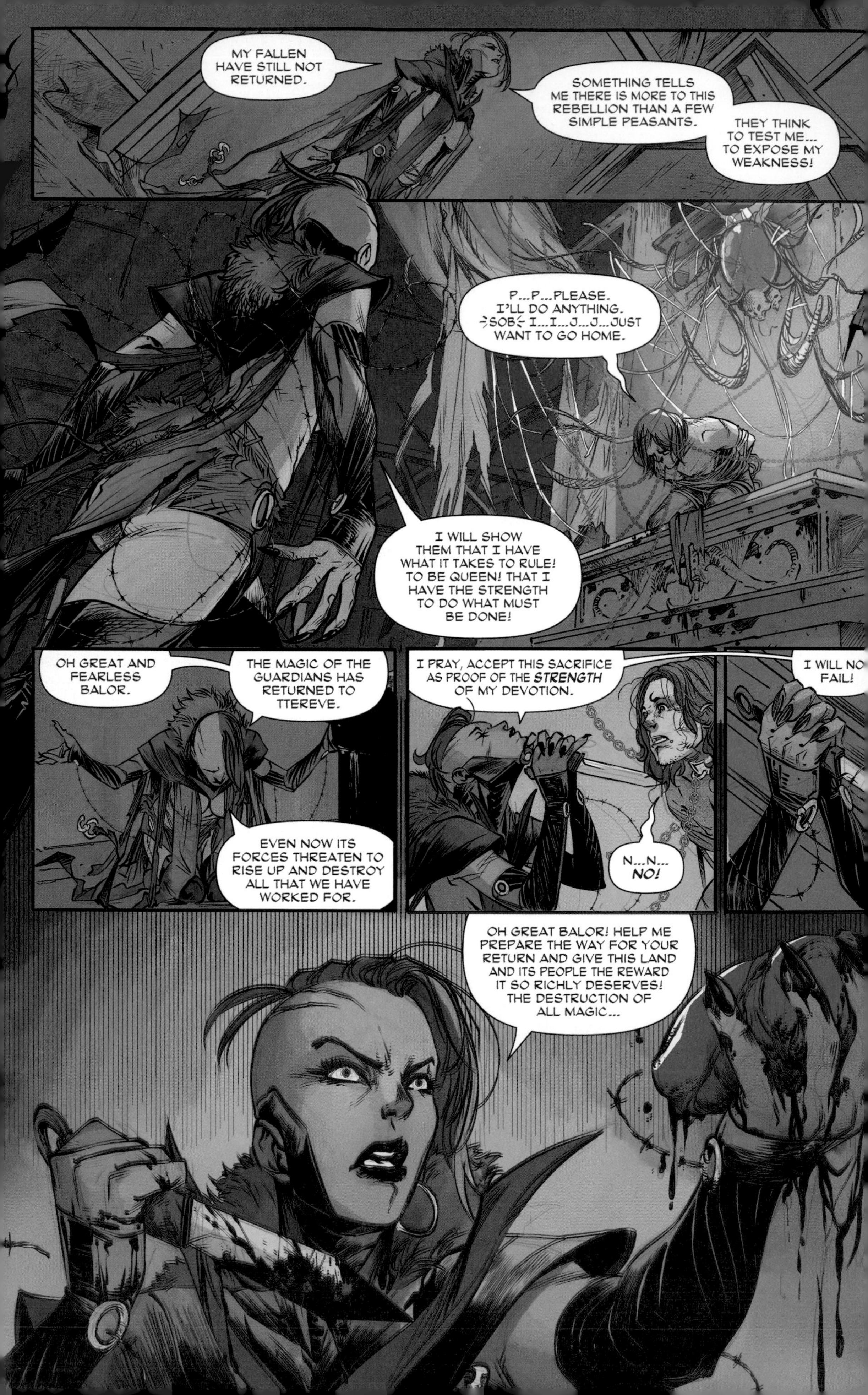
MY FALLEN HAVE STILL NOT RETURNED.
SOMETHING TELLS ME THERE IS MORE TO THIS REBELLION THAN A FEW SIMPLE PEASANTS.
THEY THINK TO TEST ME... TO EXPOSE MY WEAKNESS!
P...P...PLEASE. I'LL DO ANYTHING. ⊰SOB⊱ I...I...J...J...JUST WANT TO GO HOME.
I WILL SHOW THEM THAT I HAVE WHAT IT TAKES TO RULE! TO BE QUEEN! THAT I HAVE THE STRENGTH TO DO WHAT MUST BE DONE!
OH GREAT AND FEARLESS BALOR.
THE MAGIC OF THE GUARDIANS HAS RETURNED TO TTEREVE.
EVEN NOW ITS FORCES THREATEN TO RISE UP AND DESTROY ALL THAT WE HAVE WORKED FOR.
I PRAY, ACCEPT THIS SACRIFICE AS PROOF OF THE *STRENGTH* OF MY DEVOTION.
N...N... ***NO!***
I WILL NO FAIL!
OH GREAT BALOR! HELP ME PREPARE THE WAY FOR YOUR RETURN AND GIVE THIS LAND AND ITS PEOPLE THE REWARD IT SO RICHLY DESERVES! THE DESTRUCTION OF ALL MAGIC...

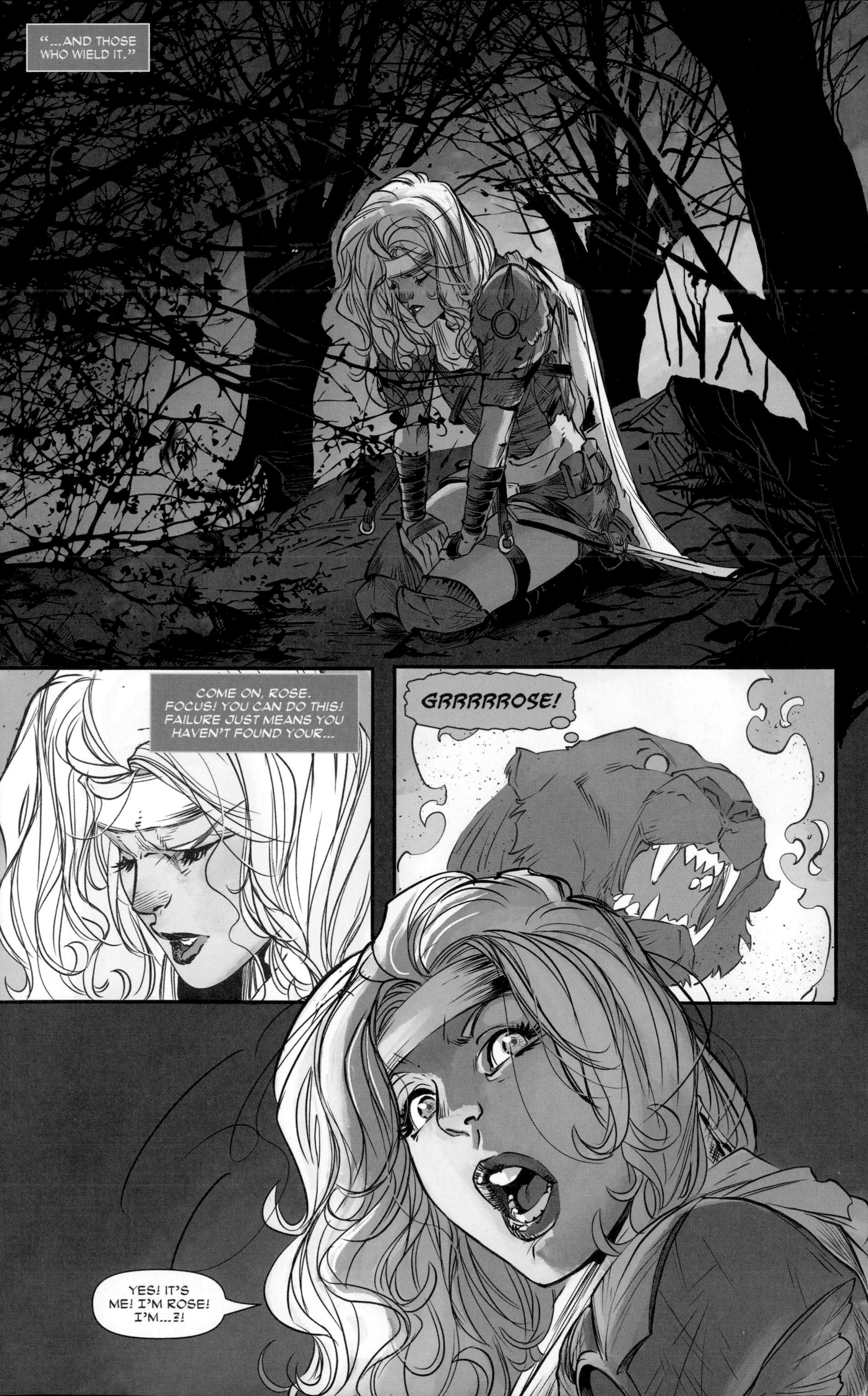
"...AND THOSE WHO WIELD IT."
COME ON, ROSE. FOCUS! YOU CAN DO THIS! FAILURE JUST MEANS YOU HAVEN'T FOUND YOUR...
GRRRRROSE!
YES! IT'S ME! I'M ROSE! I'M...?!

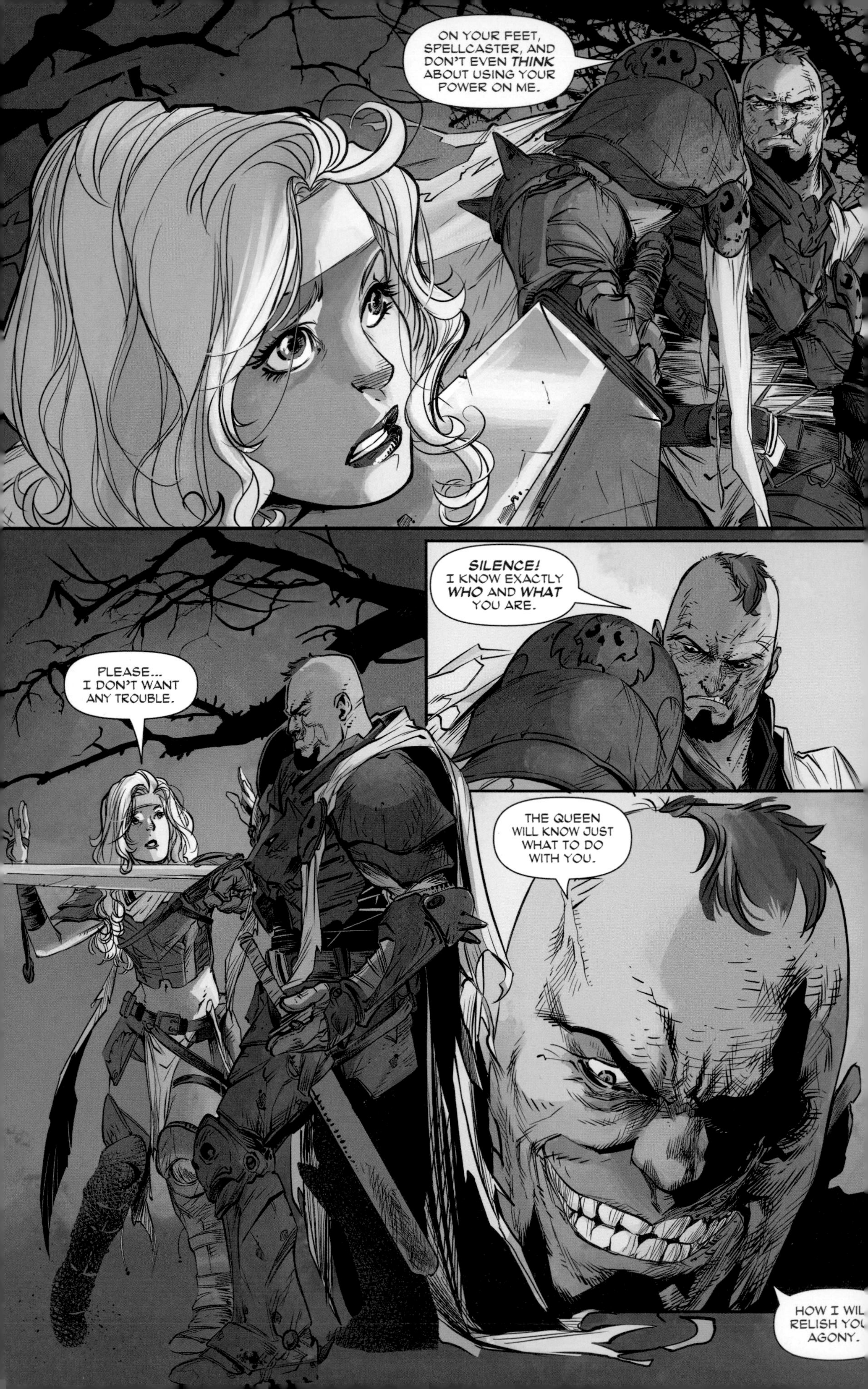
ON YOUR FEET, SPELLCASTER, AND DON'T EVEN *THINK* ABOUT USING YOUR POWER ON ME.
PLEASE... I DON'T WANT ANY TROUBLE.
SILENCE! I KNOW EXACTLY *WHO* AND *WHAT* YOU ARE.
THE QUEEN WILL KNOW JUST WHAT TO DO WITH YOU.
HOW I WIL RELISH YOU AGONY.

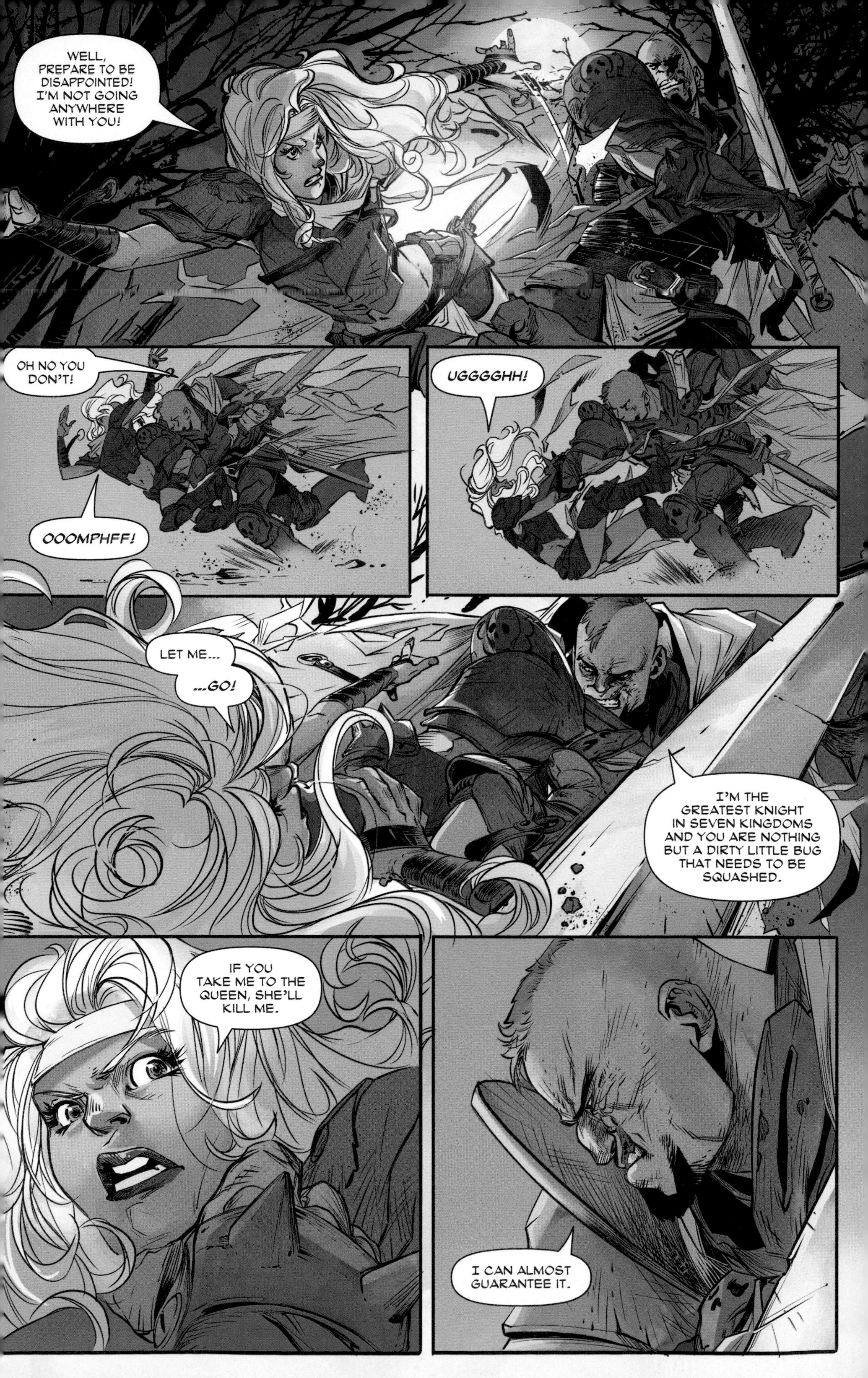
WELL, PREPARE TO BE DISAPPOINTED! I'M NOT GOING ANYWHERE WITH YOU!
OH NO YOU DON'T!
OOOMPHFF!
UGGGGHH!
LET ME...
...GO!
I'M THE GREATEST KNIGHT IN SEVEN KINGDOMS AND YOU ARE NOTHING BUT A DIRTY LITTLE BUG THAT NEEDS TO BE SQUASHED.
IF YOU TAKE ME TO THE QUEEN, SHE'LL KILL ME.
I CAN ALMOST GUARANTEE IT.

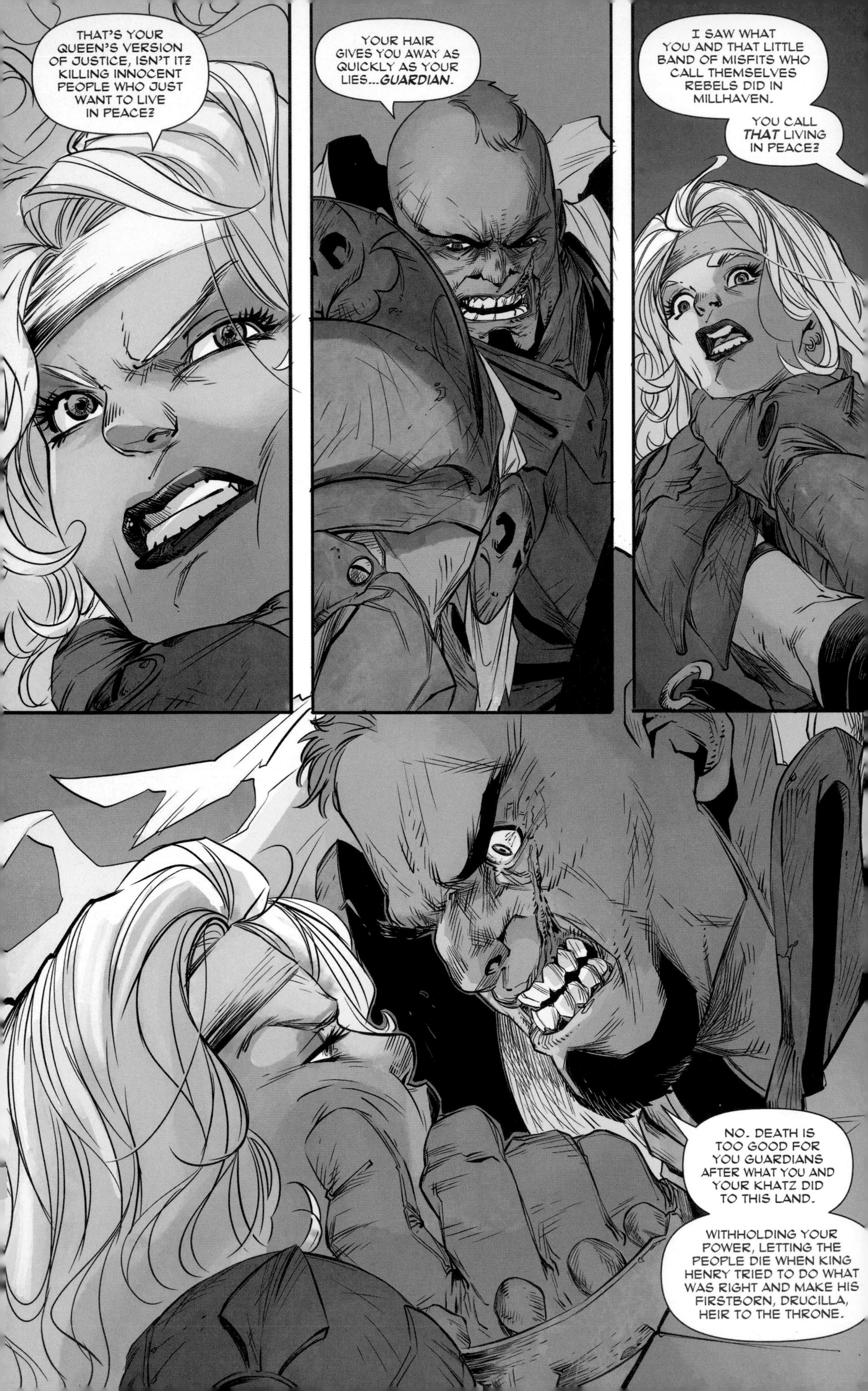
THAT'S YOUR QUEEN'S VERSION OF JUSTICE, ISN'T IT? KILLING INNOCENT PEOPLE WHO JUST WANT TO LIVE IN PEACE?
YOUR HAIR GIVES YOU AWAY AS QUICKLY AS YOUR LIES...GUARDIAN.
I SAW WHAT YOU AND THAT LITTLE BAND OF MISFITS WHO CALL THEMSELVES REBELS DID IN MILLHAVEN.
YOU CALL THAT LIVING IN PEACE?
NO. DEATH IS TOO GOOD FOR YOU GUARDIANS AFTER WHAT YOU AND YOUR KHATZ DID TO THIS LAND.
WITHHOLDING YOUR POWER, LETTING THE PEOPLE DIE WHEN KING HENRY TRIED TO DO WHAT WAS RIGHT AND MAKE HIS FIRSTBORN, DRUCILLA, HEIR TO THE THRONE.

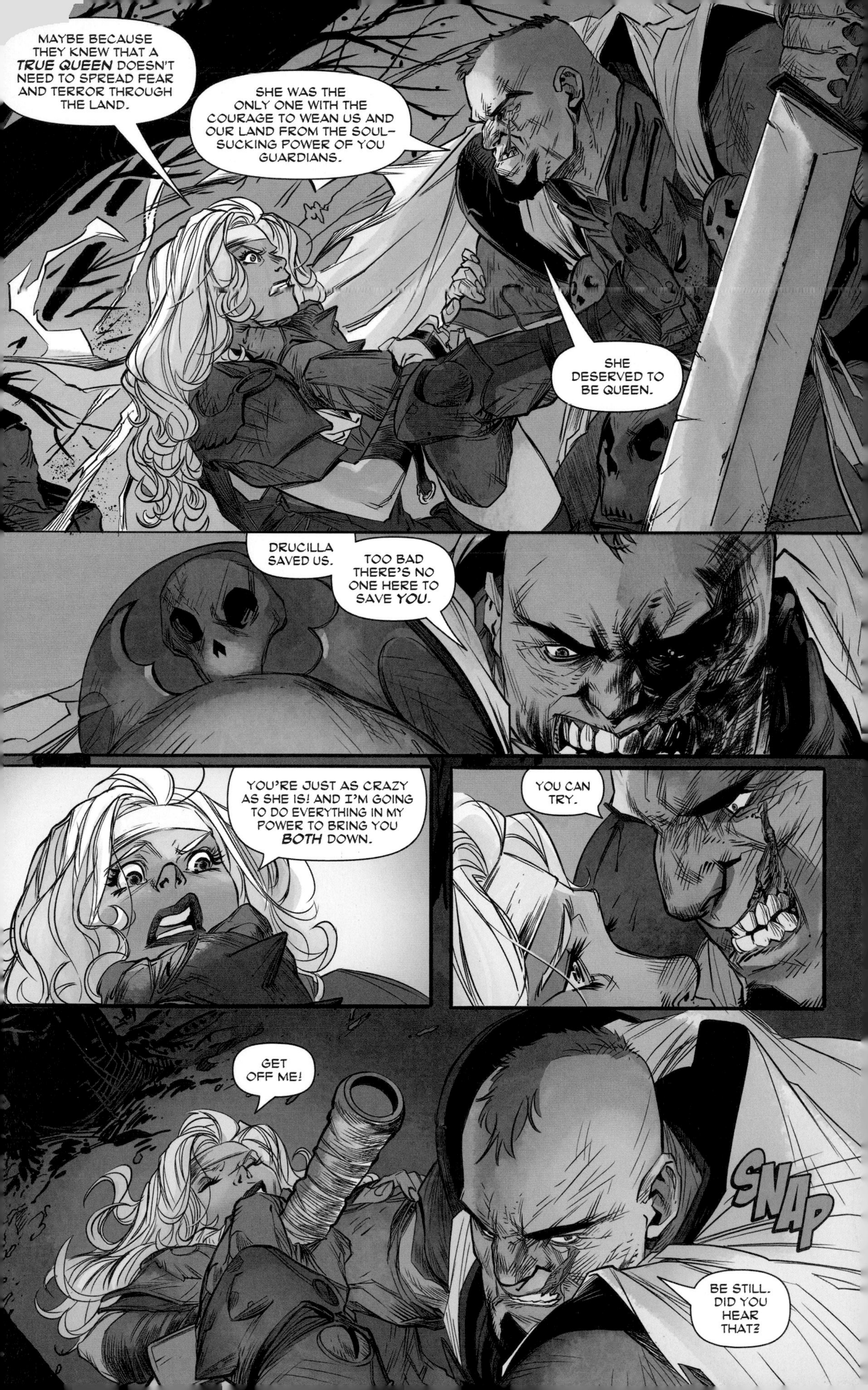
MAYBE BECAUSE THEY KNEW THAT A **TRUE QUEEN** DOESN'T NEED TO SPREAD FEAR AND TERROR THROUGH THE LAND.
SHE WAS THE ONLY ONE WITH THE COURAGE TO WEAN US AND OUR LAND FROM THE SOUL-SUCKING POWER OF YOU GUARDIANS.
SHE DESERVED TO BE QUEEN.
DRUCILLA SAVED US.
TOO BAD THERE'S NO ONE HERE TO SAVE *YOU*.
YOU'RE JUST AS CRAZY AS SHE IS! AND I'M GOING TO DO EVERYTHING IN MY POWER TO BRING YOU *BOTH* DOWN.
YOU CAN TRY.
GET OFF ME!
SNAP
BE STILL. DID YOU HEAR THAT?

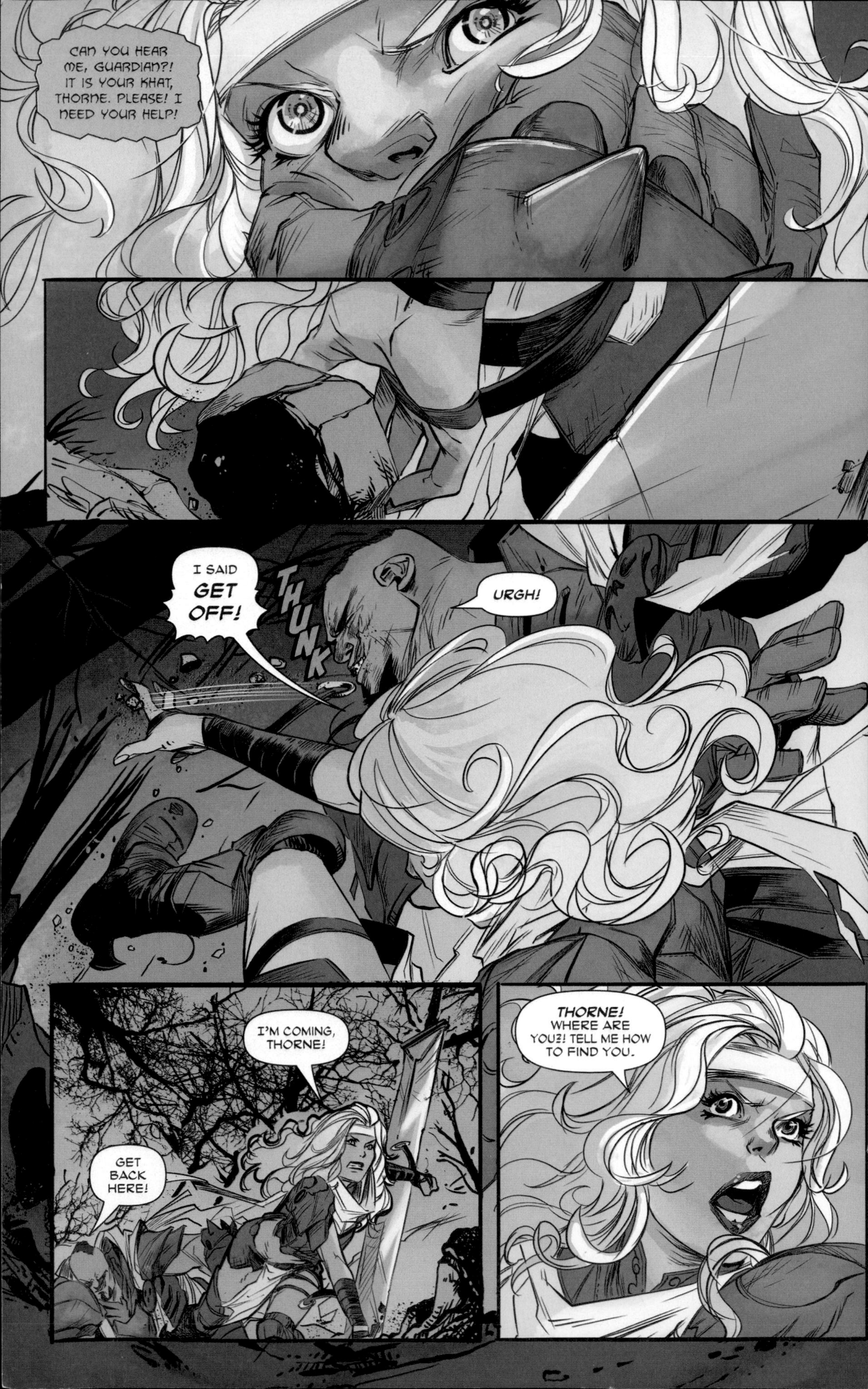
CAN YOU HEAR ME, GUARDIAN?! IT IS YOUR KHAT, THORNE. PLEASE! I NEED YOUR HELP!
I SAID GET OFF!
THUNK
URGH!
I'M COMING, THORNE!
GET BACK HERE!
THORNE! WHERE ARE YOU?! TELL ME HOW TO FIND YOU.

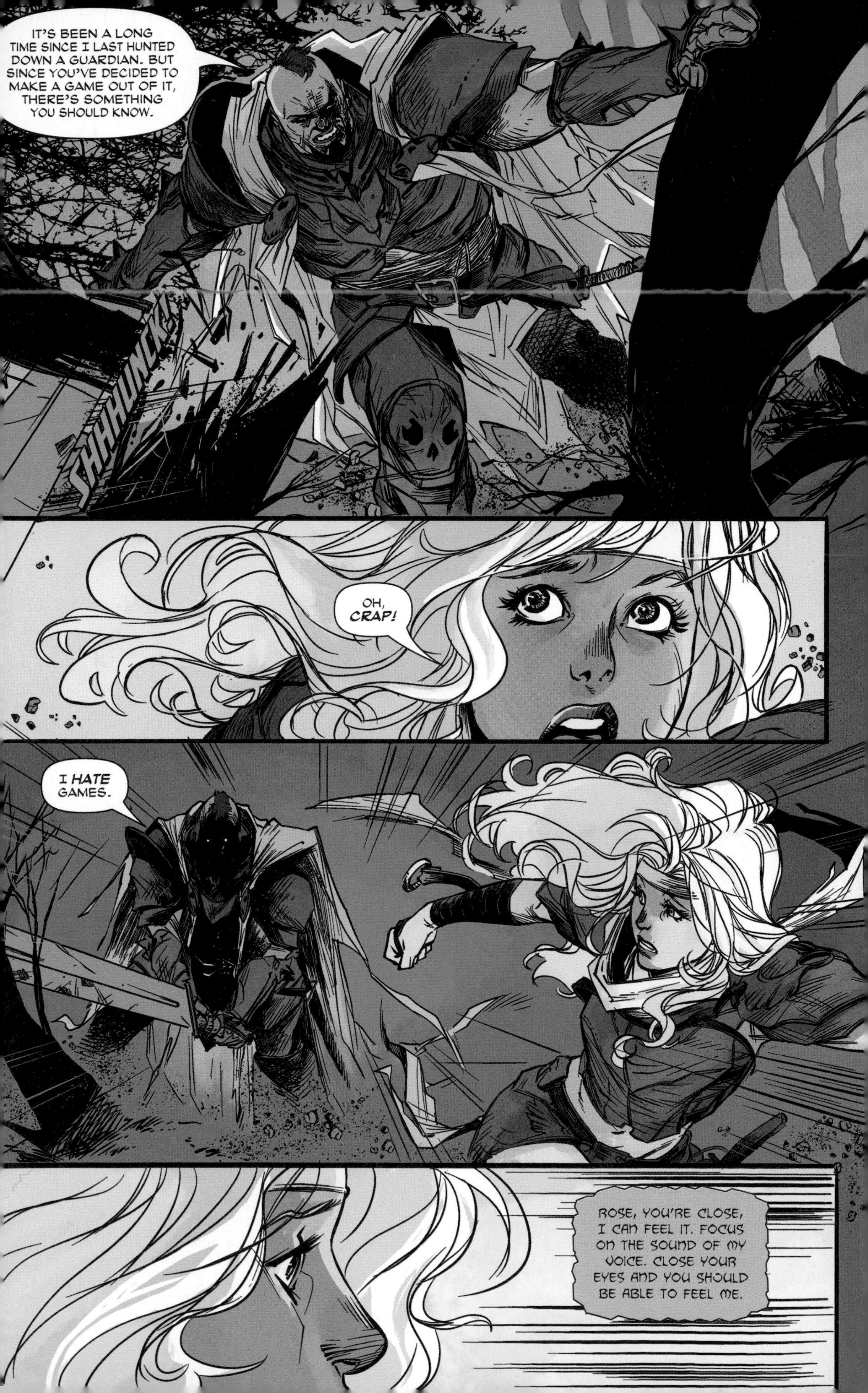
IT'S BEEN A LONG TIME SINCE I LAST HUNTED DOWN A GUARDIAN. BUT SINCE YOU'VE DECIDED TO MAKE A GAME OUT OF IT, THERE'S SOMETHING YOU SHOULD KNOW.
SHHUNCK
OH, CRAP!
I HATE GAMES.
ROSE, YOU'RE CLOSE, I CAN FEEL IT. FOCUS ON THE SOUND OF MY VOICE. CLOSE YOUR EYES AND YOU SHOULD BE ABLE TO FEEL ME.

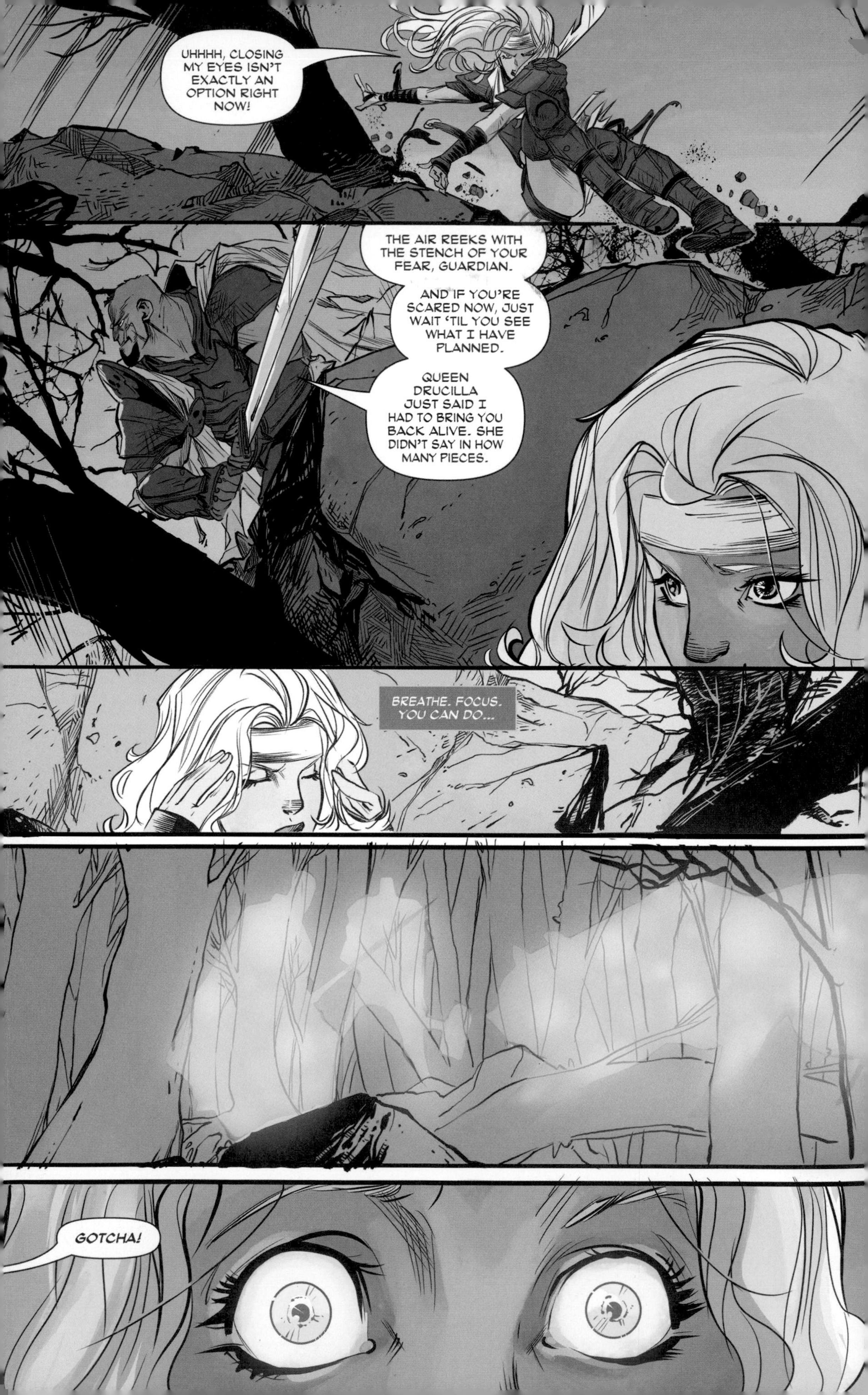
UHHHH, CLOSING MY EYES ISN'T EXACTLY AN OPTION RIGHT NOW!
THE AIR REEKS WITH THE STENCH OF YOUR FEAR, GUARDIAN.
AND IF YOU'RE SCARED NOW, JUST WAIT 'TIL YOU SEE WHAT I HAVE PLANNED.
QUEEN DRUCILLA JUST SAID I HAD TO BRING YOU BACK ALIVE. SHE DIDN'T SAY IN HOW MANY PIECES.
BREATHE. FOCUS. YOU CAN DO...
GOTCHA!

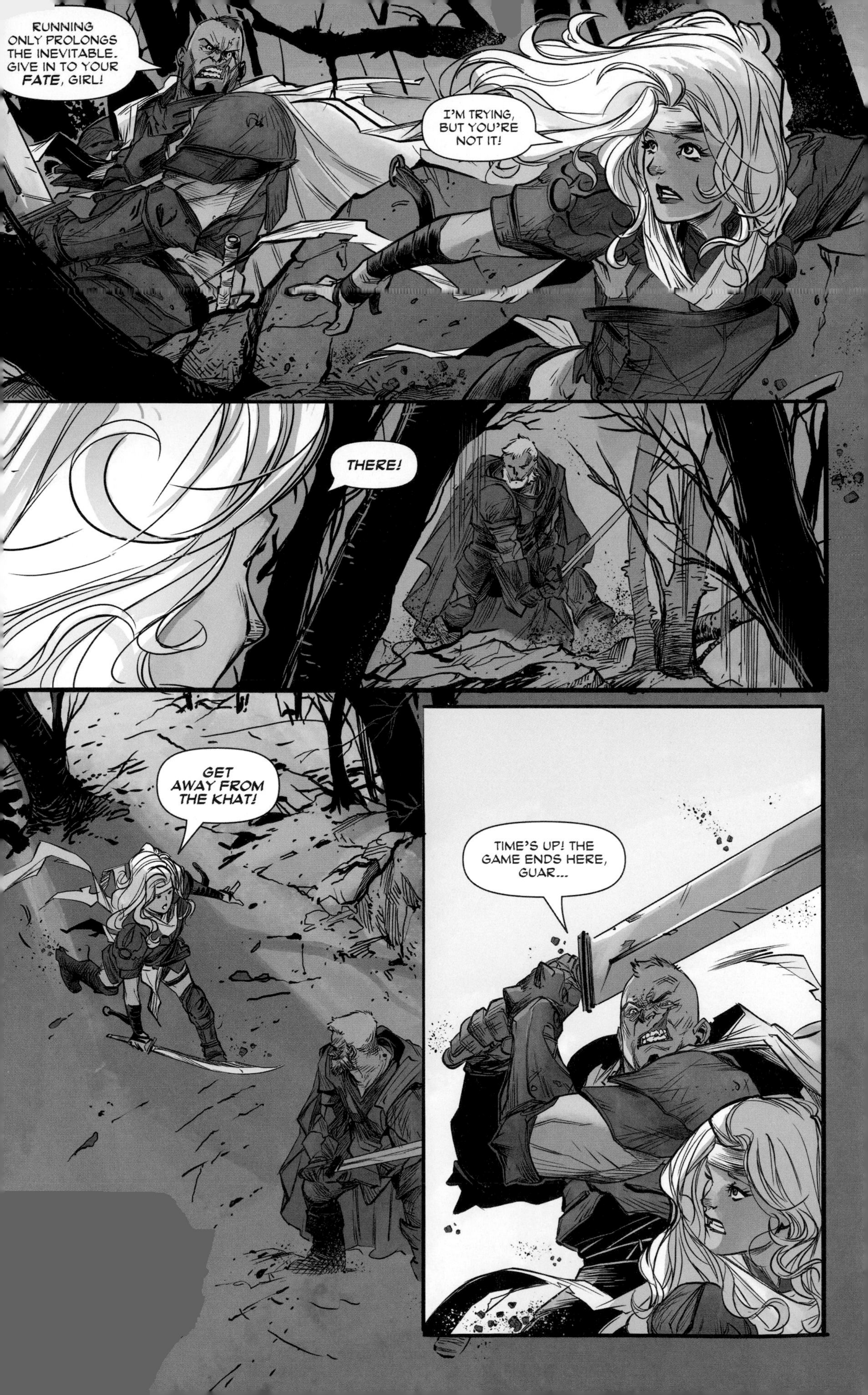
RUNNING ONLY PROLONGS THE INEVITABLE. GIVE IN TO YOUR *FATE*, GIRL!
I'M TRYING, BUT YOU'RE NOT IT!
THERE!
GET AWAY FROM THE KHAT!
TIME'S UP! THE GAME ENDS HERE, GUAR...

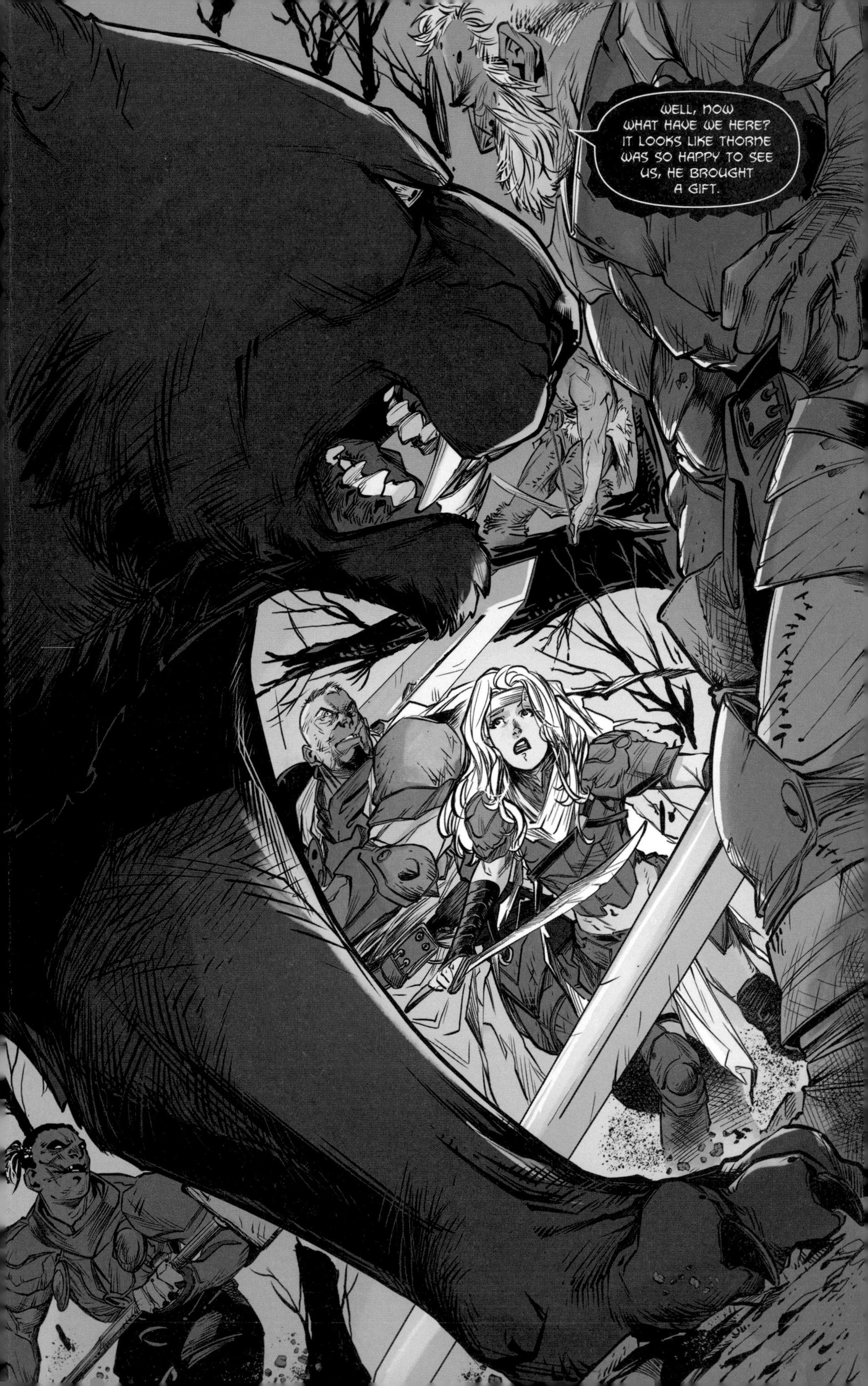
WELL, NOW WHAT HAVE WE HERE? IT LOOKS LIKE THORNE WAS SO HAPPY TO SEE US, HE BROUGHT A GIFT.

FIVE

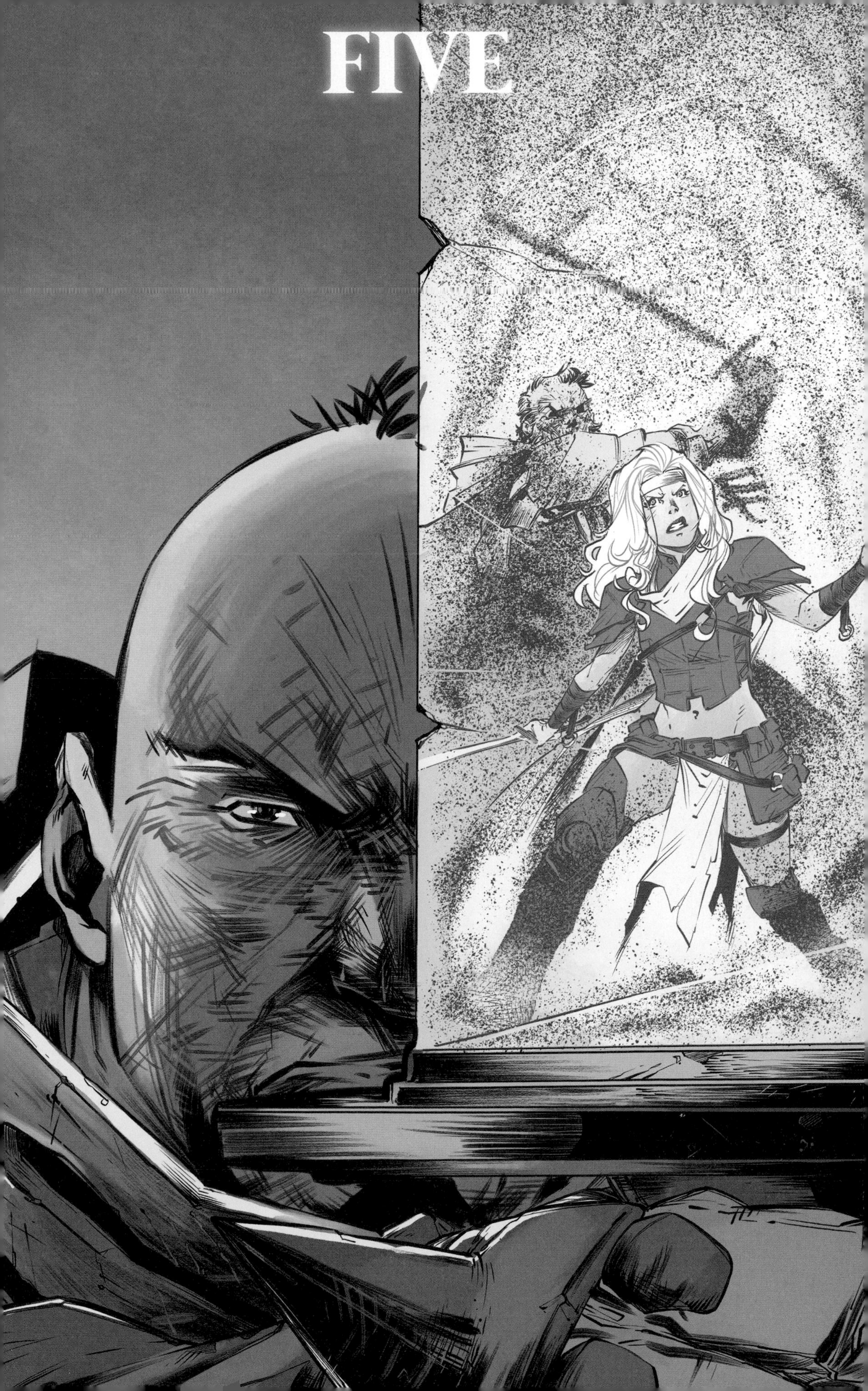

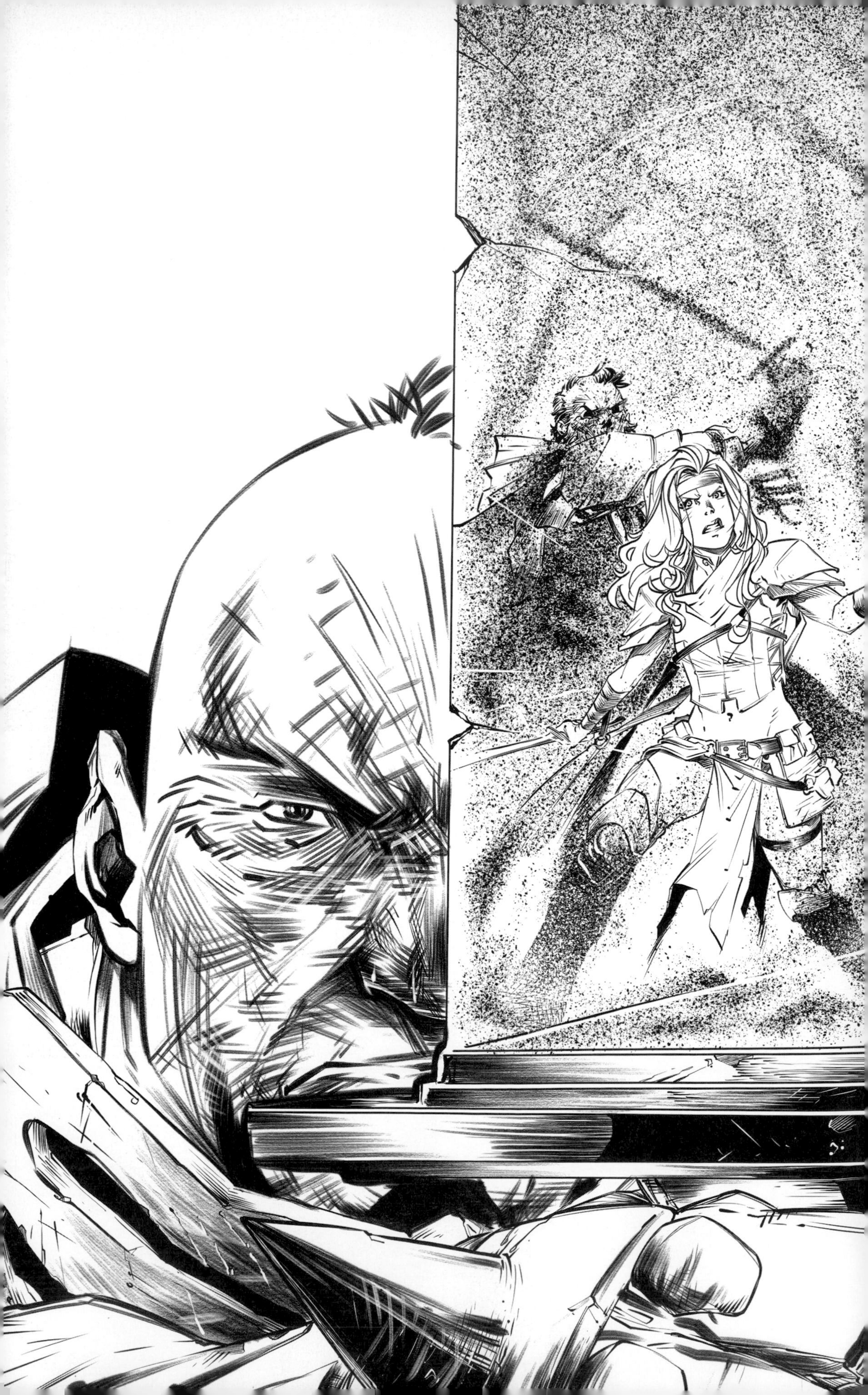

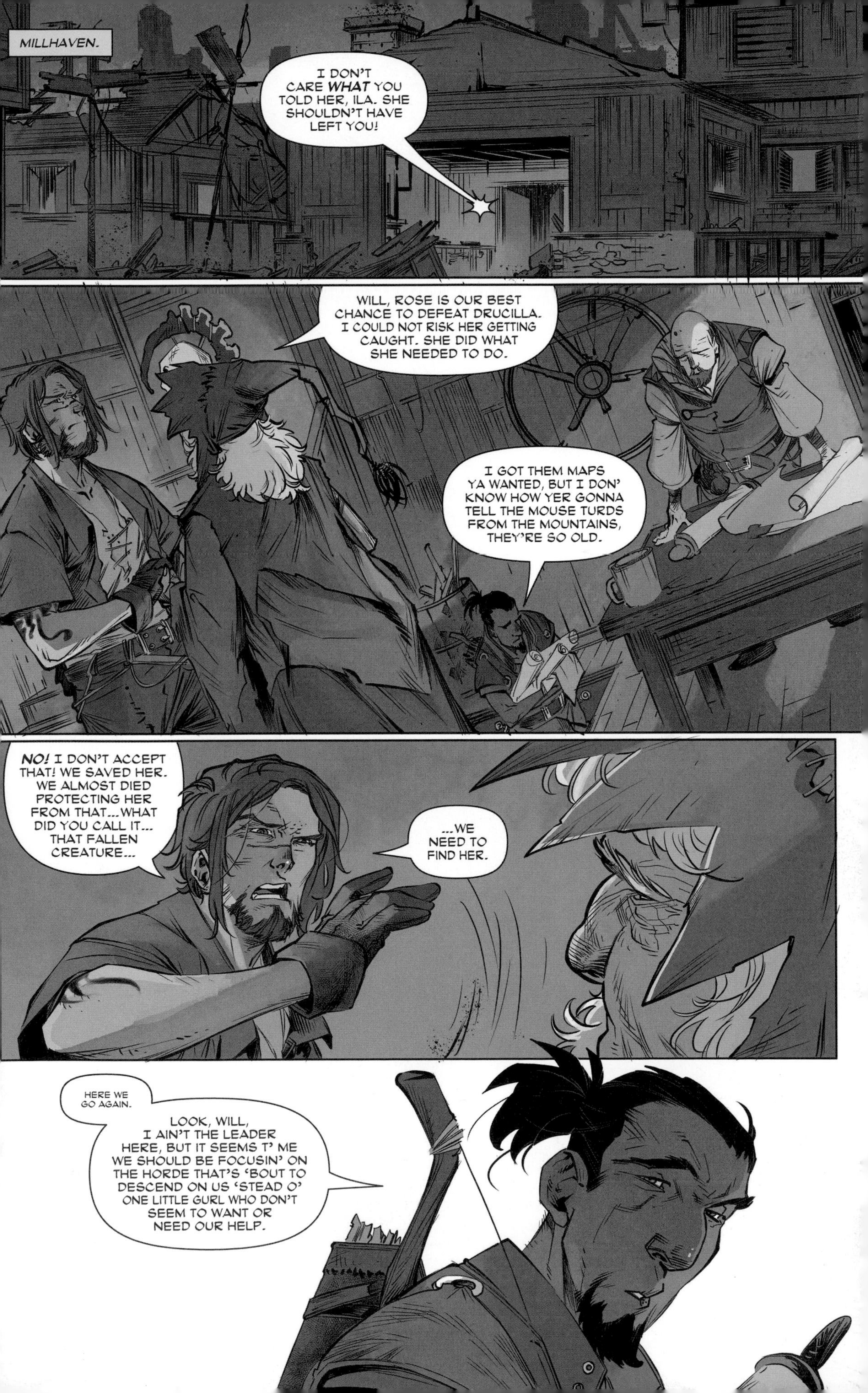
MILLHAVEN.
I DON'T CARE WHAT YOU TOLD HER, ILA. SHE SHOULDN'T HAVE LEFT YOU!
WILL, ROSE IS OUR BEST CHANCE TO DEFEAT DRUCILLA. I COULD NOT RISK HER GETTING CAUGHT. SHE DID WHAT SHE NEEDED TO DO.
I GOT THEM MAPS YA WANTED, BUT I DON' KNOW HOW YER GONNA TELL THE MOUSE TURDS FROM THE MOUNTAINS, THEY'RE SO OLD.
NO! I DON'T ACCEPT THAT! WE SAVED HER. WE ALMOST DIED PROTECTING HER FROM THAT...WHAT DID YOU CALL IT... THAT FALLEN CREATURE...
...WE NEED TO FIND HER.
HERE WE GO AGAIN.
LOOK, WILL, I AIN'T THE LEADER HERE, BUT IT SEEMS T' ME WE SHOULD BE FOCUSIN' ON THE HORDE THAT'S 'BOUT TO DESCEND ON US 'STEAD O' ONE LITTLE GURL WHO DON'T SEEM TO WANT OR NEED OUR HELP.

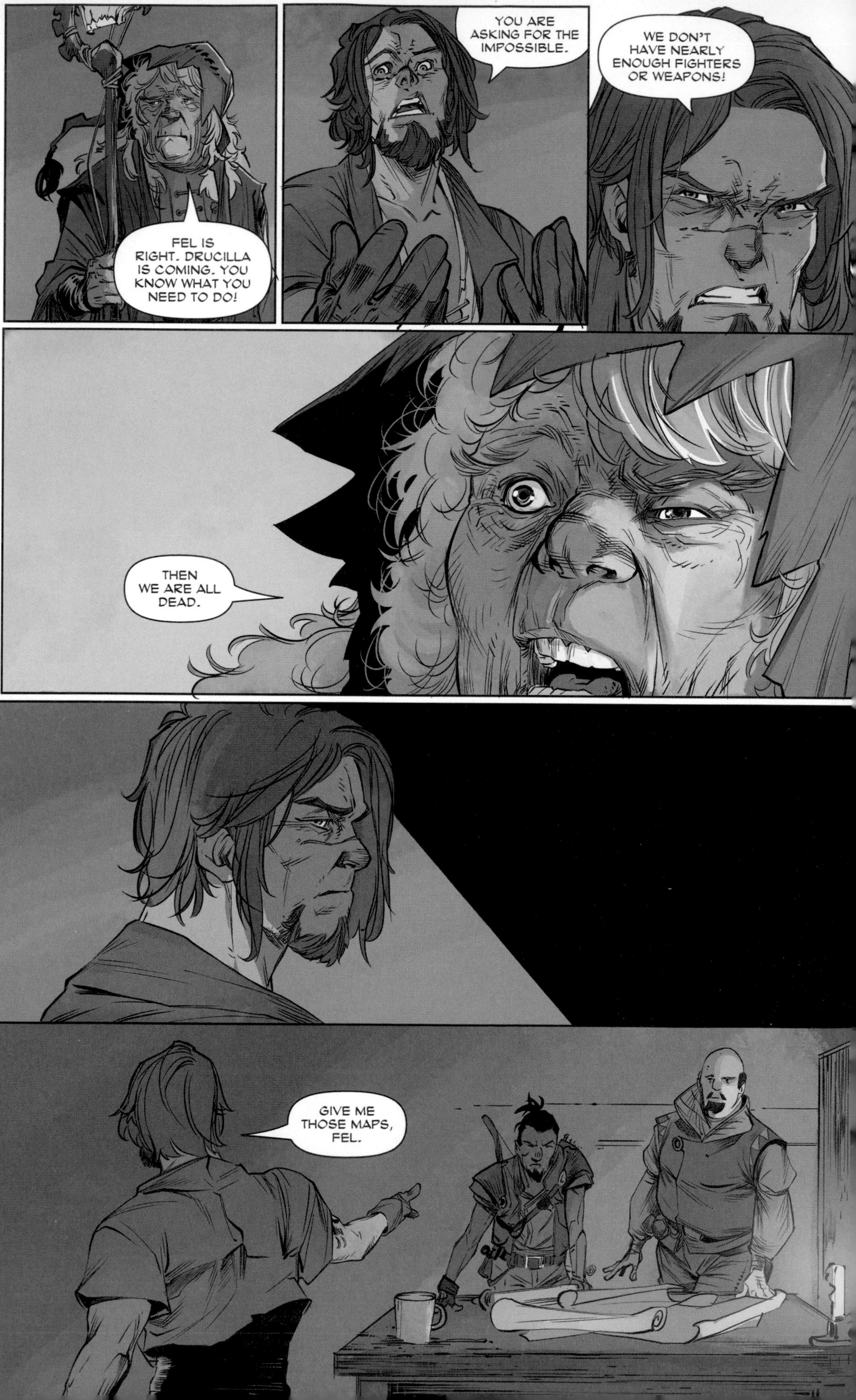
FEL IS RIGHT. DRUCILLA IS COMING. YOU KNOW WHAT YOU NEED TO DO!
YOU ARE ASKING FOR THE IMPOSSIBLE.
WE DON'T HAVE NEARLY ENOUGH FIGHTERS OR WEAPONS!
THEN WE ARE ALL DEAD.
GIVE ME THOSE MAPS, FEL.

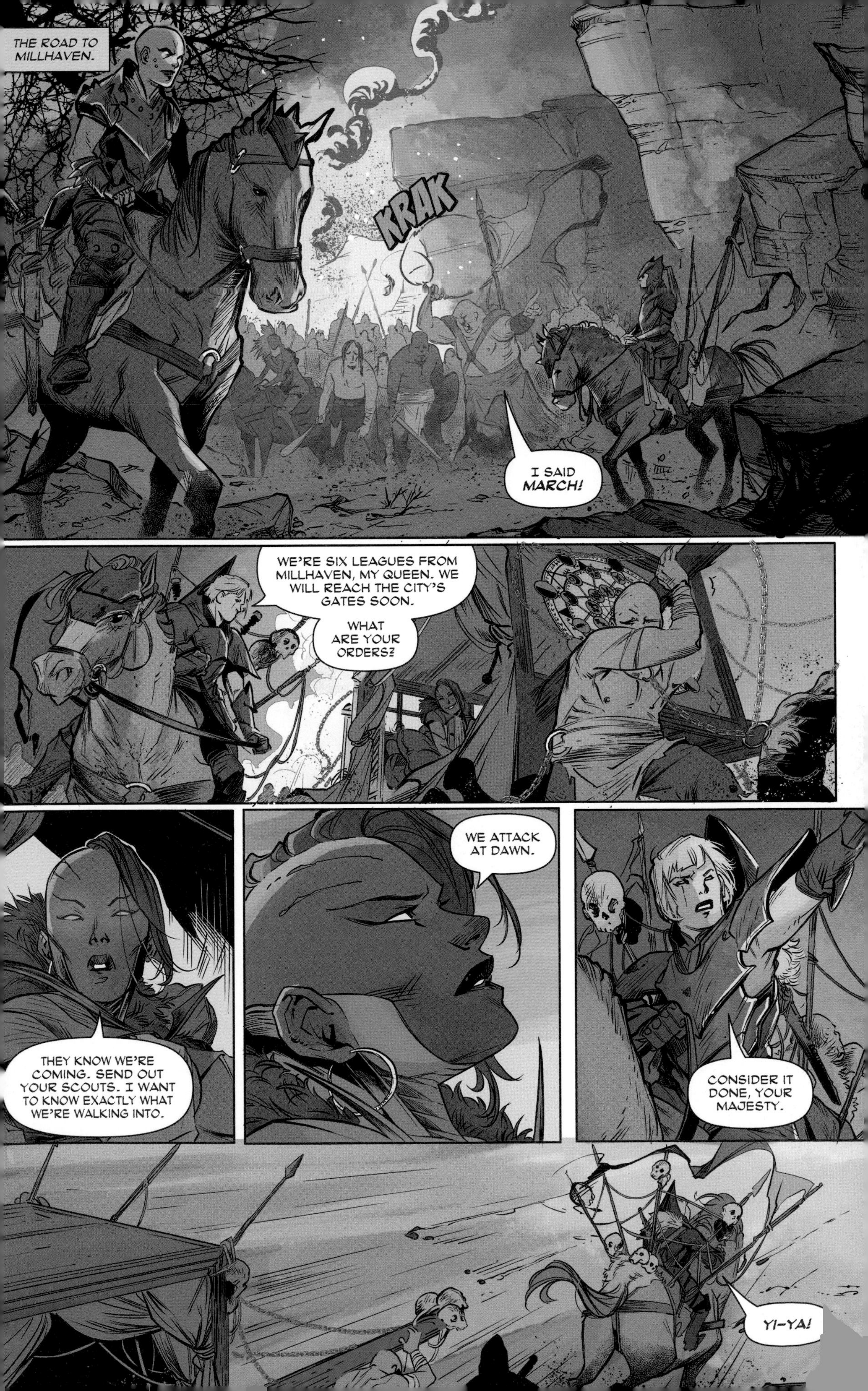
THE ROAD TO MILLHAVEN.
KRAK
I SAID MARCH!
WE'RE SIX LEAGUES FROM MILLHAVEN, MY QUEEN. WE WILL REACH THE CITY'S GATES SOON.
WHAT ARE YOUR ORDERS?
THEY KNOW WE'RE COMING. SEND OUT YOUR SCOUTS. I WANT TO KNOW EXACTLY WHAT WE'RE WALKING INTO.
WE ATTACK AT DAWN.
CONSIDER IT DONE, YOUR MAJESTY.
YI-YA!

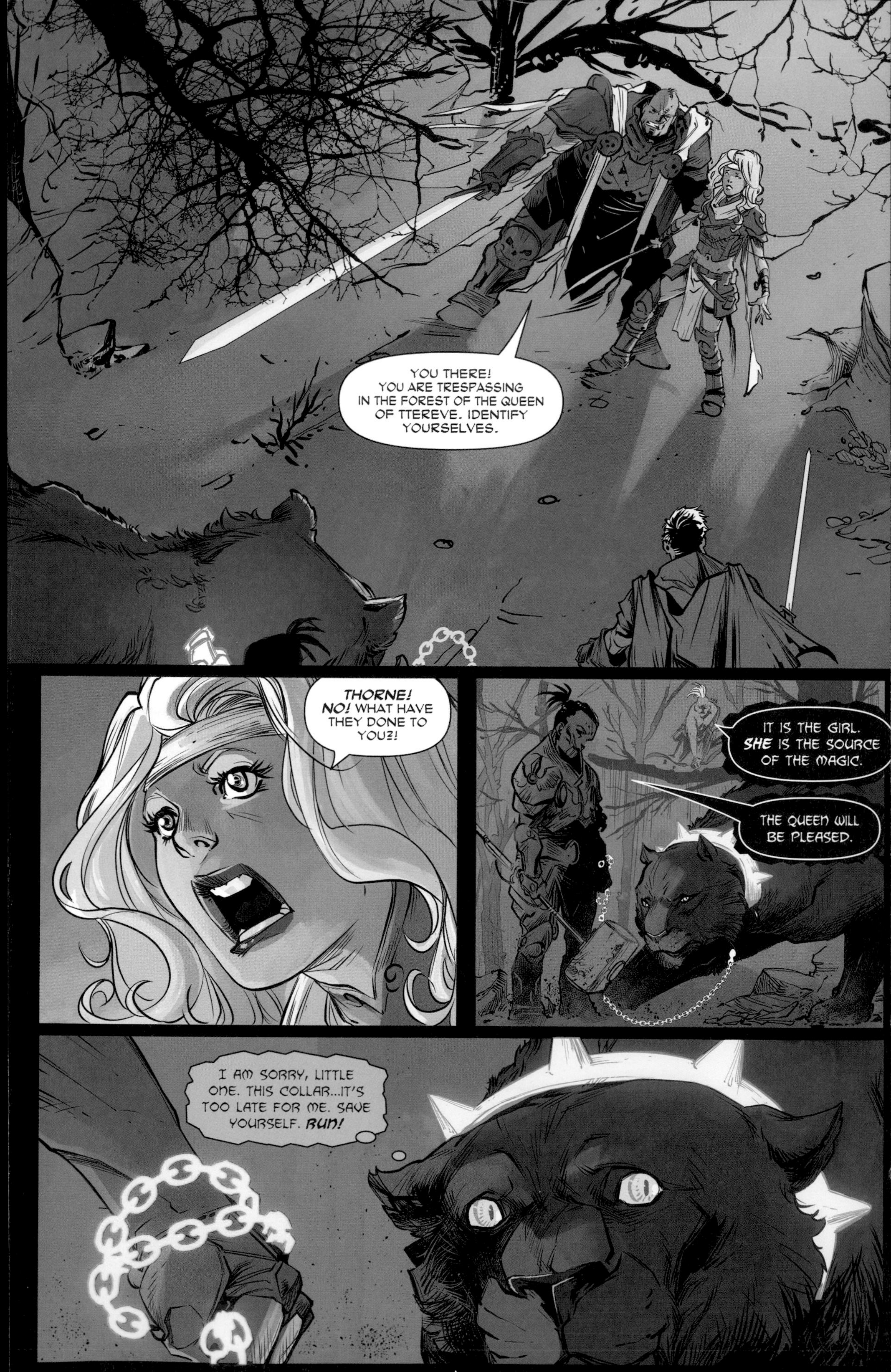
YOU THERE! YOU ARE TRESPASSING IN THE FOREST OF THE QUEEN OF TTEREVE. IDENTIFY YOURSELVES.
THORNE! NO! WHAT HAVE THEY DONE TO YOU?!
IT IS THE GIRL. SHE IS THE SOURCE OF THE MAGIC.
THE QUEEN WILL BE PLEASED.
I AM SORRY, LITTLE ONE. THIS COLLAR...IT'S TOO LATE FOR ME. SAVE YOURSELF. RUN!

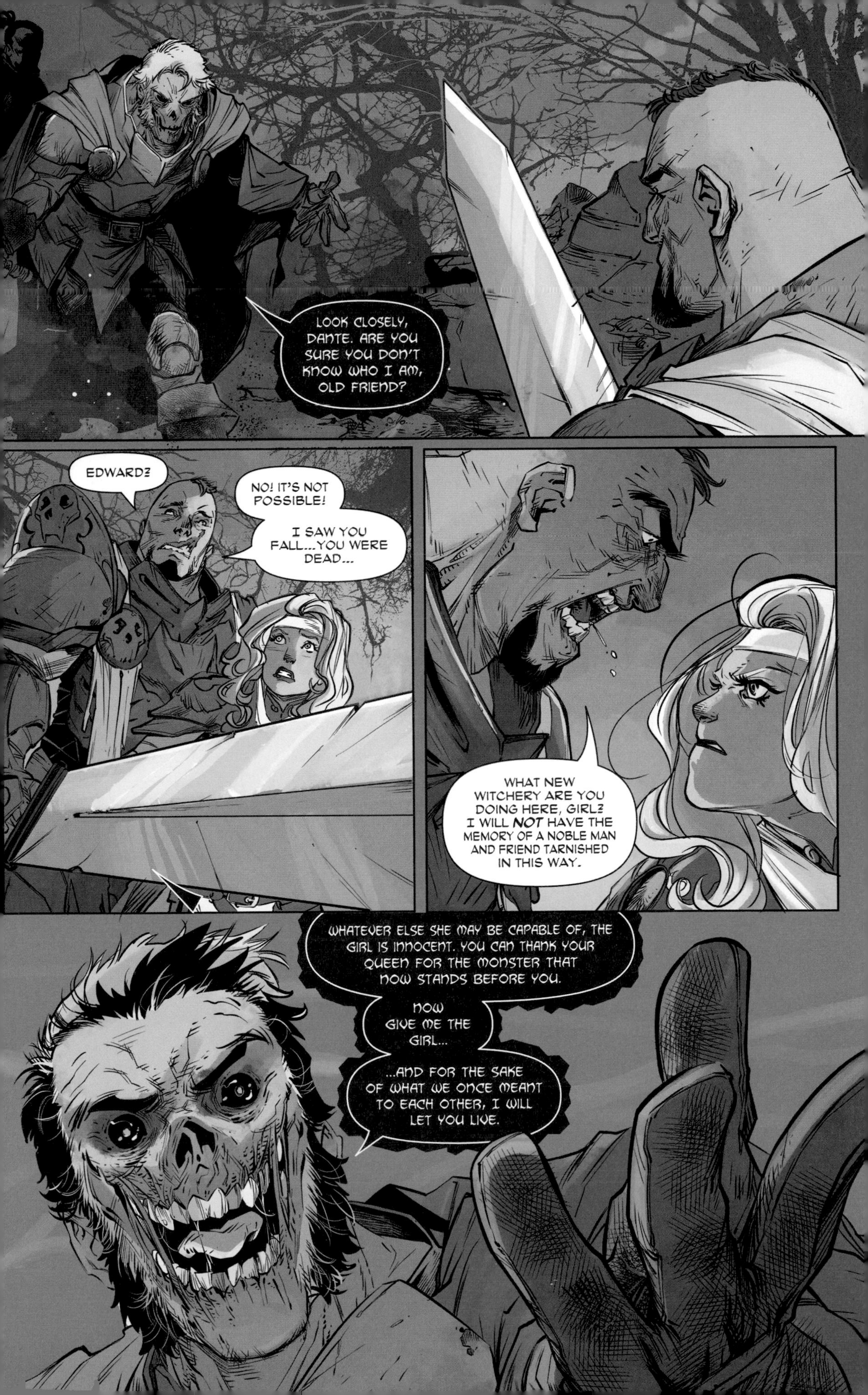
LOOK CLOSELY, DANTE. ARE YOU SURE YOU DON'T KNOW WHO I AM, OLD FRIEND?
EDWARD?
NO! IT'S NOT POSSIBLE!
I SAW YOU FALL...YOU WERE DEAD...
WHAT NEW WITCHERY ARE YOU DOING HERE, GIRL? I WILL *NOT* HAVE THE MEMORY OF A NOBLE MAN AND FRIEND TARNISHED IN THIS WAY.
WHATEVER ELSE SHE MAY BE CAPABLE OF, THE GIRL IS INNOCENT. YOU CAN THANK YOUR QUEEN FOR THE MONSTER THAT NOW STANDS BEFORE YOU.
NOW GIVE ME THE GIRL...
...AND FOR THE SAKE OF WHAT WE ONCE MEANT TO EACH OTHER, I WILL LET YOU LIVE.

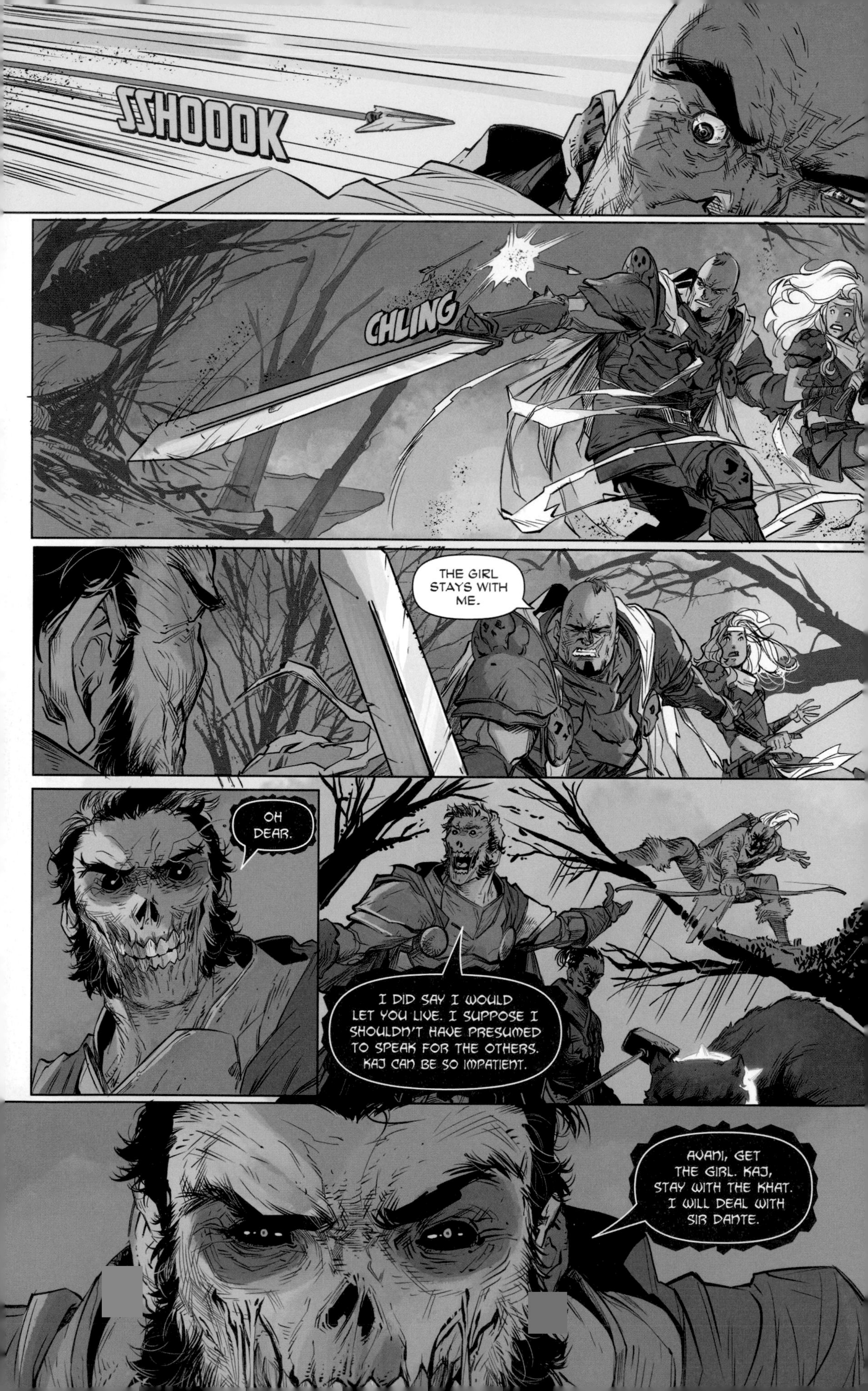
SSHOOOK
CHLING
THE GIRL STAYS WITH ME.
OH DEAR.
I DID SAY I WOULD LET YOU LIVE. I SUPPOSE I SHOULDN'T HAVE PRESUMED TO SPEAK FOR THE OTHERS. KAJ CAN BE SO IMPATIENT.
AVANI, GET THE GIRL. KAJ, STAY WITH THE KHAT. I WILL DEAL WITH SIR DANTE.

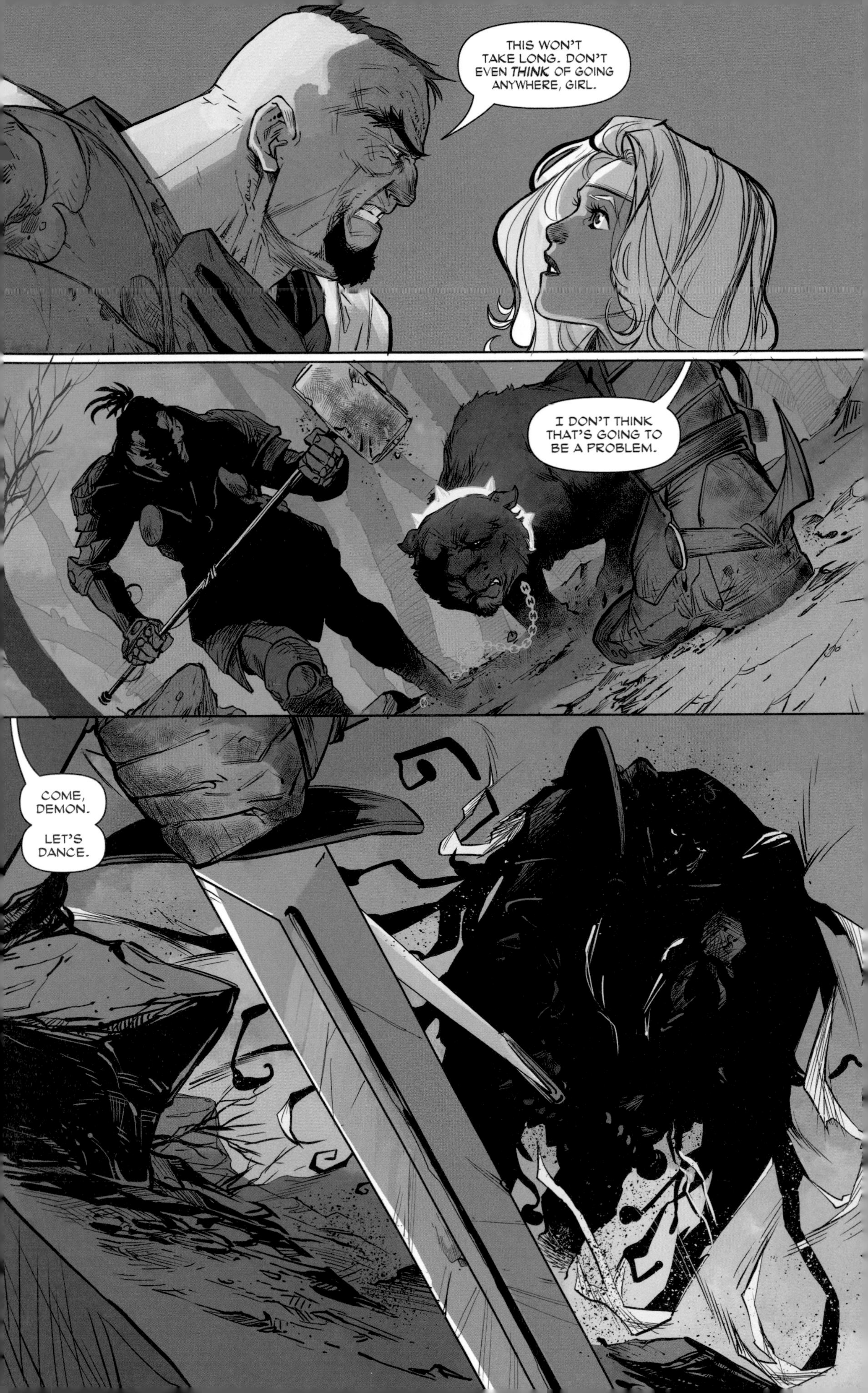
THIS WON'T TAKE LONG. DON'T EVEN *THINK* OF GOING ANYWHERE, GIRL.
I DON'T THINK THAT'S GOING TO BE A PROBLEM.
COME, DEMON.
LET'S DANCE.

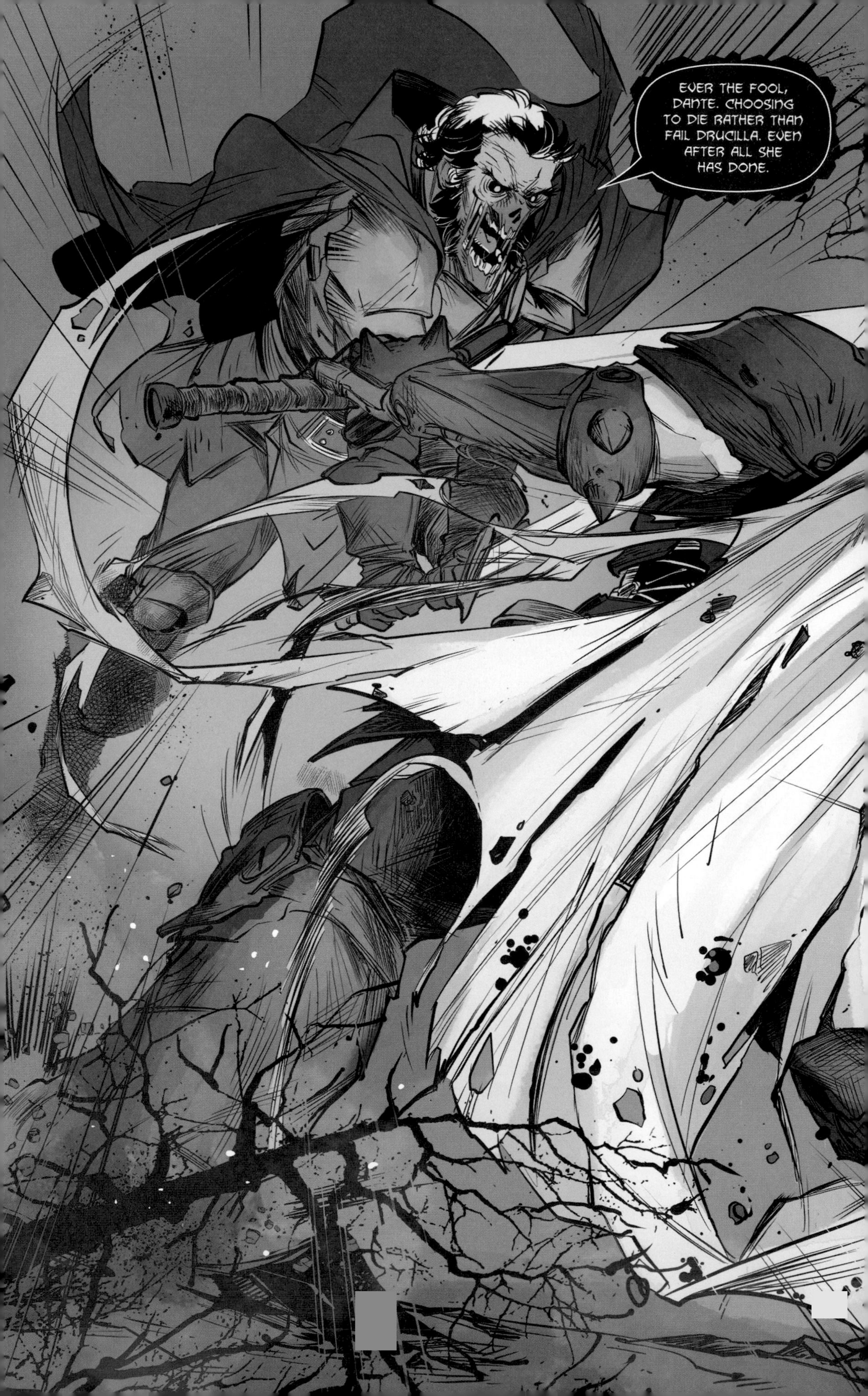
EVER THE FOOL, DANTE. CHOOSING TO DIE RATHER THAN FAIL DRUCILLA. EVEN AFTER ALL SHE HAS DONE.

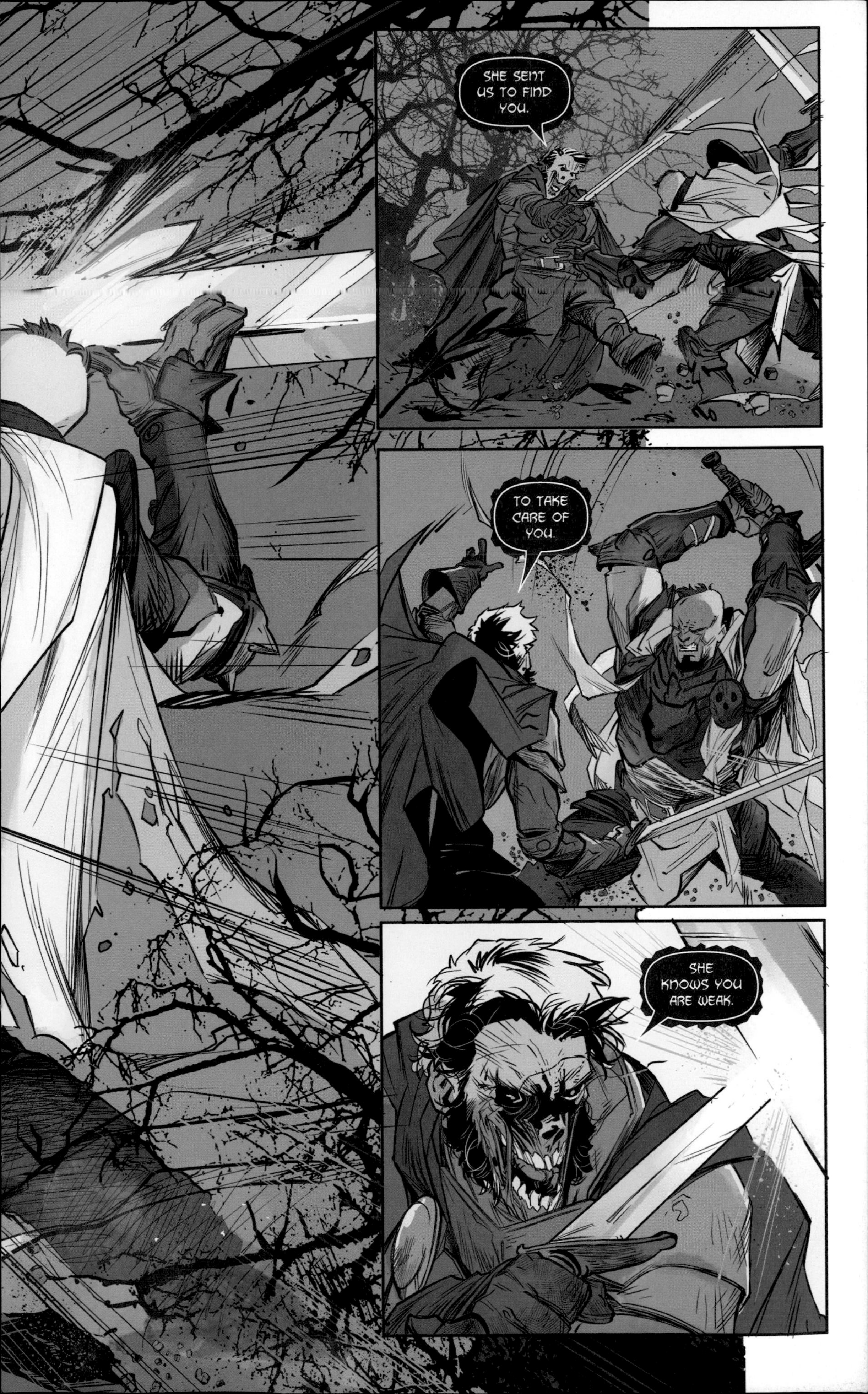
SHE SENT US TO FIND YOU.
TO TAKE CARE OF YOU.
SHE KNOWS YOU ARE WEAK.

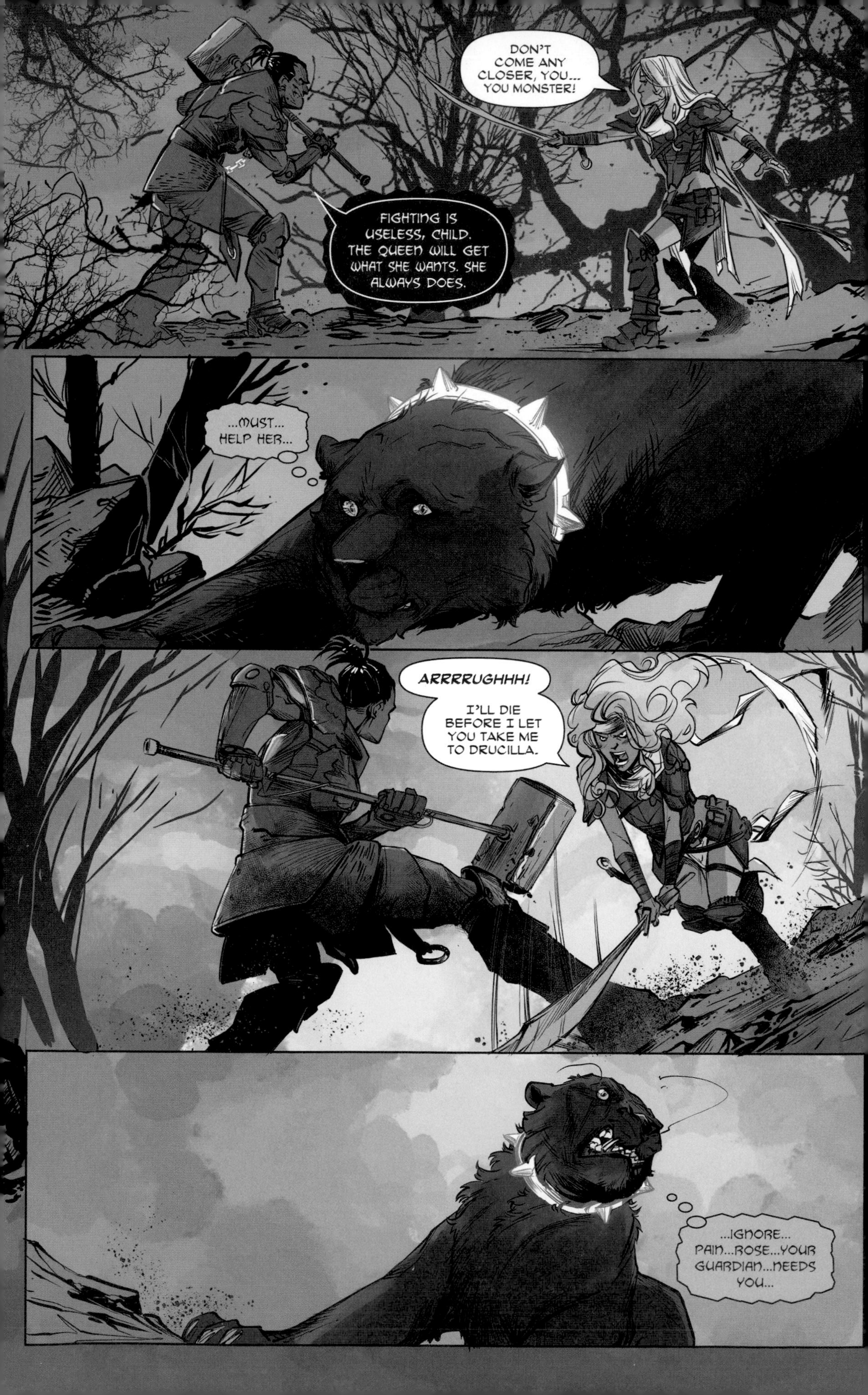
DON'T COME ANY CLOSER, YOU... YOU MONSTER!
FIGHTING IS USELESS, CHILD. THE QUEEN WILL GET WHAT SHE WANTS. SHE ALWAYS DOES.
...MUST... HELP HER...
ARRRRUGHHH!
I'LL DIE BEFORE I LET YOU TAKE ME TO DRUCILLA.
...IGNORE... PAIN...ROSE...YOUR GUARDIAN...NEEDS YOU...

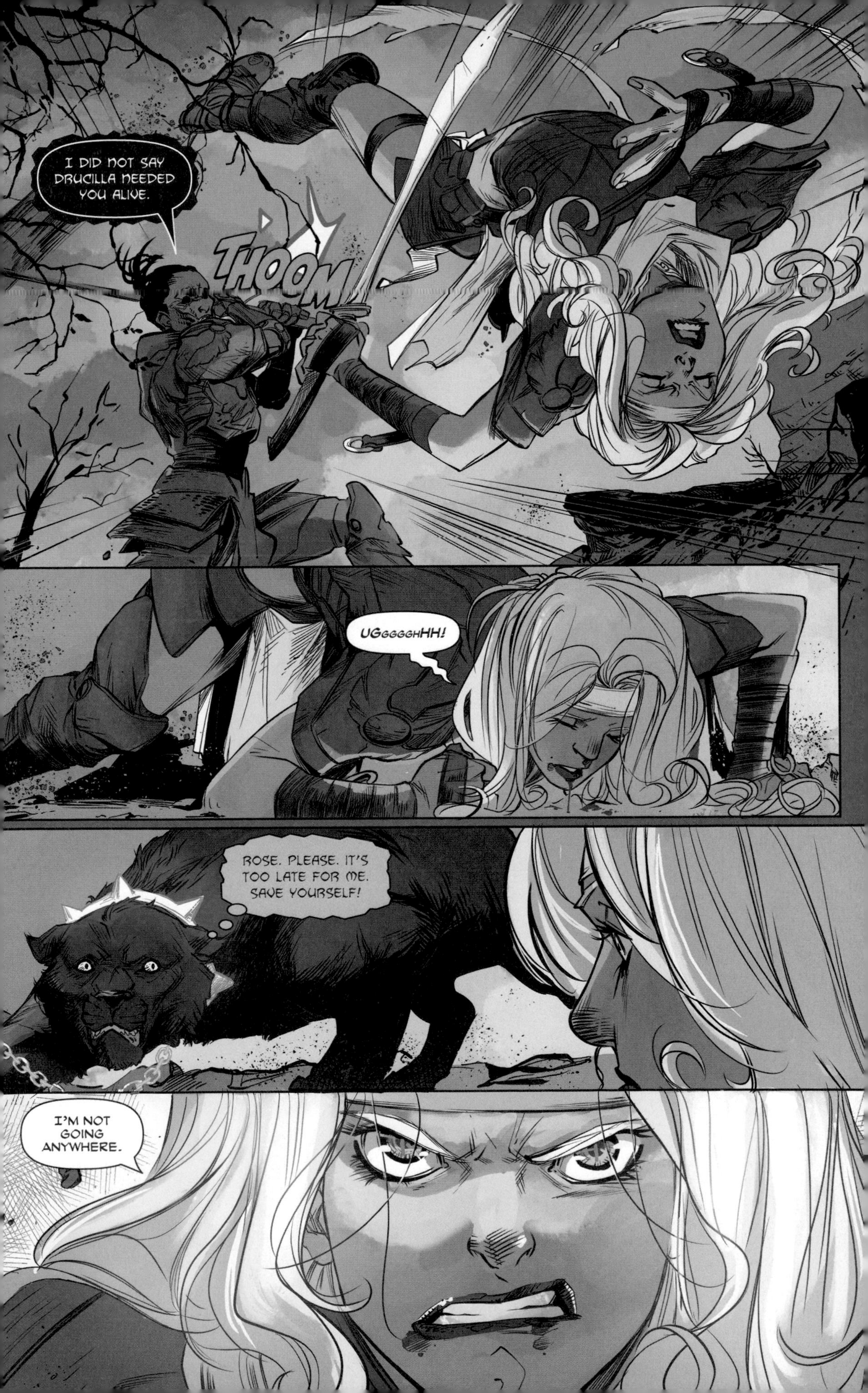
I DID NOT SAY DRUCILLA NEEDED YOU ALIVE.
THOOM
UGGGGGHH!
ROSE. PLEASE. IT'S TOO LATE FOR ME. SAVE YOURSELF!
I'M NOT GOING ANYWHERE.

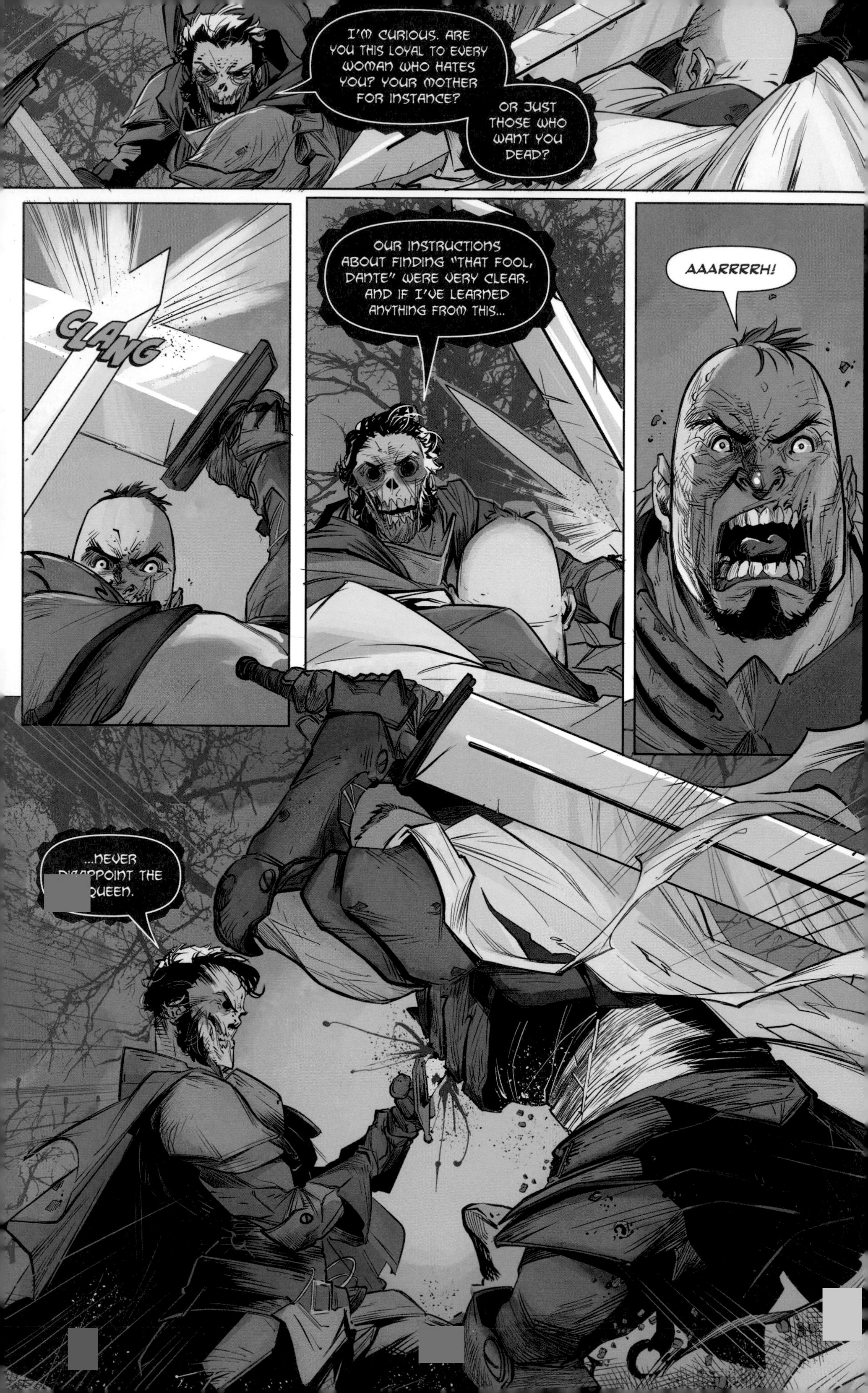

I'M CURIOUS. ARE YOU THIS LOYAL TO EVERY WOMAN WHO HATES YOU? YOUR MOTHER FOR INSTANCE?
OR JUST THOSE WHO WANT YOU DEAD?
CLANG
OUR INSTRUCTIONS ABOUT FINDING "THAT FOOL, DANTE" WERE VERY CLEAR. AND IF I'VE LEARNED ANYTHING FROM THIS...
AAARRRRH!
...NEVER DISAPPOINT THE QUEEN.

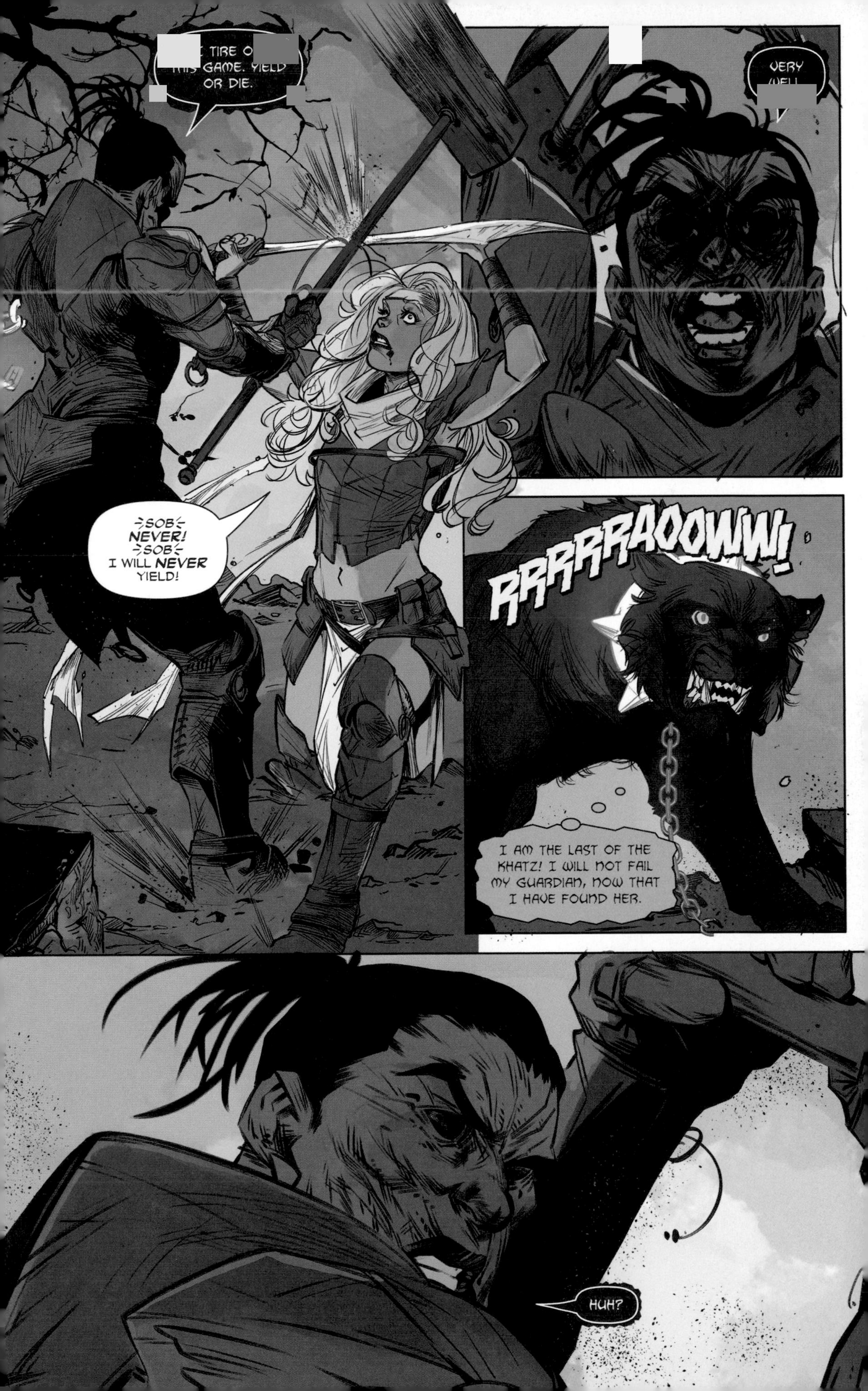
TIRE O THIS GAME. YIELD OR DIE.
SOB NEVER! SOB I WILL NEVER YIELD!
VERY
RRRRRAOOWW!
I AM THE LAST OF THE KHATZ! I WILL NOT FAIL MY GUARDIAN, NOW THAT I HAVE FOUND HER.
HUH?

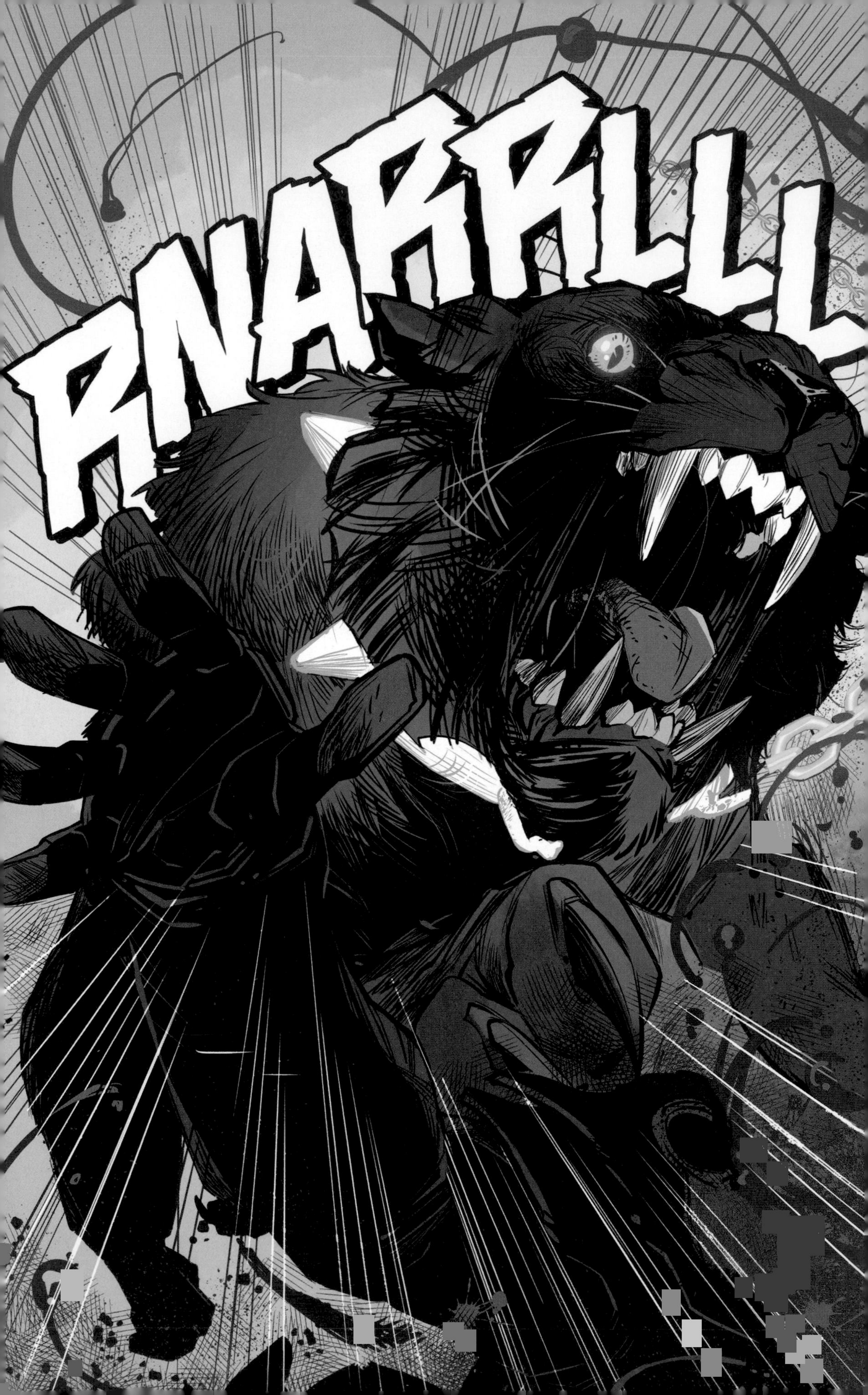
RNARRLL

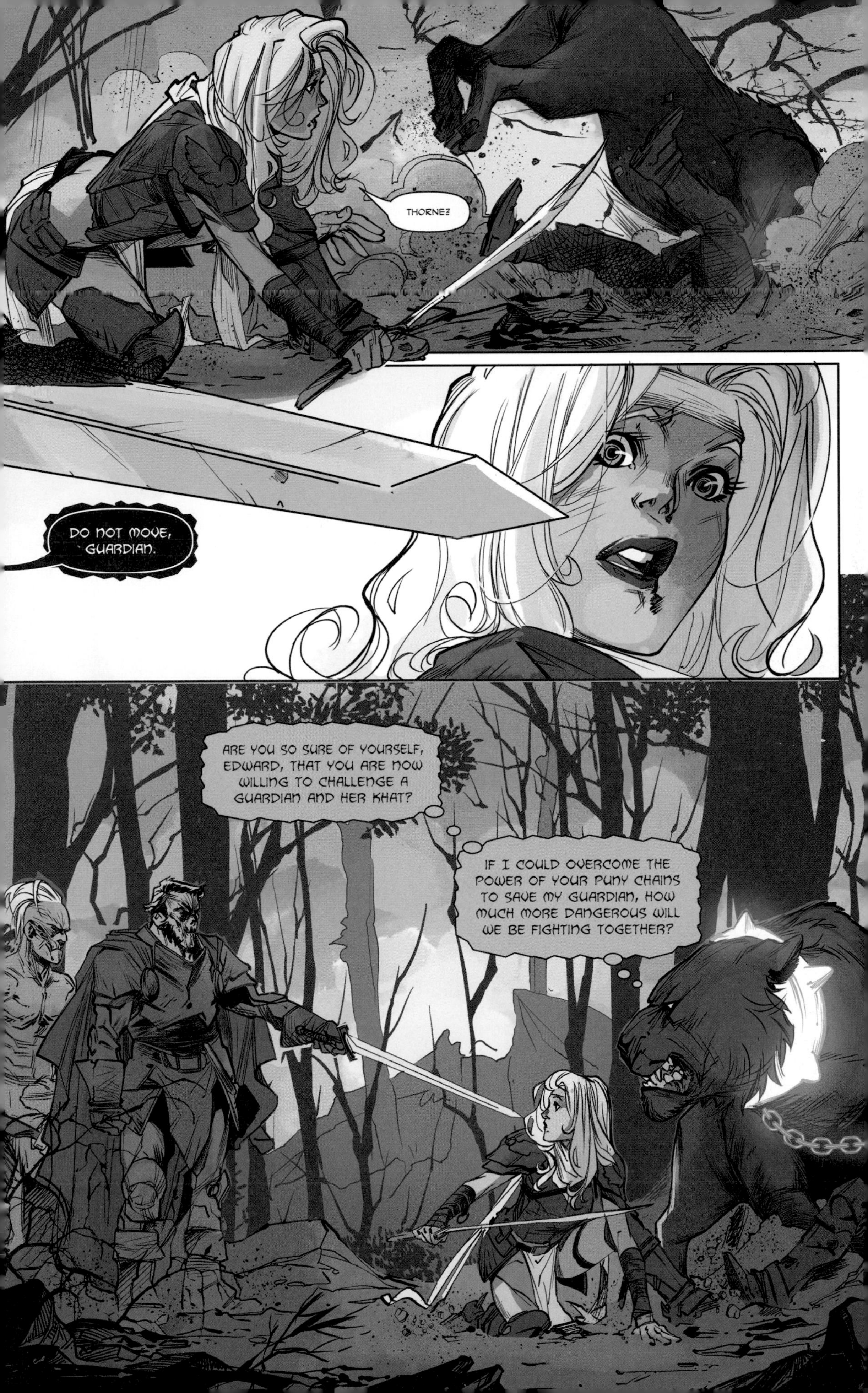
THORNE?
DO NOT MOVE, GUARDIAN.
ARE YOU SO SURE OF YOURSELF, EDWARD, THAT YOU ARE NOW WILLING TO CHALLENGE A GUARDIAN AND HER KHAT?
IF I COULD OVERCOME THE POWER OF YOUR PUNY CHAINS TO SAVE MY GUARDIAN, HOW MUCH MORE DANGEROUS WILL WE BE FIGHTING TOGETHER?

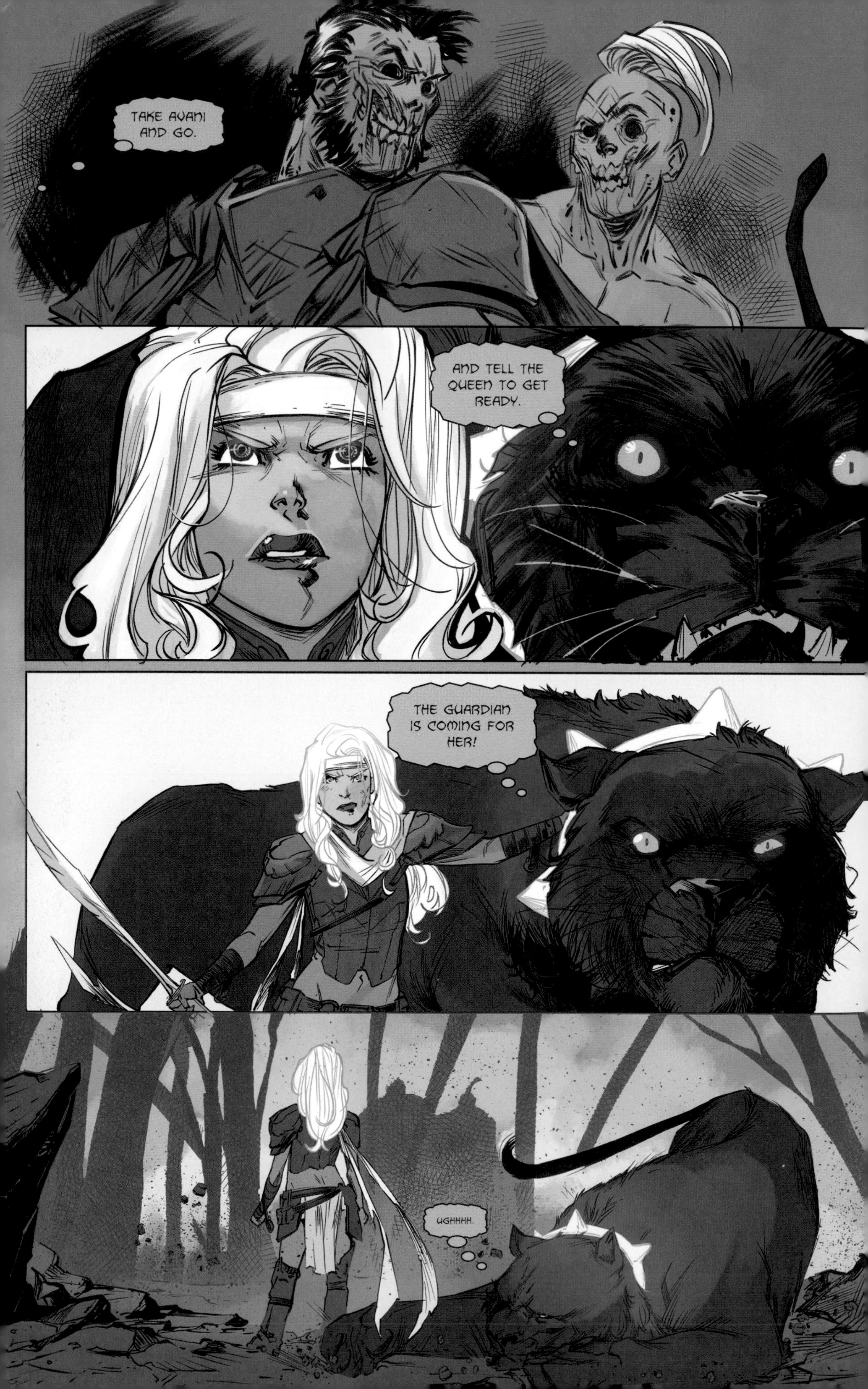
TAKE AVANI AND GO.
AND TELL THE QUEEN TO GET READY.
THE GUARDIAN IS COMING FOR HER!
UGHHHH.

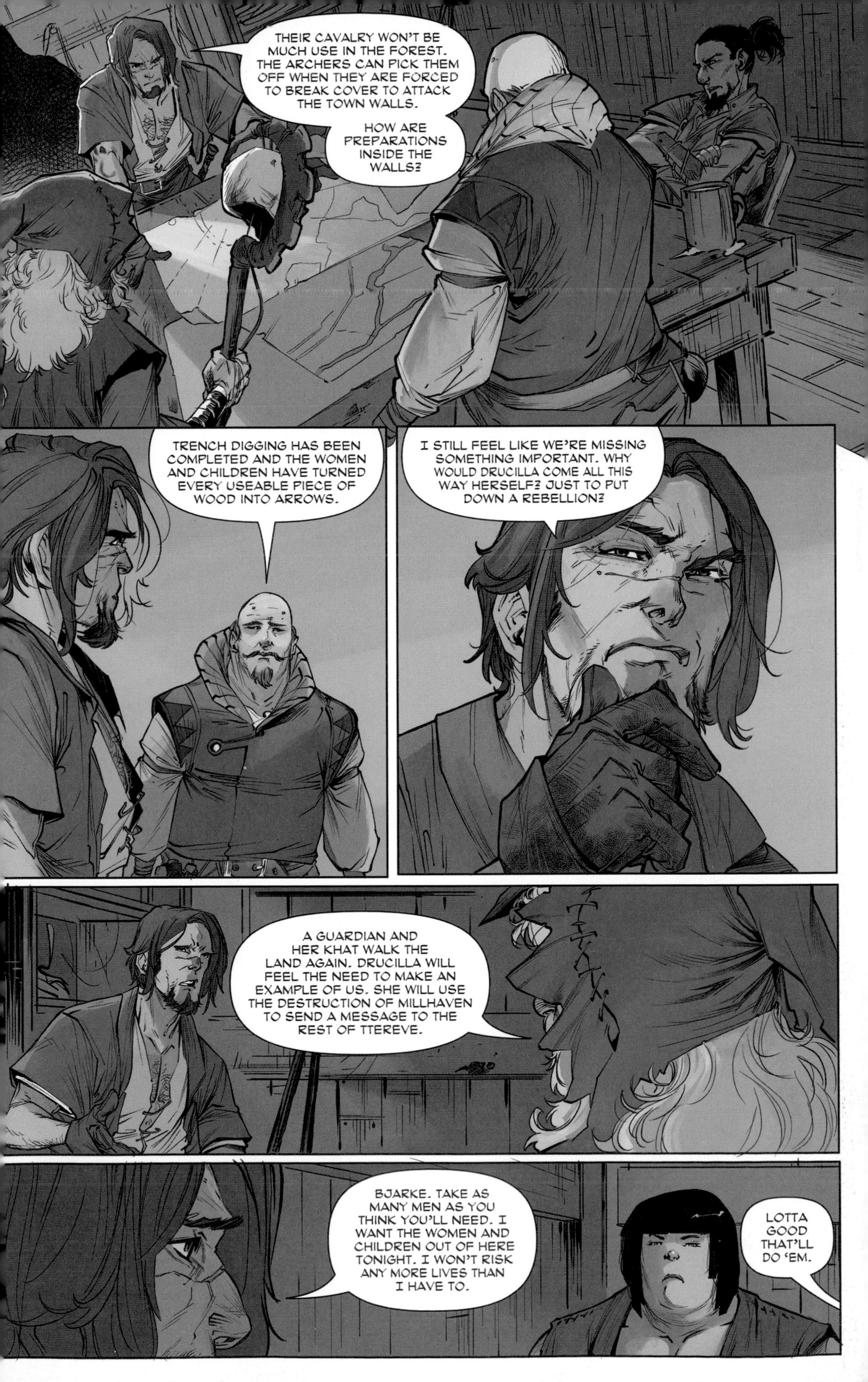
THEIR CAVALRY WON'T BE MUCH USE IN THE FOREST. THE ARCHERS CAN PICK THEM OFF WHEN THEY ARE FORCED TO BREAK COVER TO ATTACK THE TOWN WALLS.
HOW ARE PREPARATIONS INSIDE THE WALLS?
TRENCH DIGGING HAS BEEN COMPLETED AND THE WOMEN AND CHILDREN HAVE TURNED EVERY USEABLE PIECE OF WOOD INTO ARROWS.
I STILL FEEL LIKE WE'RE MISSING SOMETHING IMPORTANT. WHY WOULD DRUCILLA COME ALL THIS WAY HERSELF? JUST TO PUT DOWN A REBELLION?
A GUARDIAN AND HER KHAT WALK THE LAND AGAIN. DRUCILLA WILL FEEL THE NEED TO MAKE AN EXAMPLE OF US. SHE WILL USE THE DESTRUCTION OF MILLHAVEN TO SEND A MESSAGE TO THE REST OF TTEREVE.
BJARKE. TAKE AS MANY MEN AS YOU THINK YOU'LL NEED. I WANT THE WOMEN AND CHILDREN OUT OF HERE TONIGHT. I WON'T RISK ANY MORE LIVES THAN I HAVE TO.
LOTTA GOOD THAT'LL DO 'EM.

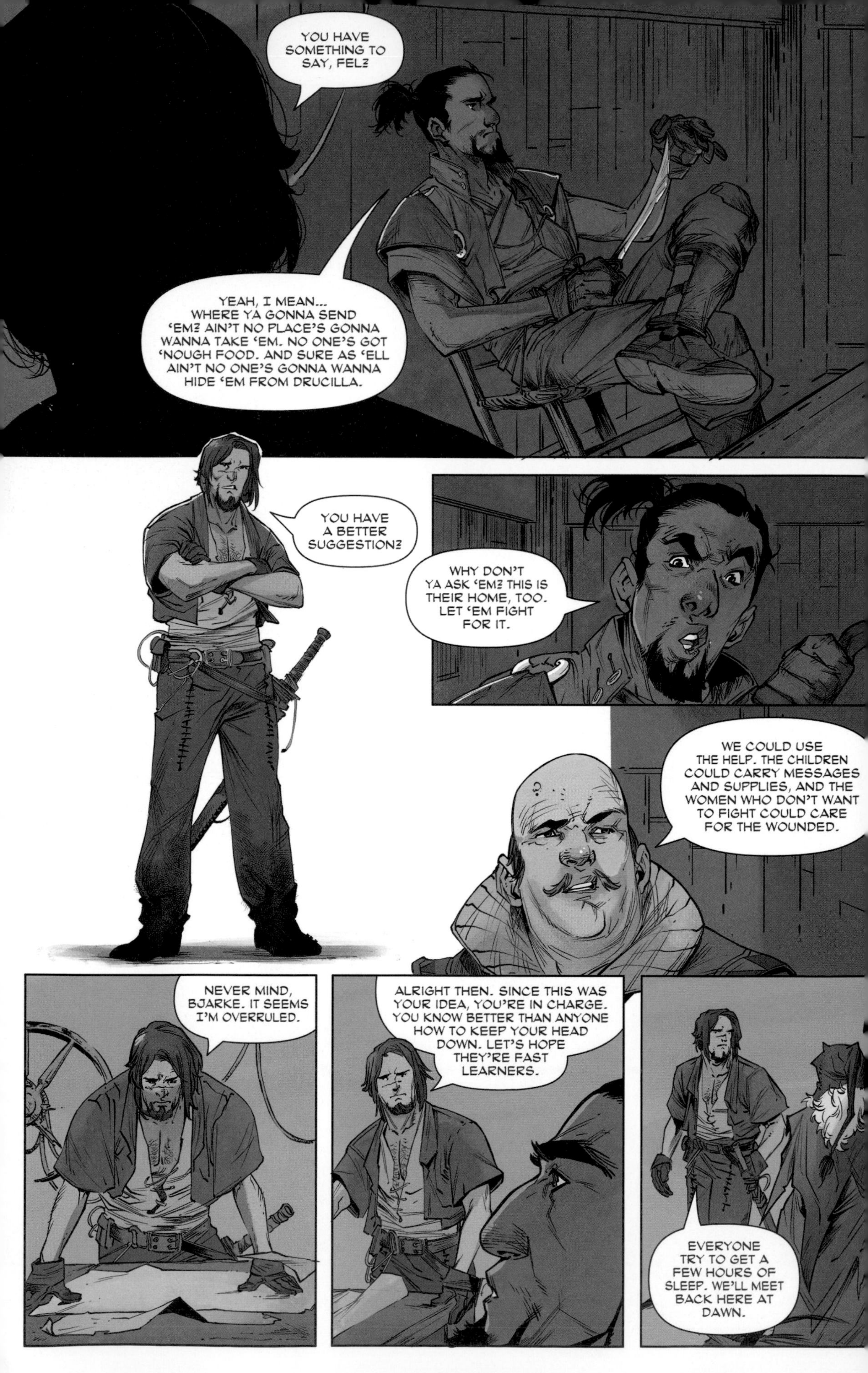
YOU HAVE SOMETHING TO SAY, FEL?
YEAH, I MEAN... WHERE YA GONNA SEND 'EM? AIN'T NO PLACE'S GONNA WANNA TAKE 'EM. NO ONE'S GOT 'NOUGH FOOD. AND SURE AS 'ELL AIN'T NO ONE'S GONNA WANNA HIDE 'EM FROM DRUCILLA.
YOU HAVE A BETTER SUGGESTION?
WHY DON'T YA ASK 'EM? THIS IS THEIR HOME, TOO. LET 'EM FIGHT FOR IT.
WE COULD USE THE HELP. THE CHILDREN COULD CARRY MESSAGES AND SUPPLIES, AND THE WOMEN WHO DON'T WANT TO FIGHT COULD CARE FOR THE WOUNDED.
NEVER MIND, BJARKE. IT SEEMS I'M OVERRULED.
ALRIGHT THEN. SINCE THIS WAS YOUR IDEA, YOU'RE IN CHARGE. YOU KNOW BETTER THAN ANYONE HOW TO KEEP YOUR HEAD DOWN. LET'S HOPE THEY'RE FAST LEARNERS.
EVERYONE TRY TO GET A FEW HOURS OF SLEEP. WE'LL MEET BACK HERE AT DAWN.

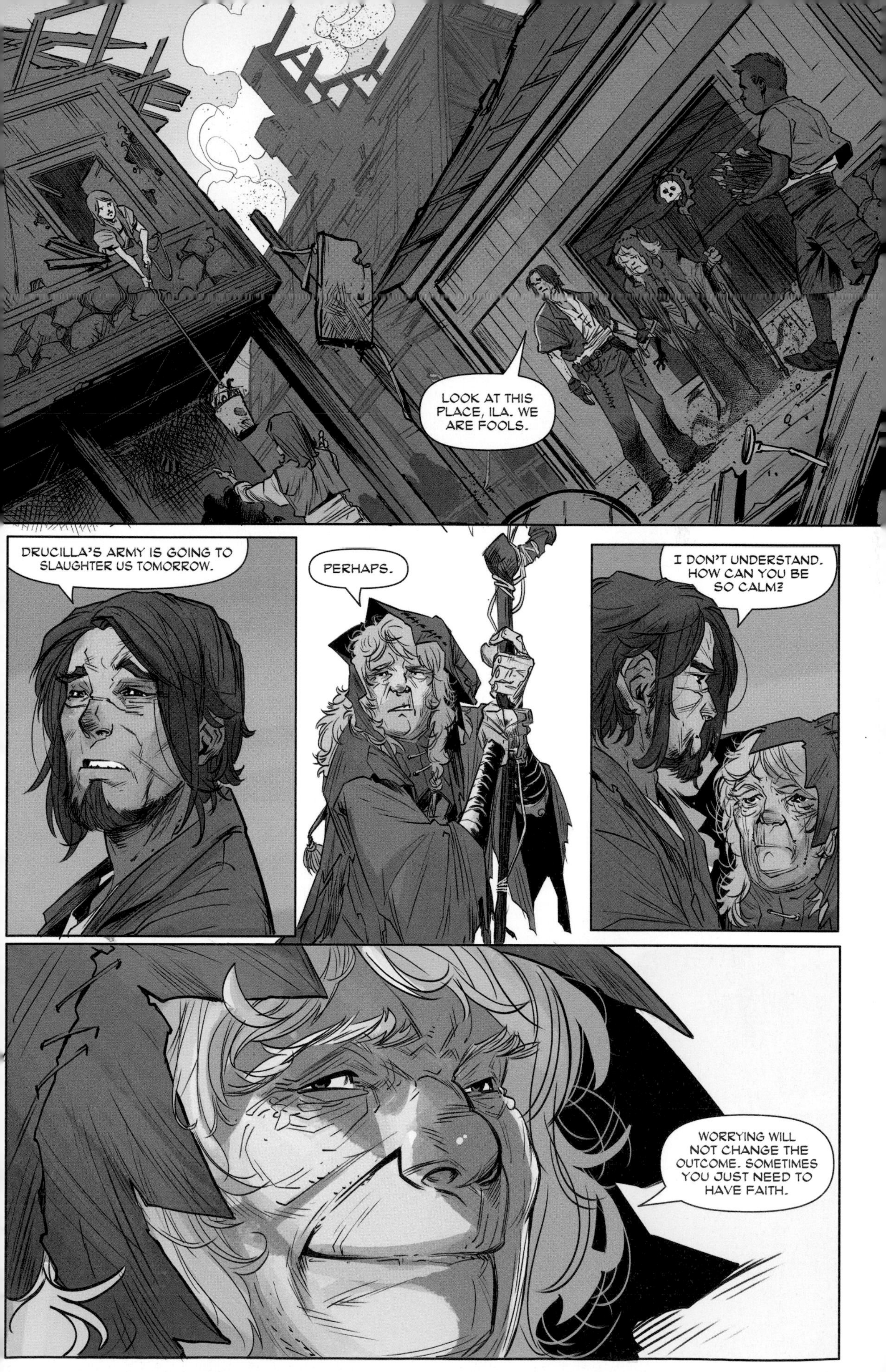
LOOK AT THIS PLACE, ILA. WE ARE FOOLS.
DRUCILLA'S ARMY IS GOING TO SLAUGHTER US TOMORROW.
PERHAPS.
I DON'T UNDERSTAND. HOW CAN YOU BE SO CALM?
WORRYING WILL NOT CHANGE THE OUTCOME. SOMETIMES YOU JUST NEED TO HAVE FAITH.

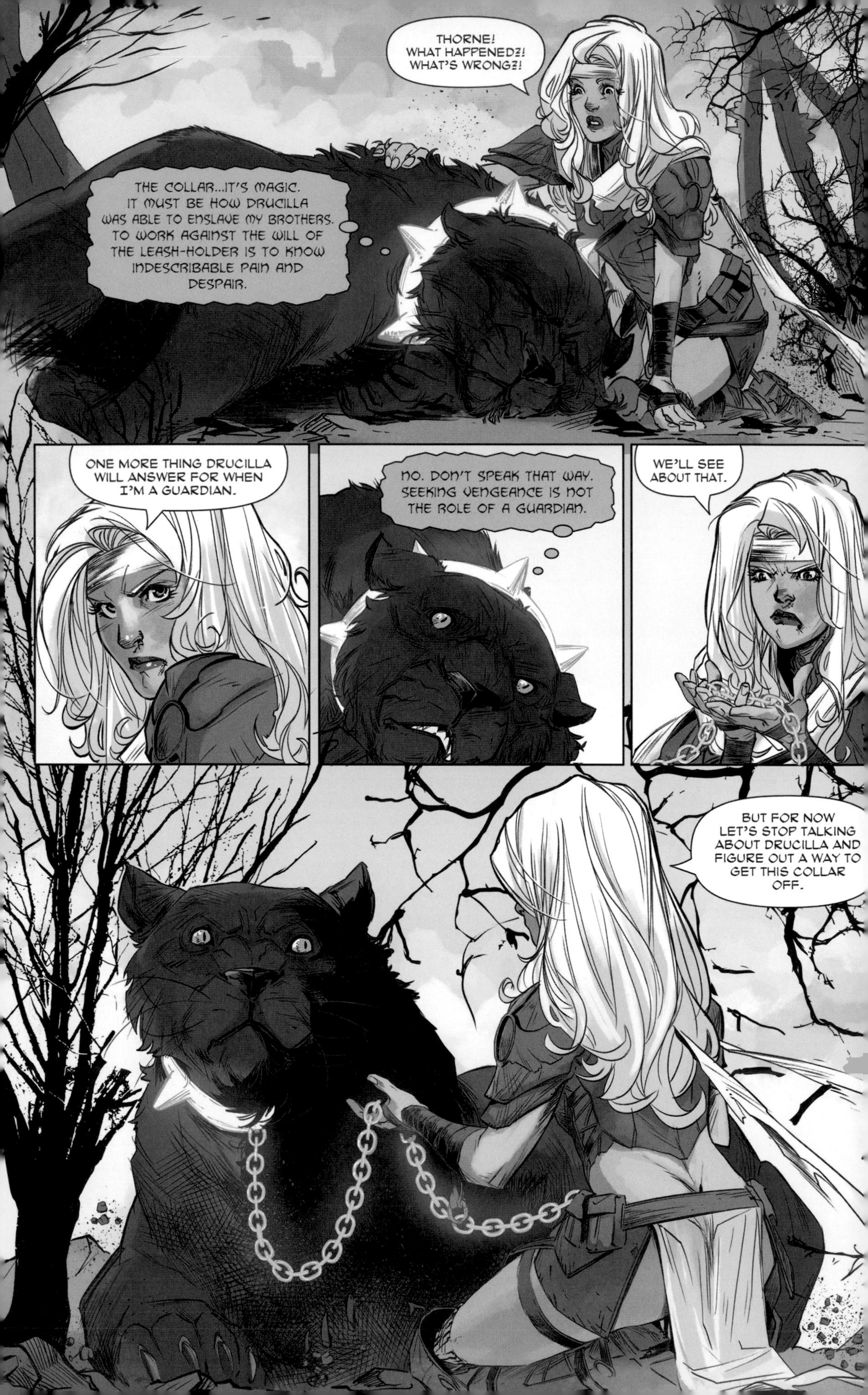
THORNE! WHAT HAPPENED?! WHAT'S WRONG?!
THE COLLAR...IT'S MAGIC. IT MUST BE HOW DRUCILLA WAS ABLE TO ENSLAVE MY BROTHERS. TO WORK AGAINST THE WILL OF THE LEASH-HOLDER IS TO KNOW INDESCRIBABLE PAIN AND DESPAIR.
ONE MORE THING DRUCILLA WILL ANSWER FOR WHEN I'M A GUARDIAN.
NO. DON'T SPEAK THAT WAY. SEEKING VENGEANCE IS NOT THE ROLE OF A GUARDIAN.
WE'LL SEE ABOUT THAT.
BUT FOR NOW LET'S STOP TALKING ABOUT DRUCILLA AND FIGURE OUT A WAY TO GET THIS COLLAR OFF.

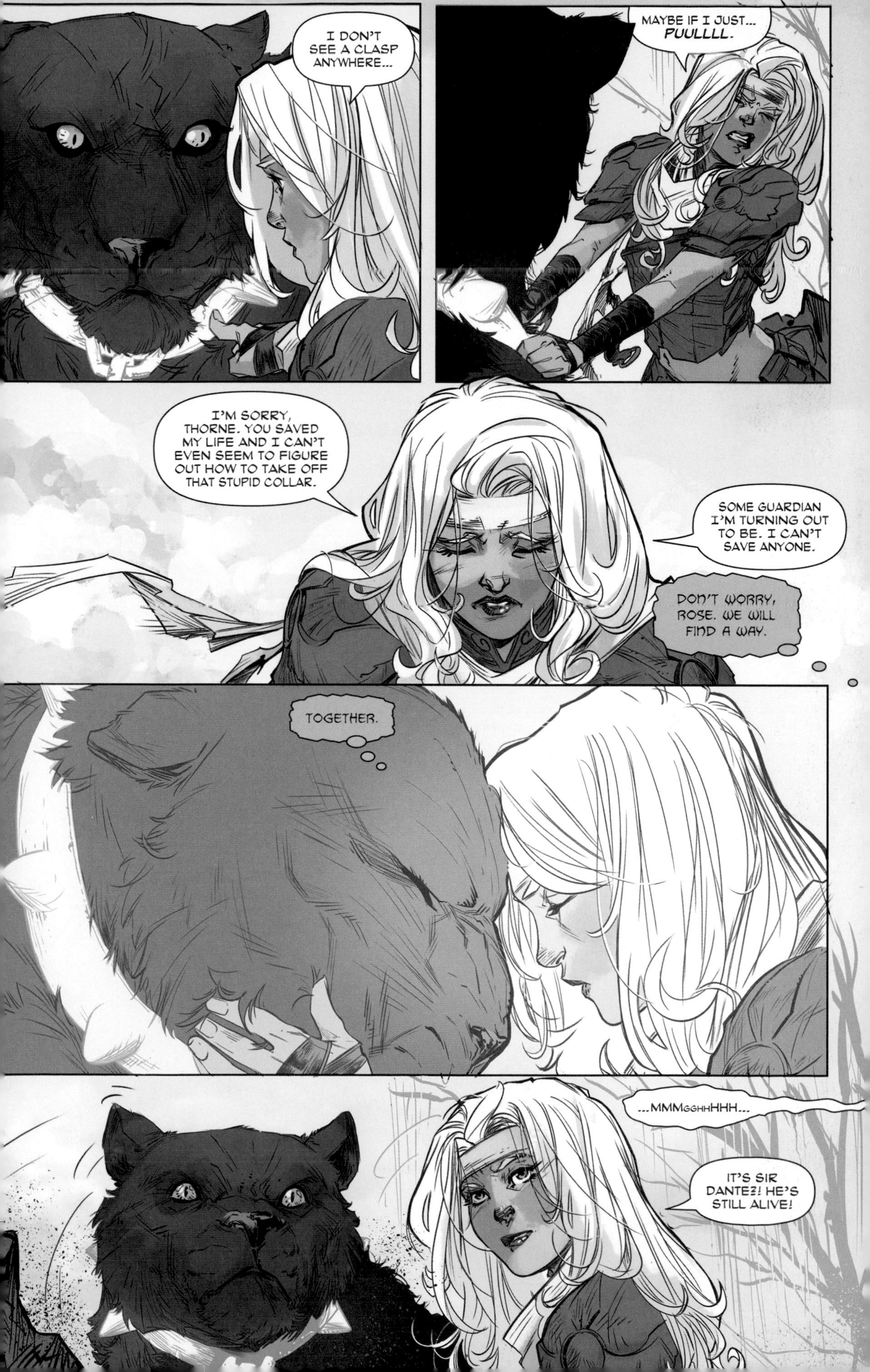

I DON'T SEE A CLASP ANYWHERE...
MAYBE IF I JUST... PUULLLL.
I'M SORRY, THORNE. YOU SAVED MY LIFE AND I CAN'T EVEN SEEM TO FIGURE OUT HOW TO TAKE OFF THAT STUPID COLLAR.
SOME GUARDIAN I'M TURNING OUT TO BE. I CAN'T SAVE ANYONE.
DON'T WORRY, ROSE. WE WILL FIND A WAY.
TOGETHER.
...MMMGGHHHHH...
IT'S SIR DANTE?! HE'S STILL ALIVE!

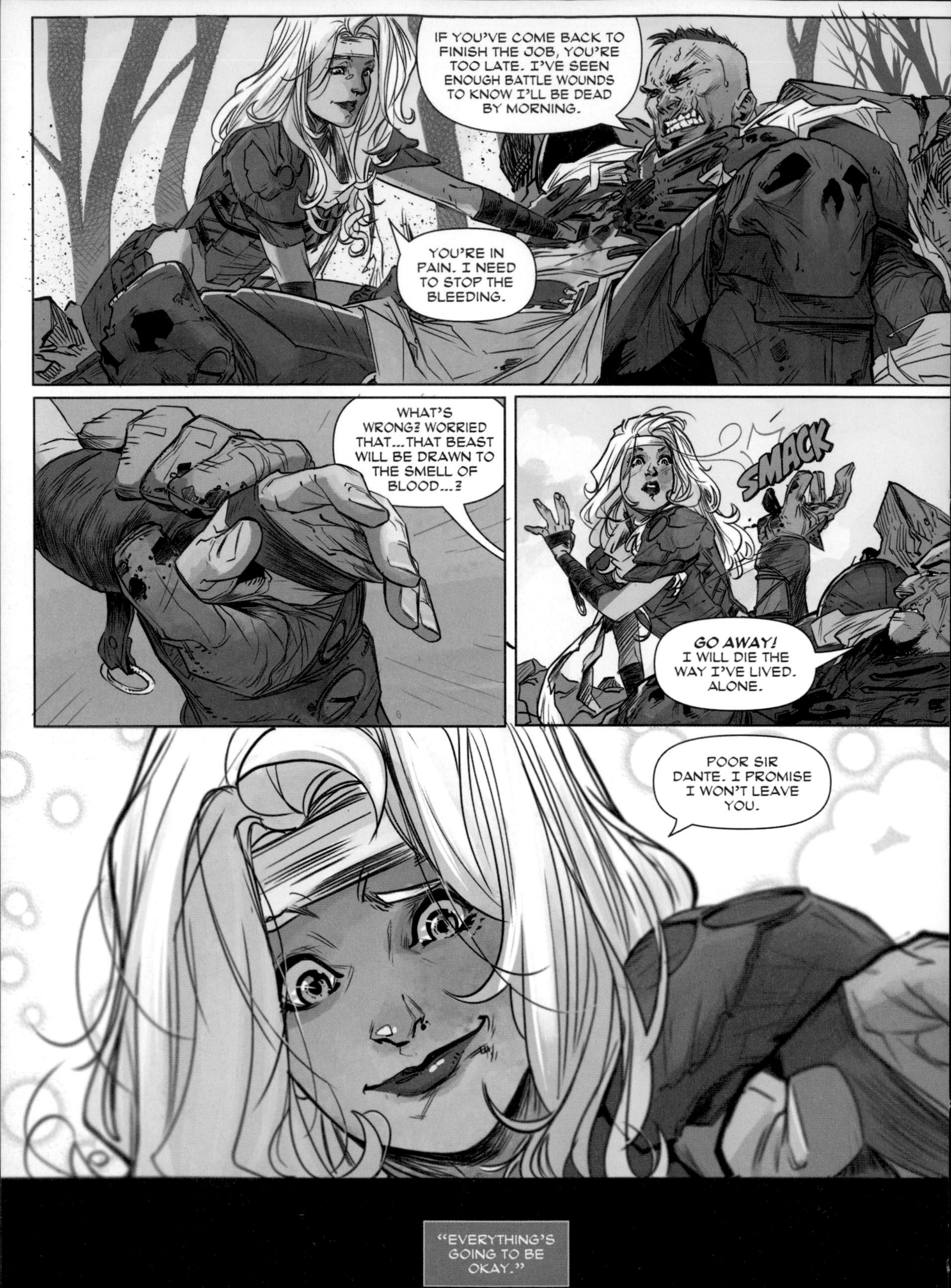
IF YOU'VE COME BACK TO FINISH THE JOB, YOU'RE TOO LATE. I'VE SEEN ENOUGH BATTLE WOUNDS TO KNOW I'LL BE DEAD BY MORNING.
YOU'RE IN PAIN. I NEED TO STOP THE BLEEDING.
WHAT'S WRONG? WORRIED THAT...THAT BEAST WILL BE DRAWN TO THE SMELL OF BLOOD...?
SMACK
GO AWAY! I WILL DIE THE WAY I'VE LIVED. ALONE.
POOR SIR DANTE. I PROMISE I WON'T LEAVE YOU.

"EVERYTHING'S GOING TO BE OKAY."

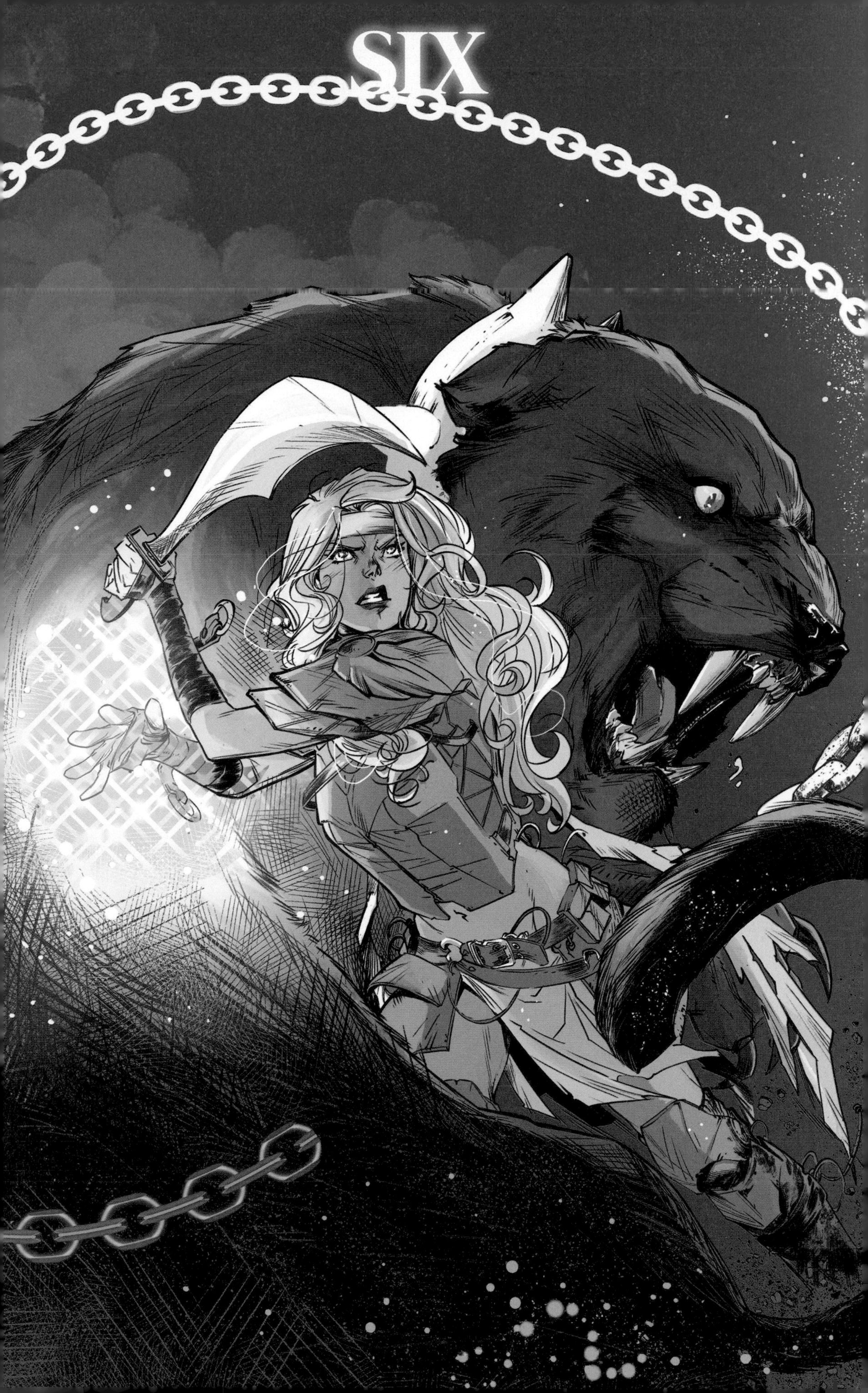
SIX

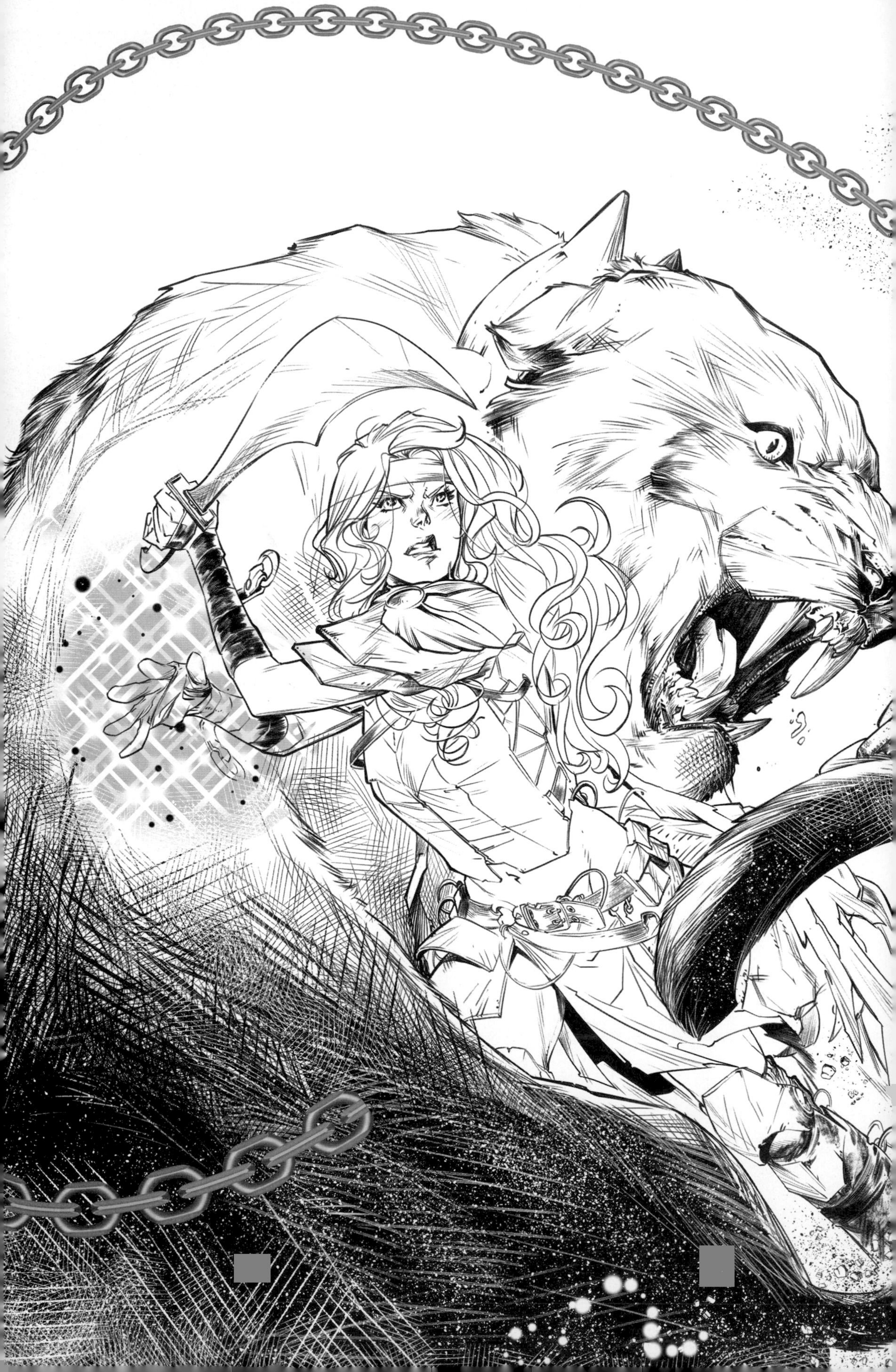

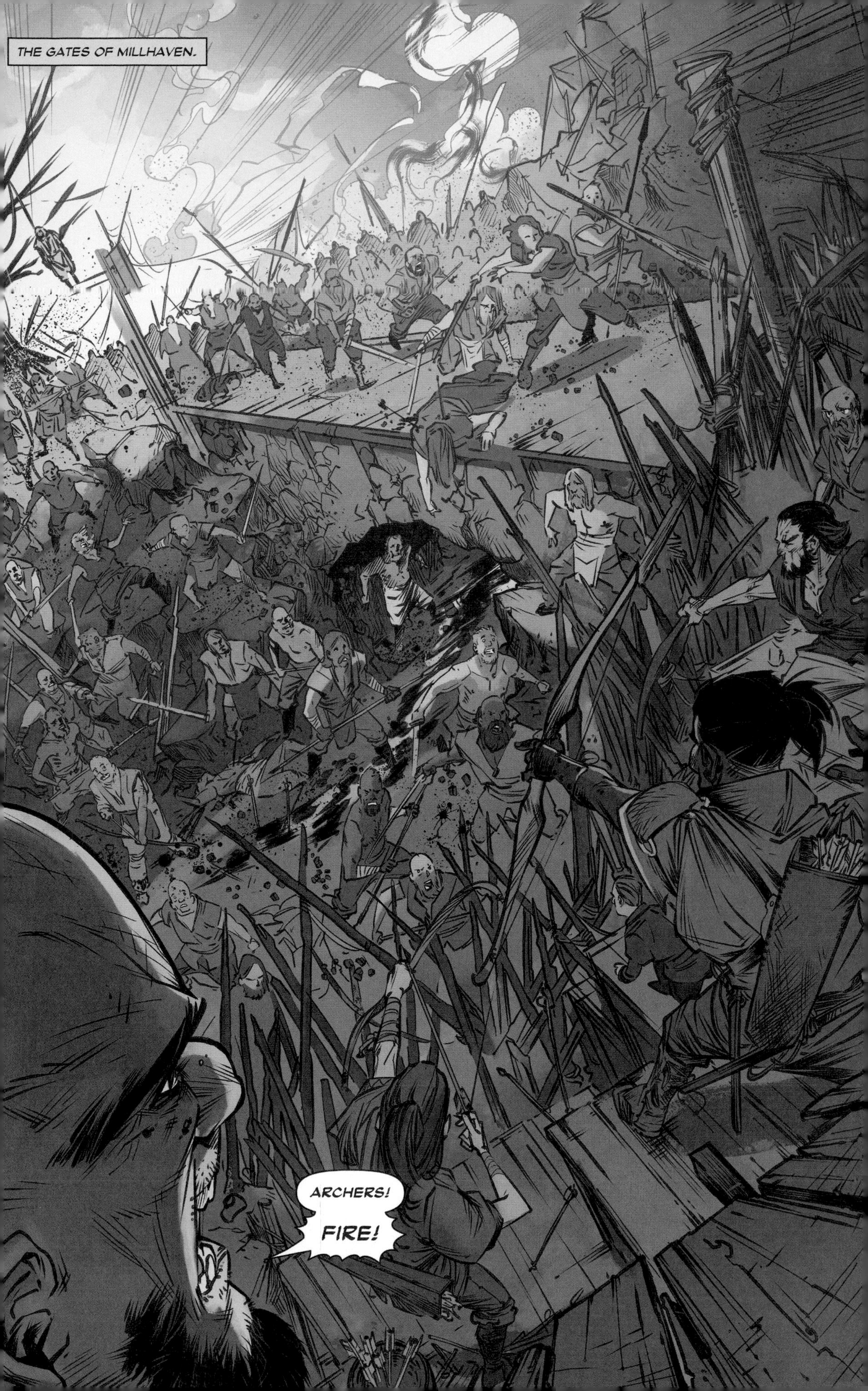
THE GATES OF MILLHAVEN.
ARCHERS!
FIRE!

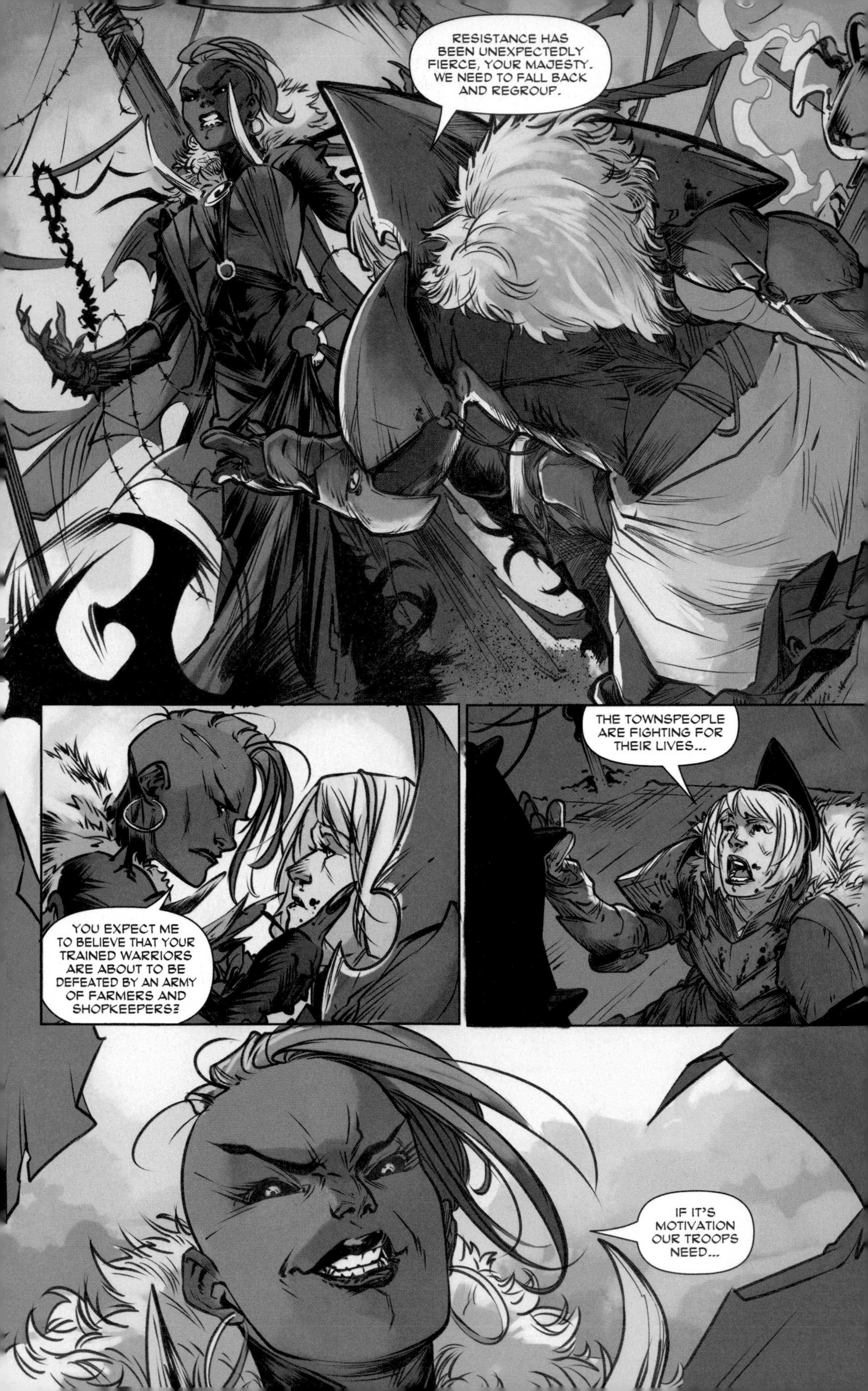
RESISTANCE HAS BEEN UNEXPECTEDLY FIERCE, YOUR MAJESTY. WE NEED TO FALL BACK AND REGROUP.
YOU EXPECT ME TO BELIEVE THAT YOUR TRAINED WARRIORS ARE ABOUT TO BE DEFEATED BY AN ARMY OF FARMERS AND SHOPKEEPERS?
THE TOWNSPEOPLE ARE FIGHTING FOR THEIR LIVES...
IF IT'S MOTIVATION OUR TROOPS NEED...

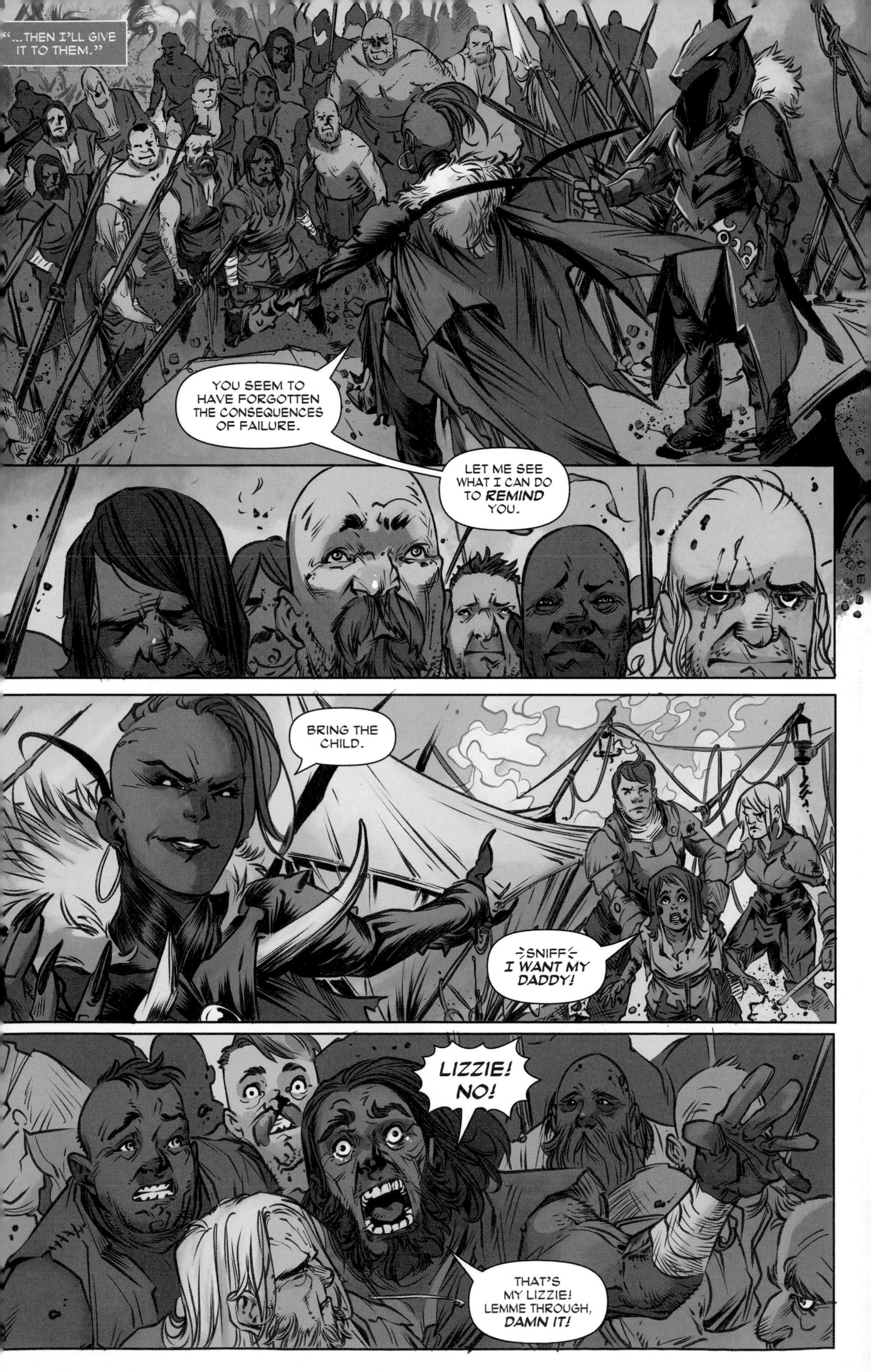
"...THEN I'LL GIVE IT TO THEM."
YOU SEEM TO HAVE FORGOTTEN THE CONSEQUENCES OF FAILURE.
LET ME SEE WHAT I CAN DO TO REMIND YOU.
BRING THE CHILD.
SNIFF I WANT MY DADDY!
LIZZIE! NO!
THAT'S MY LIZZIE! LEMME THROUGH, DAMN IT!

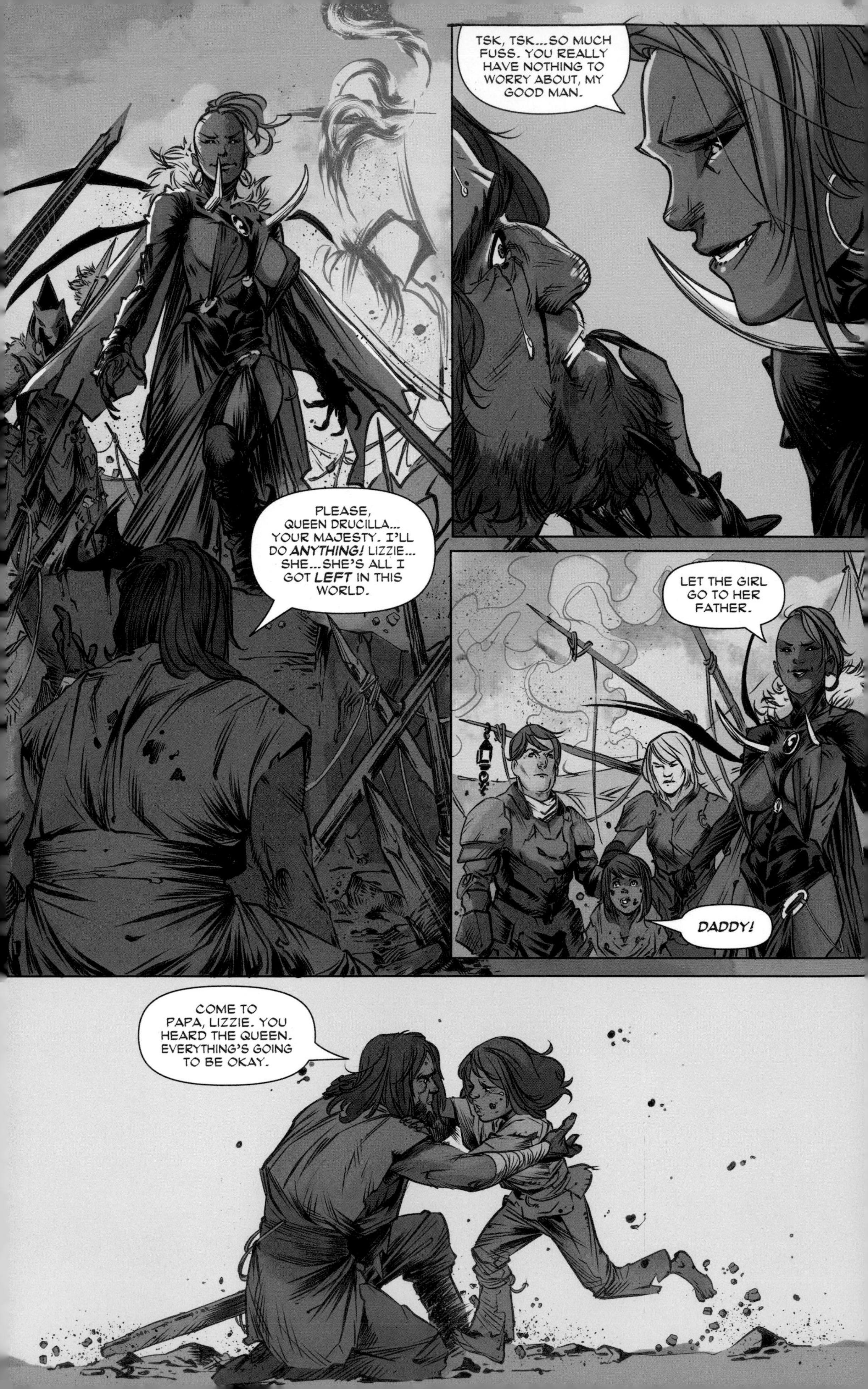
TSK, TSK...SO MUCH FUSS. YOU REALLY HAVE NOTHING TO WORRY ABOUT, MY GOOD MAN.
PLEASE, QUEEN DRUCILLA... YOUR MAJESTY. I'LL DO ANYTHING! LIZZIE... SHE...SHE'S ALL I GOT LEFT IN THIS WORLD.
LET THE GIRL GO TO HER FATHER.
DADDY!
COME TO PAPA, LIZZIE. YOU HEARD THE QUEEN. EVERYTHING'S GOING TO BE OKAY.

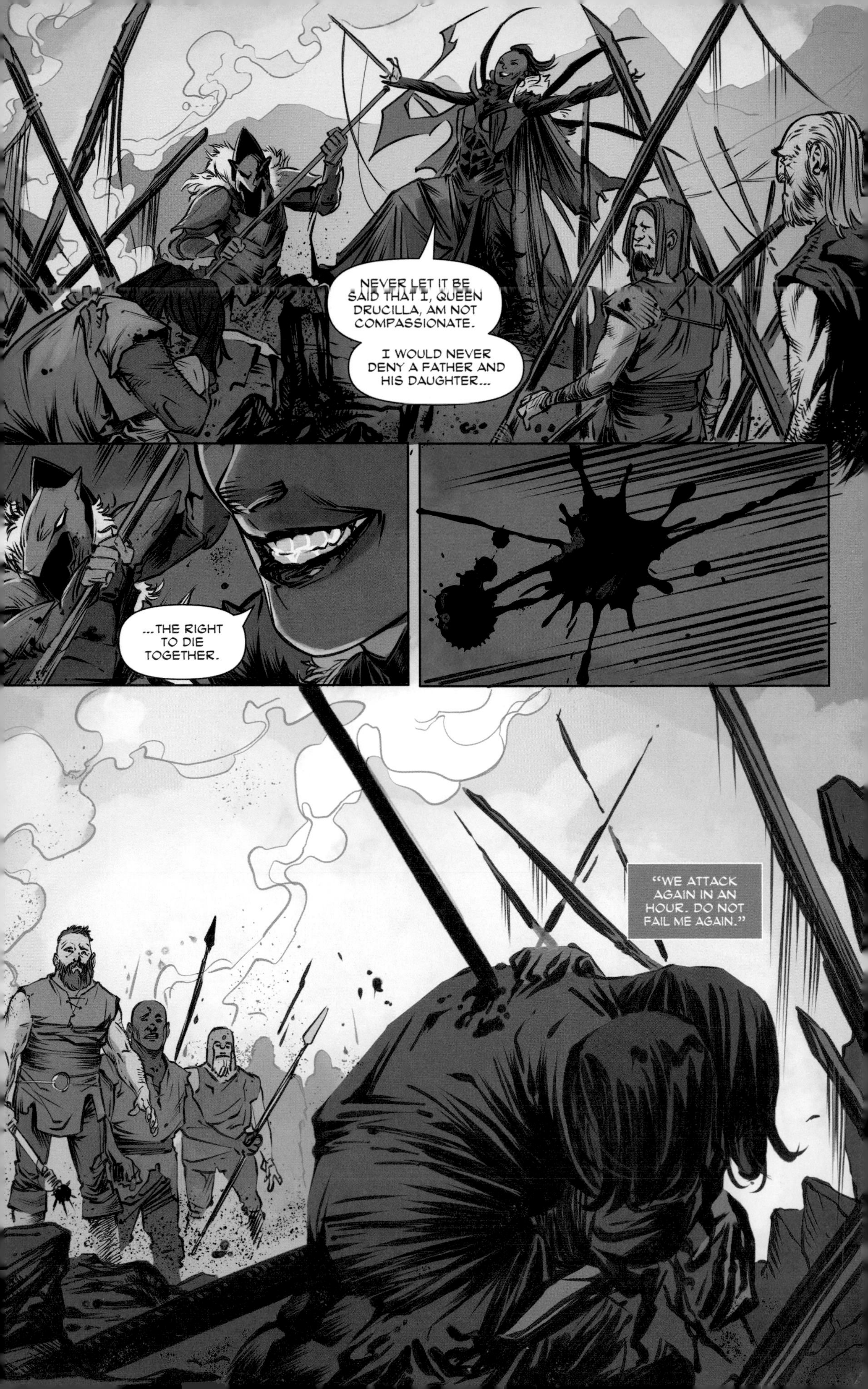
NEVER LET IT BE SAID THAT I, QUEEN DRUCILLA, AM NOT COMPASSIONATE.
I WOULD NEVER DENY A FATHER AND HIS DAUGHTER...
...THE RIGHT TO DIE TOGETHER.
"WE ATTACK AGAIN IN AN HOUR. DO NOT FAIL ME AGAIN."

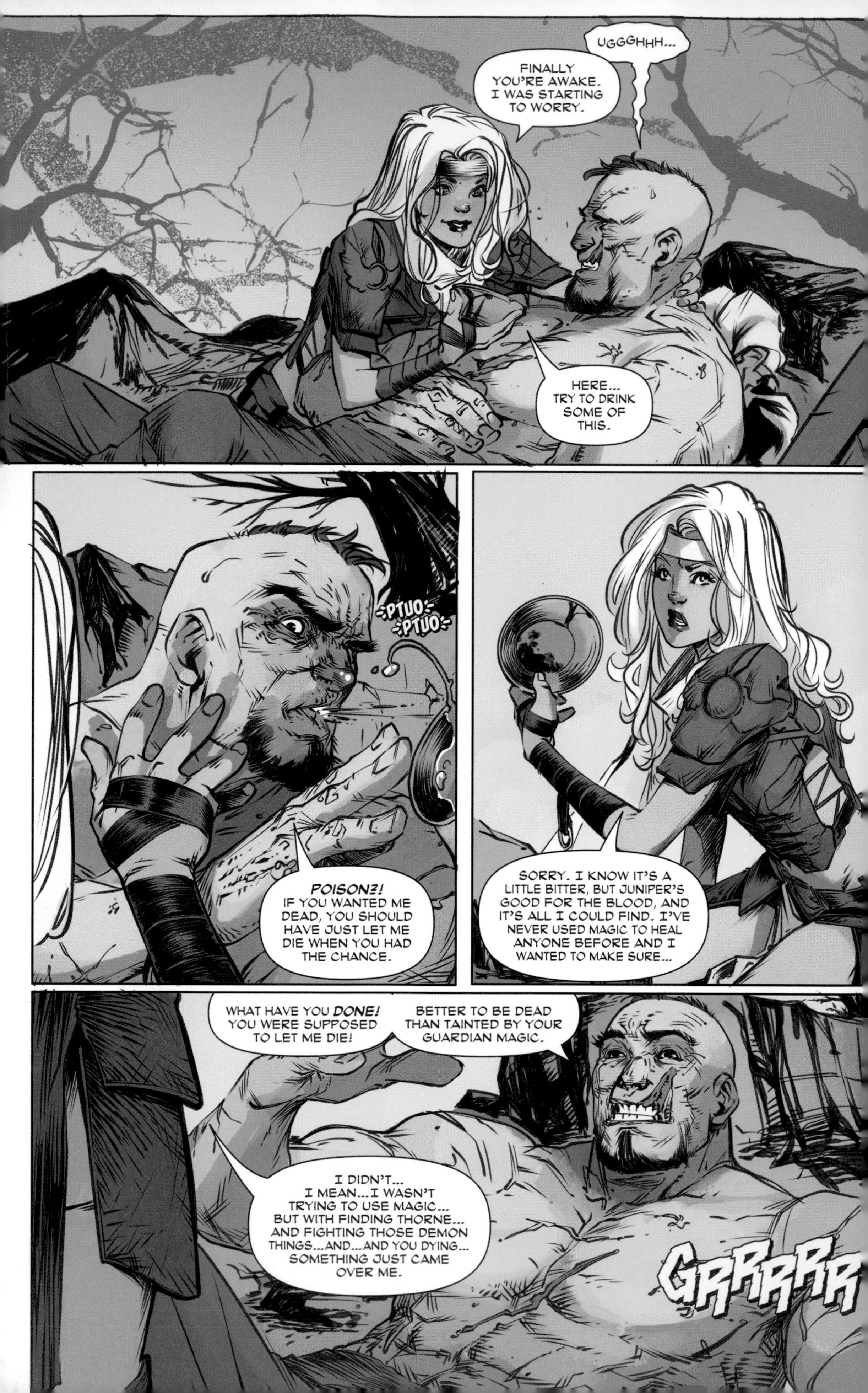
UGGGHHH...
FINALLY YOU'RE AWAKE. I WAS STARTING TO WORRY.
HERE... TRY TO DRINK SOME OF THIS.
PTUO PTUO
POISON?! IF YOU WANTED ME DEAD, YOU SHOULD HAVE JUST LET ME DIE WHEN YOU HAD THE CHANCE.
SORRY. I KNOW IT'S A LITTLE BITTER, BUT JUNIPER'S GOOD FOR THE BLOOD, AND IT'S ALL I COULD FIND. I'VE NEVER USED MAGIC TO HEAL ANYONE BEFORE AND I WANTED TO MAKE SURE...
WHAT HAVE YOU DONE! YOU WERE SUPPOSED TO LET ME DIE!
BETTER TO BE DEAD THAN TAINTED BY YOUR GUARDIAN MAGIC.
I DIDN'T... I MEAN...I WASN'T TRYING TO USE MAGIC... BUT WITH FINDING THORNE... AND FIGHTING THOSE DEMON THINGS...AND...AND YOU DYING... SOMETHING JUST CAME OVER ME.
GRRRRR

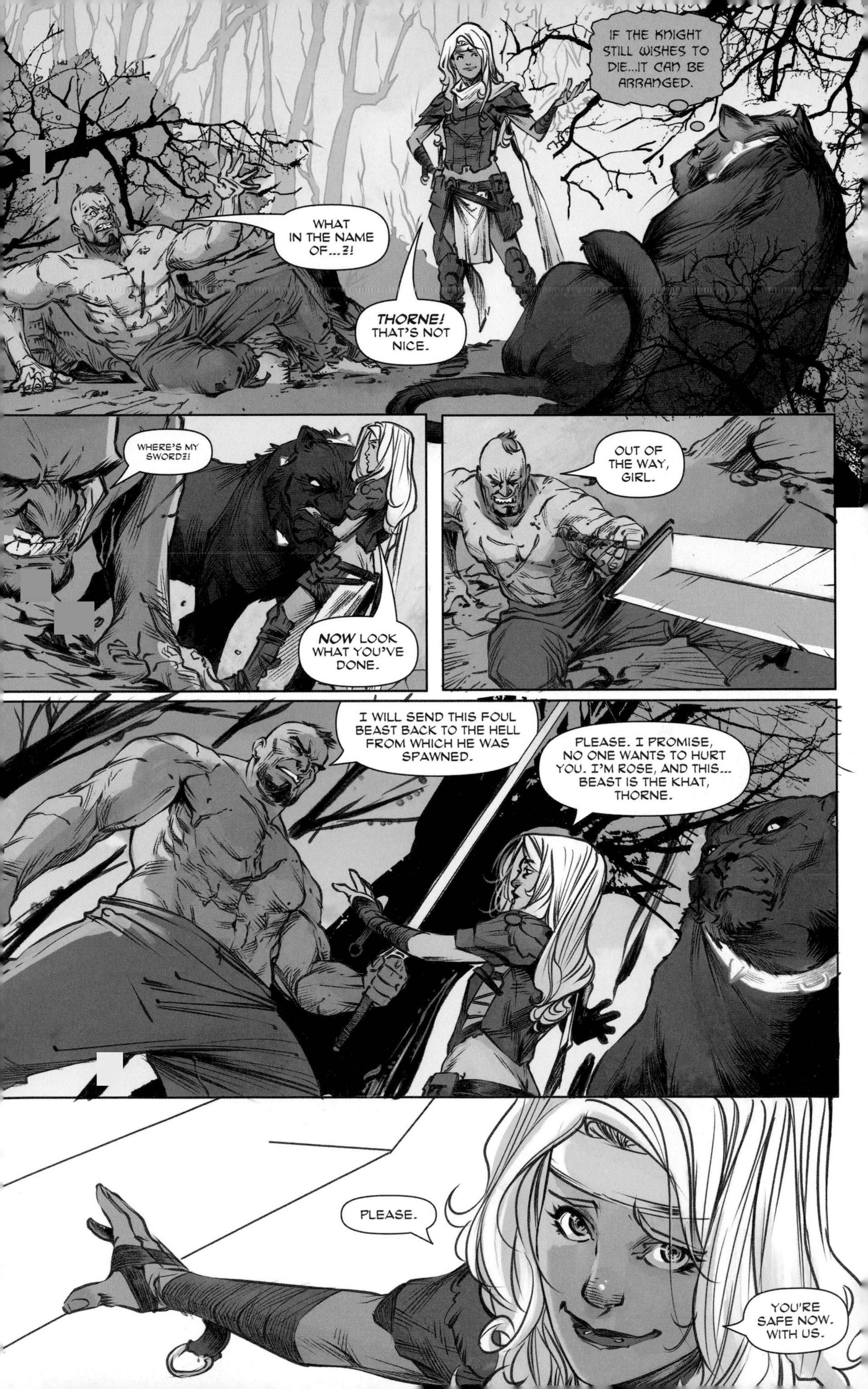
WHAT IN THE NAME OF...?!
IF THE KNIGHT STILL WISHES TO DIE...IT CAN BE ARRANGED.
THORNE! THAT'S NOT NICE.
WHERE'S MY SWORD?!
NOW LOOK WHAT YOU'VE DONE.
OUT OF THE WAY, GIRL.
I WILL SEND THIS FOUL BEAST BACK TO THE HELL FROM WHICH HE WAS SPAWNED.
PLEASE. I PROMISE, NO ONE WANTS TO HURT YOU. I'M ROSE, AND THIS... BEAST IS THE KHAT, THORNE.
PLEASE.
YOU'RE SAFE NOW. WITH US.

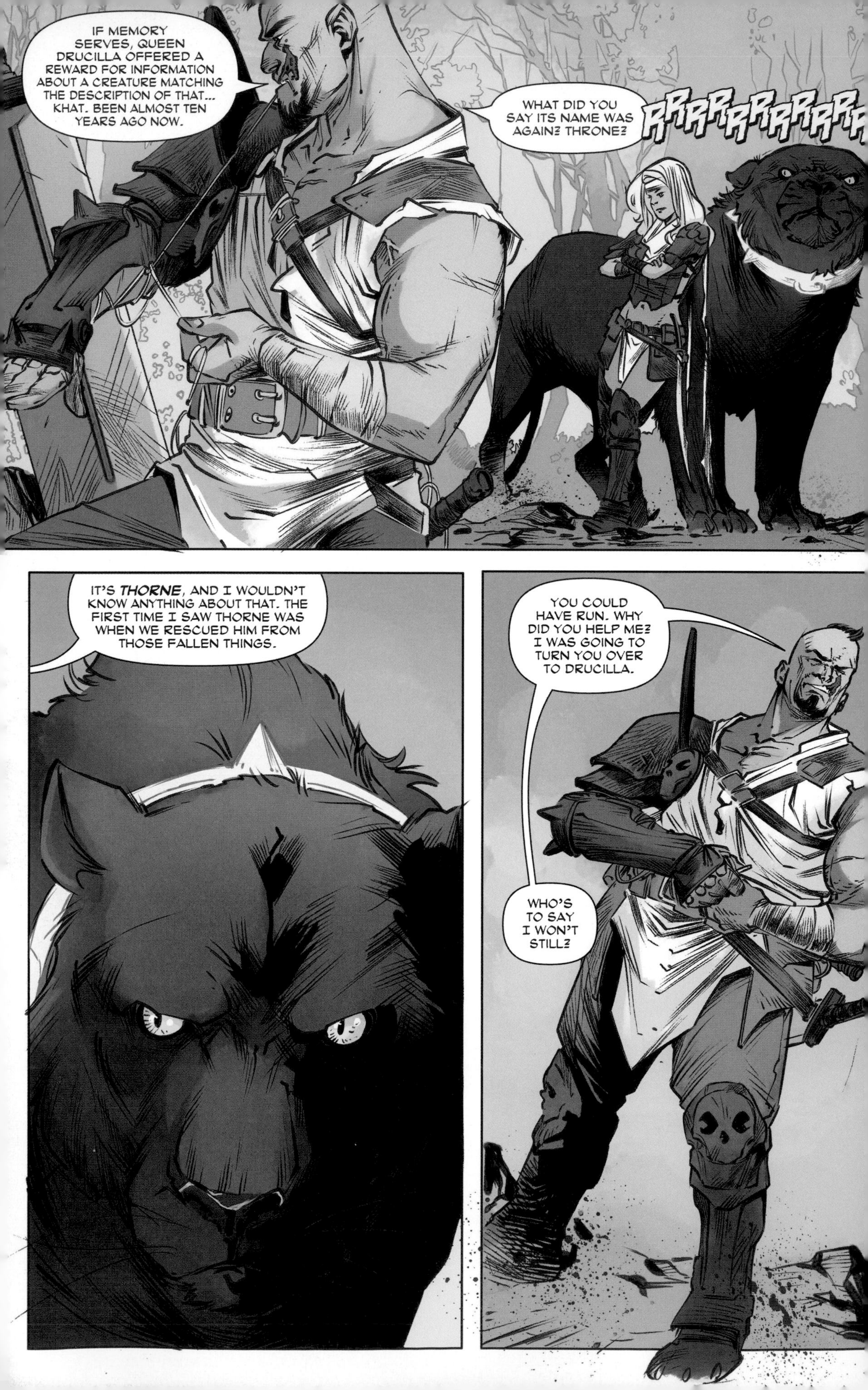
IF MEMORY SERVES, QUEEN DRUCILLA OFFERED A REWARD FOR INFORMATION ABOUT A CREATURE MATCHING THE DESCRIPTION OF THAT... KHAT. BEEN ALMOST TEN YEARS AGO NOW.
WHAT DID YOU SAY ITS NAME WAS AGAIN? THRONE?
RRRRRRRRRRRR
IT'S *THORNE*, AND I WOULDN'T KNOW ANYTHING ABOUT THAT. THE FIRST TIME I SAW THORNE WAS WHEN WE RESCUED HIM FROM THOSE FALLEN THINGS.
YOU COULD HAVE RUN. WHY DID YOU HELP ME? I WAS GOING TO TURN YOU OVER TO DRUCILLA.
WHO'S TO SAY I WON'T STILL?

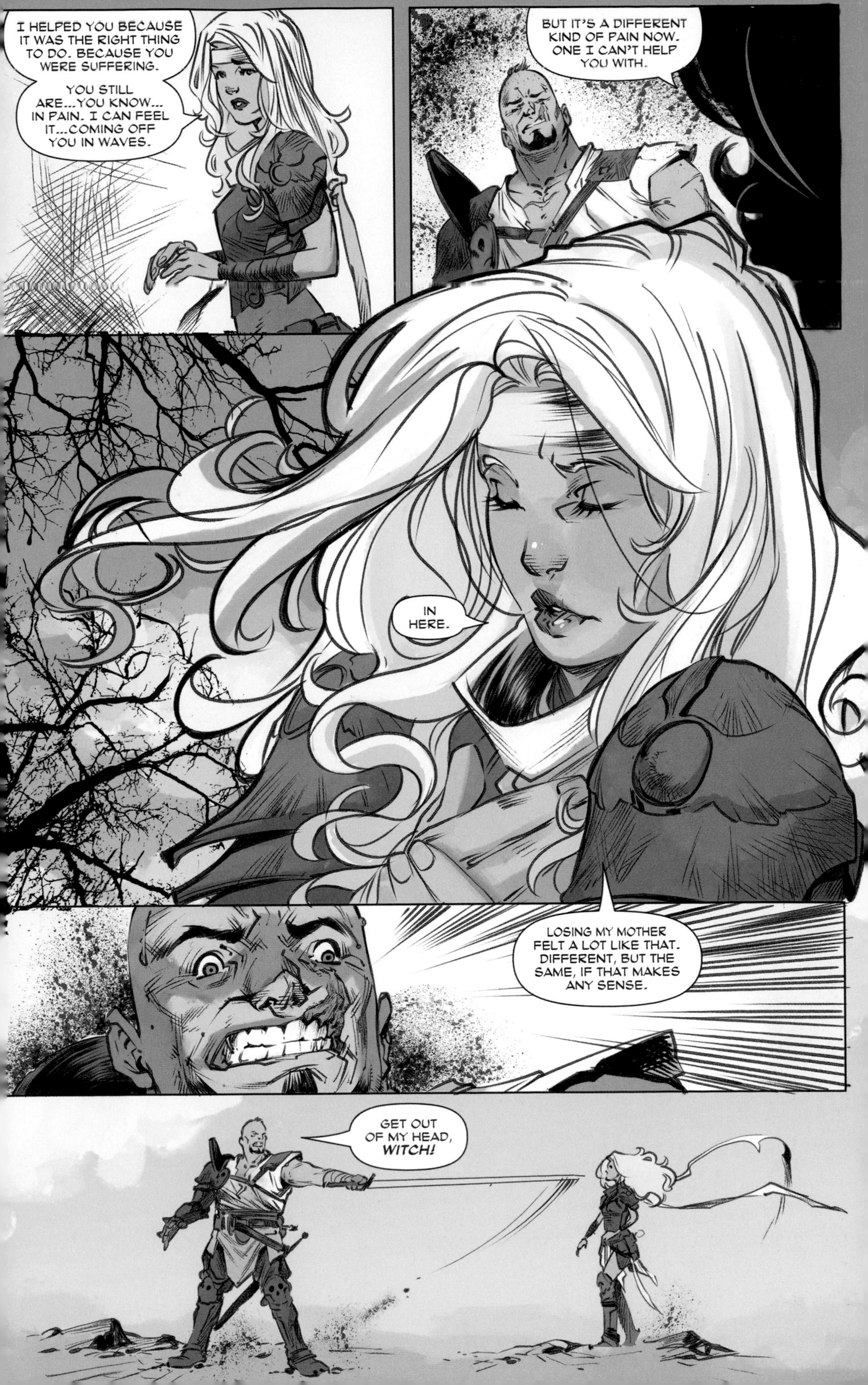
I HELPED YOU BECAUSE IT WAS THE RIGHT THING TO DO. BECAUSE YOU WERE SUFFERING.
YOU STILL ARE...YOU KNOW... IN PAIN. I CAN FEEL IT...COMING OFF YOU IN WAVES.
BUT IT'S A DIFFERENT KIND OF PAIN NOW. ONE I CAN'T HELP YOU WITH.
IN HERE.
LOSING MY MOTHER FELT A LOT LIKE THAT. DIFFERENT, BUT THE SAME, IF THAT MAKES ANY SENSE.
GET OUT OF MY HEAD, *WITCH!*

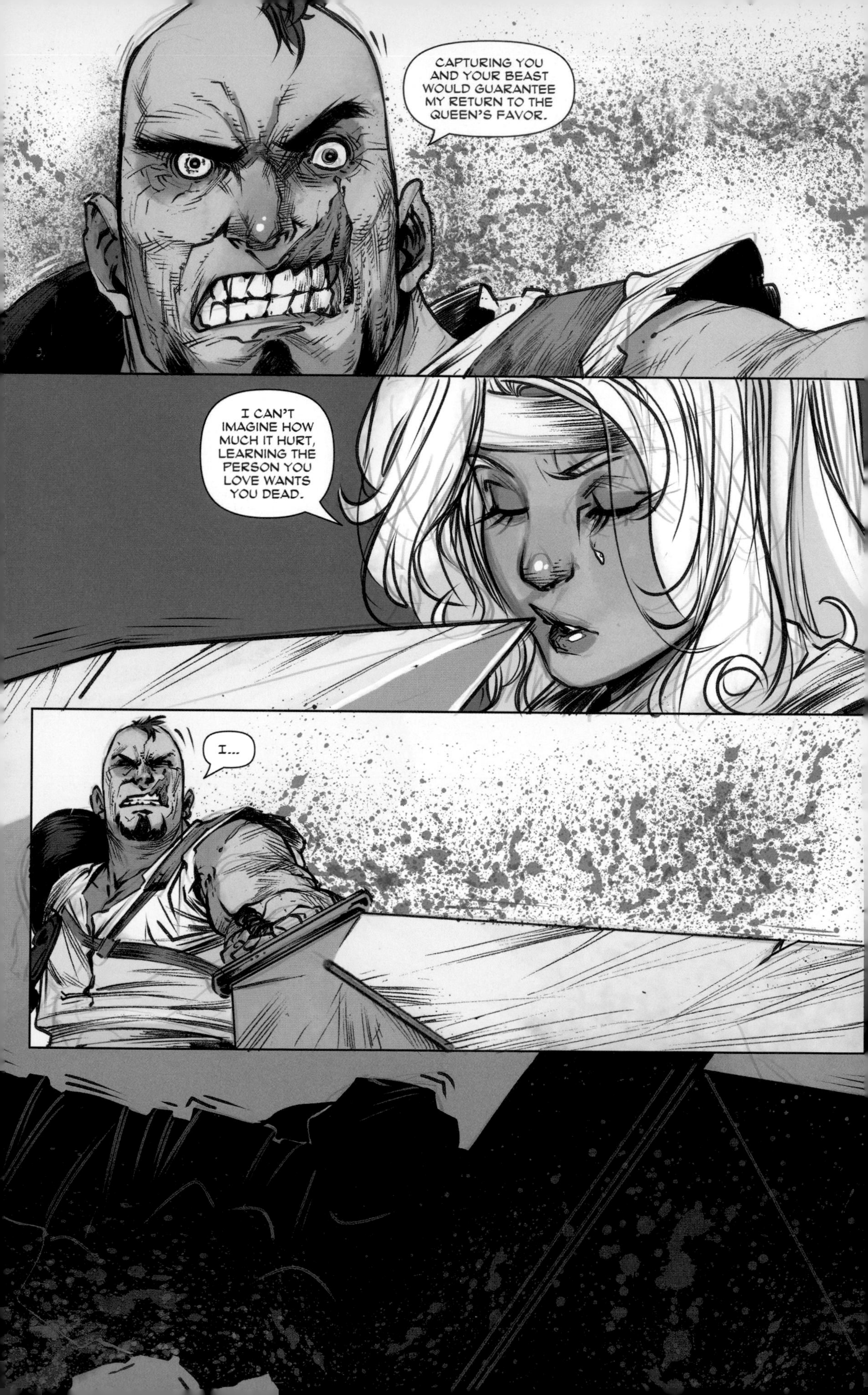
CAPTURING YOU AND YOUR BEAST WOULD GUARANTEE MY RETURN TO THE QUEEN'S FAVOR.
I CAN'T IMAGINE HOW MUCH IT HURT, LEARNING THE PERSON YOU LOVE WANTS YOU DEAD.
I...

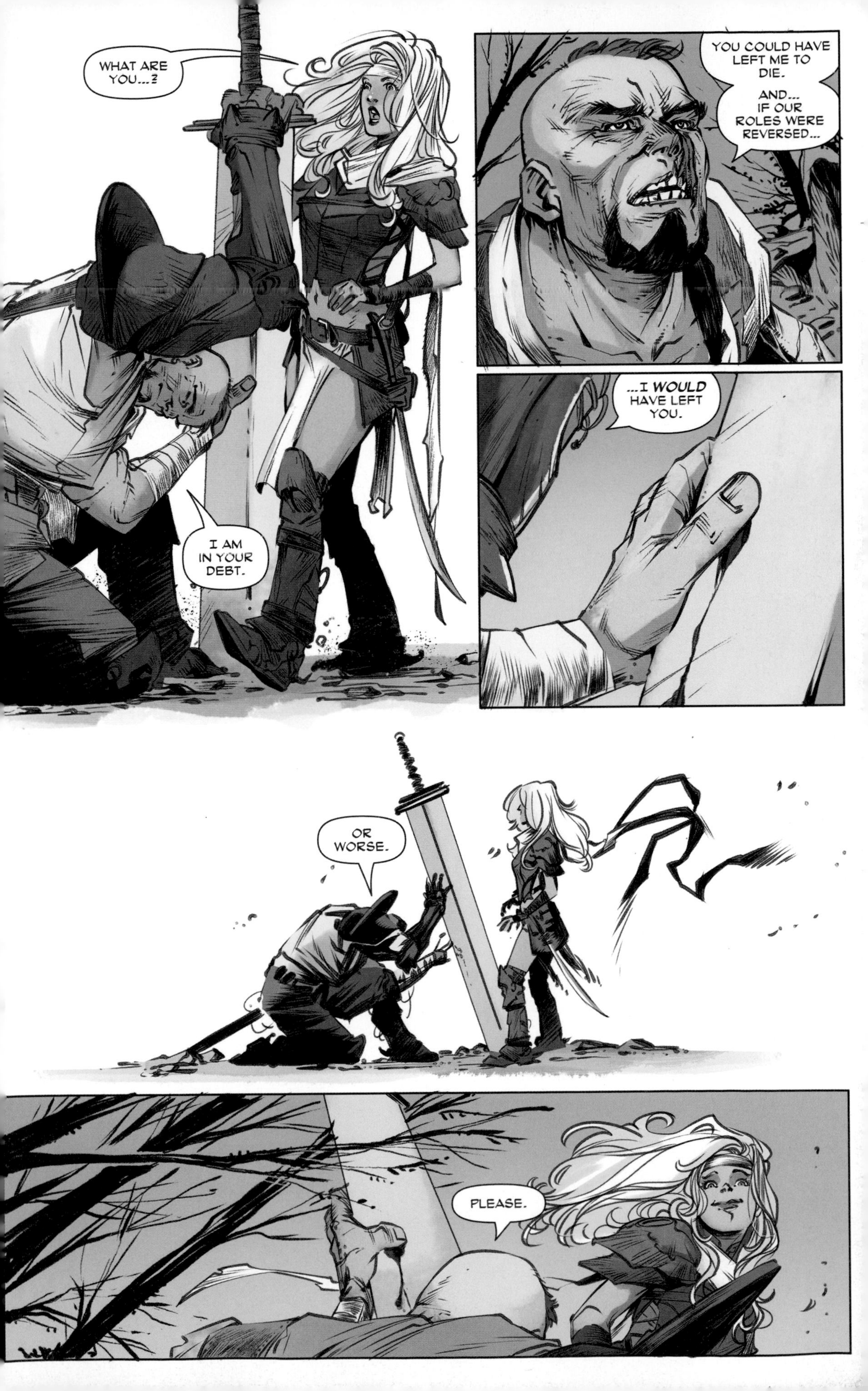
WHAT ARE YOU...?
I AM IN YOUR DEBT.
YOU COULD HAVE LEFT ME TO DIE.
AND... IF OUR ROLES WERE REVERSED...
...I WOULD HAVE LEFT YOU.
OR WORSE.
PLEASE.

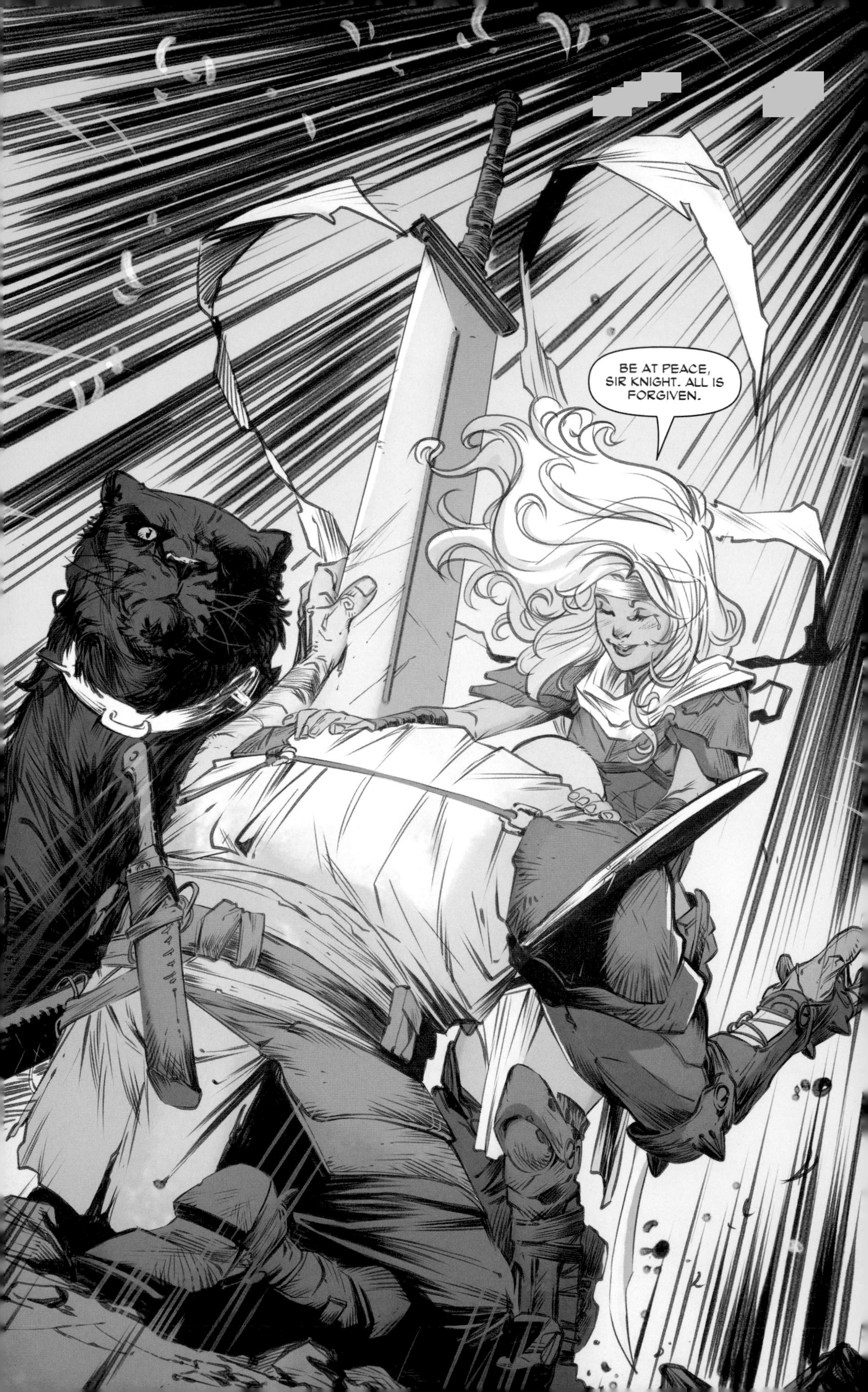
BE AT PEACE, SIR KNIGHT. ALL IS FORGIVEN.

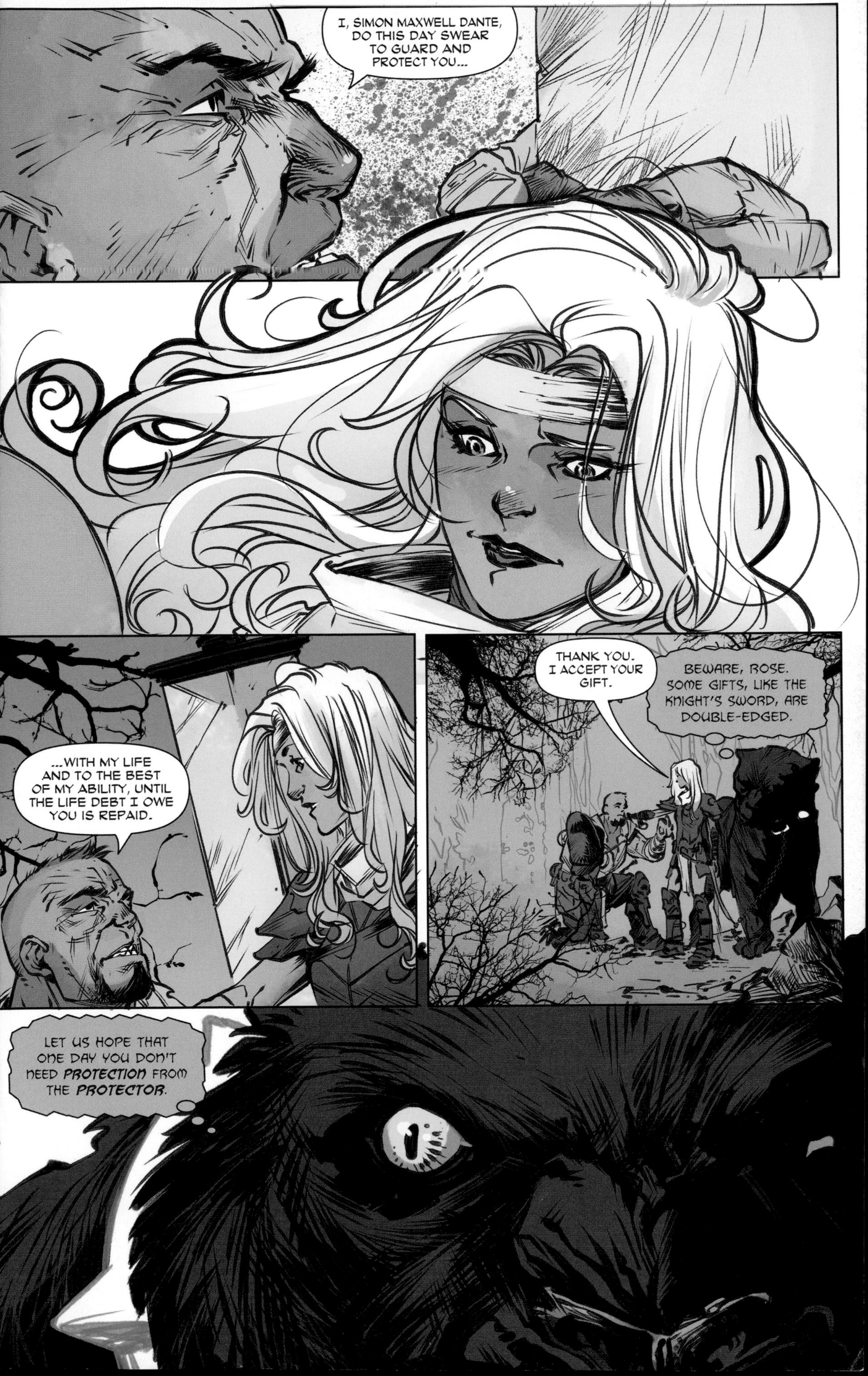
I, SIMON MAXWELL DANTE, DO THIS DAY SWEAR TO GUARD AND PROTECT YOU...
...WITH MY LIFE AND TO THE BEST OF MY ABILITY, UNTIL THE LIFE DEBT I OWE YOU IS REPAID.
THANK YOU. I ACCEPT YOUR GIFT.
BEWARE, ROSE. SOME GIFTS, LIKE THE KNIGHT'S SWORD, ARE DOUBLE-EDGED.
LET US HOPE THAT ONE DAY YOU DON'T NEED PROTECTION FROM THE PROTECTOR.

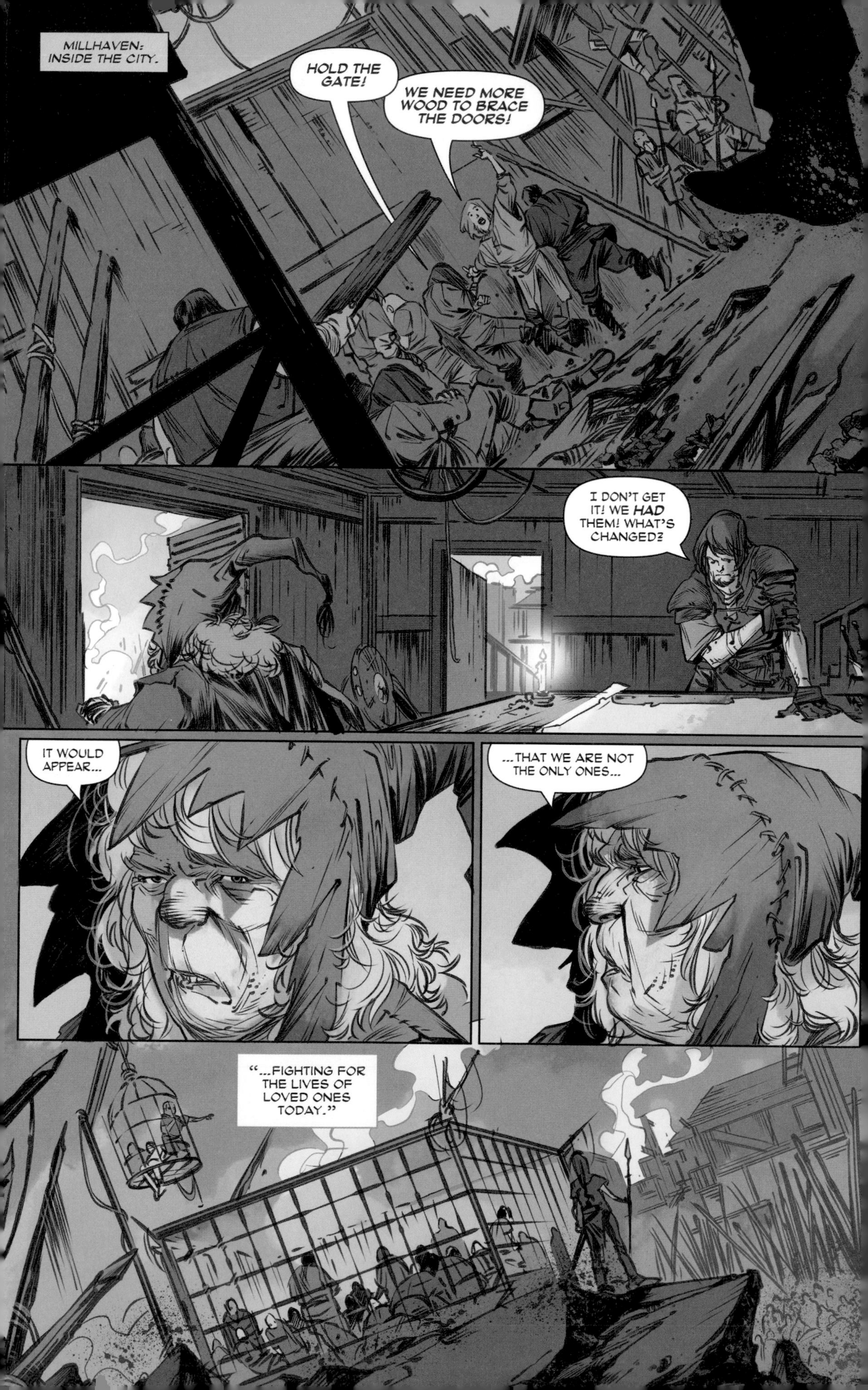
MILLHAVEN: INSIDE THE CITY.
HOLD THE GATE!
WE NEED MORE WOOD TO BRACE THE DOORS!
I DON'T GET IT! WE *HAD* THEM! WHAT'S CHANGED?
IT WOULD APPEAR...
...THAT WE ARE NOT THE ONLY ONES...
"...FIGHTING FOR THE LIVES OF LOVED ONES TODAY."

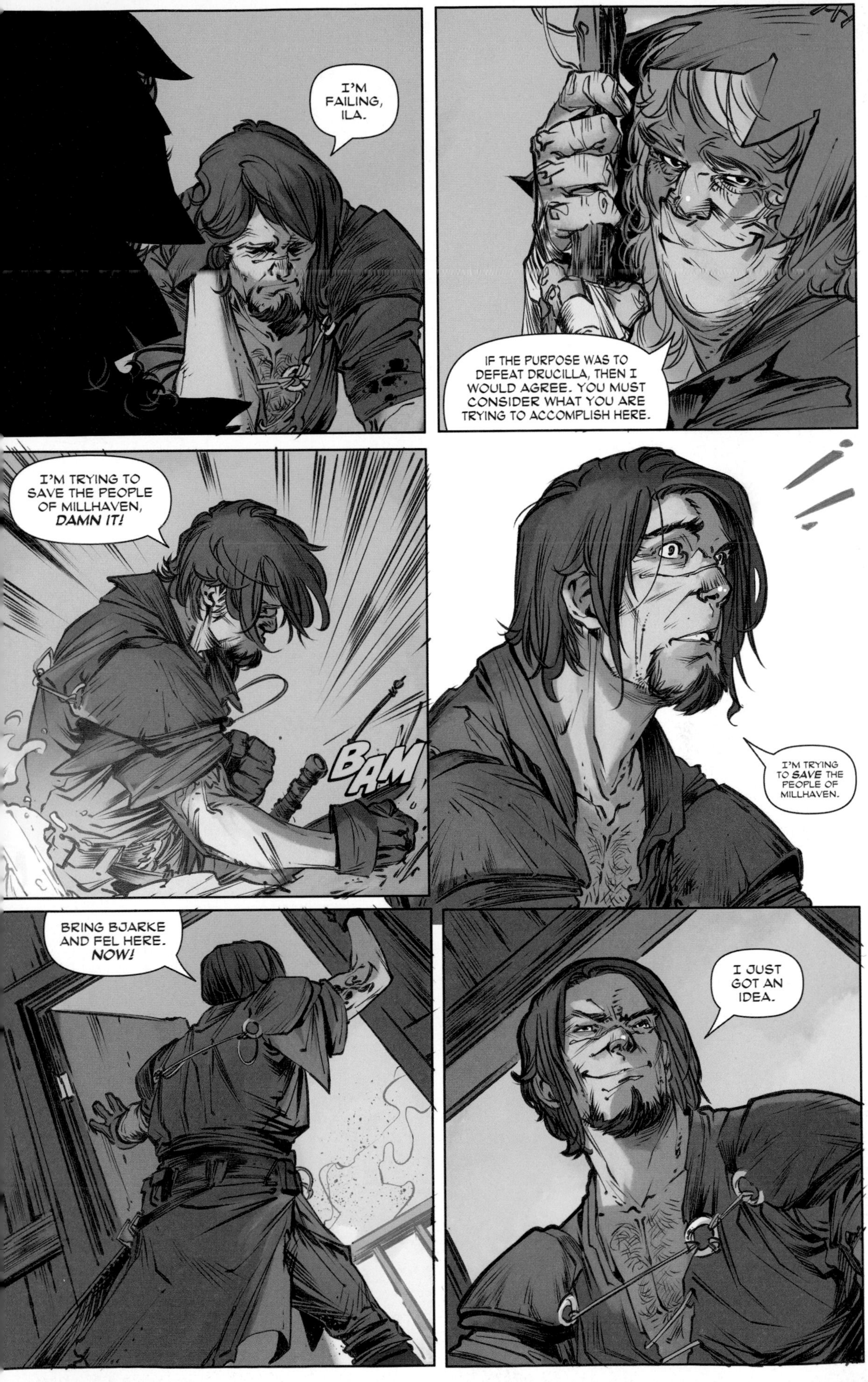
I'M FAILING, ILA.
IF THE PURPOSE WAS TO DEFEAT DRUCILLA, THEN I WOULD AGREE. YOU MUST CONSIDER WHAT YOU ARE TRYING TO ACCOMPLISH HERE.
I'M TRYING TO SAVE THE PEOPLE OF MILLHAVEN, DAMN IT!
BAM
I'M TRYING TO SAVE THE PEOPLE OF MILLHAVEN.
BRING BJARKE AND FEL HERE. NOW!
I JUST GOT AN IDEA.

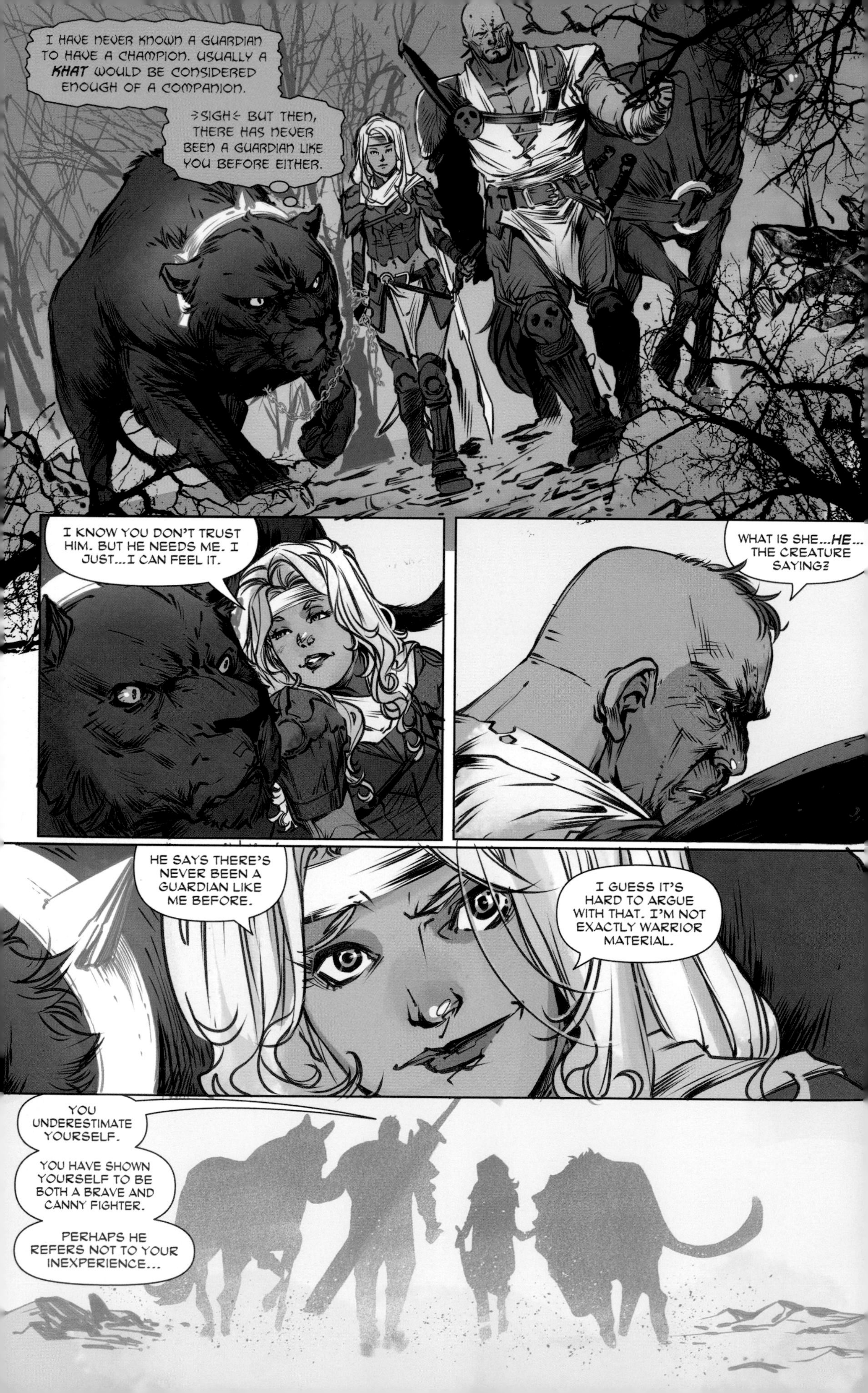
I HAVE NEVER KNOWN A GUARDIAN TO HAVE A CHAMPION. USUALLY A KHAT WOULD BE CONSIDERED ENOUGH OF A COMPANION.
>SIGH< BUT THEN, THERE HAS NEVER BEEN A GUARDIAN LIKE YOU BEFORE EITHER.
I KNOW YOU DON'T TRUST HIM. BUT HE NEEDS ME. I JUST...I CAN FEEL IT.
WHAT IS SHE...HE... THE CREATURE SAYING?
HE SAYS THERE'S NEVER BEEN A GUARDIAN LIKE ME BEFORE.
I GUESS IT'S HARD TO ARGUE WITH THAT. I'M NOT EXACTLY WARRIOR MATERIAL.
YOU UNDERESTIMATE YOURSELF.
YOU HAVE SHOWN YOURSELF TO BE BOTH A BRAVE AND CANNY FIGHTER.
PERHAPS HE REFERS NOT TO YOUR INEXPERIENCE...

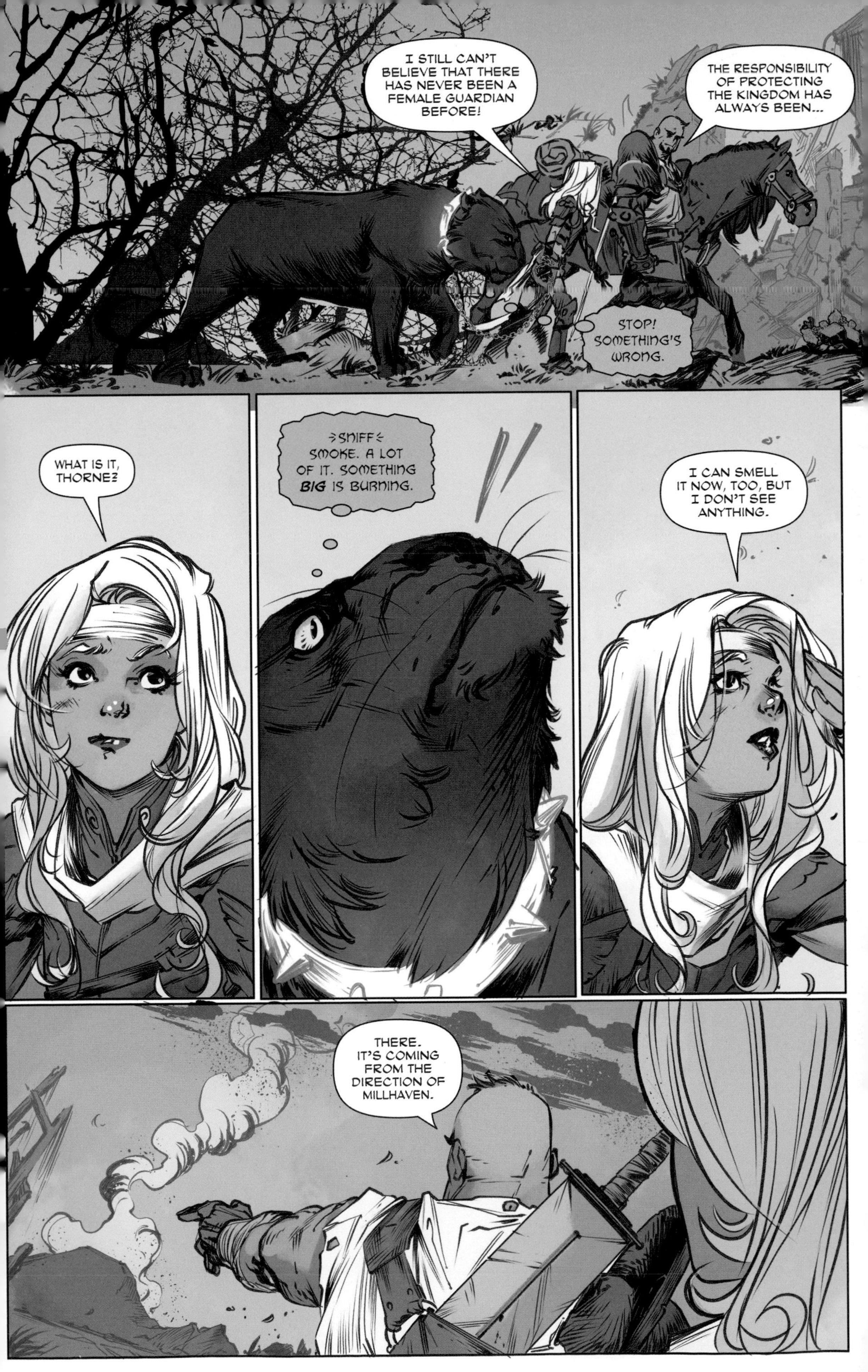
I STILL CAN'T BELIEVE THAT THERE HAS NEVER BEEN A FEMALE GUARDIAN BEFORE!
THE RESPONSIBILITY OF PROTECTING THE KINGDOM HAS ALWAYS BEEN...
STOP! SOMETHING'S WRONG.
WHAT IS IT, THORNE?
≶SNIFF≷ SMOKE. A LOT OF IT. SOMETHING BIG IS BURNING.
I CAN SMELL IT NOW, TOO, BUT I DON'T SEE ANYTHING.
THERE. IT'S COMING FROM THE DIRECTION OF MILLHAVEN.

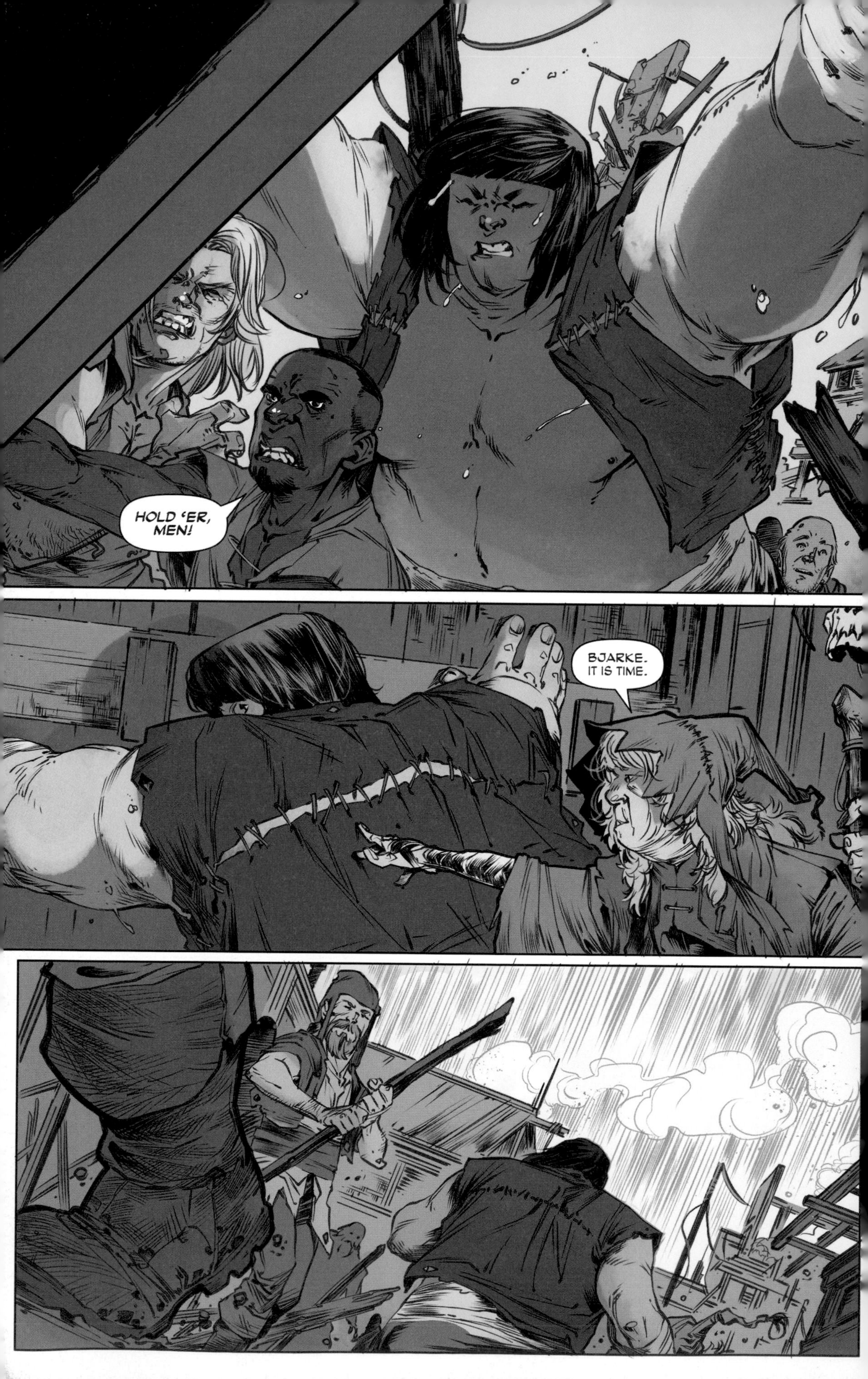
HOLD 'ER, MEN!
BJARKE. IT IS TIME.

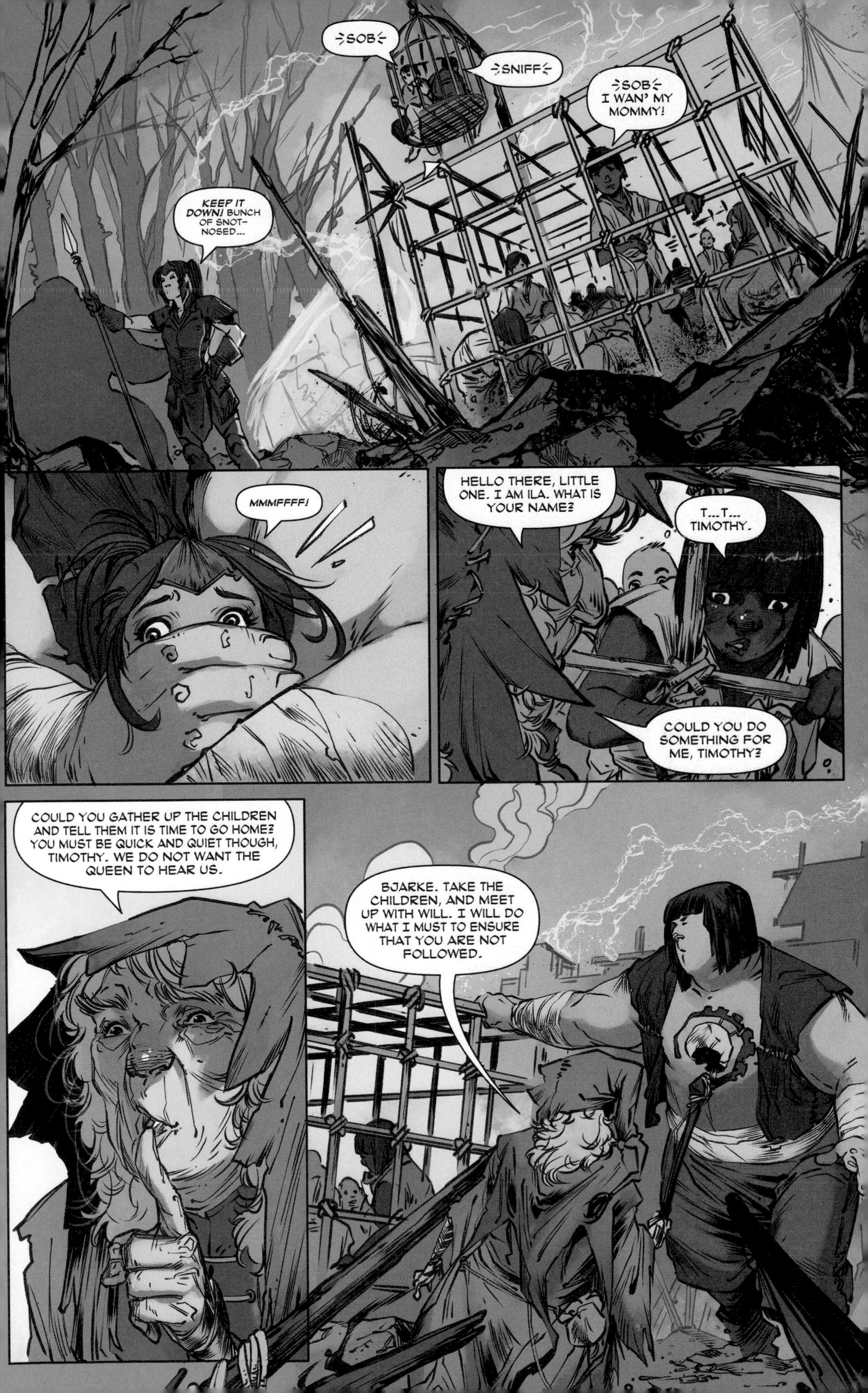

SOB
SNIFF
SOB I WAN' MY MOMMY!
KEEP IT DOWN! BUNCH OF SNOT-NOSED...
MMMFFFF!
HELLO THERE, LITTLE ONE. I AM ILA. WHAT IS YOUR NAME?
T...T... TIMOTHY.
COULD YOU DO SOMETHING FOR ME, TIMOTHY?
COULD YOU GATHER UP THE CHILDREN AND TELL THEM IT IS TIME TO GO HOME? YOU MUST BE QUICK AND QUIET THOUGH, TIMOTHY. WE DO NOT WANT THE QUEEN TO HEAR US.
BJARKE. TAKE THE CHILDREN, AND MEET UP WITH WILL. I WILL DO WHAT I MUST TO ENSURE THAT YOU ARE NOT FOLLOWED.

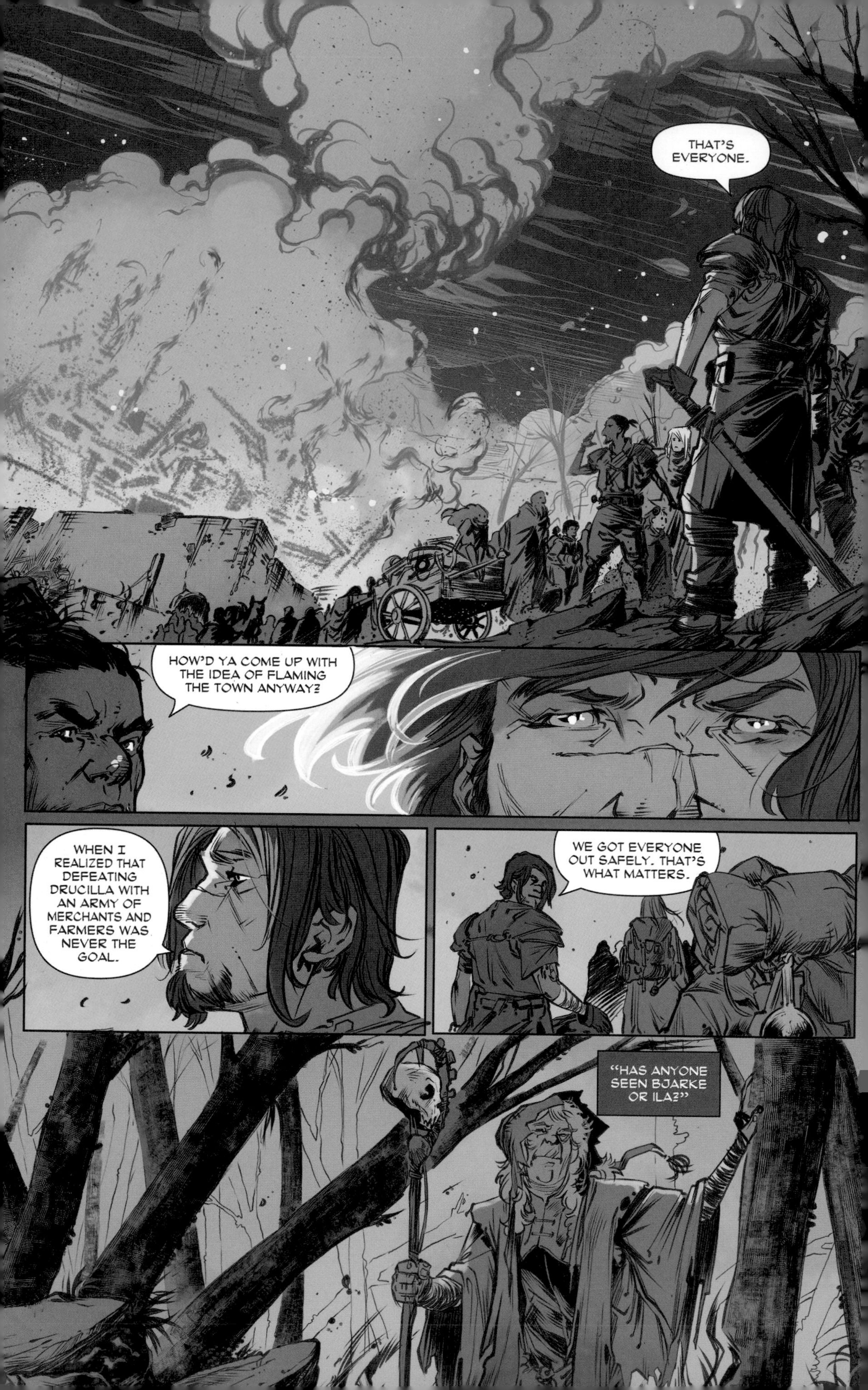
THAT'S EVERYONE.
HOW'D YA COME UP WITH THE IDEA OF FLAMING THE TOWN ANYWAY?
WHEN I REALIZED THAT DEFEATING DRUCILLA WITH AN ARMY OF MERCHANTS AND FARMERS WAS NEVER THE GOAL.
WE GOT EVERYONE OUT SAFELY. THAT'S WHAT MATTERS.
"HAS ANYONE SEEN BJARKE OR ILA?"

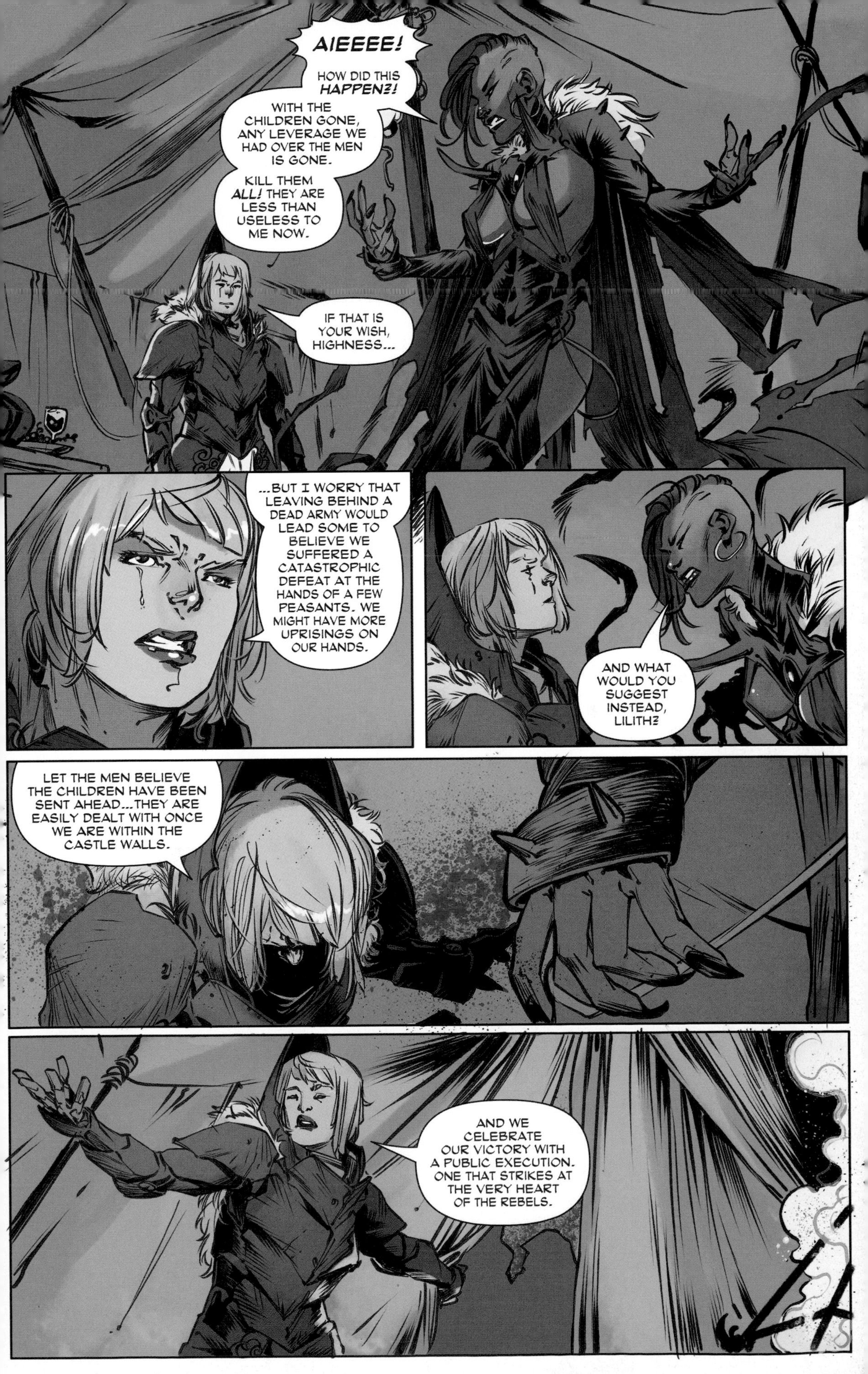
AIEEEE!
HOW DID THIS HAPPEN?!
WITH THE CHILDREN GONE, ANY LEVERAGE WE HAD OVER THE MEN IS GONE.
KILL THEM ALL! THEY ARE LESS THAN USELESS TO ME NOW.
IF THAT IS YOUR WISH, HIGHNESS...
...BUT I WORRY THAT LEAVING BEHIND A DEAD ARMY WOULD LEAD SOME TO BELIEVE WE SUFFERED A CATASTROPHIC DEFEAT AT THE HANDS OF A FEW PEASANTS. WE MIGHT HAVE MORE UPRISINGS ON OUR HANDS.
AND WHAT WOULD YOU SUGGEST INSTEAD, LILITH?
LET THE MEN BELIEVE THE CHILDREN HAVE BEEN SENT AHEAD...THEY ARE EASILY DEALT WITH ONCE WE ARE WITHIN THE CASTLE WALLS.
AND WE CELEBRATE OUR VICTORY WITH A PUBLIC EXECUTION. ONE THAT STRIKES AT THE VERY HEART OF THE REBELS.

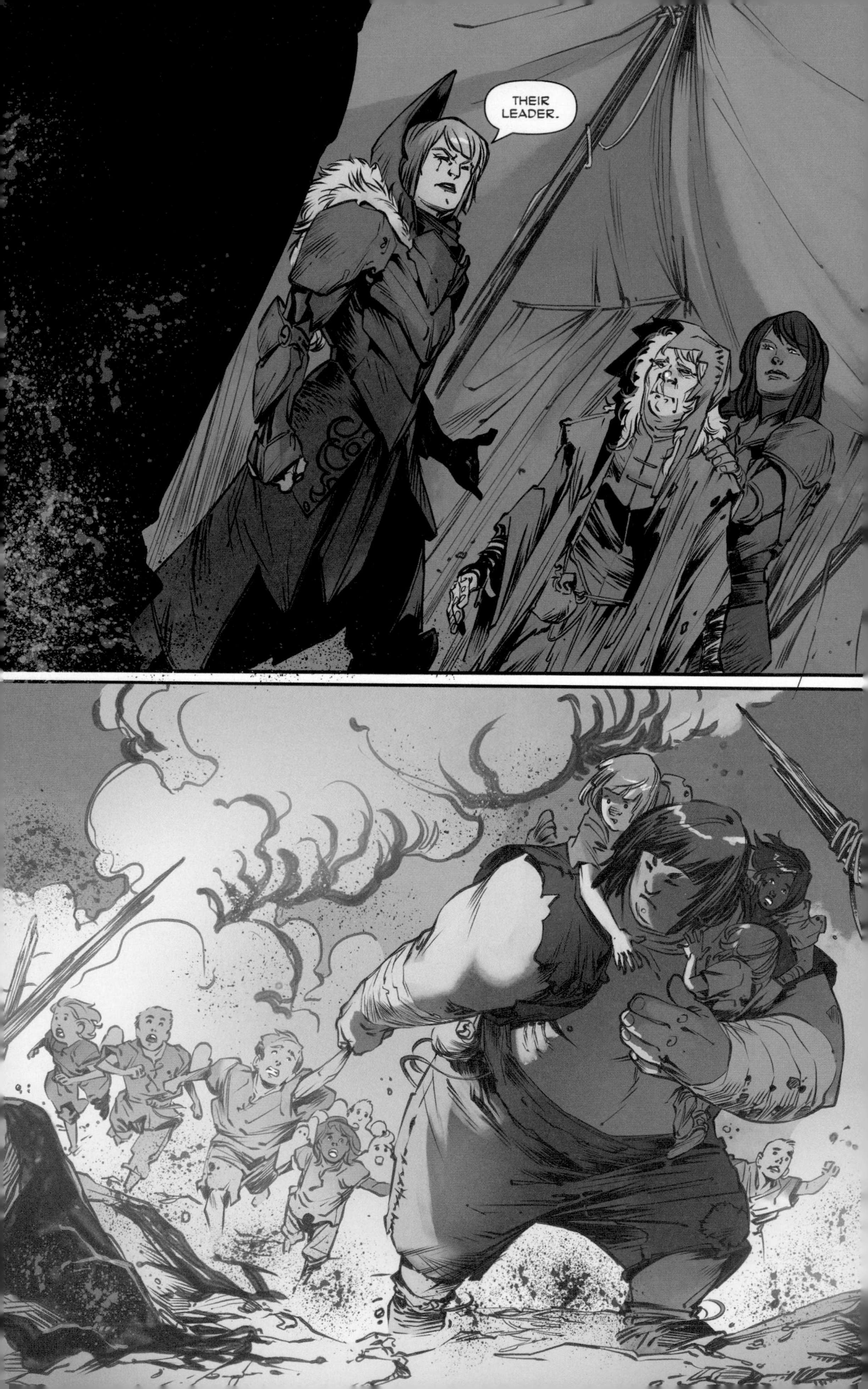
THEIR LEADER.

Cover Gallery

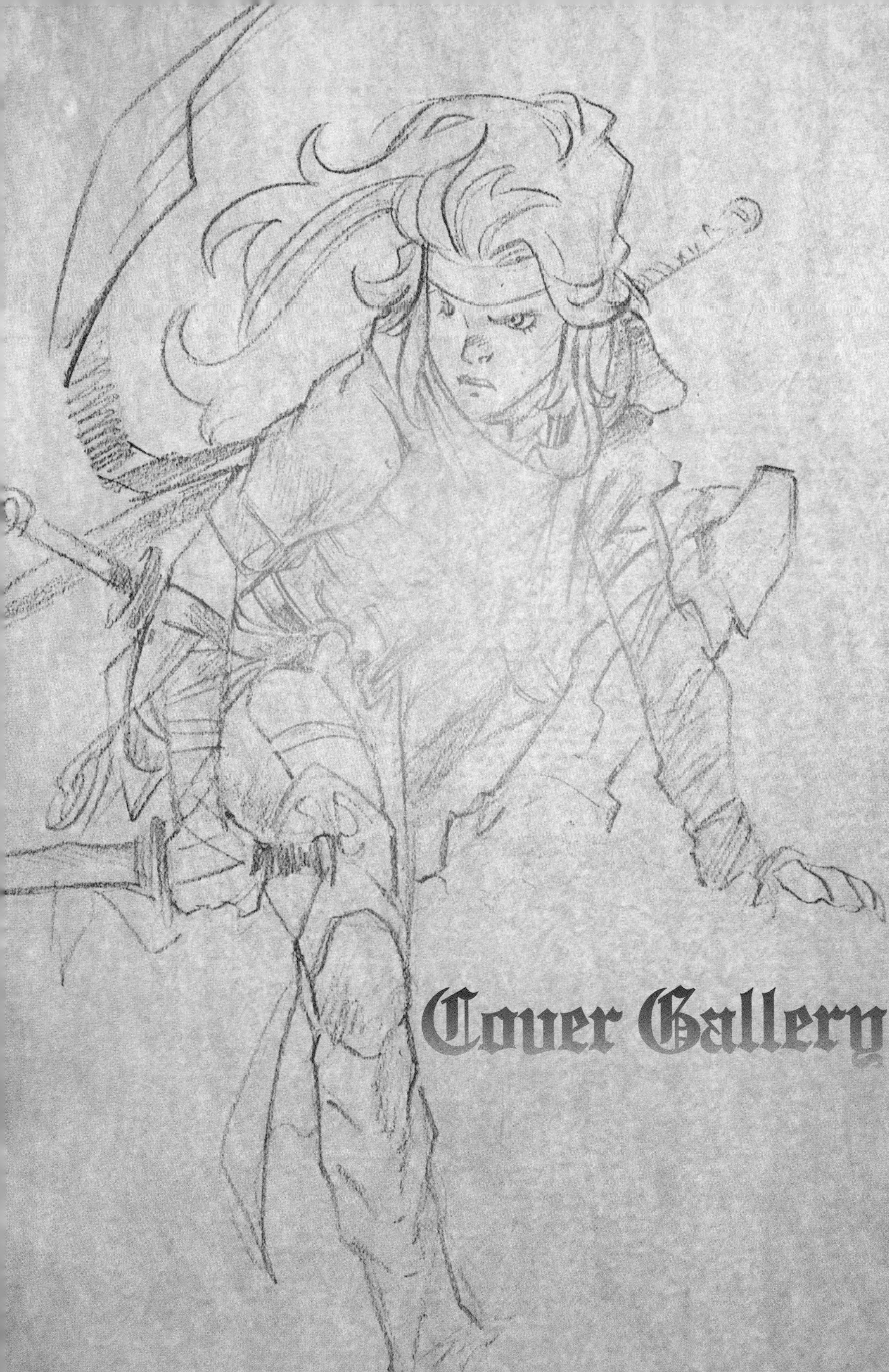

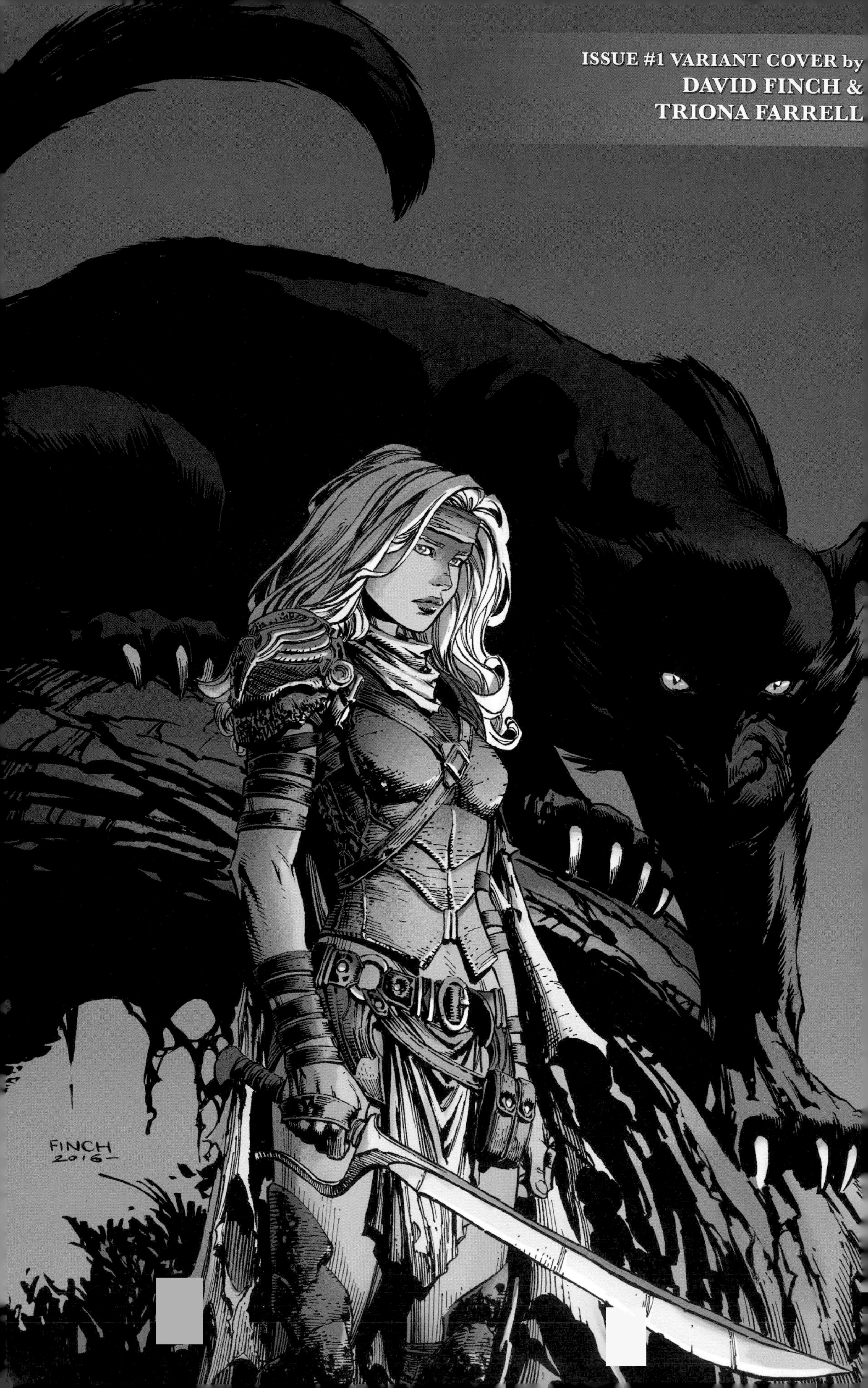
FINCH
2016-

ISSUE #1 VARIANT COVER by
DAVID FINCH &
TRIONA FARRELL

ISSUE #1 VARIANT COVER by
IG GUARA &
TRIONA FARRELL

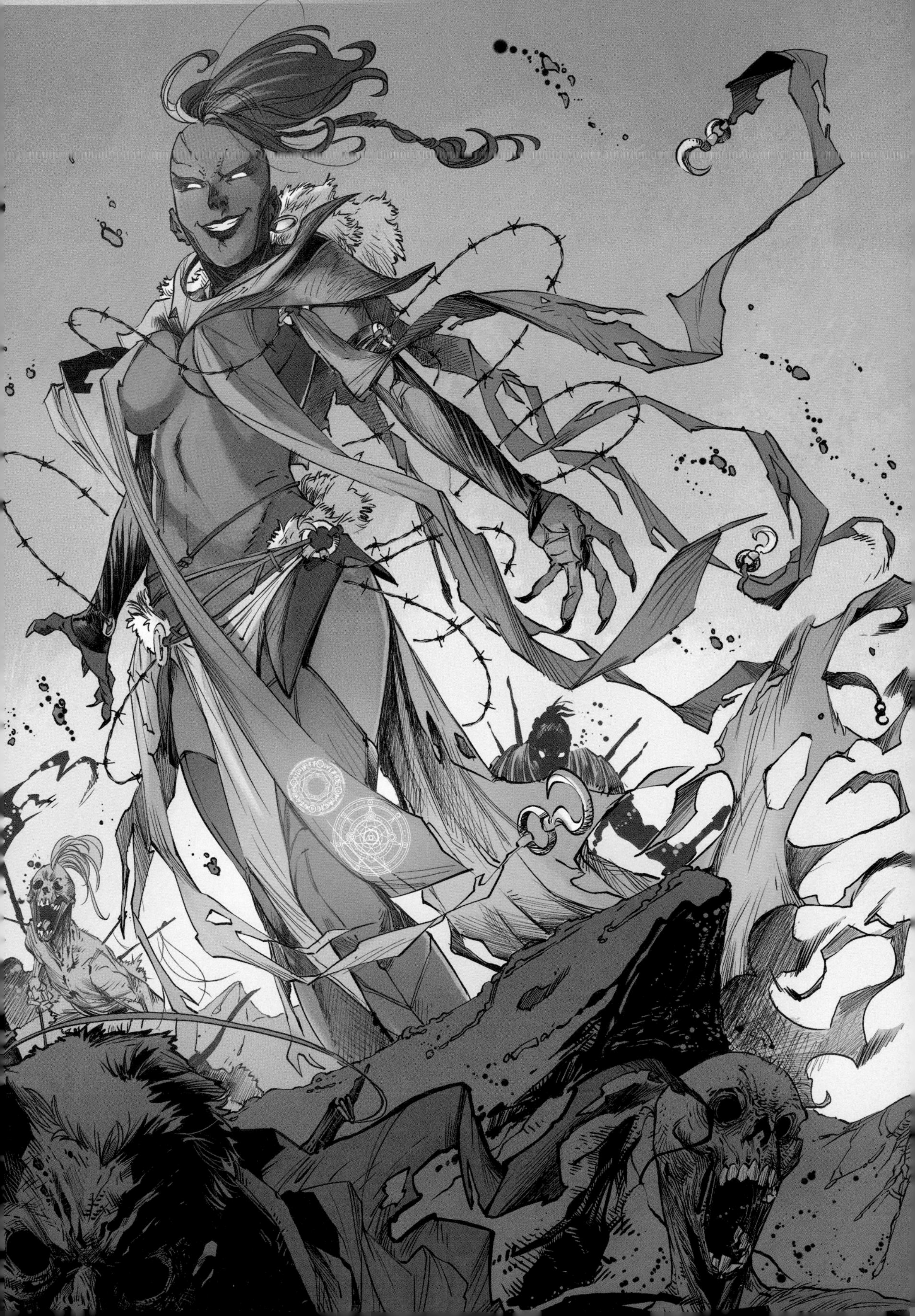

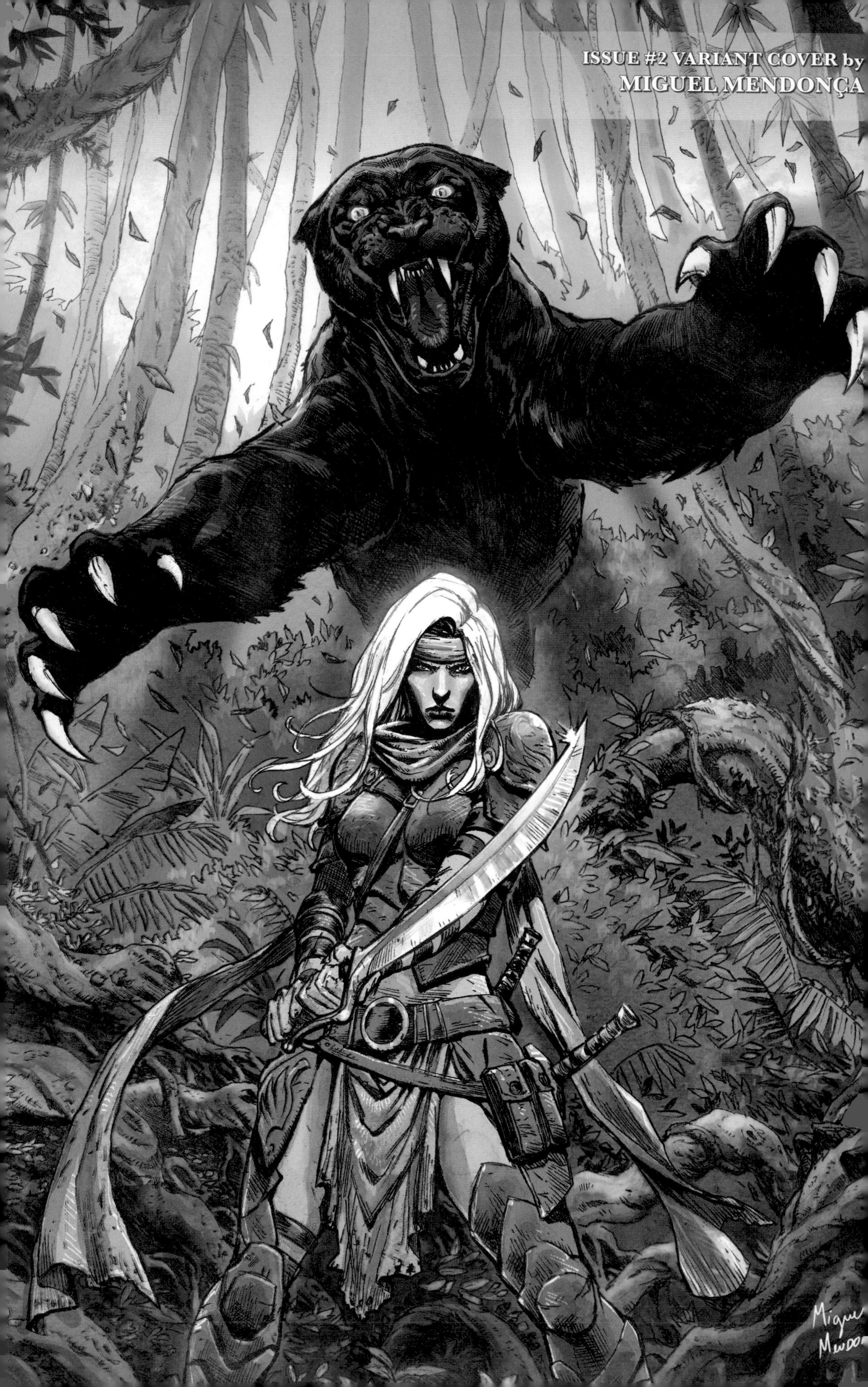

ISSUE #2 VARIANT COVER by
MIGUEL MENDONÇA

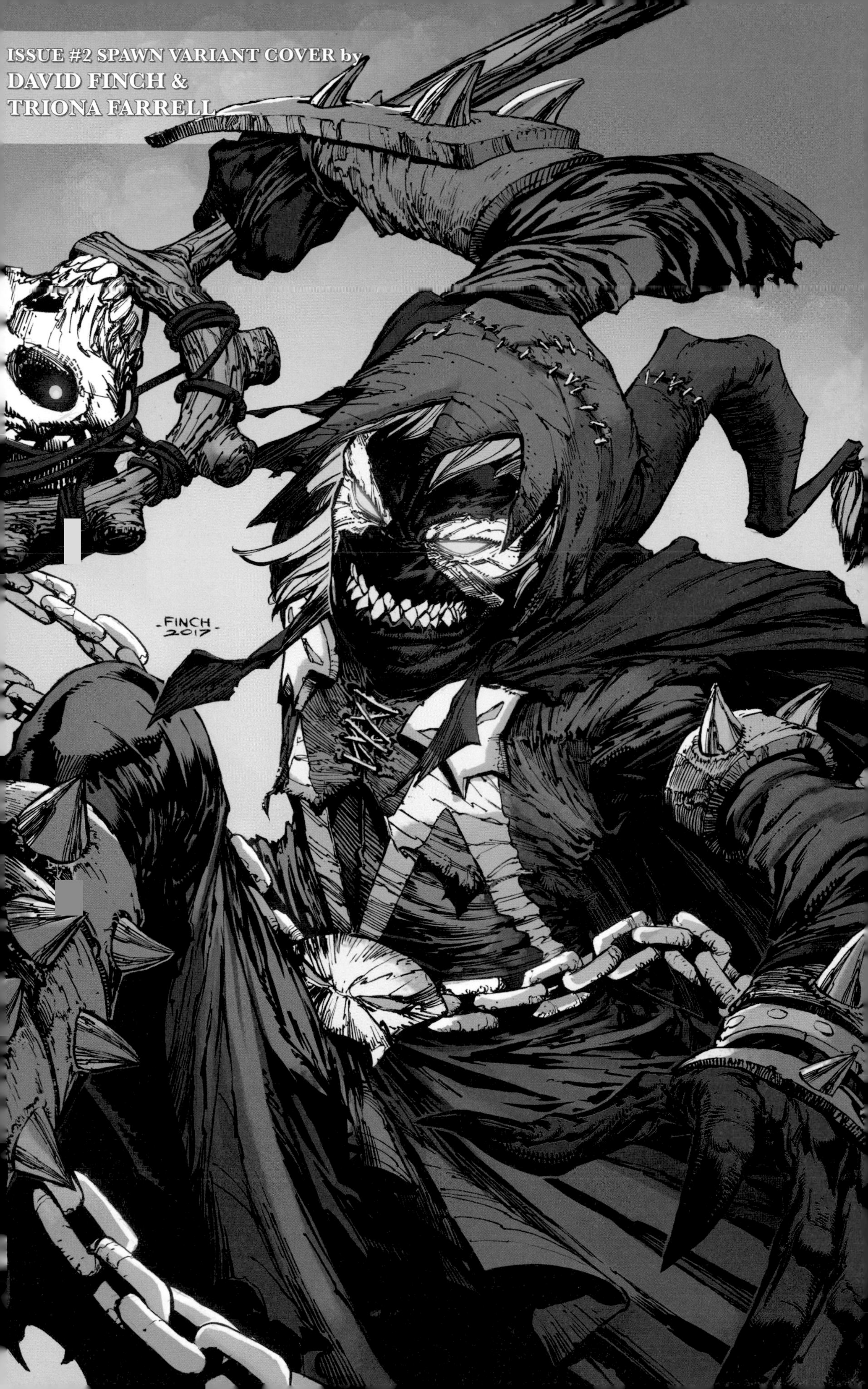
FINCH 2017

ISSUE #2 SPAWN VARIANT COVER by
DAVID FINCH &
TRIONA FARRELL

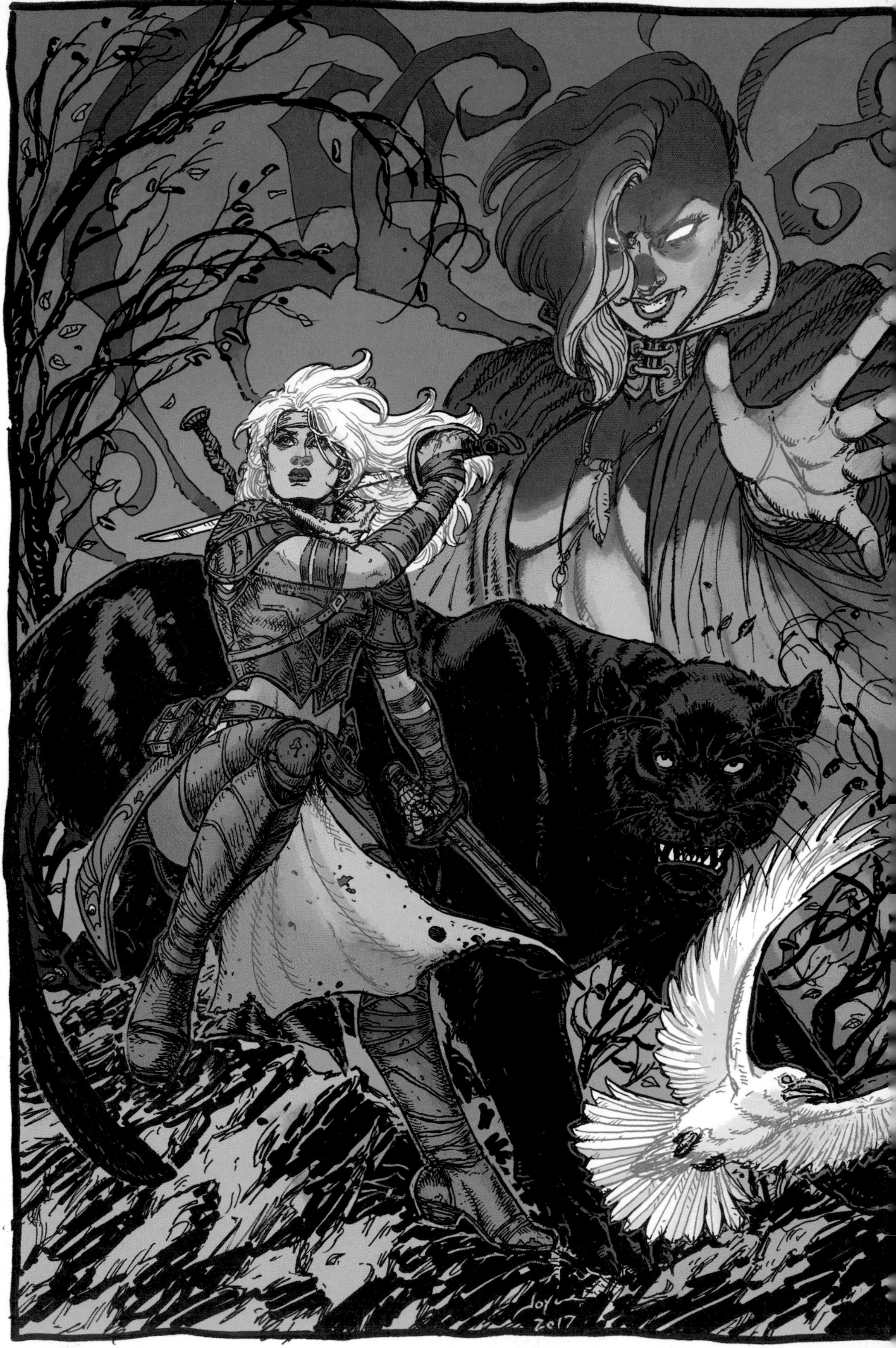

ISSUE #3 VARIANT COVER by
JOYCE CHIN & TRIONA FARRELL

ISSUE #3 PRIDE VARIANT COVER by
IG GUARA & TRIONA FARRELL

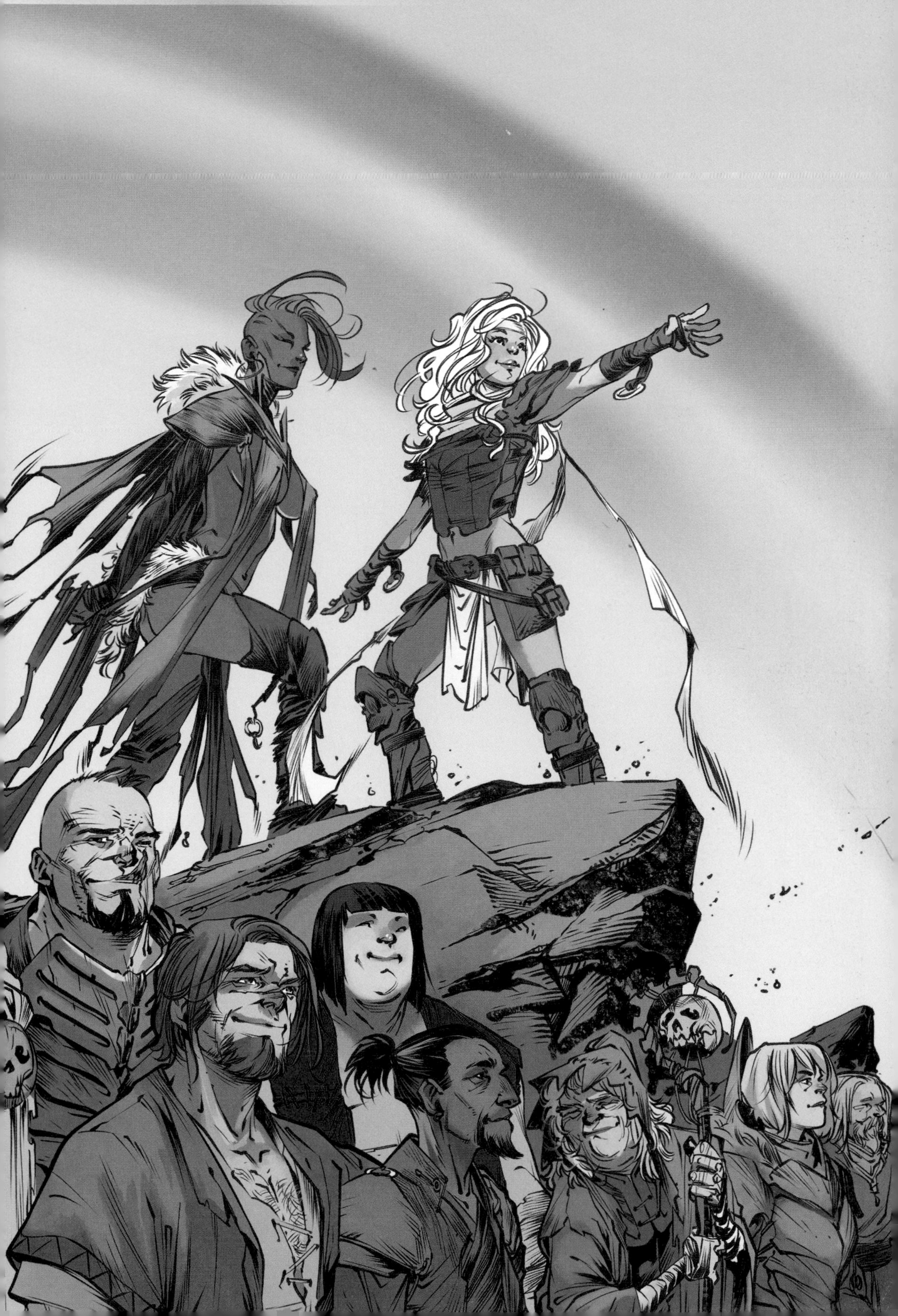

ISSUE #4 VARIANT COVER b
DAVID FINCH & TRIONA FARRELL

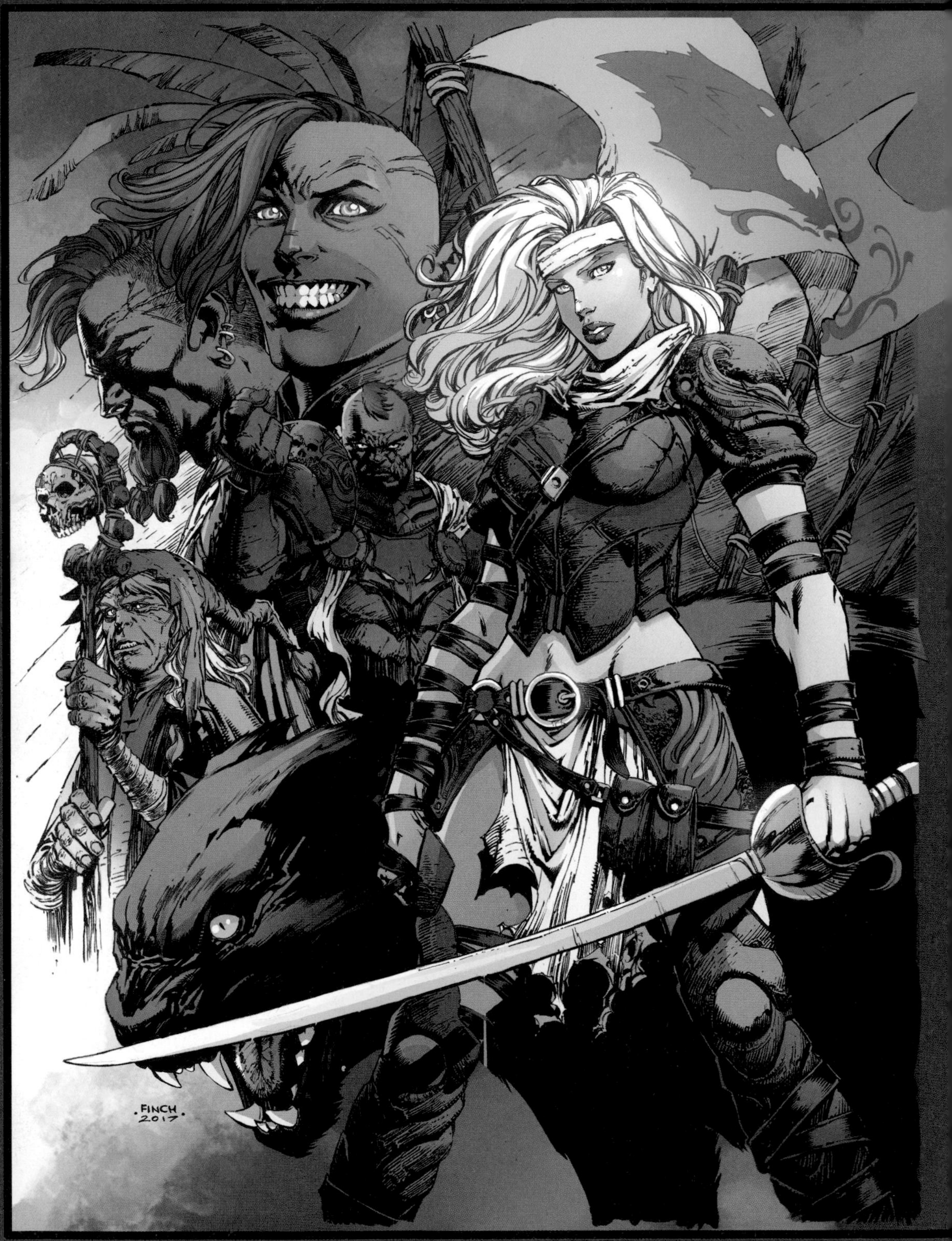
FINCH 2017

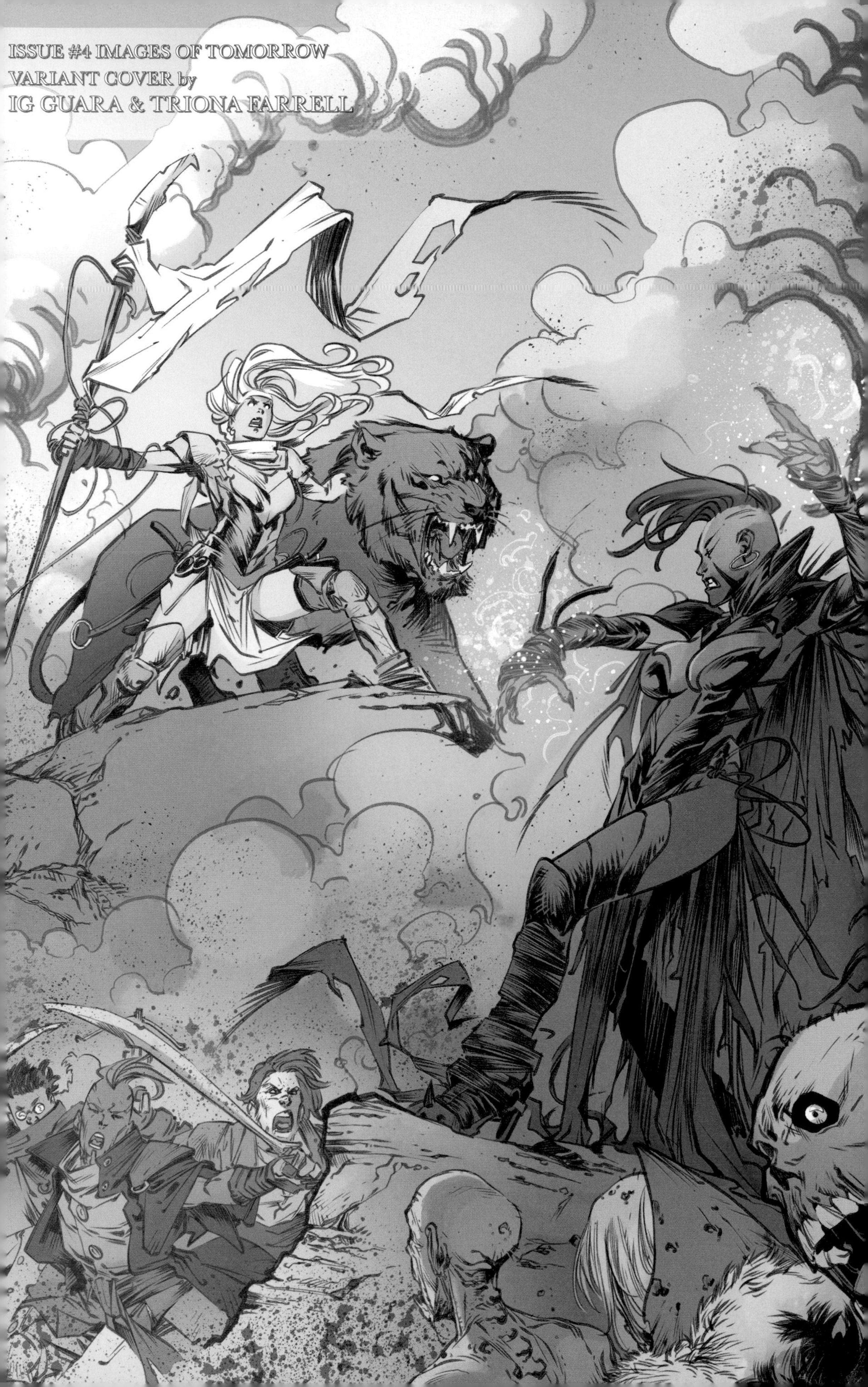

ISSUE #4 IMAGES OF TOMORROW
VARIANT COVER by
IG GUARA & TRIONA FARRELL

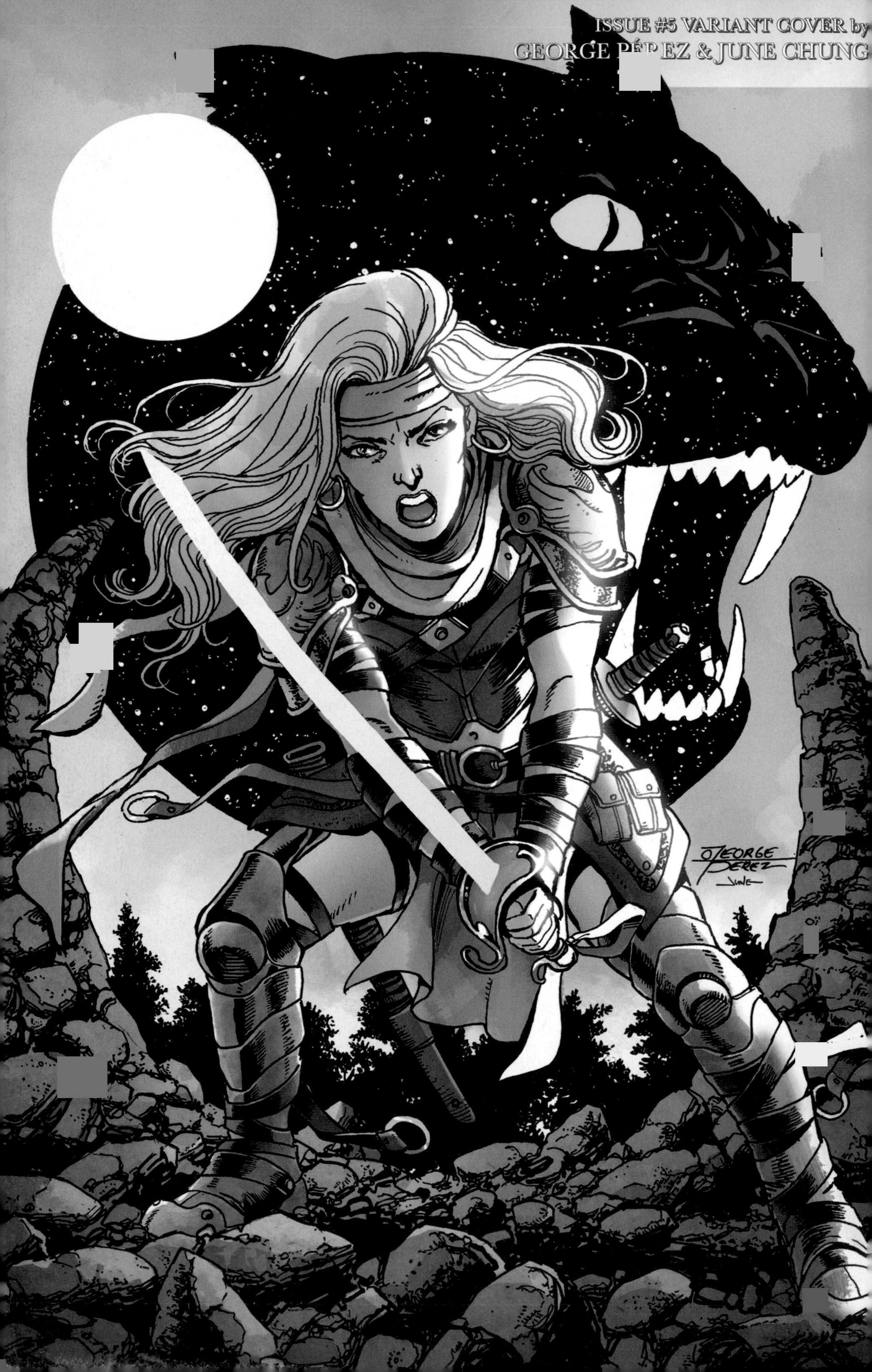
GEORGE PÉREZ
JUNE

ISSUE #5 VARIANT COVER by
GEORGE PÉREZ & JUNE CHUNG

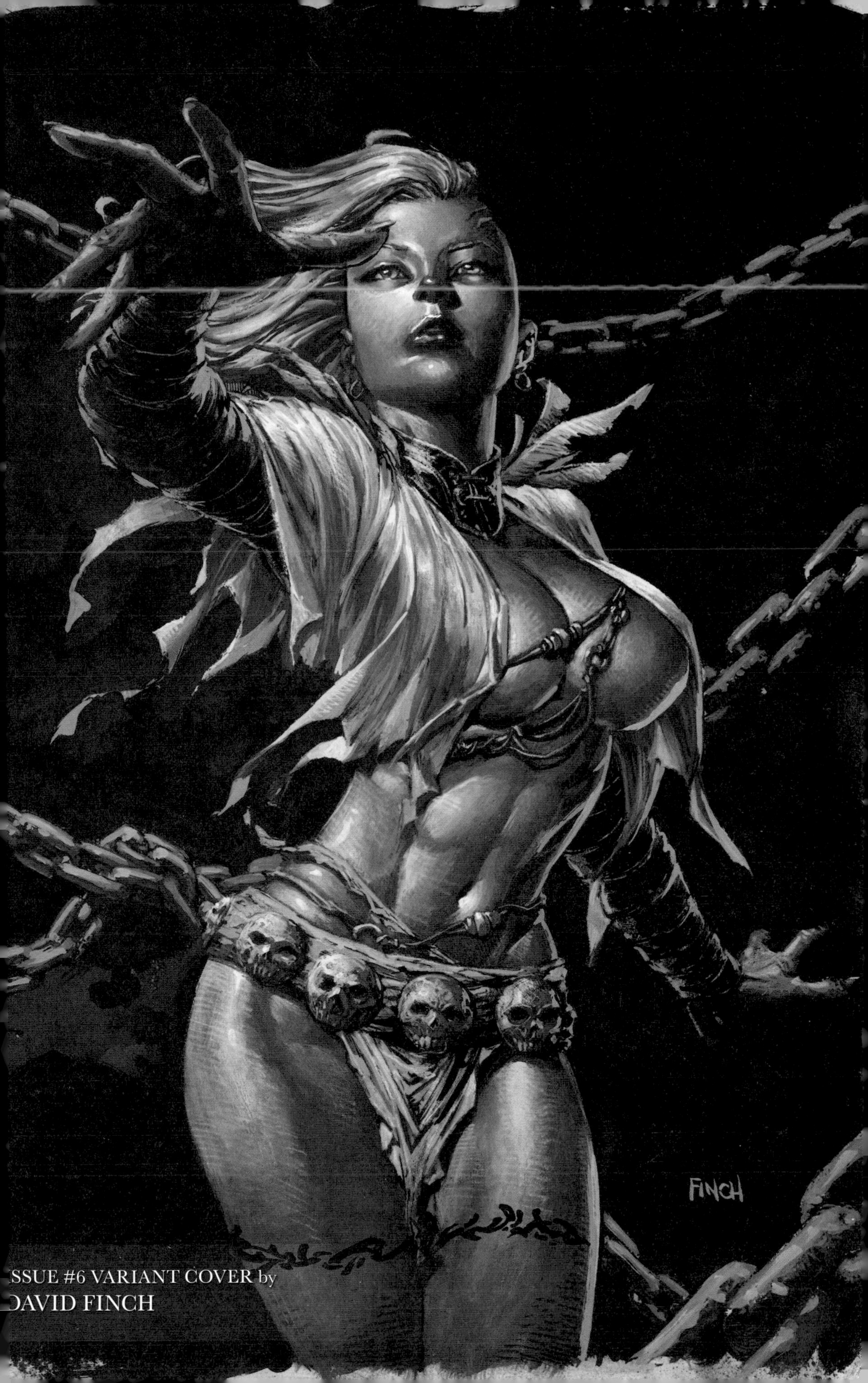
FINCH

ISSUE #6 VARIANT COVER by
DAVID FINCH

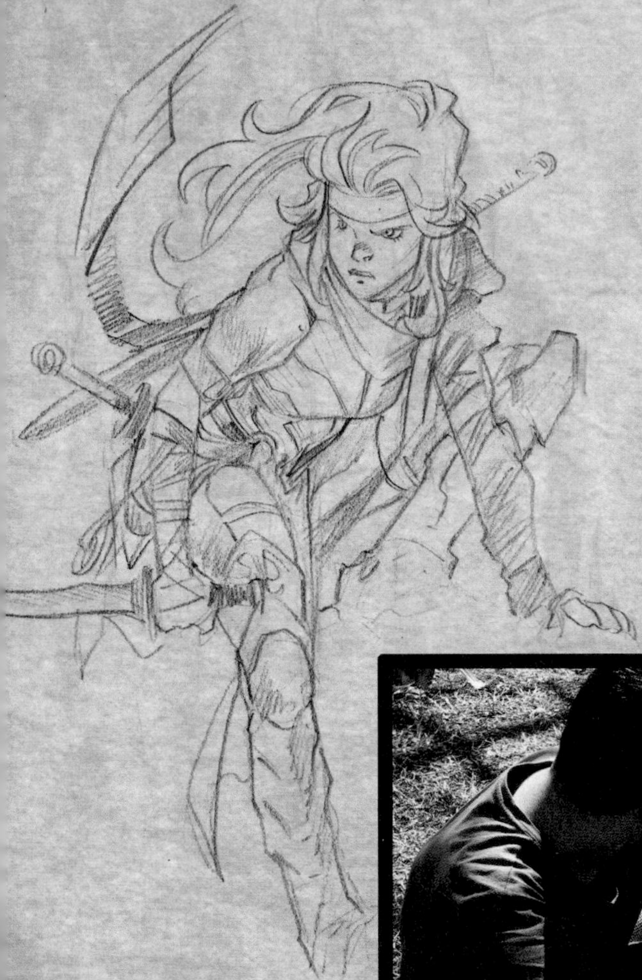

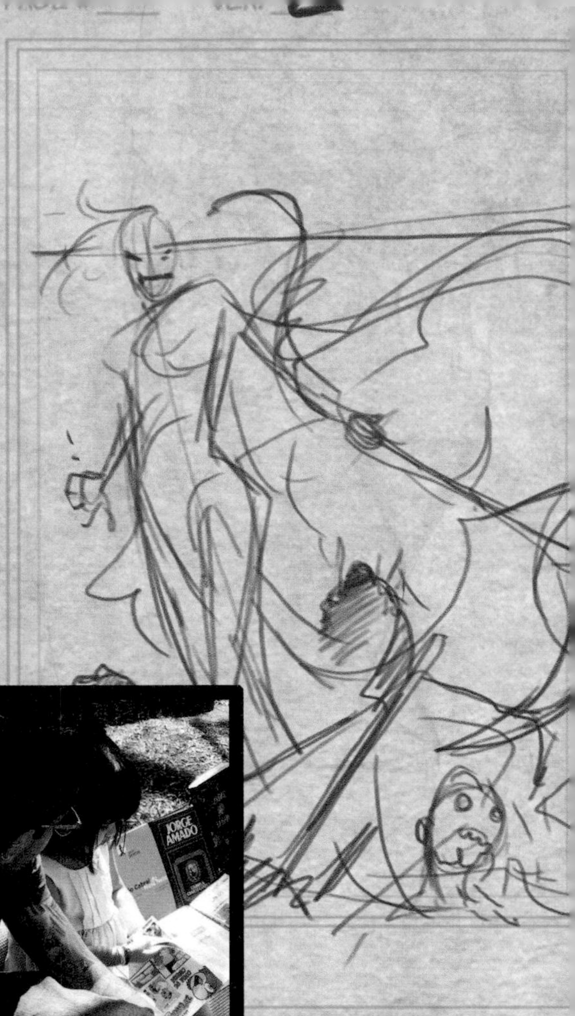

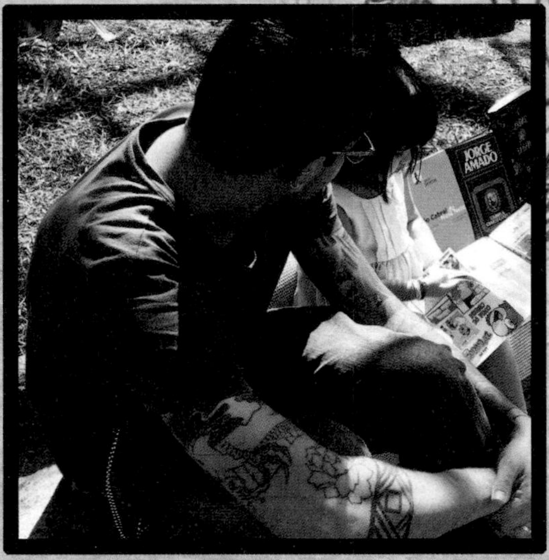
JORGE
AMADO

A WORD FROM THE ARTIST

This book is one of the most immersive experiences I have ever had! Talk about retro-feeding, when I read the script, my head fills with images, and I can see the drawings having the same effect on the rest of the team, that allows us to create something rich, that not only draws from our creativity, but also refills it. Often times I find myself thinking about the world, the clothes and the people, how they think, how they fight and how they love, and trying to pass it on in the designs and world-building. I lost myself in Rose's world, and put a part of me there, as I know Meredith and Triona also do. And, the results are nothing short of an amazing experience, and, I dare to say, an amazing book.

Thank you for reading and thank you Meredith for letting me be a part of it.

thanx =]

Ig